THE COLD YEARS
Joel Hames

Praise for Joel Hames

"In *Dead North*, Hames' lawyer turned accidental sleuth, Sam Williams, finds himself far from home and neck deep in Manchester's seamy gangster scene. But what stands out in this intelligent, intricately woven crime procedural - with a plot to make your brain hurt - is the undercurrent of slick and highly enjoyable humour reminiscent of Raymond Chandler, updated for the twenty-first century. Loved it."

S.E. Lynes, author of *Mother, Valentina*, and *The Pact*

"I really enjoyed [Dead North]. The characters spring off the page with such natural ease. I was gripped by the story – I love a book that takes turns where you least expect. It's going to leave me with a thriller hangover for some time."

John Marrs, author of *The One, The Good Samaritan* and *When You Disappeared*

"Hames is such a talent that he has created a white-knuckle, breathlessly-paced read that also has heart. Beautifully written and thrilling, Dead North deserves to go to the top of any chart."

Louise Beech, author of *Maria in the Moon, How To Be Brave* and *The Mountain in my Shoe*

"A pacy thriller, rich in voice and with a gratifying degree of complexity. Hames knows how to deliver."

John Bowen, author of *Where the Dead Walk, Vessel* and *Death Stalks Kettle Street*

About the Author

Joel Hames lives in rural Lancashire with his wife, two daughters, and one dog who has expressed more than a little disappointment at being missed off previous versions of this bio.

He has published five novels and three shorter works, including the Sam Williams series.

When not writing or spending time with his family, Joel likes to eat, drink, cook, and make up excuses to avoid walking the dog.

You can find out more about Joel and sign up to his mailing list through social media or his very own website:

Facebook: facebook.com/joelhamesauthor
Twitter: @joel_hames
Website: http://www.joelhamesauthor.com

Also by Joel Hames

Dead North
No One Will Hear
The Art of Staying Dead
Bankers Town
Brexecution
Victims
Caged

THE COLD YEARS

Joel Hames

Cover art by John Bowen

For my daughters

Contents

FOREWORD..2

PART 1: POWDER...................................3

   1: Questions 4

   2: Far From Stellar 11

   3: Looking Good.............................. 19

   4: Under a Cloud...............................32

   5: Stalker 43

   6: The Old Man and The Kinks 53

   7: Favours 65

   8: Bacon 76

   9: The Great Gaping Void 86

   10: Ghosts at our Elbows 97

PART 2: SUSPICION...................... 113

   11: All The Lawyers....................... 114

   12: To See The Point...................... 125

   13: Fallen...................................... 137

   14: The Head of the Snake 147

   15: A Little Truth 163

   16: A Clean Break.......................... 173

   17: Rage.. 181

   18: A Small Bag............................. 188

PART 3: TALK OF THE DEAD 197

    19: The Lucky One 198

    20: Things Left Behind............................... 209

    21: A Plausible Killer.................................... 214

    22: Crossed Out 224

    23: Restoration.. 235

    24: Déjà Vu 244

    25: Too Late... 252

    26: When You Can Get It, You Get It 263

    27: Between The Lines 277

    28: From Ashes 290

The World was all before them, where to choose
Thir place of rest, and Providence thir guide:
They hand in hand with wandring steps and
slow,
Through Eden took thir solitarie way.

John Milton, Paradise Lost Book XII

FOREWORD

EVERY STORY, THEY say, should stand on its own two feet, and I very much hope this one does just that. But for any reader who would like a quick refresher on the characters and the events of the earlier Sam Williams novels before embarking on this one, it can be found on my website here:

https://www.joelhamesauthor.com/?page_id=354.

PART 1: POWDER

1: Questions

"WHERE WERE YOU on the afternoon in question, Mr Williams?"

"With Maloney. As I've told you. Repeatedly."

I held her gaze as I replied. I'd declined her offer of a lawyer, and she'd sneered, as if to say that if I thought I was good enough to represent myself then I was no judge of quality. I'd provided her with my alibi twice on the phone, and once more as we'd walked to the interview room past a corridor of silent detectives trying to stare at us without being spotted. She'd sneered then, and she was sneering now. Detective Inspector Martins had never made much secret of her contempt for me.

"So that's your alibi, is it? Maloney?"

I nodded.

"For the tape, please, Mr Williams."

"Yes," I said, the 's' at the end of the word escaping in a long, frustrated hiss.

"And this would be Kevin Maloney of Parker Long House, Tottenham? Kevin Maloney, the well-known drug dealer and organised criminal?"

"I'm not aware of any convictions," I replied, eyes still fixed on her face. I tried not to smile. I knew Maloney had never been convicted, and I knew that because I'd been in his corner, knocking back every charge that came his way. I hadn't had to do that in a while, though. Maloney had been straight for more than a year.

"So you're sticking with this alibi?"

I shrugged. "It's the truth, Detective Inspector. If you want a better one I'll have to make it up."

She sat back and sighed, shaking her head. Her tongue slid back and forth across her lower lip like a fat pink mollusc, an involuntary, unconscious action on which I tried hard not to focus. Beside her sat Simon Winterman, echoing his boss's sneers and shakes like a bad parody. Winterman had done little to impress me since I'd met him an hour earlier: he sat with his legs splayed and one elbow on the table, and seemed unduly conscious of his status as detective and not conscious enough of his rank as constable. I was alone on my side of the table: I'd been *invited to attend*, that was how Martins had put it when she called. I wasn't under arrest. I wasn't under the threat of arrest. I was answering police questions voluntarily and I had an alibi that would stand up. With all that on my side, I didn't need a lawyer, and I didn't want one either. A bad lawyer wouldn't have done anything I couldn't do myself. A good one might have asked me questions that wouldn't cross Martins' mind. Difficult questions. Martins sighed again and leaned forward.

"Detective Constable Winterman will be following up on that, Mr Williams. Don't you worry."

"I'm not," I replied, with a smile. I could afford a smile. I wasn't worried; that was the truth.

It had been more than a month since I'd last seen Martins, a month that, I'd hoped, would be the first of many such months, stretching out, ideally, until one or other of us died. We'd been dragged together by murder, Martins and I. And now another murder had pulled us back into one another's reluctant orbit. This time, I imagined, no one would be mourning the victim.

Edward Trawden had died in his hospital bed, murdered while he recovered from the last attempt on his life, and Trawden was a man who'd earned his killing more than most. He was guilty of the murder of a child, Maxine Grimshaw, decades earlier. He was guilty of blackmail and manipulation, of killing Elizabeth Maurier, his own lawyer, of more murders and, no doubt, other crimes besides. Not that Martins had joined up the dots. Not that she'd even come close.

"Where was Claire Tully while all this was going on? Weighing out the coke with you and Maloney?"

Martins smiled as she spoke, which was helpful, as it was difficult to be sure when she was joking and when she was being serious. I chose not to join her in the smile.

"Ask her," I replied. "Oh, I forgot. You already have."

They'd seen Claire yesterday. I'd driven her in. No lawyer for her, either; Claire had insisted, which had made me a little nervous. I'd waited outside and hoped she'd remember what she was supposed to do, which was just to repeat "I was at home all day" over and over again until Martins got bored. Not a difficult task, especially for a clever woman, but my nerves weren't just down to being overprotective. Claire was recovering, still fragile, still on leave from work. She was just as much Trawden's victim as the others had been.

Martins, of course, knew nothing about what had happened to Claire. Simon Winterman knew less than nothing. The woman he'd replaced, ex-Detective Constable Vicky Colman, now plain Police Constable Vicky Colman, knew the whole story. But after what we'd all been through together, I felt she could be trusted to keep it to herself.

Colman had called me every other day since Trawden had been killed – it had been Colman that had called to tell me about him getting killed in the first place, a cause of wary celebration on both sides. She'd worked with me – against Martins' direct orders – to implicate Trawden in the murder of Elizabeth Maurier, and she'd lost her job for it. Once we'd stopped laughing and toasting Trawden's unknown killer – an overdose of insulin, applied intravenously while he slept – she'd asked if I wanted to help her find out who did it. Work *under the radar*, she'd said. *Just like last time.*

Last time had cost her a job. It had cost my one-time

enemy and recent friend David Brooks-Powell his life. It hadn't taken more than a second's thought to say *No*.

"Yes," said Winterman, jolting me suddenly back to the present. "We asked her. She said she was at home. Alone. No witnesses, of course." He shook his head, sadly, and continued. "And she's recovering from some sort of breakdown, is that right?"

"She was home when I got back," I replied, and shrugged, but Winterman was nothing if not persistent.

"So what's this breakdown all about, then?"

I turned and fixed him with a glare – I'd been looking at Martins until then, even when I was answering Winterman's questions, because I'd decided I liked him even less than I liked his boss.

"She's had a breakdown," I said, slowly and clearly. "If you want any more than that, you'll have to ask Claire. Or speak to her doctor, if she'll let you."

Winterman returned my glare with a smile.

"Oh, don't you worry. We'll be doing just that. She gave her consent when we saw her yesterday."

I tried to keep the surprise off my face, but I could tell from the way Winterman's smile broadened that I'd failed. She hadn't told me any of that. She'd have been perfectly within her rights to deny consent, which was precisely what she should have done, but, I realised, I hadn't warned her, because I hadn't seen the request coming.

Which meant two things. One: this, like almost everything else, was all my fault. Two: it was possible to dislike Winterman even more than I'd disliked him five minutes earlier.

Time to regain the upper ground, I thought, and leaned back.

"So," I began. "Do you plan on asking me the whereabouts of every individual who had even the most

7

tentative connection with Trawden?"

Winterman opened his mouth to speak, but I held out a hand to stop him, and continued.

"Because even if you just keep it to those who didn't like the man, it's a pretty long list."

Winterman sighed. Beside him, Martins was impassive, a gentle smile playing across her lips but never making it as far as her eyes.

"Look, Mr Williams," he said. "This isn't going to help any of us. I appreciate you don't like being here and you liked your girlfriend being here even less, but you know how this works. A man's been killed. You might not have liked him. That doesn't matter."

"I never said *I* didn't like him."

Winterman smiled. "That's fine. Whatever you say. I'm sure your alibi will check out. I'm sure Claire was at home by herself the whole time. But anything you know, anything you can tell us – well, the sooner we can rule the pair of you out, the sooner we can concentrate our resources somewhere more profitable."

It was interesting to see him take this line, but I'd seen it all before. Open hard, then play soft. What was interesting wasn't the line, but the fact that Martins had chosen to let him take it. The fact that Martins was taking a back seat herself. Either this guy was the real deal, or Martins had something else up her sleeve. Neither option looked good for me.

I decided to go with it. There were enough things I could talk about without getting too close to the edge of the cliff.

"Well, there's Lizzy Maurier, of course."

"Is she on your list, Mr Williams?" asked Martins. "The ones who didn't like Trawden?"

"Well, she's convinced he killed her mother, so I reckon he wasn't her favourite person. But you know all about that, don't you?"

She did, too. Everything Colman, Brooks-Powell and I had dug up about Trawden's past had made it onto Martins' desk, where it had been dismissed as swiftly and carelessly as Colman herself.

I could see Martins framing her response, pausing, that tongue sliding along her lower lip while she considered whether it was worth it, deciding it wasn't. She contented herself with sitting back in her chair and glaring at me instead. Wise move, Martins. I continued.

"But she's in France. She went off to Brittany, back end of December. She's taken a house there. Plans to stay, for a year or so. Writing, she says."

"We're aware of Miss Maurier's whereabouts," interrupted Winterman, and I turned my attention to him.

"I believe she prefers *Ms*, Detective Constable. And yes, she's in France. She's been sending me letters. Not sure if a letter fulfils your criteria for an alibi, mind. You might have to think about that."

I waited, to see if he'd bite. He didn't.

"The thing is," I said, "how would Lizzy Maurier know how to inject someone with insulin?" I looked around as I spoke, as if to the room in general, as if the thought had only just occurred to me and I was hoping someone, anyone, might have an answer. "How would any of us know, for that matter? Where do you even get insulin, or enough insulin to kill a man?"

Winterman sat forward, elbows on the table, and grinned at me.

"Actually it's not that difficult, Mr Williams," he said, and I found myself unable to resist returning the grin. I threw in a single raised eyebrow, in case he thought I was starting to warm to him. "It's not difficult at all. Five minutes on the internet for the knowledge, a little basic research for the supplies. Anyone could do it. You'd be surprised," he continued, and then stopped and fixed me with a stare. "Unless, of course, you were the killer."

I laughed, and he stared, but after a moment, the stare faltered and he laughed himself, briefly and quietly, but a laugh nonetheless. I found myself wondering if maybe he wasn't as bad as I'd thought he was.

There was a knock on the door. "Yes," called Martins. It opened, and a man's head appeared in the gap. Martins was on her feet a moment later, conferring quietly with the intruder, and then returning to her place. The door opened fully, the man stepped in, and Martins turned to Winterman.

"You can take a few minutes, Detective Constable. DI Genaud wants to sit in."

Winterman stood and left the room. Genaud took his place. I'd been veering between bored and angry, but now I was intrigued. I'd never been interviewed by two detective inspectors before, and neither had any of my clients.

Detective Inspector Genaud was a middle-aged man with a slight paunch, a thick layer of curly hair that preserved hints of its original brown beneath a spreading grey, and a chin that jutted forward just far enough to give the impression of a man who wasn't used to things getting in his way, or at least not used to them staying there. I'd never come across Detective Inspector Genaud before. I'd never even heard his name. The formal introductions were made, the interview restarted, and I sat back and waited to see what Genaud would bring to the party.

2: Far From Stellar

GENAUD DIDN'T BRING much, it transpired. He leaned forward the whole time he was in the room, his elbows on the table, his forehead creased into the agonised frown of someone trying to remember where they'd left the car keys. I waited some more, remembering Lizzy Maurier, remembering her letters, four of which I'd received since she'd moved to Brittany, all of which had opened with an extract from the poem she'd written for Brooks-Powell's funeral. I was beginning to understand Lizzy Maurier. I was even beginning to understand her poem. That didn't mean I liked it.

Martins was uncharacteristically quiet, too, and the whole set-up struck me as confusing and more than a little unusual. What was Genaud doing here if he didn't have anything important to say? I turned my attention to Martins and noticed something I hadn't seen before. She was fidgeting. Twisting in her seat, every now and then, brushing the thumb of one hand across the side of the other.

Detective Inspector Martins, I realised, was uncomfortable. And in the context of that discomfort, Genaud's presence made sense.

He wasn't there to watch me. He was there to watch her.

Olivia Martins might have had a meteoric rise to her august rank; she might have the best clean-up rates in the Met, for all I knew. But her recent performance had been far from stellar. Elizabeth Maurier's murder was still officially open, together with the murders of three other victims of the same murderer. Martins had appealed to the public for help, but she'd waited too long to do so, and got nothing useful in return. Detective Inspector Martins, I realised, had been handed Trawden's murder not as a reward but as a last chance. And the powers that be weren't prepared to sit by while she blew it.

I spared little sympathy for Detective Inspector Martins. David Brooks-Powell was dead. Lizzy Maurier was halfway mad, although there was an argument she'd always been close to the edge. Claire was a nervous wreck with enough antidepressants and sleeping pills in the bathroom to satisfy a cult. Colman had lost her job. Martins still had hers, for now.

"Well," I said. Genaud looked up from the green Formica table and stared at me through narrowed eyes. There was something calculating there. Something disbelieving, too. I ignored his gaze and looked for a bone to throw him. David Brooks-Powell's widow would do, I thought. She was in the clear anyway. "Let's see. There's Melanie Golding, of course. Her husband's dead, and Trawden was involved, even if he didn't pull the trigger. I'd imagine she doesn't think too fondly of him."

Martins shook her head. "Mrs Golding has an alibi. A proper alibi," she added, pointedly, "with other people there. Reliable people. Mrs Golding spent the entire day at an autism fundraiser. Big event. Newspapers, celebrities, all that crap. She blew about fifty grand, apparently. Peanuts to her, of course."

Genaud didn't say a word. He was still watching me, though.

"It's a good cause," I replied, shrugging, and Martins gave a grunt. I already knew about Melanie's alibi; I'd spoken to her several times since her husband's funeral, and she'd told me about the fundraiser. I didn't have anything useful to say, but I was having a little private fun putting Martins on the spot. I tried again.

"What about Evans?" I asked, and Martins gave one of those nasty little sideways smiles that I was starting to think she reserved for me.

"Evans is dead. He might have been scum, but he's going to struggle digging himself up and reshaping his decomposed body into something that can get into the Royal Free Hospital and shove a bagful of insulin into Edward Trawden."

I noticed Genaud had stopped staring at me and turned to face Martins as she spoke. His frown seemed to have deepened.

"Not Evans himself," I replied. "Obviously. But friends? Relatives? Anyone who liked Evans would have good reason to hate Trawden. Mind you, I can't believe that's a very long list."

Robbie Evans had already been serving his own life sentence for another child rape and murder when he'd been killed in prison, and not long after that he'd been put on the spot as the man who'd killed young Maxine Grimshaw. Trawden, who'd been convicted of the Grimshaw murder twenty years earlier, had walked. The fact that it had been me – or, as the press reported it, Elizabeth Maurier with my assistance – who had put Evans on that spot and freed Trawden, was a source of permanent displeasure, ever since I'd seen the reaction of Maxine's parents to the release of the man they'd spent two decades blaming for their daughter's death. The more so since I'd become convinced that we'd been set up, Elizabeth and I; that Trawden had manipulated us and everyone else involved to point the finger at a dead man for his own horrific crime.

Martins was nodding even as I spoke. "Well, you're right about the list. Not the most popular bloke, Evans. But he did have a son. He's due in shortly. We'll be having a word with him, don't you worry. Doubt anything'll come of it, but you know me, Mr Williams. Every 't' crossed."

She smiled, suddenly, not the usual Martins smile, the one that had me wondering what she was hiding and worrying how much it would hurt, but something open and

13

genuine and gone half a second after it had appeared. Perhaps I'd imagined it. I decided to carry on thinking out loud.

"And there's probably half the prison population, isn't there? I mean –"

I was interrupted by the door opening, again, and the appearance of Winterman's head. He walked quickly in, without waiting to be invited, and whispered something in Martins' ear. The detective inspector gave a brief nod in response. Genaud stood up and announced that he'd seen all he needed to in a neutral voice that didn't do anything to lessen the suggestion that what he had seen hadn't been to Martins' credit. I caught myself feeling sorry for her, for a moment, and then remembered how little she deserved my compassion. And I hadn't liked the way Genaud had been watching me, either. If he had his eye on both of us, it would be me I'd worry about, not Martins.

I carried on talking as Winterman resumed his post, a long and entirely vague speech about the enemies that Trawden had surely made in prison, about those who'd never believed in his innocence and those who'd just taken against him because he didn't side with the right gang or help smuggle the right brand of mobile phone in. Winterman listened with at least an outward impression of interest, but Martins might as well have been nodding off for all the attention she paid, her eyes staring at her entwined hands and her silent inactivity broken by sighs and grim little nods utterly unrelated to my words.

"Oh, shut up, Williams," she said, finally, with just a hint of her usual venom and a bucketload of bored weariness. I stopped, surprised, and wondered whether it was time to push the knife in. I could ask her about Genaud, I thought. *They're keeping an eye on you, are they*? I could say. *Not in the good books? Remember what you said about Roarkes?* I certainly hadn't forgotten what she'd said about Roarkes, her fellow detective inspector, one of just a handful of police officers I liked and, bar Colman, the only one I could call a friend. *Yesterday's man*, she'd called him, alluding to the disaster that his most recent case had ended in, with a little help from me. Maybe Martins was yesterday's woman. If that was the case, I didn't think the present would miss her.

In spite of all that, I kept the knife sheathed. Whatever was happening to Martins, she'd keep her rank, and any detective inspector could be dangerous if you chose to make an enemy of them. Instead I changed tack.

"What about CCTV?" I asked. "You can't just walk off the street and all the way through a hospital without being picked up by the cameras, can you?"

I could see Martins turning the question over in her mind. Deciding between a dismissive reply and a brutal one. She didn't get the chance.

"We're working on it," said Winterman. "To be honest, it's not very clear."

Martins glared at him, and then at me. A short silence followed, during which I decided that if they hadn't got what they needed from the CCTV by now, the odds were they weren't going to get it at all, and Winterman, no doubt, wondered what the punishment would be for speaking out of turn.

"We're asking the questions here, Mr Williams," she said, finally, and I shook my head in disgust.

"I'm sorry," I replied. "I thought I'd been invited in to share my thoughts with you. That was what you said, wasn't it? *We'd like you to come in and share your thoughts with us, Mr Williams.*" I threw her sentence back at her in her own voice, or my best impression of it, that sharpness she tried so hard to add a little depth to. I didn't bother with the depth. "I was expecting a meeting of minds, Detective Inspector. A nice little pow-wow where we could exchange ideas and think outside the box. The spirit of reciprocity and cooperation. Like when you invited the public to help with those *unsolved murders*."

I stopped. I'd gone too far. I held up a hand in apology, and Martins acknowledged it with a nod.

"You're free to leave, Mr Williams. You were always free to leave," she said.

"I guess I haven't been much help after all," I replied. "For what it's worth, I'm sorry. I wish I had."

She nodded again, and told me to let her people know if I planned on leaving the country or going anywhere for more than a couple of days. That might have sounded menacing, but it was standard enough, even for an innocent witness like me, especially with a DI like Martins running the case. "We'll be checking your alibi," she added, for good measure, as I stood to leave.

Winterman accompanied me from the interview room to the front desk, and I noticed his shoulders drop the moment he was out of sight of his boss.

"Sorry about all that," he said as we squeezed our way past an exhausted-looking woman aiming half-hearted kicks at the coffee machine, and I frowned at him. He shrugged. I'd taken against him for the way he'd conducted himself in the interview room – aggressive and appeasing by turn, the oldest play in the book and one I could see he hadn't yet mastered. I'd taken against him for getting that consent out of Claire. I'd taken against him because he wasn't Vicky Colman. But he was just doing his job, I realised. It was a difficult job, too – so many players, so much history and enmity between them. And he wasn't doing it badly.

Winterman had reached the exit, but following a step behind him I found my way blocked by a man who looked like he'd benefit from a few hours in an interview room. Thickset, about my age, I thought, although it was difficult to be sure, because his long, greasy hair hung over one side of his face and the other was most notable for a couple of scars and a tattooed spider's web that, like its owner, had probably seen better days. He stood there in front of me, torn and dirty jeans and a sweater that was unravelling as fast as Trawden's reputation, opened his mouth and said "Sam Williams" in a voice entirely devoid of emotion or personality, as though he were ticking a name off a list. Then he nodded, one of those nods you give someone you're about to hurt. I flinched, instinctively, but I didn't move fast enough, and before I knew it he'd lowered a shoulder and pushed me to one side, hard enough to hurt, but not hard enough to do any damage. I took a moment to catch my breath, then looked back at him, but he was already turning a corner in the corridor, and the uniformed officer with him didn't seem to have noticed the shove at all.

Winterman had. He was waiting for me by the main door, a few steps ahead of me.

"John Evans," he said, registering the question on my face. "Evans' son. Reckon he doesn't like you too much."

"Doesn't look like he's that fond of anyone," I replied, and laughed, but even Winterman would have heard the false note in that laugh. John Evans had left me feeling distinctly uneasy.

"Between you and me," continued Winterman, as I stepped out onto a street grey with January slush, "he's the most likely candidate. Whatever Martins says. His alibi's even worse than yours."

I forced myself to smile in reply, and hurried off down the street. The records proclaimed his father guilty of a crime Trawden had committed. I could see why he might want to put an end to Trawden.

I could see why he might not like me too much, either.

I waited until I'd turned a corner and was out of sight of the police station before I fished my phone out of my pocket and called Maloney. I'd come out in a thin coat and sleet was suddenly pouring from the skies, soaking right through me. I walked fast as I waited for him to answer.

"Well?" he asked. No *Hello*. No *How are you?*

"Yeah. I've been in."

"And?"

"I told them what we agreed. I was with you."

I stopped walking for a moment, waiting anxiously for his reply. He sighed.

"For fuck's sake," he said, and then another sigh. "Okay. It'll be taken care of. I thought I'd put my days of lying to the police behind me, Sam. But it'll be taken care of."

I thanked him and shot off towards Leicester Square underground station, grateful for one less thing to worry about.

3: Looking Good

I SHOULD HAVE known that wouldn't be the end of it. Not with Maloney. I emerged at Highbury & Islington to two missed calls and one text asking me to ring him back, and I'd just decided to ignore him for the next hour or so when my phone buzzed and I answered it without thinking.

"So there's no way round this?" he asked, somewhat optimistically given the number of times we'd already had the conversation. It was almost enough to make me laugh, the idea that this man, who'd presided over a ruthless criminal organisation in his time, who'd regarded the law as little more than a minor inconvenience, this man was worrying about providing an alibi for someone he knew hadn't committed the crime anyway.

"No, Maloney. There's no way."

He sighed again. "Okay. It's all covered at my end. I just wish…"

He tailed off.

"You wish what?"

"I wish you could say you were with Claire."

"You know that won't work. They called our flat the day after the murder and she told them she'd been at home by herself all day. If I'd known they were going to ask questions I'd have made sure she had her story straight. But I didn't know. She can't change her line now. She needs to be consistent. We all do."

"Maybe. But I still think it would be better if you came clean. I don't know who you're protecting, Sam, but I don't like it."

I had the key in the lock as he finished, and it was only the fact that I knew Claire would be able to hear me that kept me from exploding. Instead I kept myself to a murmur that turned, without my willing it, to a bitter lament.

"I'm not protecting anyone except myself. And Claire. And I'm not doing a very good job of it. Just – just help me out, okay?"

I let it hang there, that *okay*, with its history of favours given and received and respect and trust earned and repaid over and over, with the knowledge, finally, that it had been Maloney's gun in Claire's handbag when I'd found her outside the Central Criminal Court preparing to put a bullet in the Crown's chief witness. She'd been twisted and woven by Trawden into a sharp, bitter point, twisted until she was minutes from killing a human trafficker named Jonas Wolf right outside the court where he was due to give evidence in another, more public matter. But it wasn't Trawden who'd provided the weapon. That little mistake had been Maloney's.

I waited, key still sitting unturned in the lock, and when he finally spoke it was as if there had never been the slightest doubt.

"Okay," he said. "I've got a couple of guys who'll say they saw you with me. And I've made sure the CCTV's disappeared – for a couple of weeks, not just that day. Kind of thing that can happen in this neck of the woods. Shouldn't seem too unusual."

I thanked him and ended the call. Maloney lived in a council flat in the rougher end of Tottenham, only this particular council flat comprised six council flats joined together and turned into something more suitable for a man who liked the finer things in life and could afford to pay for them. A few years back, this had been his centre of operations, but where once there had been drugs and weapons, now there was just fine wine and expensive cooking equipment. Still some weapons, I realised, remembering the Sig Claire had managed to steal from under his nose.

"Is that you?" called Claire as I let the door fall shut behind me. Not the dumbest question you could ask, in a city of ten million people and probably half a million criminals, in a flat in which I'd been punched unconscious myself a few months earlier. But before Jonas Wolf, before the Sig, it wasn't a question Claire would have asked. Whatever had happened in the outside world, Claire had always thought of herself as safe – in her flat, in her mind, in her conviction that what she thought was the right thing to think and what she was doing was the right thing to do.

Trawden had blown that conviction to hell.

"It's me," I called in reply, and strolled into the bedroom. She was lying on top of the cover, fully dressed, pale and looking far more tired than anyone who hadn't done anything more strenuous in the last month than make a cup of tea had any right to look.

"You look good," I said, smiling at her, and she shook her head in quiet disbelief. I'd never been a great liar, and it wasn't a good lie.

"If I look good like this I must have been a fucking supermodel last year," she replied, and I laughed. She joined me in the laugh, and then stopped, suddenly, her hands flying to her head, her smile frozen.

"Sorry," she murmured. "Those pills are doing my head in."

I nodded. There wasn't anything more I could offer than a nod. I was looking after her as well as I could; she might not be back to her best, but she was a lot closer to it than she'd been a month back. Close enough for her parents to have left London, finally, for their native Yorkshire, confident, they said, that I was suffering no ill effects myself, that I knew what I was doing and that I could take care of their girl. I hadn't been entirely sure what they'd meant by *ill effects*. I hadn't been shot. I hadn't been there when the shooting had happened. Nobody I loved had been shot or abused or killed themselves. I was fine, I'd assured them, and they'd nodded together, in agreement. Not that my health and competence had stopped them calling three times every day since. Not that it had deterred them from making plans for a repeat visit, in a couple of weeks' time, and another one set up for the following month. I'd never needed a diary before Claire's breakdown. I needed one now.

"Melanie Golding called," she said. "Are you seeing her tonight?"

I shrugged. "Could do. We haven't got anything planned. Did she seem okay?"

"Not too bad."

"Fancy coming out?"

She considered the question, for a moment, that frown and those narrowed eyes, but I knew her well enough to know it was all show.

"Not yet." She shook her head. "I'm not quite ready. Maybe soon, though, yeah?"

"Maybe soon," I said, and hoped I'd done a better job hiding my disappointment than she had pretending to think about it.

"But you go, right? You can have a drink with her. She could do with the company."

I laughed, briefly, and reminded her that for all Melanie Golding was a widow, she was more than capable of enjoying herself.

"How about Roarkes, then? You haven't seen him for a bit?"

I shook my head. Roarkes had lost his wife shortly after Melanie had lost her husband, but in Helen Roarkes' case the end had been expected, and in some ways, welcome. Cancer. The death of David Brooks-Powell had been a very different story. They say dead is dead, but the way you go doesn't half make a difference. Roarkes was difficult company these days, and I didn't think I'd done much of a job lifting him the times I had seen him.

"I think I'd rather have a quiet one tonight. Pizza and TV?"

Her response was a smile. A genuine one, I thought, which was an improvement. Claire's parents might have bought the quick recovery line, but I knew better. Half those nods and three quarters of the smiles had been fake. The numbers on the laughs were even worse. She'd got rid of her *life coach*, a man I'd never met and never liked, either, and I'd hoped that would improve things, but it hadn't. Since her parents had gone back home, she hadn't seemed to feel the need to pretend quite so much, but they still came out from time to time, that peal of laughter at just the wrong pitch, that grin that was a quarter turn from a grimace. She should have borrowed a line from Roarkes' playbook, I thought; he didn't have much trouble showing the world his misery. Mind you, he could have borrowed a line from hers, too. Misery might love company, but company was in danger of getting bored.

Not that I could blame him. He was back in an office, stuck behind a desk. Before the disastrous case in Manchester that had started with two dead police officers and ended with three, plus a dead lawyer for good measure, he'd been roaming the country sharing the benefit of his wisdom and the bitterness of his experience with struggling police forces on tough, uncrackable cases. Roarkes had cracked them anyway, case after impossible case, until Manchester. Manchester had made him yesterday's man – much as I'd hated her for saying it, Martins had been right about that. Bereavement had given them the excuse to put him out to pasture, but Roarkes wasn't having that. The cases he was working were, he said, too boring to talk about, but boring was better than sitting at home wondering how to fill the day.

There had been a time when I'd looked forward to a drink with Roarkes. These days I needed twenty-four hours to recover from one, and it wasn't the drink I was recovering from. But I owed him – or so he seemed to think, and for some reason Claire agreed with him, and I wasn't arguing with Claire. And I was still the closest thing he had to a friend.

An hour later she'd dragged herself out of bed and the pizza and the movie were nicely teed up. If I hadn't known any better I might have been able to forget the last couple of months entirely, might even have been able to convince myself that everything was normal, that Claire was normal, that we had a completely normal life. We laughed together at Matt Damon dodging another salvo of bullets and I put the end of a slice of pizza in my mouth and Claire turned to me and said "Have you replied to Eileen Grimshaw yet?"

And that was it. The illusion was shattered.

Eileen Grimshaw was the woman whose daughter had been murdered by Trawden, then Evans, then, for those of us that knew better, by Trawden again. I'd made some weak joke with Colman, weeks back, when it was a choice between sharing weak jokes and sharing the misery of the aftermath of Brooks-Powell's death. *Getting killed once is bad luck*, I'd said. *Twice is remarkable. Three times starts to looks like carelessness.* Colman hadn't even summoned up a smile.

I'd had no contact with Eileen Grimshaw since the day I'd seen her in court, the day – twelve years ago, now – she and her husband had seen Trawden walk free, the day they'd worn the faces of people going through their daughter's death all over again. I'd suffered those faces, night and day, hitting me when I least expected them and when I knew they were coming, for a decade; I'd only recently got round to exorcising them.

And then Brooks-Powell had died and Trawden had been shot and it was all over the news, and Eileen

24

Grimshaw had written me a letter.

It had arrived the day Trawden died, but it must have been posted the day before. By the time I read it – which wasn't until the following day, what with everything else going on – the press were all over Trawden, the innocent victim of a crazed gunman and a vindictive establishment, cruelly murdered by a mystery assailant whilst fighting for his life in a hospital bed. I knew that was all bullshit; I had the feeling the rest of the world would figure it out, too, eventually.

Eileen Grimshaw already had.

Dear Sam, the letter began. *I hope you don't mind me addressing you as Sam. And I hope you don't mind me writing to you.*

My first reaction was that I did mind it, very much, but it wasn't like I could stop her. And it wasn't like she didn't have the right, either.

I know you must be hurting, it continued. *I've followed the news stories, poor Mr Brooks-Powell, who was, I recall, a colleague of yours some time ago. I've followed your career, too, but please don't think of me as some sort of stalker. It's not like I've been camped outside your house with binoculars. Until today, I didn't even know where you lived, although now I realise that the address on your website, Samuel Williams & Co., is your home. But I've always wondered how you managed, after the trial, after you left Mauriers. Not just you, of course. I followed poor Mrs Maurier – shocking, what happened to her. I followed everyone involved.*

I've seen what you've done since, Sam. I've seen the things you've done, the things you've tried to do, the people you've tried to help and save. I know you would have helped that poor woman in Manchester if you'd been able to. I know you helped that couple, the husband accused of murder and the wife hiding from the TV cameras and trying to keep her son safe.

I suppose what I'm trying to say, Sam, is that I know you're a good man. And I know that now you must realise you were wrong, all those years ago. Oh, I know the verdict hasn't changed, Edward

Trawden is still an innocent man in the eyes of the law, but you and I, we know better, don't we? I wonder what happened, in that village in Hertfordshire. I wonder how Trawden was shot, how your friend, Mr Brooks-Powell, was killed. I don't suppose we'll ever know, unless Trawden decides to tell us, and I don't believe he'd be too comfortable telling the truth.

By this point, my mouth had fallen open. She might not have known the precise circumstances that had led to Brooks-Powell's death. But she knew about Manchester, where I'd managed to prove that Thomas Carson hadn't killed anyone, where I'd saved his wife's life, where I'd failed to save Carson's lawyer, Serena Hawkes, who'd been blackmailed and threatened and pushed so far that the only way left for her was to take her own life. And she knew the truth about Trawden, or enough of the truth as made no difference. By the time I'd got round to reading the letter, of course, Trawden couldn't have told her anything even if he'd wanted to.

We had some cold years. After Maxine was taken from us. And then again, after 2005, when it felt like she'd been taken from us all over again. But this is what I want you to know, Sam:

It wasn't your fault. You mustn't blame yourself. The cold has passed and the thaw has come and whatever he does, whatever he says, Trawden cannot hurt us again.

There was more, but everything was up in the air that day, more news filtering through about Trawden, more rumours and lies to bulk out the news, the phone ringing every five minutes with updates from Colman or questions from the more persistent journalists. I spent hour after hour parroting "no comment" and telling Colman it wasn't a good time and I'd speak to her later. It wasn't a good time. Claire had taken a step backwards, not to the start, not to the woman who couldn't open her eyes without them filling with tears and couldn't rise from the bed without falling back onto it, but a step backward, nonetheless. I could see

26

the fragility in every action she took, the nervousness that accompanied something as simple as lifting a cup of tea to her lips or speaking to her mother on the phone. I'd got halfway through the letter and Claire had appeared from the bedroom, a smile etched tentatively across her lips in material so breakable it would have fallen apart if I'd so much as breathed on it. I'd stuffed the letter in my back pocket and there it had stayed, emerging to be read and reread and then stuffed back in, safe from prying eyes.

Claire wanted to read the letter. She'd asked to read it that day and I'd told her it wasn't a good idea. She'd asked again, a couple of days later, and I'd explained that it brought things up she might not be ready for. The third time she'd asked I'd turned *you might not* into *you're not*, no *might* about it. Trawden had hurt her a lot more than he'd hurt me, and a lot more recently. I found it painful enough. Claire didn't need this on top of everything else.

After a while she'd given up asking if she could read the letter and switched her focus to my reply to it, or lack of one. For someone who spent half the day in bed and much of the rest so zoned out she looked like she'd just stepped out Woodstock, she seemed to have a remarkable grasp of the finer details of my life. And now she was at it again.

I shook my head.

"No," I said. "I'll get round to it eventually. I've got to work out what to say, and it's not top of my list of priorities."

For once, this was true. I'd spent so long pretending to have more clients than I really did that I kept forgetting I wasn't spinning a line this time. I had a client. I had two, but one of them was Hasina Khalil, an Egyptian asylum seeker with an awkward relationship with the truth and a range of roles so vast that sometimes she forgot precisely which victim she was supposed to be playing. I'd get her what she wanted, eventually, but it was taking longer than either of us had expected, with short bursts of activity followed by days of silence. The way things stood, Hasina Khalil didn't need more than a couple of hours a week out of me.

But that was okay. Because I had another client, finally. Or at least, a potential client. I had Richard Fothergill. Richard Fothergill was an interesting client with an interesting case, which I wasn't entirely certain I wanted to take on, but what I wanted and what my bank statement told me to do were very different things. Richard Fothergill lived in Oxford, and tomorrow, I would be paying him a visit.

Claire listened to me explaining that Fothergill could well take up a good amount of my time over the coming months, with the appearance of taking in every word, and then turned back to the television in time to see Matt Damon escape from the bad guys into the arms of a woman whose beauty and poise stretched credibility even further than the gunfight had. We sat in silence, lost in our own thoughts, and we'd finished the pizza and most of the film when my phone rang.

I saw from the display that it was Colman, who had, I'd thought, taken the hint: I did not want to investigate Trawden's death, and if I had my way about it I wouldn't be hearing his name again as long as I lived. I thought about ignoring it, and then I remembered her stubborn persistence, and the fact that we had a history of speaking to one another at odd hours of the day and night. She had my home phone number as well as my mobile, a landline that couldn't be disconnected in case Claire needed to speak to her mother and that I didn't want ringing in the middle of the night. I sighed in frustration and stepped away from Matt Damon locked in the embrace of a second, equally beautiful woman (the first had either been killed or turned out to be an ally of the gentlemen who were trying to put bullets in the hero's head).

"Hello Vicky," I said, from the relative quiet of the bedroom. Judging by the gunshots and explosions coming from the living room, Damon's romantic interlude had been interrupted. Poor guy had it even worse than I did.

"Have you heard?" she asked, breathless, and I remembered the first time I'd called her, at something around two in the morning, and she'd answered in the same voice, only that time it had been because I'd interrupted her own romantic interlude.

"I doubt it."

"Evans. The son, John. Word is, they think it's him."

"Really? I was with your old boss this morning. She indicated otherwise."

"Like she'd tell you anything," snorted Colman, and I found myself agreeing with her. Martins liked to keep her cards close to her chest.

"So how did you find out?" I asked.

"Ear to the ground, me. Contacts. Friendships."

The way she said that *friendships* made me think there was something more to it than a cup of coffee and a shared cigarette break.

"So who is he?"

"Simon."

"Winterman?" I gasped, picturing the bastard who'd lured Claire into allowing him to question her doctor. Halfway through the final syllable I remembered I'd come away from the police station with a different, less unpleasant impression of him, and tried to change my tone from disgust to surprise, but there weren't enough letters left in the name to make it work.

"Yes," she replied. She sounded a little sharp, a little defensive, and I couldn't blame her. "He's not so bad. Not so bad looking, either. Fancies me."

"Don't they all?"

She laughed. "The ones who know what they're looking at do. I'm playing it cool with Simon, but he'll get what he wants in the end, if he's a good boy."

"So you're paying for information with sex?"

She paused, and I waited for her to tell me it wasn't like that at all, that Winterman was boyfriend material anyway and all she was doing was stringing him along for a while. Instead she waited, those breaths slowing as my rudeness and negativity rubbed away all the excitement she'd called with, and finally she just said "Yes."

I owed her an apology, which I produced right on cue, together with an account of my interview with Martins and my brief encounter with Evans that morning. It seemed to do the trick: Colman started up again the moment I'd finished my narrative, detailing John Evans' history of addiction (alcohol and heroin being his weapons of choice), his dislike of the world in general ("and you in particular," she added, as if I needed the reassurance), and the fact that his alibi was, according to Winterman, even weaker than mine – pretty much the same words Winterman had said to me earlier that day.

"Do you know what that alibi is?" I asked, but she didn't.

I reflected on that, later, in bed, with Claire snoring gently beside me and the rain beating hard against the windows. At least the snow would be gone by morning. I wondered what Evans' alibi was, where he'd been, who'd seen him doing it. I knew what my alibi was, and it was shit, but at least I knew what I'd been doing when Trawden was killed.

As for Claire, well, I knew what she hadn't been doing, whatever she'd told Martins. What she hadn't been doing, where she hadn't been. And that was sitting at home all day waiting for me.

4: Under a Cloud

TEN O'CLOCK NEXT morning found me hunkering down against a cold wind as I trudged out of Oxford railway station amid a melee of tourists and business travellers. Oxford was much changed since my time as a student there – this side of the city had turned into a hive of hotels and conference centres – but that wind was the same one I remembered, a sharp, relentless bite, all the chill of central England brought to bear on anyone foolish enough to be out in it. I concentrated on my feet – it was dry, but there was slush in the station foyer and ice on the pavements outside – and managed to walk straight into a young blonde woman who had stopped dead right in front of me, bang in the middle of the pavement, to take a sip out of a plastic cup. She scowled as I apologised, and a grey, weary-looking chap beside me raised one eyebrow and looked as though he were about to laugh. A minute later I was walking into a dingy little café and looking around for my client.

He stood as I entered, a frail-looking man with a few threads of white hair over a face blotched brown and red, but I pretended not to notice, and continued to gaze from table to table. I liked to get a sense of where I was before I committed myself to being there, and this place gave run-down a bad name. The table cloths were torn, paper coverings in a red check pattern, Mediterranean style in the middle of the coldest, windiest city in the south of England. The tables themselves were a mix of white painted wood with half the paint flecked off, and metal that showed more rust than shine. Half the fluorescent lights were out, and those that weren't flickered between dim and painfully bright and emitted an irritating high-pitched hum. There were orange laminate menus at every table and a board above the counter at the far end of the room with a list of items on it, half of them crossed out, prices updated in highlighter on bits of green card. The place was packed and it smelled fantastic.

I raised a hand in acknowledgement and made my way over to Fothergill's table. He'd remained standing while I'd made my mind up whether I was staying or going, but once he shook my hand he sat down with an audible sigh and I noticed a cane leaning against his chair.

Introductions made, I went to the counter to order tea and a bacon sandwich, nodding in approval as I saw the meat thrown fresh onto a steaming hotplate. I'd told him I could come up to visit him at his convenience, and assumed he'd want to meet at home, but he'd chosen instead to have our first session here. *I'd rather not be in the house any more than I have to*, he'd said, which had puzzled me. I hadn't really been looking forward to this meeting, if truth be told. I needed an interesting case, a proper crime involved, if there was one, and this met the bill hands down. Bad people, or those accused of being bad people, they were what kept the money rolling in and might serve to keep my name in people's minds. But after Trawden, I reckoned I'd had my fill of bad people.

Richard Fothergill was seventy-five years old, and the crimes he was accused of had taken place at the back end of the nineteen seventies. He'd been a music teacher at an Oxford school. He'd been accused of sexually abusing one of his pupils.

Fothergill's name was out there now, of course. It wasn't supposed to be; the press were supposed to be subtle about this sort of thing, to avoid influencing a future jury with lurid headlines about sordid pasts and filthy deeds. But someone had leaked, and once social media had their way with it, there was nothing to keep quiet about any more. The name of the victim – there was one victim, if there was a victim at all, I kept reminding myself – that was still under wraps. Not to me, of course. If I was to represent my client, I had to know everything.

Pieter Van der Lee had been thirteen years old when it had happened, he claimed. Pieter Van Der Lee was now fifty-one and had chosen not to report the crime until the tail end of the year that had just passed, so there were certainly questions to be raised there, but that didn't mean it hadn't happened. I could see plenty of reasons someone would keep quiet until they decided not to. Pieter Van der Lee alleged a multitude of offences, any one of which would see Fothergill serving out the rest of his life in prison, were he to be convicted. I took my seat at the table – "We bring it to you," the thickset woman behind the counter had said, waving at the hotplate and handing me my tea in a chipped red mug – and began the formalities.

Whatever Fothergill was, he wasn't considered a risk, so he'd been granted bail immediately after being charged. He'd already had his first court appearance, during which he'd given his name and insisted upon his innocence, and he'd been bailed again to appear before the Crown Court at an unspecified future date. The courts were heaving under the strain of growing crime and shrinking budgets and this might be a case that could drag on for a while; I wondered, with that *unspecified date*, whether they were hoping Fothergill would conveniently drop dead before anything more had to happen.

Fothergill had laid it on thick when he'd called, talking about my reputation and how well I was spoken of, but I hadn't bought that for a second. Fothergill had come to me because all the other, better lawyers were busy, or had claimed to be busy because they didn't want to dirty their hands with a case that had *loser* written all over it. I'd had the chance, right at the start, to plead busy myself, but I'd dallied too long over the decision and by the time I'd realised I needed to make it, it was too late: with all the questions I'd been asking and comments I'd been making, I'd shown too much interest for someone who had too much on his plate to take on another case. But, I figured, there's always a way out. This meeting was officially our introduction, a kicking-off of the process that would, Fothergill presumably hoped, see charges dropped and apologies made. As far as I was concerned, it was my chance to work out whether I wanted Fothergill at all.

My sandwich arrived just as I invited him to tell me a little about himself, and he took himself straight back to the year in question as I smeared brown sauce onto soft white bread.

"I remember a lot – that surprised me, you know, you think you'll forget, because there have been so many of them, so many thousands, over the years, but when I set my mind to it, it was there."

"So do you remember Van der Lee?" I asked through a mouthful of bacon. He shook his head.

"No, alas. As I say, there were thousands. Some stick in the mind; most, regrettably, do not. Mr Van der Lee is in the latter camp."

"So what do you remember?"

He shrugged, now, and frowned as if he were searching his mind for something he'd put away just a moment ago.

"The staff, the headmaster, of course, an immensely memorable man, an excellent man, if truth be told. The rooms. Some of the music, even, certain sonatas that were so far beyond the ability of the students to play, and yet somehow they were expected to perform them. The piano. The collection of woodwind instruments and the double bass that sat untouched year after year. I often wonder what happened to that double bass. And, as I say, certain of the students."

I waited while a middle-aged couple at the table behind

got up noisily, the metal of their chairs clattering and scraping against the floor, the door creaking as they pushed it open and falling shut with a sharp crack behind them, a high-pitched wail of wind in the intervening seconds.

"Any of Van der Lee's friends?" I asked, when quiet had finally returned.

"Since I don't recall the boy, I'm unlikely to know who his friends were."

It was a sharp reply, the same frown now expressing a very different emotion, but it was no more than the stupidity of the question deserved. I tilted my head in apology, and noted mentally that the old man was smarter than he looked. I decided to take him back a little, not so much for information on the case, but so that I could get a better understanding of Fothergill himself.

"So how long were you teaching at Thameside?" I asked.

"Oh, practically forever," he laughed. "Let's see. I left the university in sixty-three – I studied here, you know. I'd hoped to tour the world with one of the great orchestras, and I spent ten years trying to, but I learned fairly quickly that the great orchestras were too great for my meagre talents, and the ones that would have me – well, you know what Groucho said?" He waited for me to nod, and concluded. "So I became a teacher."

He was smiling as he spoke, an openness and a feeling that we were in this together. I tried to work out whether that was real or just an image he was projecting, but I couldn't. He continued.

"I was at Chalmere for three years, and then I started at Thameside. So, you see, I hadn't been there more than two or three years when these events supposedly took place."

The fact that he'd been a relative newcomer might be important; it might not. I filed it away in case I needed it. I was more interested in Chalmere, one of the city's best-known and most expensive private schools.

"What happened at Chalmere?" I asked, and he shrugged again.

"Very little, I'm afraid, and what there was wasn't of the highest quality. I didn't fit in there at all. Thameside was far more to my liking."

I wondered at that. At whether something *had* happened at Chalmere, something that had precipitated his departure from an easy and, presumably, well-paid job. The seventies had been the era of the cover-up, of sharp words with the perpetrator, keeping things quiet – *for the sake of the school* – of palming the predator off on the next unwary establishment. Chalmere was definitely worth investigating, and I cursed myself for having come by train. I didn't know where Chalmere was, but it wouldn't be in the city centre. If I'd come by car, I could have driven there, asked all the questions I wanted, and still been home in time for dinner.

Fothergill had taught at Thameside for thirty years in total and, he told me, wouldn't have quit if it hadn't been for a touch of arthritis and a growing tinnitus, conditions which might have been manageable in most jobs but were the beginning of the end for a music teacher. The tinnitus had eased off when he'd stopped teaching, but the arthritis, he said, gesturing at the cane, was a worsening problem.

I nodded at the cane, at the words, and tried to work out how quickly I could extricate myself from Fothergill and his memories. I'd been undecided about taking him on before I'd met him; a few minutes in his company had made up my mind, or at least steered me away from the middle ground. He was quite convincing, certainly; given time, I might even buy his line about not remembering Van der Lee. But a jury wouldn't have that time. Instead, they'd listen and get the same impression I'd got within those few minutes: a man who seemed frail, a man who looked like his thoughts might be as fragile as his body, but ultimately, a man who remembered almost everything and a man who understood all of it. In my experience, juries equated confusion and ignorance with innocence, incisiveness with guilt. A jury wouldn't like Richard Fothergill one bit.

I allowed him to drift gently along as I turned through my options – now he was analysing the ways in which musical education had changed during his time in the field, yet another demonstration of a man whom twelve of his peers might consider too clever by half. And then I drained my tea, stood, and thanked him for his time. He frowned again, surprised, but regained his composure quickly enough and reached for his cane.

"Please, don't," I said, and regretted the words immediately. I'd shot for polite but come out both patronising and impatient. The frown shot across his face again, replaced quickly by a smile.

"Really, it's no bother," he replied, but I noticed his teeth were gritted as he rose to his feet. We shook hands.

"I'll be in touch," I said, as I turned to go. "I'm sorry I didn't have as long as I'd hoped, but one of my clients has a hearing shortly and some information came through this morning that I need to get to grips with."

"That's fine. I'm pleased to see you take your responsibilities seriously."

He was smiling, still, and I couldn't tell whether there was a rebuke behind the words or whether he meant them just as they came out. I nodded.

"Let me know if you get a court date. Let me know if the CPS or anyone else gets in touch."

I turned and walked out and wondered whether he'd noticed what I hadn't said, which was that I was willing to take him on. I'd deliberately said "one of my clients", not "one of my *other* clients"; I'd kept things as vague as I could. He'd seemed a little put out by my abrupt departure, and it was quite possible he hadn't been fooled for a second by that *information came through this morning* line.

It had been dry when I'd left the station, but by the time I walked out of the café London's overnight rain had dragged itself west and Oxford sat under a grey sky, the streets empty apart from the occasional surprised pedestrian racing for shelter between puddles. Half a dozen people huddled under an awning across the road, stranded without umbrellas, but I had the good fortune to find a taxi seconds after I stepped outside, and I decided then and there not to let that fortune go to waste.

"How far is it to Chalmere?"

"The school?"

"That's it, yes."

I waited while she thought about it. I hadn't seen her face through the rain-streaked window, but the back of her head was a dirty blonde flecked with grey, her voice gravelly and harsh.

"'Bout eight, nine miles. Have you there in twenty minutes. Cost about fifteen quid."

"How about thirty if you take me there, wait twenty minutes and then bring me back into town?"

She turned her face to me, finally. She was younger than the voice had suggested; maybe she'd just had a rough night. She wore a smile with a curl in it, halfway to a sneer, as if what I'd asked was plainly absurd and she was waiting for me to deliver the punchline, but after a moment she nodded, slipped the car into gear and slid off into the barely-existent traffic.

Oxford lost all its charm in the rain, but retained its grandeur, leaving an impression of magnificence and unapproachability, buildings like tombs built for other people, for other times. I was reminded, briefly, of *Ozymandias*: "Look on my Works, ye Mighty, and despair", and then I caught sight of a gaggle of students in dayglo tearing across St Giles towards a bar I remembered from my own time, their laughter audible through the rain and from the other side of the road, and the sense of otherness disappeared. We passed through Summertown and took a right, and gradually the buildings were replaced by parks and small gatherings of trees. In considerably less than the twenty minutes she'd offered, we passed onto a private road and through a set of wrought iron gates with the grass grown so high around them they couldn't have been closed in years.

The gates were a one-off; the rest of Chalmere might have been dropped from the sky within the last few months, a complex of modern buildings linked by paths through the grounds and corridors in the air above them. It was term-time, and despite the weather I glimpsed a huddle of figures in black on one of the fields, chasing after a ball rendered invisible by distance and rain.

Mrs Piper, the school secretary, was a pleasant, jovial lady in her late sixties, hair as white as the fresh paint in her office and an air of dependability and solidity that her lean figure and stick-thin legs did nothing to diminish. She sat me in a deep but surprisingly uncomfortable armchair in her office and listened as I explained that I was working to absolve an innocent, elderly gentleman of some slanderous accusations that threatened to destroy the retirement he'd worked for all his life. As we drank tea and I reminded myself that I'd need to visit the facilities if I wasn't to be caught short on the train, she shook her head and told me that Fothergill had departed the school shortly before she'd arrived.

She held up a hand and left the room for a minute, and I took the opportunity afforded by her absence to examine the photographs that adorned the walls. Sports teams, every last one of them, the First XV and the First Eight, the hockey team and the shooting team and even croquet, a sport which seemed to belong to a different world from the

40

rain-soaked one outside. She returned with Fothergill's files – nothing was ever disposed of here, by the look of things – but they were little more than a bland collection of qualifications, references and tax notifications that did nothing to help me make up my mind.

As I thanked her and turned to leave, she leaned in towards me and told me, in a quiet, conspiratorial voice, that she remembered them talking about him.

"Who?"

"The other staff, of course. The music masters, the house masters."

"What did they say?"

She laughed, gently. "They'd go quiet when they saw me listening, so I never really learned anything specific. But there was something they weren't comfortable with people knowing. Hushed voices, secrets," she said, apparently unconscious of the irony of her own near-whisper. "I had the impression Mr Fothergill had left under something of a cloud. I'm afraid there's nobody left here from that time, Mr Williams, otherwise I could point you in the direction of some first-hand information."

I thanked her again, and left her with my phone number and a plea to contact me if she remembered anything else. I didn't think she would. Mrs Piper wouldn't have forgotten anything worth remembering in the first place.

The taxi driver sighed audibly as I slid into the back seat, even though I'd been less than the twenty minutes I'd indicated, and we made our way back to the city centre in silence. My phone rang, and I answered without checking the display.

"Sam Williams?" asked a voice before I'd had a chance to say it myself, a flat male voice I'd heard recently trying out the same two words.

"Yes," I replied, as the taxi drew to a halt at a red light we'd looked like running half a second earlier. The rain showed no sign of clearing, the streets teeming with black and grey. "Is that John Evans?"

"I need to talk to you."

"We're talking now," I said. He hadn't answered my question, but it was Evans.

"We need to meet."

"I don't think that's a good idea," I replied. That was understating it. Meeting a fellow suspect in a murder trial wasn't just a bad idea. It was insane.

"I don't care." For the first time there was some feeling in his voice, a petulant sharpness, a bitter little anapest, two sullen shorts and one resentful long.

"Well, Mr Evans, it takes two to meet, and I'm afraid I do care." I spoke slowly and clearly. I didn't want any ambiguity getting in the way.

"We need to meet," he repeated, urgently this time. Insistently.

"Not now, Evans. When this is all over, fine. But until then what we need to do is keep well away from each other."

I killed the call and made a note of the number. I had a feeling I'd be hearing from John Evans again.

5: Stalker

FOR ONCE, I was lucky. I made the train with seconds to spare, a stroke of good fortune not afforded to the grey-haired, rain-soaked gentleman I watched from the window, standing and gesticulating in fury on the platform as we drew away. The carriage was crowded, but there was a space beside the window at a table for four, and I found myself apologising as the woman in the aisle seat gathered up the magazines and snacks with which she'd hoped to disguise the seat beside her, and rose, with ill grace, to let me past.

I'd seen the train coming just as I'd been about to head for the toilet, and I hoped my bladder would hold out; the facilities on the train to Oxford had been unusable, and I wasn't expecting any better on the way back. I sat down and checked my phone, and saw nothing I needed to deal with, so I closed my eyes and tried to work out what I really made of Fothergill and what I was going to do about it. Ten minutes later, as we headed out of the city, I realised I had no idea and I wasn't going to get any idea just by sitting and thinking about it. So I thought about something else instead.

It had all started with the pills.

Thirteen days after David Brooks-Powell had been buried, and not long after Claire's parents had finally pissed off back to Yorkshire – I was sick of them by then, sick even of Claire's mother, who I liked in general – I woke tired and late for a meeting with a potential client that I was convinced would come to nothing, but I had to try. I crept from the bedroom, where Claire slept fitfully; she'd thrown off the duvet at some point in the night, and when I turned back to look at her, on her side against the enormity of the off-white sheet, she looked small and vulnerable and I cursed myself for arranging to leave her alone at all.

But she'd insisted I should. She wouldn't be a victim. She wouldn't make me one, either. I switched on the light in the bathroom and found myself staring into the same face I saw every morning; somehow it still surprised me that the events of the last month had wrought no discernible change in my appearance.

The stubble had to go, I decided; the man I was due to meet was a millionaire who believed himself the victim of a malicious campaign by both local and national authorities. The planning application he'd submitted for his home had not been granted; his daughter had failed to win a place in the sixth form of the prestigious grammar school she had applied to; the restaurant he owned had been raided by immigration authorities and half his staff taken away; an investigation had been ordered into his tax affairs. He was a pillar of the community – at least, he'd told me he was a pillar of the community, using those very words, *pillar of the community*, no fewer than six times during the five-minute conversation that had precipitated our meeting – and a pillar of the community, even a self-styled one, deserved a clean-shaven lawyer.

Never one to trust his own clients, potential or actual, I'd done a little research of my own. The planning application included the demolition of a sixteenth century building and the removal of a fair chunk of ancient woodland. The daughter had, according to her own Facebook profile, prepared for her GCSEs by getting herself escorted, drunk, from the biggest night club in Ipswich and adorning the kerbside with the contents of her stomach – the images were still with me forty-eight hours after I'd seen them. The immigration authorities could, I knew, be heavy-handed, but Mr Shinwa appeared to have a history of conflict with them over the way he "imported" – his word – his staff from Pakistan. And since three of his former business associates were currently in prison for tax fraud, it was hardly surprising that the Revenue would turn its attention to him.

But for all that, Mr Shinwa was a millionaire.

I'd just disposed of an old razor blade and was reaching for a new one when I fumbled, grabbed what I thought was the thing I was after, and watched in horror as Claire's glasses case sailed out of the bathroom cabinet and described a neat arc towards the floor. Even as it flew, I had time to think through the consequences: Claire wore contacts most of the time, but glasses when her eyes were tired or she couldn't be bothered to put the lenses in. I watched it land, willing it to stay shut, willing the glasses to stay safely inside, and to my relief it did, and they did, only when I opened it to check, they weren't there at all.

Instead, it was full of pills.

I placed it back in the cabinet, wondering. I thought, as I bent down to start shaving, finally, that I'd caught a glimpse of Claire watching me in the mirror. But I couldn't be sure.

I shook my head and finished shaving, and when I walked out five minutes late she was back in bed, or still in bed, asleep. She'd been there all along, I decided. I was imagining things. If there was anything to worry about, I'd worry about it later. I dressed, made coffee for us both, woke her and kissed her goodbye.

My meeting with Mr Shinwa started badly, with him informing me that we only had fifteen minutes – he was meeting other potential candidates for the role, candidates with more prestigious offices than a Starbucks outside Liverpool Street Station. It didn't improve with my informing him that whilst it was possible he had a reasonable claim in each of his four grievances, there was little chance they were connected. It descended into barely-concealed hostility when he countered by telling me that other lawyers he had spoken to had been of a very different opinion. I looked pointedly at his wallet, lying open on the table between us, and reminded him that not all lawyers had their clients' best interests at heart, particularly where there might be large sums of money involved, at which Mr Shinwa snatched up the wallet, thanked me for my time, and strode away, leaving his mocha latte untouched. I took a sip, watching through the glass wall as he marched off in the direction of his next meeting, and gagged at the sweetness.

As I headed back, my thoughts returned to the pills. For Claire to hide her medication from me like that was – my mind had been about to tell me it was *uncharacteristic*, but then I remembered what had brought all this on, the secrets and the lies and the plans that had ended with Claire in the middle of London with a loaded gun in her bag. I had, I realised, become complacent; I'd allowed myself to think all that was history.

And yet when I pictured them in my mind, I had no doubt that the pills I'd found were at least part of the medication that Claire insisted she was still diligently taking. I returned from my fruitless appointment with Mr Shinwa to find her still in bed, still in her pyjamas, awake at least but with the duvet still hanging half-on, half-off, as if it had been caught in the middle of a daring escape and decided to play it casual.

"Been up?" I asked, shooting for casual myself, and she shook her head.

"Made it as far as the loo," she croaked. "Bad day."

There was a cup in the dishwasher which I hadn't put there, but maybe I was taking her too literally. If she'd managed to boil herself a kettle and drink some hot water before collapsing back into bed, I reckoned *made it as far as the loo* was a forgivable exaggeration. When I slipped into the bathroom myself, half an hour later, I shut the door and opened the glasses case. The pills were gone.

Later that night, as I shed my clothes and put them away, I opened the drawer that contained her tops and skirts. Everything where it should be, nothing out of place, her favourite pale green number on top and untouched for longer than at any time since she'd bought it. I told myself I was looking at a clock and seeing a bomb, and I tried to forget about the pills.

I couldn't forget about the pills. The next day, as I lifted the toilet seat, I thought I could see a few specks of white powder at its edge, but when I bent down to take a proper look, they'd gone. The day after that, heading out for an afternoon with Roarkes which held about as much appeal as an afternoon in a police station with Martins, I slipped a few pennies in between her tops and tried to convince myself I wasn't being paranoid, just cautious. When I returned, tired and depressed, four hours later, Claire was in her dressing gown, on the sofa, watching television, which meant at least she'd made it out of bed. She'd texted me three times while I was out, anxious for my return. I took a look in the drawer while she filled me in on the box set she was watching. Everything in the right place. But the topmost coin – the coin that had nestled into the folds of the pale green top – had found its way out of that top to the back of the drawer.

I hadn't spotted any stray pills or white powder lately, and Claire was exhibiting what I assumed was standard behaviour for someone recovering from a breakdown with the help of antidepressants and sleeping pills. There was nothing to say she hadn't just decided to have a rummage amongst her clothes, to remind herself who she was, who she'd been before Trawden had got to her. A normal man in a normal relationship would, I realised, just ask her: *Have you been out, Claire? Are you taking your pills?* But there was nothing normal about any of this at the moment, and if she was hiding something, I didn't want her to realise I suspected her.

A few days later I went out again for most of the day. I'd made sure she knew all about it, well in advance; I'd told her I was going to see Maloney, and I'd cleared it with Maloney himself, who agreed to cover for me even if he didn't know why. I felt like an idiot, standing in the shelter of the entrance to the underground garage for the posh flats across the road, hidden in shadow and the gloom of a January morning. From where I stood I could lift my head an inch for a clear view of my own front door, and I did that every thirty seconds for half an hour, feeling more foolish with each passing minute, and then the door opened and she stepped out.

I hadn't really thought about what I was going to do at this point, but luck was with me; a crowd emerged from a bus a moment later and I kept them between her and me as we headed for the tube station. I followed her, at a distance, down the escalators and onto a Piccadilly Line train heading north, and congratulated myself for having the sense to get on a different carriage as passengers departed station by station and the human cover shrank.

I saw her stand as we drew into Southgate, and waited until she was off the train before I made my own move, beating the closing doors by moments. In another stroke of good fortune, Claire had emerged beside the exit and I caught a glimpse of her turning into the tunnel before she was hidden from sight. There was only one way out from here, and I hung back until she had made it onto the street, where I watched as she paused, consulted her phone, and set off through a light drizzle past the shops and cafés, and towards Winchmore Hill.

Again, I was dependent on others to shield me; a gaggle of excited mothers, their babies sheltered by plastic covers across the tops of their prams, proved particularly valuable, and I silently cursed when they turned into a pizza restaurant and left me momentarily unguarded. Thankfully, Claire had eyes only for her phone and her surroundings; the human traffic seemed not to interest her at all.

There was a nasty moment when she stopped, briefly, and looked behind, as if convinced she'd taken a wrong turn and needed to retrace her steps. I shrank into a convenient wall and found myself holding my breath until she frowned, turned back to her phone, and carried on in the direction she'd been taking.

Eventually she took a right off the main road onto a street that looked like it was mostly residential. I worried that my brief adventure was coming to an end; I'd stick out like a fat man on a catwalk on the almost deserted street. But as I stood at the corner, pondering my options, she paused, looked at the granite building in front of her – a small office block, I thought – and strode determinedly to the front entrance.

Determination could only take her so far. I crouched at the corner of the road, ignoring the bemused glances of passing drivers, and watched as she spoke into an intercom, waited, spoke again, and was eventually rewarded with access as the nondescript black door clicked open. I counted to one hundred and approached the door myself, but there was nothing to say who was based here, or what they made or sold. I retreated to my vantage point, took a photograph of the building and made a note of the address, and decided my work was done. As far as Claire was concerned, I was out for the day, which meant she might stay inside for hours. I gave it five minutes, just in case, and then turned and headed back to the underground.

Lunchtime was approaching and I'd skipped breakfast, so on a whim I turned into the same pizza restaurant I'd seen the mothers enter earlier. I took a table facing the street, ordered something spicy and large, and an early beer to go with it. Behind me the mothers were entertaining one another with the failings of their husbands, the failings of their au pairs, and in one case, the mutual and rather distressing failings of husband *and* au pair. Neither husband nor au pair had been forgiven, much to the approval of the rest of the group, and the wronged woman appeared to have taken the opportunity to remake herself and re-enter life with a spirit I couldn't help but admire. I was so caught up in the conversation taking place behind me that I almost failed to notice Claire striding past on the pavement outside, but the brief glimpse I caught of her face before she passed was enough to tell me that things had not gone as she'd hoped. Her jaw was set as she marched purposefully back towards the station, and I found myself pitying anyone who had the misfortune to get in her way.

I finished my pizza and left while the mothers were sorting out their bill. I'd need to stay out at least another couple of hours, I realised, unless I wanted to confront Claire today, and, I realised, I really didn't want to confront Claire today. I gave Maloney a call and met him in a pub half a mile from my own flat, where he listened to everything I told him, shook his head, told me to *grow a pair and have a bloody word with the missus*, and watched as I fruitlessly searched the internet for information on the occupants of the building she'd visited.

I found Claire in bed when I got home; she claimed she'd hardly left it all day. Fortified by the beer, I asked her if that was really true – asked her gently, and in a way that, I hoped, could be taken as concern for her wellbeing rather than outright accusation. Her reaction wasn't gentle at all; she fell back into the bed and began to hyperventilate, and even through the beer I could tell she wasn't faking it. I ran to the kitchen and returned with a glass of water and one of the pills I was now convinced she wasn't taking any more, and watched as she swallowed both and her breathing gradually eased.

"I'm sorry," I said, and she shook her head.

"It's okay. I know you're only looking out for me. You're the only one who believes in me, Sam. I can't tell you how much that means."

I nodded. She frowned at me, as if I hadn't grasped what she was saying, as if I hadn't understood its importance.

"No," she said. "I'm serious. It's like – remember Mandy? Remember what happened there?"

Mandy was her cousin. Had been her cousin. Had taken her own life after she'd tried to speak out about the abuse she was suffering at the hands of her mother's boyfriend, and not been taken seriously. I nodded. "Of course."

"That's what happens. When you have no one to believe in you, and no one you can believe in. When you've got no one on your side. I'm glad you're on mine."

She smiled as she finished, and we changed the subject, and I tried to work out if there was something there, a threat, hidden among the thanks and the smiles. Five minutes later she remembered that a letter had come for me, and I was all set to open it when the phone rang, and I answered it and listened to Colman telling me that Trawden had been found dead in his bed at the Royal Free Hospital in suspicious circumstances.

I forgot about the letter until the following morning, when I opened it and read Eileen Grimshaw's critique of my own pain. And I forgot about Claire's mysterious trip until halfway through the afternoon, when Detective Inspector Martins called and informed me of Trawden's death. Claire had answered the phone – in retrospect, I realised, I should have kept her away from phones that day, at least until I'd had a chance to talk properly with her. But it was too late; I heard her telling Martins that yes, she knew about Trawden – it had been all over the news by then – and that she'd been at home by herself all day. I already had half an alibi in Maloney, so I went down that path when Martins asked me the same question five minutes later. It wasn't even completely untrue, I reminded myself, as I lied through my teeth to a woman conducting a murder investigation. But it wasn't completely true, either.

The good news was that even if she hadn't been at home, like she said she had, I knew Claire hadn't been at the Royal Free Hospital administering a lethal dose of insulin to Edward Trawden. The bad news was that apart from the location, I had no idea what she had been doing, who she'd been meeting, what – and this was the thing that bothered me most, because the Claire I knew was clever enough to have learned from her mistake with the Sig and possibly clever enough to get someone else to do the dirty work for her – what, precisely, she'd been arranging. I had no idea, and after she'd said what she'd said about Mandy, I couldn't ask.

The train drew into Paddington Station and I burst through the doors and up the platform, desperate to relieve my bladder. I'd spent a lot of time since Trawden's death looking into that building and keeping as close an eye on Claire as I dared, without inducing another panic attack. I still knew nothing about what she'd been doing. But whatever it was, I had the feeling I didn't want Martins finding out about it.

6: The Old Man and The Kinks

CLAIRE WAS IN when I got back from Oxford, but fully dressed. She'd tidied up the flat and done a little cleaning, and it was easy, for a moment, to forget everything else that was happening under the surface.

"Colman called," she said. Colman had called my mobile, too, and it was just like her to try the landline when I didn't answer. The woman didn't know how to give up.

"Thanks. How have you been?"

She shrugged. "Not too bad, actually. Best day in a long while, I think."

I took a moment, a long half-second, to examine her smile. It seemed genuine enough, but I was starting to distrust my own judgment.

"No TV?"

She shook her head. "Nope. Too busy." She smiled again, and stretched, and this time I was sure of it. She wasn't as tired as she had been. More lively. More alert. "Are you going to call Colman back?" she asked. Like she wanted to distract me.

I was distracted enough. I'd spent an hour on the train rereading Eileen Grimshaw's letter and then looking her up on the web, not that the web had much to say about her beyond the usual melodramatic portrait of the grieving mother. I wanted more. I wanted to know where Eileen Grimshaw got her insights, where Eileen Grimshaw got her language, what Eileen Grimshaw had been before she'd been *the mother of the victim*. I knew a little. I remembered snippets of information from the trial, useless, all of it. It wasn't enough. And it looked like the web didn't have much more.

"Maybe," I replied. "Not now."

"Why not?"

It was a good question, but I couldn't go into it. Not with Claire.

"It won't be anything important. Just a bit more gossip. I'll ring her later, or tomorrow, probably. Seeing Roarkes tonight. Want to come?"

"Let's see," she replied. "Would I rather go out and watch you get drunk and miserable and talk about death with an old man, or would I prefer to stay at home and cook myself a nice meal and watch something exciting on the TV?"

I laughed. If I'd had the choice, I'd have been sitting down in front of the television with her. I didn't have the choice.

There was a surprise waiting for me outside the front door, but only because it had come sooner than I'd expected. John Evans, leaning against a Jaguar parked on the other side of the road – not his Jaguar, I assumed – with a cigarette hanging from his mouth and one hand cupped around it to shield it from the rain. He moved quickly, across the road and then stepping forward to block my way before I made it as far as the pavement, and I stopped and stared him in the face and tried to see tiredness and confusion there instead of a tattoo of a spider's web.

"I told you I didn't want to meet," I said, and started to push past him, emboldened by the way he'd sounded on the phone, by a certain pleading quality I thought I'd spotted in his expression, but I'd misjudged: he grabbed my forearm before I'd left him behind and tugged me sharply back towards him.

"I just want to talk," he said. I looked down, to the point where his hand wrapped itself around my wrist.

"Let go of my arm."

I heard footsteps and glanced beyond him, to a figure walking by on the other side of the road, slowing as he approached, wondering, no doubt, whether he should intervene or call for help or just walk on by. The footsteps quickened as he passed under a streetlight, and I caught a glimpse of grey hair and a black coat slick with rain, and then he was gone.

"Give me five minutes." The cigarette still hung from his lips as he spoke around it, but there was urgency in his voice, a hint almost of desperation.

"I'll give you ten words," I said. "Let go of my arm or I'll call the police."

I thought, given his standing with the police, a threat like that might have some effect, but once again, I was wrong. Instead, I felt his grip tighten and his other hand snaking round, grabbing my bicep, dragging me towards him until I was inches from those scars and that spider's web and could smell the pungency of his hair and the sickly sweetness of whatever it was he was smoking. Without thinking – I must have absorbed more from those long-abandoned martial arts classes than I'd imagined – I made a fast circle with my wrist to free it, and tugged my arm away. For a moment we were staring at one another, his eyes wide with surprise, and then I pushed past him, catching him hard with my shoulder as I went, the same way he'd caught me at the station, and had the pleasure of watching him fall to one knee. I kept going, not looking back again until I was about to turn the corner thirty yards down the road, surprised I hadn't heard him running up behind me. He was still there, rooted to that same spot, on both knees now, searching out something on the rain-soaked ground.

Roarkes had greeted me warmly and with some of the old bitter vigour he'd made a habit of spraying around him as he strode through life. But two pints in and something had changed. It might have been the alcohol, it might have been the music – someone had shoved a sixties collection on the jukebox and it was possible Roarkes was reliving his past. His wife was dead, and there wasn't anything I could do for him except sit there and talk at him while he stared silently at his beer.

I'd probably drunk more of that beer than I should have done, and eventually I couldn't take any more, so I leaned across the table, tapped him on the shoulder, and said "Is it the music?"

He looked up at me, blank.

"The music," I repeated. "Memories, right? You and Helen, the past, all that?"

He continued to stare at me, for a few seconds, and then his face creased into a smile.

"How old do you think I am, Sam?"

I examined his face as Tom Jones wound down and The Kinks launched into *Tired of Waiting for You*. I'd never thought to ask. Roarkes was old. He'd been old when we'd first met, a couple of years back, and he'd only got older since. I shrugged.

"Sixty-five," I said, figuring I was probably flattering him by a year or two.

Smile still in place, he shook his head, slowly. "No, Sam. I'm fifty-six years old. I was probably a fucking toddler when this came out." He gestured broadly, at the pub, the music, The Kinks and Tom Jones and Diana Ross and the rest of them.

"Christ," I replied, without thinking, and Roarkes, who'd lifted his glass to his lips while he was waiting for my reaction, snorted and spilt most of his mouthful down his shirt.

"Sorry," I said, and handed him a tissue. My judgment might not have been good – on his age or the effect of the music – but it had broken the ice and brought something of the old Roarkes back to the table. We finished our drinks and grabbed two more, and I decided, finally, that if I wasn't getting anywhere trying to figure things out for myself, if Maloney wasn't getting any further than I was, then I might as well try Roarkes.

So I told him everything. Claire and Trawden. Claire and Jonas Wolf and the Sig. I widened the circle – with Claire and Colman, and Maloney, and me of course, now there were five of us who knew. He nodded, kept his surprise, if there was any, to himself, didn't ask why I hadn't come to him earlier, because he must have known what the answer would be, and neither of us wanted to hear me saying he'd been busy watching his wife die at the time. "OK," he said, when I'd brought him up to the Central Criminal Court and its aftermath, Claire's parents, the medication, and the worse-than-useless *talking therapy* she'd abandoned after a single session. "It sounds bad, but it's over, right?"

I shook my head. "I wish it were."

And then I laid out the rest. From the start, the pills and the white powder, the trip to Southgate, the news of Trawden's death, the pair of bullshit alibis Claire and I had fallen into through bad luck and miscommunication, my interview with Martins and the all-but-silent Genaud. I laid it all out, right up to my little altercation with John Evans, which I omitted because I didn't see how it could play any part in what I was about to ask of him, and then I waited for him to say precisely what I knew he'd say.

"Why don't you just ask her about it?" he said, and I congratulated myself on my accuracy.

"I tried. She had a panic attack. She might be better than she's pretending to be, but she's still not right. I can't risk that happening. Not after everything she's been through."

Roarkes sighed in frustration, as if he'd spend an hour arguing rationally with an idiot instead of ten seconds saying the obvious thing. I thought about telling him about Mandy, about the hint Claire had dropped, *abandon me and I'll have nothing, disbelieve me and I'll die*. If she'd dropped it at all. I decided to keep it to myself. If I'd imagined it, then there was no point in raising it. If I hadn't, then Roarkes wouldn't stop until he had her sectioned and medicated and physically safe. And that, I was convinced, would end up killing her.

"Okay," he said, when he'd finished sighing and shaking his head, drained his beer, and sent me to the bar for two more. "First thing I've got to ask. Because I'm a cop, see."

"Ask away."

"Are you sure she didn't do it?"

"Do what, kill Trawden?"

He nodded.

"Of course. I've just told you. Unless there's a secret underground monorail between that building in Southgate and the Royal Free Hospital, then she couldn't have been anywhere near Trawden."

He nodded again. "Yes, I get that. But you know what I mean. There's more than one way to skin a cat. Are you sure she wasn't involved?"

I hesitated, and saw Roarkes noticing me hesitate, and cursed my slow reactions.

"Yes. One hundred per cent. She didn't do it, Roarkes."

"Because you know her and you know that's not the sort of thing she'd do?"

I knew where he was going. I kept my mouth shut and waited for him to get there.

"Because you knew what she was like last month, and heading into town with an illegal firearm with the intention of shooting dead a significant witness to a major crime, without you knowing about it, that's different, right?"

"Yes," I replied, when he'd finally finished. "It is different. This is Trawden. This is something we're in together, me and Claire. And we talk to each other, now. All the time. I know what she's been through."

"Hmm," he said, and took a long drink. "And the fact

that she's lying to you right now, telling you she's stayed in when she's actually been gallivanting around London doing god knows what, that fits into your talking to each other all the time thing precisely how?"

I shrugged. I knew Claire hadn't killed Trawden. I just couldn't explain how. Roarkes nodded at me, and went on.

"Right. I'm going to take all this on trust, because you seem convinced, and contrary to popular opinion, you're not as stupid as you look. So now I'm going to say something else I have to say because I'm a cop, not because I mean it or I think it's a good idea. Just because I have to. Okay?"

"Okay."

"Why don't you tell Martins?"

I laughed, and he laughed too, a little, but despite the build-up and the laugh, I could tell he was waiting for an answer.

"That would involve telling her we've both lied to her, that our alibis are bullshit. And you know Martins. No one's more likely to add up two and two and get five. She'd have us arrested and charged before I'd finished saying sorry."

"You're not wrong there." He paused, and took another drink. "And she's not the worst of it."

"What do you mean?"

"Genaud. Tricky fucker, that one. Dirty."

"What, actual dirty? Like, seventies beat-'em-and-fit-'em-up dirty?"

He laughed, a laugh devoid of warmth or humour. "No, but only because it's not the seventies any more. That was when I knew him, though, give or take a decade. I caught the bastard out and made sure everyone knew about it. He wasn't playing by the rules, and he was giving the rest of us a bad name. But Micky Genaud was a political animal. People like him always are. Political enough to get it swept under the carpet."

We sat in silence for a moment, while I thought about Genaud and what the hell he was doing getting himself caught up in Martins' case.

"So, what, he'll try to fit someone up?"

Roarkes shook his head. "Probably not. Twenty seventeen's not nineteen eighty-seven. Bit harder these days." He took a sip from his drink, and went on. "But he'll want to push things his way, whether that's the right way or not. Just watch your back, Sam. If Genaud decides he's after you, you want to be very, very careful."

Another silence fell. Roarkes drank; I just sat and stared and tried to work out whether Genaud could really be worse than Martins. Finally, Roarkes frowned and asked the question that he'd have asked five minutes earlier if Genaud hadn't cropped up.

"So, if you don't mind me asking, why the hell are you telling me all this? Senior officer of the law as I am?"

"Because I want to figure out what Claire was doing if she wasn't killing Trawden and wasn't sitting around the flat watching TV. And I've drawn a blank."

"I take it Maloney's got no further."

I examined his face as he spoke. I hadn't mentioned Maloney's help, but it didn't take a genius to figure out that I'd have called on the one man who could get information quicker than the police. Roarkes and Maloney had a grudging respect for one another, but they sat on opposite sides of the line – Maloney might claim to have gone straight, and it was true he didn't run a criminal empire any more, but normal members of society didn't keep illegal handguns plus ammunition locked away in their homes. Roarkes looked serious. He wasn't trying to wind me up.

"No. Nothing. I need to know about the building, Roarkes. There's nothing online. Reckon you can help?"

He shrugged, lost in thought. The old Roarkes, the Roarkes who'd been my friend before Manchester, before

Serena Hawkes, before his wife had died, that Roarkes would have been on this like a shot, before I'd even finished speaking, would have been on the phone shouting orders at terrified subordinates. The fact that this wasn't a police investigation, the fact that there was a real police investigation going on and I'd misled it, all that would have been forgotten in the thrill of the hunt.

But this Roarkes just sat there, silent and unsure. He was grieving, and older than he had been, and maybe he'd just had enough of stepping the wrong side of the line and spending most of his time and energy having to justify it. I waited – I didn't want to push him – and he finished his beer, and I offered him another, but he declined with a shake of the head, still silent, and looked down at his empty glass.

He sat like that a full five minutes, and I resisted the urge to push him while The Kinks became The Four Tops and The Four Tops became The Moody Blues. I could hear grumblings from other tables as realisation dawned that they could well be spending the rest of the evening in the sixties. As "Go Now" faded out, he raised his eyes to meet mine and gave a small nod.

"Thanks," I said.

"I'm not promising anything, Sam. If Maloney couldn't find anything – well. It's not going to be easy."

"You'll do what you can."

"Right. I'll do what I can without treading on too many toes."

I froze. This was what I'd feared. Roarkes' brilliance had always been that he didn't care whose toes he stepped on, or how hard. He got results. A tamed Roarkes was no Roarkes at all. I couldn't let that go.

"What do you mean, stepping on too many toes?"

He waited a moment before answering, as if he wanted his response to be as precise as possible, as if he didn't want me running to complain down the line because I'd misunderstood what he could deliver.

"It's just a figure of speech, Sam. But if Maloney hasn't cracked it, this isn't going to be easy. I'll probably need access I'm not entitled to. And if I want to get that access I'm going to have to piss some people off. Like you said. I'll do what I can."

I could live with that, I thought. Roarkes could do a lot more than I could. He accepted that beer, finally – I'd forgotten I'd offered it and we both chose to forget it was his round – and half an hour later I was home. There was no sign of Evans outside, but I noticed a half-smoked cigarette a few feet from the front door. He'd have dropped it as I shouldered my way past him, I realised. He'd have been looking for it as I turned and watched him searching on the ground. The police thought he might be the murderer, that was what Colman had said. He was calling me and hanging around my front door. And he had good reason not to like me. I'd have to give John Evans some thought.

It was only eleven, but Claire was already asleep. I lay down beside her and ran through the day in my head, trying to figure out if I'd told Roarkes everything I needed to, trying to guess what it was Colman had called to tell me, or whether she'd called for any real reason at all; trying to think like John Evans and work out whether he meant me harm and if so, how much; trying to imagine what it was that had forced Fothergill out of Chalmere and whether the mere hint of suspicion was enough justification to turn him down; looking inside myself to see if I really wanted to turn him down at all. And then the phone was ringing beside the bed – my side, not that a few extra feet of distance stopped Claire sitting up and rubbing her eyes, and it was three in the morning, and a man I'd never met was telling me that Fothergill had just attempted suicide.

"How did you get this number?" I asked, and then apologised as it dawned on me that of all the questions I should asked, that was some way down the list.

"He gave it to me. He asked me to call you. I'm sorry for waking you. I assumed you were a friend, or a relative, or something."

"No," I replied. "I'm his lawyer." Which was getting ahead of myself a little, but now wasn't the time for pedantry. "Can you tell me what happened?"

What had happened was that Richard Fothergill had been taken in an ambulance to the John Radcliffe Hospital in Oxford, around the time I was enjoying my last drink with Roarkes, with a stomach full of sleeping pills and whisky. He'd been given oxygen and had his stomach pumped, and been treated with medication to reverse the effects of the benzodiazepine which had been the cause of his overdose. And when he'd come round, he'd thanked the doctors, stood up, grabbed the cane from beside his bed, and walked out, tearing the cannula from his arm, ignoring all attempts to persuade him to lie back down and at least allow his body time to recover. He'd stopped only to ask the man who was calling me – a junior doctor who'd just come on shift and hadn't really appreciated what was going on at the time – to let me know what had happened and that I could find him at home, should I wish to do so. "A funny turn of phrase, that," said the doctor, and I agreed, but I knew precisely what it meant. Fothergill knew I was having second thoughts about taking him on.

"Was this for real?" I asked. "I mean, the guy's walked out of hospital a couple of hours later. Do you think he was just after a bit of attention?"

"No." There was no pause, no uncertainty. Just that *No*. "Absolutely not. I've spoken with my colleagues. He was lucky, that's all. A neighbour came round to see if he was okay and saw him lying on the kitchen floor. Another hour and there wouldn't have been anything we could do."

I thanked him for his time and hung up. I'd assumed, the whole time the doctor was talking, that Fothergill had just been trying to send me a message.

Not for the first time, I'd been wrong.

7: Favours

CLAIRE WOKE ME with coffee and yet another letter from Lizzy Maurier.

This was the fifth. It opened, as did each of its predecessors, with a line or two from her poem, which was enough to make it clear the reader was in the presence of something unusual. Her first two letters had dwelt on her favourite themes, severed tongues and nightingales, tapestries and pies. Trawden had cut out her mother's tongue when he'd killed her, the rare, deranged act of an animal who wore his human clothing well, and Lizzy's mind had leapt straight to Greek myth and Shakespearean tragedy. The third letter still had a little pie in it, but below it a comment about the weather, an observation on the food, a barb about her neighbour in the farmhouse nearby that was almost witty. Trawden had died by then, and she mentioned it, but almost in passing, as if Trawden wasn't important any more, as if whether he lived or died made no difference to her whatsoever. The fourth ignored the weather and the food but went into some detail about the locals, sharp and funny enough that I was almost sorry it was so short. After the news overnight, I found, to my astonishment, that I was pleased to be hearing from Lizzy Maurier again.

She suspected the Mayor of having an affair with the neighbour in the farmhouse, but, as she pointed out, this was France: that hardly constituted gossip, and certainly wouldn't make the grade as news. Her car – Lizzy's, not the neighbour's – had broken down on the way into town and she had been touched by the number of people that had offered to help. She'd thought they despised her. Perhaps they didn't. *Perhaps I deserve their derision, Sam*, she wrote. *Perhaps even their hatred. I was a fool, at best, and people are dead because of it. But all they see is a lonely Englishwoman in need of assistance, and they come running to me.* After the incident with the car, she had felt suddenly more at home in her tiny Breton village. She'd sold the gîte in the Dordogne her mother had left her, she'd rented out her London flat, and the Oxfordshire manor held too many difficult memories. Brittany *was* home. She asked after me. She asked after Claire, after Melanie Golding, after Roarkes, all people she'd never met in her life. She even asked about Martins, but what she actually wrote was *I hope you haven't had cause to see that bitch again*, which was something any sane person who'd had the pleasure of making the DI's acquaintance might ask. I took her letter to the kitchen drawer and inserted it into the envelope that held the others, and then, on a whim, I pulled them all out and arranged them on the worktop, each overlapping the next, so that only the top few lines were visible. Silently, I read the poem.

> So at last all the tears have been shed.
> All the sayable words have been said.
> The songs were all sad and each story a lie,
> And now even the lies have run dry.
>
> *A hand reached for me*
> *It held food love warmth sex*
> *It held ropes chains and scissors*
>
> Attics aren't healthy for paintings or wives,
> Not blindness nor death can be stayed.
> Music and words won't restore stolen lives,
> The road into hell goes one way.
>
> *I was fed clothed and pleasured*
> *My cords were severed*
> *For every joy a rock soldered onto my chain*

For every action
An equal and opposite reaction

The staff has been broken, that pearl's just an eye,
The volume lies torn on the stage.
The sprites needed scaffold and winches to fly
And the trickster was never a sage.

Five letters. Five verses. Lizzy Maurier's life unravelling in poetry. I had the feeling there was more to come, and what I'd read, I still didn't much like, but a part of me admired her honesty.

I slid my eye over the stamps and grinned. As a child, I'd been a collector. There was one other thing I hadn't mentioned to Martins, partly because I wasn't sure what it meant or if it meant anything at all, and partly because she'd pissed me off. The postmarks. All from that little Breton village, except one, the one posted the day before Trawden's death. That one had been sent from Le Touquet. Brittany was close enough to London to offer opportunity to the determined murderer, but Le Touquet was just an hour from Calais. An easy morning's drive to London, a quick needle in a bag, and home again in time for tea.

I pushed the letters back into the envelope, and instinctively patted my back pocket, frantic for a moment before I remembered I wasn't yet dressed. Claire was in the bathroom, the shower was on. I found my jeans slung across the back of the chair where I'd left them the night before and pulled out Eileen Grimshaw's letter.

It was unusual, all this post in the age of email and instant messaging. Real paper and stamps. I wondered whether Eileen Grimshaw had entered the electronic age at all, or if she'd remained stuck in the eighties, frozen at the moment of her daughter's death. Except she hadn't. What had she said? *The thaw has come.* The cold years were over. I delved back through those years and pulled out that look again, and everything that had gone before it. Hands blocking the line from cameras to face, on the way in to court for Trawden's final hearing. Her witness statement, read out at his original trial. She'd been too traumatised to give evidence in person, but it hadn't made much difference. Eileen Grimshaw, I realised, had always come across well on paper. I smoothed out the pages and read on, words I'd read before, words that I still needed to digest.

Trawden cannot hurt us again, she'd said. And then she'd explained why.

I understand Mr Brooks-Powell left a widow, and I hope she is coping better than we were when Maxine died. If you feel it appropriate, please pass on a message to her, from us. Tell her that we know her pain, we know it intimately. Tell her that Trawden is lying in a hospital bed, and when he gets up and walks out of that hospital bed, her thoughts will travel with him, wherever he goes, whoever he speaks to or sees or touches. But tell her, too, that in time those thoughts will learn independence. They will rid themselves of Edward Trawden. Her thaw will come.

Her thaw will come. I stifled a laugh as I folded the page and stuffed it back in my pocket. Melanie's cold years had been the ones with David. She'd learned to thaw a long time ago.

I was, I realised, deliberately delaying. I had a job to do today, and it wasn't one I was looking forward to. I hadn't greatly enjoyed Fothergill's company first time round. I wasn't sure I liked the man and I wasn't sure I trusted him. But he'd tried to kill himself. I owed him a visit, at least.

Of course, a second trip to Oxford threw up another problem, one I'd managed to push to the back of my mind when I'd met Fothergill the previous day. The problem was monitoring Claire's movements. It was hard enough when

I was in London, but with a whole day to play with she could be doing anything, going anywhere, and I wouldn't know a thing about it.

Claire stepped out of the shower, wrapped in a towel, flashed me a smile, and headed straight into the bedroom. A moment later I heard the sound of the hair drier. After Fothergill's attempt, what Claire had said about Mandy loomed larger, as if someone else's near suicide made hers more likely. I reached for my phone, found the contact I wanted. My finger hovered over the big green dial button. I didn't really want to make this call. I knew exactly how I'd be received.

I hit the button and Maloney answered a few seconds later with a cheery "What do you want now, Sam?", which was precisely what I'd expected.

"As if I'd only call you for a favour," I replied, and he gave a wary laugh. Something had changed between us, I realised. Before Claire had walked out of his flat with his gun and his ammunition, he'd always had the upper hand. But he'd never shown it. I'd done him a favour, once, a long time back, and he'd repaid that favour a hundred times over, never a complaint. Usually I hadn't even had to ask – he'd known what I wanted from him before I said a thing.

Now it was as if something had shifted and he needed to remind me – there was a balance sheet, and Sig or no Sig, I was still in the red.

"But yeah," I said, into the silence that followed the laugh. "Yeah, I do. If you can."

"Well?"

He sounded almost impatient, now. He'd never been impatient before.

"Well, I need someone to follow Claire."

There was a short pause, then he said "No."

"Just for today. Keep an eye on her. I've got go to Oxford."

"What's so important in Oxford?"

That was good. He wasn't questioning the need for Claire to be followed. He was just asking why I couldn't do it myself. I told him about Fothergill, the case, the suicide attempt, and he asked me why I gave a damn about someone with that kind of crime in their history.

"Because he might not have done it," I said. "And if he didn't – well, they'll tear him to pieces in prison, and I wouldn't be wasting a second's thought about that if I knew he was guilty, but I have a feeling he isn't."

"It's not enough, Sam."

"Look, you know why I need this, Maloney."

There was a brief pause, and when he came back on the line, his voice had changed, an edge to it that I hadn't heard in a while. "Oh, right," he said. "It's my fault, is it? I handed the woman a gun and told her to go out and shoot someone, did I?"

"Hang on a second –"

"No, *you* hang on a second," he interrupted. "*You know why I need this*, that's what you said, right? Yes, she got the gun from my place. But if it hadn't been me it would have been someone else. If it hadn't been a gun it would have been a knife."

I took the words in and paused for a moment while I examined each one. He was right. Trawden had pushed all the right buttons. He'd posed as the father of one of the victims Claire had spent the last two years obsessing over, the women trafficked by Jonas Wolf, who was just about to give evidence in a migrant boat disaster trial so important Wolf had been granted immunity for his own crimes. Trawden had also found out about Claire's own past – the suicide of a cousin who had been groomed and abused – and hinted at a vague connection between that history, and the crimes of Jonas Wolf. He'd instilled in Claire a need for vengeance and justice that only made sense in the twisted

70

world he'd created for her, and by the end she'd been so caught up in Wolf that not having a gun wouldn't have stopped her.

"I'm sorry," I said, and he grunted. "You're right. I'm not trying to make you feel guilty. I just really, really need your help."

"Well. Okay then." He sounded halfway mollified, at least. I wasn't going to let it stop at halfway.

"So what do you say? I'm desperate, Maloney."

A pause, and then "Yeah. Okay. I'll get someone on it. Can't promise anything, though."

I thanked him and explained what I needed him to do. And then I stepped into the bedroom, where Claire was still drying her hair, kissed her goodbye, got in the car and drove to Oxford.

I pulled over before I'd left London to take a call, thinking maybe Maloney had found something out already, or Roarkes had, something I needed to know here and now, something that might give me the excuse I was looking for to turn around and forget about Oxford and Richard Fothergill entirely. I regretted it the moment I heard Martins' voice.

"I'm driving," I said, and she laughed.

"Hope you've stopped your car then. I just wanted to tell you that it looks like your alibi checks out."

"I know it checks out, Martins. It checks out because it's true."

"Everyone says that," she replied, and laughed again, and I was just about to kill the call when I remembered John Evans.

"Evans has been hanging around," I said. "The son."

"What do you mean? Hanging around where?"

I told her what had happened. I jazzed it up a little – the hands on my arm bit right into the skin, the words were shouted, not spoken – but not so much it wouldn't seem

71

real.

"Hmm," she said, when I'd finished. "Well, it's not pleasant, but it doesn't sound like much."

I couldn't disagree. I waited in silence, while on the other end of the line she thought it over. I could almost hear her trying to work out how she could turn this to her advantage.

"Do you want us to pull him in?" she asked, finally. "We probably could. He's still a suspect. This could be, I don't know, witness intimidation?"

"No," I said, with barely a second's thought. He'd be in that afternoon and out by evening and he'd have cause to hate me even more. "No. I don't think he's planning on killing me. I just thought you should know."

"Why, thank you," she replied, in a voice dripping with sarcasm, and ended the call. I started the car, wondering if I'd regret turning down her offer even more than I regretted talking to her at all, and hit the road again.

Fothergill's house was a two bedroom bungalow on a scruffy estate near Cowley that might have seen better times but wasn't expecting them back any time soon. I parked across the road and saw a woman glaring at me as she led her dog into a house a few doors down.

In the rare burst of sunshine – the rain had dribbled to a halt halfway into my drive – Fothergill's house looked cleaner than most, washed down within memory, the window frames repainted at least once since the place had been built, which put him one up on his neighbours. But it wasn't the cleanliness that drew my eyes to the wall and kept them there. It wasn't the cleanliness that made the two lads cycling down the road – I had to jump back to avoid them, focussing as I was on the house instead of the oncoming traffic – pause a few yards down, turn back and stare.

It was the words on the wall.

"DIE PEDO SCUM," they said. Red paint, thick

lettering a foot high. Spelling aside, the message was pretty clear. Fothergill's difficulties were not as private as he might have hoped.

He answered the door a full minute after I'd rung the bell, a delay that was explained when I watched him hobble back to the kitchen and set about the painful business of making me a cup of tea. I offered to help, but he wasn't having any of that.

"I'm not dead yet, you know," he snapped. There was an obvious challenge there, an invitation to ask him why he'd tried to kill himself the previous night. I declined, and sat opposite him around a small wooden kitchen table as he apologised for his "outburst" and explained, in a surprisingly matter-of-fact tone, that his neighbours would probably be delighted if he *were* dead.

"You saw that, outside?" he asked, and I nodded. "It's just the latest. My friend Julia usually spots them first thing – she passes by on her way to work – and she helps me get rid of it. But Julia's away at the moment, and everyone else round here, well." He shrugged.

"They've already found you guilty and hanged you," I ventured, and he produced a small, thin smile.

"I had a couple in the street, asked me what this was all about, I've known them for years. I said it was nonsense, explained I didn't even know the boy, didn't remember him in the slightest. Do you know what they said?"

I shook my head.

"No smoke without fire. That was it. No smoke without fire. They've avoided me ever since, actually crossed the road when they saw me. It's not like we were great friends before all this happened, but we passed the time of day, chatted, that sort of thing. Now? I suppose I should be grateful they're not throwing things at me."

"Has anyone thrown anything at you? Done anything physical?"

73

"No, but I suppose it's only a matter of time. They egg each other on, the young ones, don't they? See what they got away with last time, go a bit further next time. That, outside, that's the biggest and boldest so far. I wish I could explain. But no one's listening."

I'd been planning on delving into him a little further, asking him about Chalmere and his mysterious departure, trying to get a handle on whether I believed him or not, but suddenly, I didn't need to. He'd made me tea, and, I remembered, insisted on rising painfully to shake my hand when I'd left the café the previous day; he was acting as if he were strong. The reality, I saw, was very different.

Richard Fothergill was a broken man, or as close to broken as made no difference. A few minutes the night before and he'd have been a dead man, too. *No one's listening,* he'd said, and I remembered Claire's dead girls, Claire's cousin, the words Trawden had scrawled on the wall behind Elizabeth Maurier's dead body, in Elizabeth Maurier's own blood. *No one will hear.* Fothergill had something to say. Everyone assumed he'd done what he was accused of. They might be right – I knew from bitter experience how effectively the guilty could mask their guilt. But he needed to be heard. He needed someone to listen.

"Okay," I said, and nodded. He frowned at me, confused, and I realised that I'd just conducted a swift monologue in silence, and it sounded as if I were agreeing with his unsympathetic neighbours. "I mean," I continued, "Okay, I'll represent you. You need a fair hearing."

He slumped, as if a metal rod had been removed from his back, and his face followed suit, collapsing like I'd just delivered bad news rather than precisely what he had, I thought, been hoping for. I stood and leaned towards him, and he managed a smile – still a weak one, but with a warmth that made it as far as his eyes, and I realised this wasn't despondency. This was relief. There was no need to project strength any more. All that was needed was the truth. I sat back down.

"Thank you," he sighed.

"I'll get back to London and get to work right away. I want to find out as much as I can about Pieter Van der Lee. You're sure you don't remember him?"

"Absolutely."

"Well, it's not a common name. Not in England, anyway. I'll find out what I can."

He nodded, and as I stood he forced himself back onto his feet. "Thank you," he said, again, and shook my hand. I looked into his face and tried to find the lie there, or even the hint of one, but all I could see was misery, and the shadow of a frantic, desperate hope.

"Just one more thing before I go," I said.

The paint had dried hard to the wall in the sunshine, but it was no match for the cleaning fluid Fothergill had retrieved from under his sink, and I found myself rather enjoying the exercise as the sun retreated behind grey clouds and the rain began to spatter the back of my shirt. The neighbour with the dog came and stood outside her front door and stared at me for a minute, but when I offered her a smile she shook her head at me in disgust and went back inside.

By the time the boys on the bikes cycled back down the road, the graffiti was gone.

8: Bacon

MALONEY WOKE ME at eight next morning to detail his surveillance on Claire. Claire answered the phone herself, and continued to lie naked beside me in bed while he went through what she'd done the night before, which would have made things difficult if I'd had any questions to ask, but I didn't, because Maloney's report was that she hadn't left the flat. Since he had no idea what had gone inside the flat – *she might have been raising an army of the undead for all I know* was the way he put it – the call was short and, I reflected, as I ended it, about as satisfactory as I could have hoped. Not entirely satisfactory, of course. I still didn't know what she'd been up to on the day of Trawden's death.

She'd been in a good mood when I'd got back from Oxford. She'd been on the phone when I came in, and I'd caught the tail end of her conversation.

"What about the others?" she'd been saying. "Oh, don't worry. Sam's back. Just tell everyone I'm fine. Yes, I'll send him your love."

"Your mother?" I asked, and she smiled and kissed me on the lips. She was dressed, in leggings and a sweater, which made a change from the same old dressing gown. I stepped back and looked at her again, and her smile creased into a quizzical half-frown.

"You're looking good," I said.

"So are you."

We'd ended up in bed a few minutes later, the first time we'd made love since Brooks-Powell's death, and for an hour or two I managed to forget about Trawden and the Sig and the lies she'd been telling me, about trust and Mandy and death. Maloney had texted me – two words, *no news* – and I'd forced all that from my mind for the rest of the evening, which had comprised a thriller and a Chinese takeaway. And now, this morning, he'd called with no further elaboration on his text, because there was nothing for him to elaborate on.

I put the phone down and tried to relax as Claire twined her fingers around my chest hairs and leaned in to kiss my ear. I couldn't relax. Everything was back, and Maloney might have done his job, but I hadn't learned a thing from it. I hadn't heard from Roarkes, either, and he'd had a full day since I'd asked him to find out about the building Claire had visited. I turned to Claire and smiled at her, and said "Tea?", and leapt from the bed and out of the room before I could look back and register the expression on her face.

She was still lying there when I returned five minutes later, only now she wasn't naked, she was back in the dressing gown, and she sat up and took the tea from me with barely a murmur.

"I never asked, how was your mum doing?" I said, for want of anything else to say, and she shrugged and slumped back down in the bed. For all the brightness of the previous day, she wasn't much more than a shell right now. The slightest crack could spread and shatter the whole. And by denying her – if that was what I'd done – I'd given the shell a tap.

I lay down beside her, picked up my phone and started searching for Pieter Van der Lee, and found within a few minutes that he still lived in Oxford, and that he owned a bar there. Claire had managed to sit up by now, to take the occasional sip from her tea, to lie back down again with a sigh and close her eyes and rear up again a minute later for more tea. Pieter Van der Lee and his bar opened up a world of interest, but I couldn't focus on them. When Claire got up and announced she was going to have a shower I nodded at her, and the moment she'd left the room I had Roarkes' number up on my screen and had pressed dial.

"Bloody hell, Sam," he said, by way of *Hello*. "You really

don't have much by way of patience, do you?"

"Yeah. Well, you know me. I struggle doing fuck all."

He laughed. "I'm with you there. Right, then. I've done the routine searches and nothing's come up, so either there's no hint of any criminal activity there, or there is but it's the kind of criminal activity we're supposed to pretend we don't know about so MI5 or Special Branch or the Grimethorpe Brass Band can do their business without twats like us getting in the way. I'll see if I can dig a bit deeper but I can't promise anything."

I waited. I knew Roarkes. He couldn't resist going over old ground. A moment later, he proved me right.

"But Sam, there's an easier way of getting there, you know. You could just ask her."

I flashed back a few minutes, Claire going from purr to hiss in the time it took to brew a cup of tea.

"Can't do that, Roarkes. I told you why. What happened when I pushed her. She's building something, I don't know what, a new personality or a stronger version of the old one, but whatever it is, it's fragile. I'm not going to risk breaking it."

"Sounds like bullshit to me. Sounds like you're scared of having a row."

I laughed. Roarkes wasn't going to wind me up that easily. "You're right. I am. The best I can hope for is to get her to a place where she trusts me enough to tell me herself. If I ask her straight out now, I can guarantee she'll just move further away." *And maybe worse*, I thought, but kept that bit to myself. "And she's not stupid," I continued. "If she's keeping something from me, she's doing it deliberately. She hasn't forgotten Jonas Wolf. She knows how dangerous secrets can be. If she's got one, she'll have a good reason for it."

Roarkes' response was a grunt, but with Roarkes a grunt was as good as a smile and a handshake. He promised to keep digging, and I promised to let him know if I found out anything that could help him, and I killed the call moments before Claire walked back into the bedroom, still wet, wearing nothing but a smile. The shell, miraculously, was whole again. Somehow I managed to put Roarkes and Maloney out of my mind for the next half hour. Truth be told, it wasn't difficult.

But half an hour was all I got. Claire had fallen asleep, my arm around her shoulders, her head on my chest and her hands resting on my belly. I picked her limbs from my body with the slow, quiet precision of someone defusing a bomb, and even when the route out had been cleared, I waited five minutes before carefully edging up and onto my feet, and out of the room.

I'd made a decision, in those five minutes. I'd decided Maloney didn't have the resources I wanted, not any more, and Roarkes didn't have the balls. I needed someone with both, or at least with the balls to get the resources. I waited another minute, listening nervously for signs of life from the bedroom, and then I picked up my phone and called Colman.

"Finally got round to calling me back, have you?" she said when she answered, and I remembered Claire telling me she'd rung, my decision not to ring her back, to keep as much distance as I could between me and a woman who knew precisely what had happened outside the Old Bailey and would jump to obvious conclusions if she knew the truth about Claire's alibi. I hadn't changed my mind about any of that. But I needed her help.

"Yeah," I replied. "Sorry about that."

"So I assume you've come round to my way of thinking?"

"What?"

"Trawden. You're going to help me get to the bottom of it. I'm not buying this John Evans line."

I'd been about to explain that no, I hadn't come round to her way of thinking, and I had no more appetite to help her off-the-books investigation than I'd had last time she'd mentioned it, but the mention of Evans derailed me.

"Why not?" I asked.

"I'm not sure. Partly because it's Martins' line, and she's got history in getting things wrong. Partly because it's too easy. Kind of road Trawden would have tried to steer us down himself if he'd been alive to do it."

I found myself nodding in silent agreement. But then, Evans had the motive. If his alibi didn't hold up, he had to be in the frame. He kept the focus off Claire, which suited me. He was hanging around my flat trying to talk to me. But right now, John Evans wasn't my problem.

"Look, are you busy today? I want to talk."

"Sure," she said. I hadn't, I realised, put her right about my role in her investigation, so she'd be disappointed when she heard it from me later. But needs must. We arranged to meet in a café a couple of streets away from her new station in Holborn, and I got myself showered and dressed as quickly and quietly as I could. Claire woke as I was hunting down a pair of shoes that didn't let in the water – it had rained heavily overnight, and the pair I'd been wearing for the last few days seemed to have developed holes in uncomfortable places.

"Oh," she said, when she saw me dressed and ready to go out. I shrugged apologetically.

"Yeah. Sorry. Colman wants to meet. Says she might have something interesting for me."

First rule of lying. Always tell the truth when you can.

"Will you be long?"

"No," I replied, turning back to the wardrobe, hunting and eventually finding the smart shoes I'd been looking for behind a battleground littered with the corpses of worn-out trainers. I kissed her gently on the forehead and headed out.

There no sign of Evans outside, and I felt strangely optimistic as I headed to the bus stop and a refreshingly uneventful journey to the café. Colman was halfway through a bacon sandwich when I arrived, and I recalled her penchant for taking food whenever the opportunity presented itself. I hadn't seen her in uniform before, and it didn't suit her, somehow reducing her to the ordinary when from what I knew, she was anything but. She stood, mouth still full, and tried to smile through the meat and bread. It wasn't a pretty look.

"So you're going to help, right? Get the old team back and running again?" she said when she'd finally chewed enough to swallow. I'd been hoping it wouldn't come up quite so soon. She carried on, not waiting for an answer. "We work well together, you and me. I don't know what Martins has got up her sleeve, because Winterman's being a bit cagy, but I'll find out soon enough. And whatever it is, they won't be as sharp as we are."

I nodded, unsure of what to say. She went on.

"We fucking nailed it last time, right? You, me and David?"

Her face fell as she said the name. It was true. Without Brooks-Powell, we'd have got nowhere. I'd dealt with his death, I thought. I felt bad, but for ten years I'd hated the man and in a week or two I'd grown to like him, and that week or two wasn't enough to make me mourn him forever.

But I was halfway to London when Brooks-Powell died.

I hadn't been there.

Colman had, her face and clothes coated with his blood. At Brooks-Powell's funeral a week later she'd seemed fine, had left her latest lover waiting in the car ready to drive off for three days in a bed somewhere in Wales. It was just possible, I realised, that she hadn't got round to processing what had happened.

She took another bite from her sandwich and I let her

chew in silence. After a minute or so, she lifted her head and changed the subject.

"John Evans."

"What about him?"

"Well, they're not holding him. I got that much out of Simon, before he went quiet on me. And a little more."

"Such as?"

"Well, he hated Trawden. Can't blame him for that. I mean, you and I know his old man was an animal, and maybe he only killed one child instead of two, but the son seems to blame Trawden for everything, anyway. Blames everyone. Elizabeth Maurier. You, too."

She watched me carefully as she spoke, and I grinned. "Not the first time I've taken the rap for someone else," I said, and told her what had happened outside my flat, the phone call that had preceded it, the encounter at the police station that had preceded the phone call. I told it straight this time. No jazz.

"Interesting," she said, when I'd finished. "Did you tell Martins?"

I nodded, and she continued. "Doesn't look good for him, does it? And he's got form, too."

"What, murder?"

She shook her head, sandwich halfway to her mouth, looked at it, at me, and put it back down on the plate with what looked like reluctance.

"Nope. Robbery. Got six months. Looks the type, from what I hear."

I recalled the man I'd seen in Martins' station and outside the flat, the scars, the spider's web on one cheek, and found myself nodding in agreement.

"Yeah. I'd say that. Doesn't mean he killed Trawden, though. And I'm not sure insulin would be his style."

Colman picked up her sandwich, which had finally proven a temptation too far. I took the opportunity to get

82

us a couple of coffees, waiting impatiently for a grey-haired man in a suit – he reminded me of someone, Fothergill, I thought, with that slow, careful walk – to edge past me carrying his own steaming mug.

"So," she continued, when I'd returned and the last mouthful had disappeared, "apparently he was normal enough as a kid. Evans. The son. But he went off the rails when his dad went inside. No big surprise there. Finding out your dad's a child abuser and a murderer, not likely to give you an idyllic childhood. Usual trouble, drink, drugs, fell in with bad crowd, you could have predicted it from the beginning. Just went downhill from there."

I nodded, which Colman took as a cue for her to go on.

"And I get what you're saying about the insulin. But that one robbery aside, Evans doesn't have form for violent crime. Well, not much. Might not have the stomach for it. Might not want to think of himself as hurting people, be too much like his dad, that kind of thing. Christ knows what goes on in someone's head when they're faced with something like that. So maybe he just thought a little bit more than he's used to thinking. I mean, you would, wouldn't you?"

This time I shrugged. On she went.

"So I'll be seeing Simon again soon. I'll wear something low-cut. Anything he knows, I'll know by morning."

She grinned at me and I nodded again, and finally the penny dropped.

"So really, Sam, what did you want to see me about?" She'd turned that shrewd look of hers on me, the eyes a little narrower, the sandwich and the monologue of a moment ago a distant memory. "You're not actually interested in any of this, are you?"

She'd have got there in the end, I figured. No way to sugar the pill. I put up both hands in a gesture of apology and acknowledgement.

"You've got me," I said. "I'm sorry. I could do with a little help. That's all."

"Not about Trawden, then?"

I shook my head. "No. Don't think so. I mean, for all I know he could have been mixed up in anything from the stuff we know about to hacking the CIA, but this time I can't see any link."

Or at least, I didn't want to see any link.

"So what's the score, then?"

"There's this building," I began. "In Southgate. I need to know what's going on there."

"Okay." She reached into her bag, nestling beside her feet under the table, and withdrew a notebook and pen. "Give me the details."

I described the building, the entrance, the address, and Colman dutifully wrote them down.

"So," she said, returning the notebook and pen to her bag, "what's this all about if it's not about Trawden?"

I'd known this was coming. You don't ask someone like Colman for help and expect her to trot off and provide it without telling her why.

"Sorry. I can't tell you that."

She paused in the action of lifting her cup to her mouth. I'd finished my own coffee while she was still talking about Evans.

"What?"

"I said I can't tell you. I wish I could. It's complicated."

"It's always complicated, Sam."

I shrugged, and Colman put her cup back down on the table.

"So let me get this straight," she said. She was smiling, but I didn't like the smile. It looked like it was holding something back. "You leave me in a house with a murderer so you can run off and stop your girlfriend killing a witness in a high profile criminal trial." She tapped her left index

84

finger against her right thumb. "You leave me there to watch people die." Her left index finger tapped its counterpart on the right. "You ask me to keep it to myself, what Claire was doing, the fact you were even there in the first place, despite the fact that I'm a police officer and two people are dead – two *more* people – in the middle of a complex murder investigation." Index to middle. "You ignore me, you won't help me when *I* ask for help, you don't return my calls, and when you're finally forced to speak to me you just grunt until it suits you to say anything more substantial." A tap on her ring finger, not that Colman was wearing a ring. "And now you come here and you ask for *my* help and you won't tell me why." Index finger to little finger, and a look on her face like she was still trying to figure this out even while she was saying it.

I shrugged. The look was bullshit. Colman might not know why I wanted her help, but she knew exactly what she was saying.

"Thanks for the sandwich," she said, stood, picked up her bag, and walked out. As the door slammed shut behind her, a slip of paper fluttered from under the plate that had contained her sandwich, a little wave for my attention. She hadn't paid for her food.

I reached into my pocket and pulled out a ten-pound note. Getting stuck with the bill for Colman's mid-morning snack was the least I deserved.

9: The Great Gaping Void

CLAIRE WAS DRESSED when I got back, jeans and a woollen sweater I didn't remember seeing before. She was standing by the cooker singing along to the radio beside her, stirring at something in a pot, and for a moment I just stood there and admired the happy ordinariness of the scene, the remarkable ability of circumstance to present a tableau in which everything was just fine in a world where it clearly wasn't.

"New sweater?" I asked, and she turned to me with a smile.

"Do you like it?" I nodded. "Ordered it last week. I wasn't sure it would suit me but I rather think it does."

"So do I," I replied. She was playing a role. *I rather think it does*? That wasn't Claire. That wasn't Claire at all. "What you cooking?"

"Just soup. Sorry. One portion. I assumed you'd have eaten."

I thought back to Colman's bacon sandwich with a pang of regret, and told Claire not to worry and that I'd make something for myself.

I found a packet of Singapore noodles in the freezer and while the microwave was loosening them up, asked Claire what she'd been doing, which turned out to be nothing other than getting dressed and trying on her new sweater. We sat in front of the television, watching the news, which was something I hadn't dared do since Claire's breakdown – in the weeks leading up to it she'd been glued to coverage of the human trafficking trial in which Jonas Wolf was the chief witness for the prosecution. Claire gave a yawn, when she'd finished her soup, and announced that she needed a nap, which seemed unlikely, but I nodded, cleared everything away, and turned my thoughts to Pieter Van der

Lee.

The internet might give me what I wanted, but people with things to hide usually knew how to hide them, and there were more direct ways. Granted, they weren't likely to pay off, but it wouldn't hurt to try.

I picked up the papers Fothergill had handed me before I'd left the day before and leafed through until I found the details for the Crown Prosecution Service lawyer who was handling the case. Her name, it emerged, was Karen Hobart, and she worked out of an office in Oxford city centre.

She answered the phone herself, and I took a moment to apologise for disturbing her, to explain who I was and what I was after, and to apologise again, because what I was doing wasn't the way things were usually done. There was a silence, when I'd finished with my apologies and my explanations, and I waited for her either to say *No* or to tell me to fuck off and then say *No*.

"You know this isn't exactly standard procedure?" she asked, instead, and I agreed with her.

"I'm sorry. It's just proving difficult to get the facts I need given how far back we've got to go. And my client – well, you may not know this, but he tried to kill himself a couple of days ago. Given his condition, he's not proving immensely useful."

That was as close to an outright lie as I was going to go, I decided. Fothergill wasn't much use, true, but that had nothing to do with his condition and everything to do with the fact that the details I was trying to find were nearly forty years old and if he was an innocent man, there was no way he'd have been expected to remember them.

"Okay, well, let me see. You want to actually meet with him, do you?"

"Yes. If Mr Van der Lee is prepared to."

"I very much doubt that. You know he isn't obliged to."

87

"Yes."

"Indeed. If every defence lawyer were allowed a private chat with every complainant, well, there would be a lot of mysteriously collapsed prosecutions and missing witnesses and probably not enough cases to go round, which would mean me out of a job for a start."

I laughed, as I assumed as I was supposed to, and listened to the sound of Karen Hobart rifling through what I guessed was the case file.

"Right, well, if it were up to me I'd say I'm perfectly happy to pass on your request but I'm pretty sure he'll say no. But unfortunately, it's not up to me, so you're going to have to waste a little more of your precious time, Mr Williams."

"Call me Sam. And why's it not up to you?"

"Because Mr Van der Lee has taken on his own private lawyer. Must be costing him a bit."

A private lawyer wasn't unusual, for the very rich, at least. From the brief searches I'd done that morning I hadn't got the impression Pieter Van der Lee was very rich.

"So you're not prosecuting the case?"

"Oh, we are. I am. But it says here that any time I want anything to do with the complainant, I've got to go through this guy. Christ knows why. People do like to make things complicated, don't they?"

She read out a name and phone number and I noted them down and thanked her for her time. Karen Hobart had provided a refreshing change from my usual treatment at the hands of the CPS.

I dialled the number she'd given me and asked for Joseph Hartley, and found myself talking to a man who insisted he could not reveal any of his clients' personal details, as a matter of course.

"Yes, I'm sure, I just want you to pass on a message. I'd like to meet with him to discuss the case."

"Case?"

"Yes. The allegations against Fothergill."

"Ah," replied Hartley, as if all had suddenly become clear. "I'm afraid there's been a misunderstanding. I'm a probate lawyer. Wills, that sort of thing. I don't deal with criminal matters at all. Now, I shouldn't really even be telling you this, since it makes it clear that I am familiar with Mr Van der Lee's affairs and that alone is probably something that should remain confidential, but since you've called and we've already gone this far I can let you know that Mr Van der Lee has engaged another lawyer to take care of more *controversial* matters. I believe the gentleman you're after is Darren Sutcliffe, at Trimers."

Another name, another phone number, another thank you and goodbye. I hadn't called this many lawyers in one day in as long as I could remember. Darren Sutcliffe, according to the recorded message that played back when I dialled his number, was not currently available, so I left my own message explaining who I was and what I was after and crept into the bedroom to check on Claire.

She was sound asleep, or at least doing a decent impression of someone sound asleep, breathing evenly and not too deeply and twitching a little as I moved closer. I backed out again, shut the door behind me, and returned to the internet.

Pieter Van der Lee's bar had been converted from a neglected church some time in the mid-eighties, but he'd only owned it for seven years. The bar itself had suffered from the usual troubles, some drugs, the occasional fight, but nothing to draw attention to itself. Mr Van der Lee himself barely troubled the internet at all; his licencing applications for the bar had gone relatively smoothly, and the locals seemed to agree that things had actually improved since he'd taken the place over. There had been a grand reopening around eighteen months back, at which, the local press reported, he had given a short speech and been congratulated by a number of councillors for his contribution to the city. *Dervish*, the place was called, and from the photographs online I thought it might have been one of the places I'd frequented myself, long before Van der Lee had owned it. It wouldn't have been called *Dervish* back then, though. I'd have remembered the name.

I shut down the laptop and sat back with a disappointed sigh. I had, I realised, been pinning my hopes on something obvious: a decent police record, a severe drug problem, a strong hint of the kind of psychological damage that might drive someone to make up a history of sexual assault and would at least damage their credibility in the witness box. Of course, something like that could just as easily have been caused by a childhood trauma, of precisely the sort he alleged, so even if I'd found it, it wouldn't have proven a thing. But it wasn't there. Van der Lee had no children, as far as I could tell, but the photographs hinted at a relationship or two in the last decade and there was no reason to suspect he wasn't childless by choice. I was, after all, and there weren't that many years between me and Van der Lee. The failure of a life I'd been looking for, that great gaping void for which he might have sought an excuse, was nowhere to be found.

Still. He owned a bar. And that was rarely as straightforward as it looked.

I flicked through the television channels for something to kill twenty minutes, and settled on a quiz show that had me mouthing silent insults at the contestants within seconds. As the leading team were sitting with brows furrowed, struggling to recall the name of a single minister from any of Tony Blair's cabinets, my phone rang, and I snatched it up before it could wake Claire.

"Sam?"

"Melanie." I'd have recognised her number if I'd looked

at it, but I knew the voice anyway. "How are you?"

"Not bad. Listen, I need to see you."

Melanie Golding was good company, for all the difficulties she'd had with her late husband. But she wasn't a hotshot financial *wunderkind* for nothing. When she wanted something, she got straight to the point.

"Erm, yeah. Sure. When?"

"Is tonight good for you?"

"Yes – I mean – I'll check. Call you back in a minute, okay?"

"Need to run it past Claire?"

I thought for a moment before replying. Melanie knew nothing about Claire's breakdown, the Sig, the link with Trawden. I'd convinced myself that I was protecting Melanie – her husband had died, after all, and more complications were something she didn't need. But the truth was, the fewer people that knew, the better, for Claire and for me.

"Yeah. I'm not sure she hasn't made plans for us."

"That's fine. If you're busy, let me know when you're not. If you're not, bring Claire along."

I'd been too slow: the phone had woken Claire, and by the time I opened the bedroom door twenty seconds after ending the call she was playing word games on her phone. *Keeps my mind young*, she'd said, when I'd asked why the sudden addiction. *Got to have something fresh when the rest of me starts to rot.* I'd laughed, at the time, and then realised she wasn't joking. Brooks-Powell was twelve days dead by then. There weren't any jokes in our flat.

She looked up as I entered. Her hair was dishevelled and her face pale, but no more than it usually was these days. She raised a single quizzical eyebrow.

"Who was on the phone?"

"Melanie. Wants us round tonight. Fancy it?"

It was worth a shot, I thought. A pretty long shot, mind.

"No. I don't think so. You go, though."

"Nah, I'll stay and keep you company."

She patted the bed beside her, and I dutifully sat.

"Don't be silly, Sam. I get you every day. She needs the company more than I do. It can't be easy."

"What, for Melanie Golding, merry widow and multimillionaire? From what I can see, she's not spending her evenings crying into silver bowls."

She laughed.

"Come on. You don't really believe that, do you? I mean, yes, her and David, it wouldn't have been easy, all those years. But they loved each other, in their way. They were fond of each other, at least. She's asked to see you. Do the right thing."

I hesitated for a moment, more because I didn't know what Claire would be up to in my absence than because I thought she'd need me there. And then I nodded and visited the bathroom, where I dropped Maloney a quick, pleading text and prayed for the right reply.

It came before I'd even flushed. *For fuck's sake*, it said. *Okay. But this can't go on forever, Sam.*

Thanks, I replied. And then, partly because I couldn't resist the urge for a dig, and partly because I was genuinely curious, I fired off another question.

Where are you getting these people from, anyway?

Maloney had gone straight – Sig aside. The guns I could just about understand, weapons of last resort and a souvenir, of sorts. But my experience of other clients had taught me that when the boss went away – dead or inside or out of the business, it didn't matter which – the minions didn't tend to stick around. So who was Maloney tasking with the little surveillance job I'd thrown his way?

I was staring into my wardrobe for something to wear when my phone beeped with his reply, and I took my time getting to it, because Claire was sitting on the bed watching me and I didn't want her thinking there was anything interesting going on she didn't know about. I picked out a white shirt and then put it straight back when I realised it was the same one I'd worn to David's funeral, and bore a highly distinctive logo. Most of my sweaters had holes in them, but there was an old Paul Smith that didn't, even if I did have to squeeze in a little. No need to change my jeans. Not much I could change them for.

I spend a minute or two pottering around the bedroom before I reached for my phone and read the text.

Same place you'd get them from yourself if you got off your arse and picked up the phone book and made a call or two, it said. *I'm paying them, you bloody idiot.*

I sat there staring at the text, a horrible mix of surprise and guilt washing through me, and then I remembered I wasn't supposed to be looking at anything worth looking at, sighed and put my phone back in my pocket.

It hadn't been resting there more than a minute when it rang, and I pulled it back out again carefully, anticipating more abuse from Maloney, or from Roarkes, or from Colman, from any of those people whose friendship I'd stretched to breaking point lately. It wasn't any of them. I recognised the number, but I couldn't think where from until I answered and heard him speak.

"Sam Williams?" he said, and I knew it right away, the same voice from the recorded message I'd listened to earlier. He'd sounded a little harried on his own recording. He didn't sound much different now.

"Yes, that's me."

"This is Darren Sutcliffe. Trimers. What the hell are you playing at?"

I held the phone away from my face and stared at it for a moment as if I might find the reason for this little outburst written on it in short, simple words. I could still hear him talking, tinny but clearly angry, a heady swirl of righteous indignation. I waited a moment before I replied.

"Sorry, what precisely is the problem?"

"You want to talk to Van der Lee?"

"That's right."

"Well that's out of the question. Absurd. The very idea of defence holding a pre-trial interview with a vulnerable witness in a sexual crime case. I've never heard of such a thing."

"I'm sorry," I said, in a tone that suggested no such thing. "Is Mr Van der Lee vulnerable?"

"Well, not now, obviously. But he was at the time. He was a thirteen-year-old child, for God's sake."

"That's okay. It's not the thirteen-year-old Van der Lee I want to talk to. Fothergill's budget doesn't stretch to the time machine."

I knew I shouldn't have said it the moment the words left my mouth, but Sutcliffe was riling me.

"This is outrageous. It's unprofessional of you even to suggest such a thing. You do realise how this kind of behaviour could reflect on your reputation, don't you? How it might be regarded by the Law Society?"

I thought about laughing and just hanging up, but instead, I decided to set him straight as politely as I could. No point making more enemies than I already had.

"I'm sorry, Mr Sutcliffe," I repeated, trying to inject a hint of authentic apology into my voice this time. "Really, the Law Society don't think a great deal of me, the profession regards me as some kind of a leper, and the public at large aren't interested, so in all honesty I'm not too bothered about my reputation. But if you're saying *no* on behalf of your client, then that's fine, that's the end of the matter, and unless anything else crops up in the course of proceedings, you won't hear from me again until we meet in court."

There was a short pause, the sound of a man trying to

gather both his breath and his thoughts.

"Well. That's fine, then. Goodbye, Mr Williams."

I hung up without returning his goodbye. There had never been much chance of an interview with Van der Lee, but it had been worth a shot. I decided to leave a message with Karen Hobart, to warn her, in case Sutcliffe decided to blame her for my call, that he was mobilising and keen for a reason to go to war.

She answered the phone, to my surprise, since it was nearly seven o'clock and my experience of the CPS had them at home or in the pub by six.

"It's Sam. Sam Williams."

"Oh," she replied. "Is everything okay? I was just about to head out."

I explained what had happened, and she apologised, not that she had anything to apologise for.

"I'm afraid it's out of my hands, Sam. Sorry I can't help you."

"You've been really helpful," I said, and I meant it. I was about to say goodbye when she cut in.

"I suppose you could see a transcript of the pre-trial interview, if that's any use. I mean, if this ends up going to trial we'd have to give it to you eventually."

"That would be fantastic," I replied, and decided on the spur of the moment to push my luck a little further. "Can you send it to me?"

She laughed. "No, I don't think so. I shouldn't really let you see it without a formal request, and I haven't even had confirmation you're representing Fothergill yet. But if you want to stop by the office here I'll let you have a read."

"Great," I said, without stopping to think. "How about tomorrow?" I didn't have anything important to do the following day, a call on Hasina Khalil I could field in the car or kick into the long grass if I needed to. I'd have to deal with Claire, which meant asking another favour from

95

Maloney before he'd even done tonight's. And this whole thing with Claire was starting to take on a flavour I didn't much like. Sure, she was keeping something from me. But I was spying on her, and that wasn't the person I thought I was. I shook my head and waited for Karen Hobart to answer. Even with Claire, even with Maloney, this was too good an opportunity to pass up.

"Fine," she replied, finally. "Ten work for you?"

It did. I thanked her and said goodbye.

I spent an hour chatting to Claire, apologising for the fact that I'd be out again the next day, trying to make her laugh, and eventually succeeding, which was just enough to get me comfortable with heading out to the home of a beautiful rich widow and leaving my girlfriend at home by herself. As I was heading out of the door my phone rang again and I cursed myself for not turning the damned thing off for once.

It was okay, though. The caller was Mrs Piper, the Chalmere School secretary, and she said she had information for me. She spoke in a conspiratorial near-whisper, clearly caught up in the intrigue of the affair, and I thought it only fair to play along, replying quietly myself, suggesting – because I was, after all, going to be in town next day – that perhaps it would be safer if we discussed her findings in person.

"Ooh," said Mrs Piper. I could tell she was enjoying the notion that somehow the telephone wasn't quite safe enough. "I look forward to it, Mr Williams. I'll be in the office until four."

I had, I reflected, as I finally left the flat and emerged into a cold and wet North London, turned a barren day into something that might actually bear some fruit.

10: Ghosts at our Elbows

I MISSED THE bus by seconds and decided to walk to the station instead of waiting for the next one, and as if spiting me, the rain started halfway there. I hadn't brought an umbrella with me, so I broke into a gentle run and was surprised to hear a set of footsteps behind me mirroring my change of pace. I turned, fearing Evans or worse, but it was neither: a man in his fifties with grey hair who looked vaguely familiar. I stepped up the pace – the rain was coming down hard, cold, insistent, and my jeans were already plastered to my legs – and by the I reached the station he was nowhere to be seen. Probably nothing, I thought, as I forced my way onto a hot, crowded carriage. But it paid to be careful.

The rain had eased off a little by the time I reached the Brooks-Powell mansion – the Golding mansion, I corrected myself, since she was the only one living in it now. I was still wet, but bearably so, and to my relief Melanie was casual, by her standards. Long skirt and blouse, only the second-best Wedgewood, and beside it the menu from the Thai Palace. There was a bottle of red open in the morning room, already a glass or two down.

Melanie looked well, all things considered, but when I told her that she rolled her eyes and replied that she was sick of being told she looked well and even sicker of that *all things considered*. She was rich and in her mid-thirties. Why shouldn't she look well?

She watched me for a few seconds as I tried to splutter out a reply, and then I noticed her face crack a little and realised she was joking. But only in part.

"He was a good man," she said, two minutes later, when she'd taken my coat and poured my wine and we were sitting on the sofa waiting for the Thai Palace to deliver. "I mean, you know all about it, of course, but he was a good man and I loved him."

She glared at me as she said the last three words, challenging me to question them, and I tried to keep my expression both serious and amenable but something must have given me away, because she shook her head at me and smiled.

"Oh, I know that doesn't sound likely. But I did. He said the same about you, funnily enough, not just in those last weeks but before."

"What, that he loved me?" I replied, incredulous, and she laughed.

"No. Of course not. You weren't his type. Or if you were, there was too much history. No, he said you were a good man."

"That seems a little unlikely, Mel. I mean, sure, we got on well enough in the end. But before that? He couldn't stand the sight of me."

"No, he couldn't. And don't pretend you could stand the sight of him either. But even when he was cursing you for being a devious bastard and ruining his career and everything else, he still said you were a good man."

I was saved from any more discussion of David's views by the arrival of the food. As I took my seat in the dining room I was unable to bat away the image that passed unbidden across my mind: the four of us, Melanie, Claire, David Brooks-Powell and I, at this very table, a meal that had begun awkwardly enough, which was only to be expected given all those years of bad feeling. A meal that had passed through phases, from that awkward beginning, that had included flashes of bitterness and bursts of humour and the occasional insight falling among the four of us like rain in a desert. A meal that had ended with laughter and handshakes and hugs and that had set the tone for the next few days, had turned Brooks-Powell and me into something like friends until he died.

And now: the same four chairs in the same four places, two of them empty, one occupant in the grave and the other recovering from a breakdown. Melanie sat down beside me and topped up my wine as I gazed in silence at the curries and fishcakes and bowls of rice that would between them have fed the four of us with ease.

I remembered Colman's bacon sandwich and the ready meal I'd bolted down hours ago, and was suddenly ravenous. And even though the ghosts of those who weren't with us couldn't be made to melt into nothing at the snap of a spring roll, there was a matter-of-factness that made things simpler and less laden with meaning than I'd feared. David was dead. Claire was at home. Melanie and I were eating Thai food out of Wedgewood bowls and drinking expensive red wine. Melanie, thankfully, was good company, despite the little we had in common, and I wondered if perhaps that was one of the gifts that had propelled her to the top of her field. Maybe she was good company for everyone.

Between us, we managed more of the meal than I'd thought possible, eating and talking about work, my clients, her investors, Colman, who she'd met at the funeral, Lizzy Maurier, who'd run away to France and sent a poem in her place. We made a decent fist of ignoring the ghosts at our elbows. When we'd finished, she started to clear away and declined my offer of help, so I strolled back into the morning room and got my phone out. No news from Maloney. No news from Roarkes, either, and granted I'd only spoken to him that morning but my patience was starting to wear thin. I texted him, *any news?*, and was surprised to feel the phone vibrate in my hand ten seconds later.

"No there isn't any fucking news," he said, before I could get a word out. "When there's any fucking news I'll

99

tell you. Until then, no news. Got it?"

I could hear music and voices in the background.

"Where are you?" I asked.

"Pub," he said. "Where are you?"

"Melanie Golding's house."

"Play nice, Sam."

I laughed. If he wasn't sitting in his office trying to find out about Claire's mystery building, at least he was out with beer and other people and didn't seem to be in his usual, bitter mood. I apologised and killed the call and looked up to see Melanie smiling down at me.

"Whisky, Sam?" she offered. I declined. It wasn't late, not by any normal measure, but I'd given up measuring things normally when I'd caught my girlfriend with a gun outside the nation's principal Crown Court. She could be anywhere, doing anything, Maloney's men on her tail but not stopping her or interfering – perhaps, I reflected, I should have given instructions, set out some sort of flow chart, *If X then Y, If A or B then C* – I found myself running through the possibilities and permutations in my head and then remembered where I was. Melanie was still smiling. I smiled back and tried to focus on where I was.

"Look, Sam, I didn't just invite you over for Thai food," she said. "I need a favour."

I kept the smile on my face and tried to ignore the various unpleasant options leaping around my brain. Favours, in my experience, were rarely good news for the person granting them.

"Happy to help," I lied. "What's up?"

"Come upstairs," she replied, turned and walked away without waiting. I spent a few seconds worrying where this was going and trying to work out if I'd misjudged things. Just a few seconds, though. She'd invited both of us, Claire too; Melanie Golding was rich and attractive and if she'd wanted to play, she'd have her pick from a far more impressive field than I could join. I saw her starting up the stairs and followed her up to the second floor and the office I'd sat in a few weeks earlier with her husband, trying to get to grips with Trawden and everything he'd hidden.

The office hadn't changed a bit; what few items of furniture had been there remained in their places, only the faintest trace of dust to suggest things weren't the way they'd always been. Chair, desk, screen, filing cabinet, and the reproduction of Holbein's *Ambassadors* on the wall. I'd been unnerved by that painting last time I'd been here, with its glum diplomats and obscure objects and the notorious skull lurking at their feet. Power and death, that was the point, supposedly, and where the power lay was obvious enough, but I'd wondered whose death, I'd wondered that since I'd first seen that painting. Now, as it glowered at me from the wall of a dead man's office, a dead man who'd been powerful enough in his time, I thought perhaps I knew.

There were no books, no shelves, but there hadn't been last time, either. Just that bloody painting. I turned, suddenly nauseous and anxious to be out of the room, to be anywhere but here. Melanie was standing with her back to me, staring at the Holbein.

"I'm starting to get rid of some of David's things," she said, without turning. "Would you like this painting?"

"Erm, no thanks," I said. I couldn't manage any more than that. I stepped past her and hoped she wouldn't think me rude. I had to be out of the room.

She joined me on the landing, a moment later, put a hand on my arm and steered me into a different room, another office, by the look of it, with a more traditional feel; one mahogany desk, one office chair, one armchair and walls lined with shelves. Books on the lower shelves, legal texts, mainly, with the occasional classic thrown in – I spotted the complete Dickens and a Riverside Shakespeare and, surprisingly, a handful of Philip Roth novels that I wouldn't have associated with David Brooks-Powell in a million years. But then, the Brooks-Powell I'd known in his final days had been a very different man from the one I'd always thought he was.

The upper shelves were full of files.

"The files, Sam. I know it's a lot to ask. But I want to get rid of them and I don't know if I can. I mean, is there client business in there? Do they need to be returned to someone? Do they need to be disposed of properly, shredded or something, or maybe sent to a storage facility? I don't have the heart to go through them and I don't think I'd understand what they were if I did. Do you think you could take a look?"

"I – er – I can make a start," I said, my eyes travelling from one end of the shelves to the other. There had to be forty files there, hundreds of pages of documents in each one, and no way of knowing what was closed and what was still active until every last page had been read. That was some favour.

"Oh, thanks Sam. Are you sure you don't want that whisky?"

This time I accepted, waited until she'd left the room, and fell back into the armchair, running mental calculations on how long it would take me to flick through a witness statement, how long it would take me to digest a set of court papers, how many of each there might be in each file, how much I really didn't want to do this and how on earth I could get myself out of it.

I waited there, eyes still drifting along the shelves. Some of those files looked old – not just dog-eared, but worn and faded as ancient relics. I smiled, for a moment, conscious that the older they were, the more likely they could be consigned to storage without much by way of scrutiny, and then it hit me. These were Mauriers files – they had to be, since Brooks-Powell had still been with the firm up to the last year of his life. The older they were, the greater the chance they'd involve cases I remembered, people I remembered. Elizabeth. Me.

There was no point delaying things any further. I stood and took the file from the far left of the shelf, one of the older ones, by the look of it, and I'd just sat back in the armchair and let my eyes rest on the title on the inside cover when Melanie returned with the whisky.

"Oh, good," she said, handing me a large glass half-filled with liquid the colour of the desk. Room temperature, no ice. I raised it to my nose and let the fumes sink through me as she continued. "You've made a start already. I'm so grateful, Sam. I really am."

I smiled at her and offered one of those *really-it's-nothing* shrugs. It wasn't nothing. It was something.

"Anyway," she went on, "I'll be downstairs if you need me. Just shout."

She turned and left the room, and as her footsteps faded on the thick stair carpet, I set the whisky down on a little wooden table nestled conveniently beside the armchair, and looked again at the title on the file.

Millicent Fairgood, it said.

I remembered Millicent Fairgood. She hadn't been one of my cases – Brooks-Powell and I had worked together just a handful of times at Mauriers, which was probably a sensible decision on Elizabeth's part. Millicent Fairgood had insisted that her husband's cancer – he had died three years before Elizabeth took on the case – had been caused by the nefarious goings-on at the Ministry of Defence land that backed onto her Lincolnshire garden. The Ministry of Defence had insisted that the land was empty and entirely unused, had been unused for nearly half a century, had offered sympathy but not a penny in compensation, and suggested Mrs Fairgood's efforts might be better directed towards the doctors who had failed to diagnose her husband's condition until it was too late to do anything about it. This was plausible enough, but when Elizabeth had asked to be allowed to visit the site, the Ministry had refused point blank, citing reasons of national security whilst continuing to insist there was nothing to see. Anyone acquainted with Elizabeth Maurier's personality and career would have seen at once that this was a foolish step, akin, as she had put it herself at the time, to waving a leg of lamb at a hungry dog and claiming it was inedible.

The details were sketchy in my memory, so I flicked through the file to refresh them. Elizabeth had won the right to a judicial review, but at the review itself had fallen short, unable to convince the judge that national security was unlikely to be an issue in an empty and unoccupied strip of wasteland. Undeterred, Elizabeth had publicly sought out whistle-blowers from the military, a step which had resulted in her being referred to in the House of Commons as a *traitorous harpy hell-bent on suborning brave British soldiers to betray their country*. A newspaper clipping covering that particular statement sat towards the top of the file, the offending words circled in orange highlighter and underneath, in the same thick orange pen, a proud acknowledgement: "That's me!"

She'd got herself a whistle-blower, a retired military chef who'd claimed all sorts of unusual experiments had taken place at the site, and for a few weeks the Ministry of Defence was threatened with its biggest scandal in decades. Unfortunately for Millicent Fairgood, following extensive research and examination by a forensic psychiatrist, Elizabeth was forced to conclude that the chef was nothing more than an attention-seeker. Putting the seal on the whole affair, the Ministry relented and permitted an independent expert to investigate the site, which proved, as they'd insisted all along, to be empty and utterly innocuous.

At the same time, witnesses came forward to claim that the clean-living front the late Mr Fairgood had presented to his wife was a work of pure fiction. Outside the house he'd been a heavy drinker and occasional smoker, had conducted at least three extra-marital affairs and run up significant debts. Millicent Fairgood went back to Lincolnshire, broken. The case was closed. Not everything Elizabeth Maurier touched turned to gold.

I set down the file on the floor beside me and let out a long, slow sigh. I'd been through the first one. It could go into storage, but more importantly, it hadn't involved me, and where it had touched on Elizabeth or on Brooks-Powell himself, it hadn't brought anything back up that I'd rather had stayed down.

The next file bore a name I didn't remember at all, but that didn't matter, because it was short and simple, an easy win for Elizabeth, David not mentioned at all, done and dusted with a few phone calls and a smattering of correspondence. I wondered, briefly, why David had taken these files from Mauriers; he shouldn't have done, that was clear enough, but it wasn't exactly the first instance of a partner treating firm property as his own. And hardly likely he'd see fit to return them once that firm had terminated his partnership and reduced him to the level of *consultant*.

I'd laughed at that, at the time. The fall of the great Brooks-Powell, and at my own hands, no less. I'd seen it as my long-overdue revenge, the final act in a drama that had played out over a decade. But now I found myself sitting in his armchair in his office and wondering what he'd done, how he'd felt when he'd sat here himself and let his eyes roam from the beginning of his career to what must have felt a lot like its untimely end. Had he taken the files down, one after another, had he sat and mourned the past? Had he cursed my name?

Well, he had cursed my name. He'd as good as admitted

that. But as for the mourning, I thought not. Brooks-Powell had been down, but far from out. He'd have been sure there was plenty more for him to live for.

I let the file I was holding drop to the floor, and made to stand and approach the shelves, but instead I remained in the chair. I could see it now, Brooks-Powell sitting exactly where I was, cursing, true, but plotting as well: his revenge on me, his exoneration, his triumphant return.

And now he was dead.

It hit me suddenly and without warning. I'd spent the best part of six weeks telling myself I was fine, that we hadn't been friends, or that if we had been friends it had been a fresh new friendship that could bloom and die without my grieving it. I was fine, that was what I'd told myself, that was what I'd told those few who'd asked how *I* was coping. There were others to worry about, other more directly affected, others who needed my help or someone else's help or at least their sympathy and concern. Claire. Roarkes. Lizzy. Melanie. Colman, who'd been there. Fothergill, who was shouting his innocence into deaf ears. Even Martins, for whom Roarkes had expressed a surprising touch of fellow-feeling for her failure to crack any of the big cases she was working.

I was fine.

But now, suddenly and powerfully, I wasn't. I tried to work out what it was, this feeling that had sprung up so abruptly, rooted in my gut but sprouting tendrils through my body. I tried to work out whether it had been there all along, dormant and waiting for something to wake it. It was a complex beast, I could tell that already, there was regret there, that I'd spent so long hating the man I hadn't had more than a week or two to like him. There was grief, the run-of-the-mill everyday grief for the dead. There was a bitter nostalgia, for with Brooks-Powell's death, following Elizabeth's, there was nothing left of my past at Mauriers.

Nobody there who could remember me. All that history locked inside my head alone. There was guilt, for certain; the guilt of a survivor, but more than that, the guilt of a man who'd dragged Brooks-Powell into his own obsession, because Trawden might have fuelled my nightmares for a decade, but he'd been nothing to Brooks-Powell. The guilt of a man who'd dragged him in and driven him to a quiet village and sat down with him and a police officer and a dangerous murderer and then left them there. Left, alone. Left Brooks-Powell behind.

Left Brooks-Powell to die.

Without warning, the feeling became physical, a nausea that had nothing to do with the scotch I'd done no more than sniff. I pushed myself up from the chair and staggered into the corridor, where a third door revealed a bathroom. I leaned over the toilet and waited, but nothing came. Instead I stood and waited for the sickness to subside, for my breathing to return to its usual steady beat, for the guilt and grief to vanish as abruptly as they'd arrived.

The sickness faded. The breathing slowed. The guilt and the grief showed no sign of wanting to leave.

I left it another few minutes, then returned to the study and took a sip of the whisky. I glanced down, at the two files I'd looked at, and back up at the forty or more I hadn't, and decided then and there that this was something I couldn't do. If Melanie didn't want to do it herself, she could pay someone else to. She had the money.

I took another sip of the whisky and started turning over the phrases I'd use, the sleight with which I'd turn rejection into something else. Melanie couldn't have known what this would mean, how difficult it would be. She probably thought I'd find it interesting.

My thoughts were interrupted by the ringing of my phone. I answered without thinking, and regretted it the moment I heard the words.

"Hello, Sam," she said.

I sighed. "Detective Inspector Martins. How are you?"

"Well. No, scrap that. Struggling."

I pondered my response for a moment. Martins struggling I could live with. Martins struggling and telling me about it was unexpected, and I'd learned not to trust the unexpected.

"I'm sorry," I replied, finally. "I've told you everything I know. I didn't kill Trawden. Claire didn't kill Trawden. That's it."

There was a noise from the phone, a clicking noise that I couldn't place for a few seconds, until I realised she was tutting. Detective Inspector Olivia Martins was tutting at me.

"I know that," she said, eventually. "You've told us everything you know and to be honest, I've pretty much given up trying to work out if it's true or not. But I believe you. You didn't kill Trawden."

She hadn't mentioned Claire. I thought about pressing her on that, pushing until we were both in the clear, but then I remembered that even if she did end up telling me she had nothing on us, it wouldn't mean she was telling me the truth. And it wouldn't stop her changing her mind when it suited her. Instead I waited, and she continued.

"So yes, you might have told us everything you know. But we haven't told you everything we know."

That was cryptic, and deliberately so, I thought. I decided to play along.

"What do you mean?"

"What I mean is that in spite of everything I might have said to the contrary, more than once, I could do with your help."

"Pardon?"

"I could do with your help, Sam."

I found myself staring open-mouthed at the phone. If

Martins was playing, this game was a new one, and I didn't know the rules.

"How? I mean, what do you want? What help?"

She sighed, loudly. "Your brain. I'm told it's good. You knew the victim. You might be able to share an insight or two."

I laughed, inwardly. I might indeed. Didn't mean I would.

"Does this mean you're going to stop giving me grief every chance you get?" I asked, and she laughed before replying.

"My best friends get nothing but grief from me. Consider it a mark of respect. So, can you come in and let me pick that brain of yours?"

It couldn't hurt, I thought. But I needed time to think it over. Time to back out.

"Sure," I replied. "How are you set the day after tomorrow?"

For a few seconds I heard the rustling of paper, and then she was back. "Early afternoon work for you? Two, say?"

"Yes."

"Good. See you at the station."

She ended the call but I stayed where I was for another minute, sitting in the armchair, phone in my hand, thoughts in my head that didn't really belong there. After that minute I heard the sound of footsteps, and a moment later Melanie was back, the bottle of scotch in her hand, glancing at the two files on the floor and the phone in my hand and packing away the frown that had appeared on her face just an instant too late for me to miss it.

"How's it going?" she asked, a forced breeziness in her voice, and I decided it wasn't worth lying and it wasn't worth whatever evasions I might think of on the spot, either. I shrugged.

"I'm sorry, Mel. I really am. But I don't think I can do

this."

She turned sharply as I spoke – she'd been looking at the shelves, no doubt trying to work out how long it would take me to get through all the files when it seemed to have taken forever to look through just two. She fixed me with a serious, probing look and opened her mouth to say something, to ask why, I imagined, possibly even to offer to pay me for my time. Then she closed her mouth and nodded.

"I'm sorry," I repeated, and to my surprise she smiled, gently, picked up my glass from the little table beside me and filled it.

"It's okay, Sam. I should have thought. I should have been a little more sensitive, but in all honesty, being sensitive isn't something I'm very good at. Don't worry about it. I can have someone else look through. Maybe Mauriers will send someone."

I nodded. She seemed to understand at least part of what I was trying to deal with. She didn't need to know any more. She pulled the office chair away from the desk and sat beside me, her own glass in her hand, full of the same orange-brown whisky. She took a sip and looked up, her lips pursed, a frown in place, but a hesitant one, as if she were trying to work out what to say and how to say it. I waited.

"There's something else you might be able to help me with," she said, finally, and my heart sank. Between Olivia Martins and Melanie Golding I was rapidly running out of time to help my clients or Claire or, heaven forbid, myself. I didn't say any of that, though. Instead I raised my eyebrows in an invitation for her to continue.

"I'm a very rich woman, Sam. There's no point denying it. And I've got a lovely house and I go on expensive holidays and I've got foundations and charities coming out of my ears." I leaned forward, ready to tell her how she'd earned all that money fairly, and how worthwhile all her causes were, even though I had no idea what they were or what they did, but she spotted the movement and held out a hand to forestall any interruption. "No, let me say this. The thing is, someone says *Cancer* and I say *Sure, how much?* Then someone else says *Autism* or *Homeless people* or *Refugees* and it's the same thing, I'm just reacting, I'm not on top of things making decisions. And I'm the sort of girl who likes to be on top."

She smiled at me, at the *double entendre*, and her smile seemed to relax things and lift the tension that had fallen upon the room as she'd begun her speech.

"So what do you want me to do?" I asked.

"I just want you to have a think. Think about what I can do with the money. Not all of it, of course. But enough. I want something I can care about, something I can understand and get involved in, something where a few million might make a difference instead of just landing in a bottomless pit and getting dredged up for something incomprehensible in a few years' time. Just, you know, have a think. Give me ideas. David's dead, or I might have asked him. He always had ideas. Most of them were useless. But not all of them."

She smiled again, a soft, sad little smile, and I nodded my agreement.

I left an hour later. We'd made our way back downstairs and sat ourselves in comfort in the living room, Chopin playing quietly in the background and the bottle of whisky almost finished by the time I kissed her goodbye and left her with a promise to think about her money. I found a cab on the main street a minute later, and I was relaxing into the black leather seat when my phone gave a beep.

A text. From Maloney.

She went out, it said. *About twenty minutes after you did. She was followed to the tube but we lost her there. She wasn't out long, though. Got back a couple of hours later. Sorry I don't have any more. Next time.*"

Next time, I thought. Typical Maloney. I had the feeling that despite his protests, he was rather enjoying this.

PART 2: SUSPICION

11: All The Lawyers

I DROVE CAREFULLY next morning, half-convinced that the whisky I'd drunk the night before was still working its way through my system. It was unlikely: Melanie had taken the lion's share whilst I'd taken it a little easier. I hadn't known what would be waiting for me at home.

In the end, what was waiting for me at home was nothing more than a sleeping girlfriend, which suited me just fine. I didn't want a confrontation, and I didn't know whether I'd be able to avoid one if I had to listen to her telling me she'd stayed in all evening watching television. There was a note in the kitchen, her writing, *John Evans called*, with a mobile number beside it, which I tore off the pad and threw in the bin, and then picked out again a moment later. It could always end up being evidence, I figured, although of what I couldn't imagine. I slipped into bed beside Claire and fell quickly into a blank, uneventful sleep. When the alarm roused me at half past six next morning she hadn't stirred, and I showered and dressed quietly, only waking her when I was about to leave, with a quick kiss and a reminder that I'd be out for most of the day.

Traffic was light and Maloney had already texted to confirm that *the usual arrangements were in place*, as he put it. It was almost shocking, I thought, how something as abnormal as asking a gangster to arrange surveillance on your girlfriend could so quickly become nothing more than *the usual arrangements*. I switched on the radio and spent an hour listening to angry people arguing about politics. Anything was better than worrying about Claire.

The CPS office at which Karen Hobart was based sat inside a squat red brick building located on the outskirts of the city. From the car park it looked old and a little worn, bullied into meek submission by all the glass and metal in the business parks that had sprouted alongside it. The same impression continued inside: the main security door yielded to a light shove, and there was nobody behind the plastic desk in the small reception lobby. There were glass doors heading off in four different directions, but no sign of life behind any of them. There was an ancient vending machine, and flowers, too, but the vending machine was empty and the flowers were as plastic as the desk.

There was nowhere to sit, so I stood beside the vending machine and dialled Karen's number from my phone. I waited, in a bleak, hostile silence that seemed uncanny for a place of work, even one populated by lawyers, and then I looked at the screen. No signal. I gave a dramatic sigh for a non-existent audience and turned, wondering whether I might have better luck outside, and then I spotted the phone on the plastic desk. *Nine for an outside line*, I reckoned, and I was right.

"Karen Hobart," she said, a burst of warmth that stood in stark contrast to the plastic and the silence. "Hello?"

"It's Sam Williams. I'm downstairs in the lobby."

"Oh," she replied. "I'll come and get you. You don't want to stay down there too long. You'll never smile again."

She emerged from behind one of those glass doors a minute later and shivered as she shook my hand.

"Come on," she said. "Let's get upstairs."

I followed her through a long corridor to a fire door that creaked as she shoved it open, and then up a dark, narrow staircase that would have been more at home in a Soviet re-education centre than a legal office in the Oxford suburbs. She apologised as we reached the top, a short line about budget cuts and maintenance problems that had the sound of something she'd had to say before, and more than once.

She sat me down in her office, a small room which was granted a good swathe of natural light by one outsize window. The view was of the car park, where I could see my battered Fiat trying and failing to look inconspicuous among the host of newer, cleaner, more Japanese cars around it. The view didn't matter: after the first floor corridor, which had been as dark and as narrow as the stars, any sign of the world outside was refreshing. As Karen returned with two coffees in Styrofoam cups, I realised that apart from her, I hadn't seen another soul since I'd arrived.

She sat at her desk, opposite me, and for the first time I got a decent look at her. Late forties, I thought. Auburn hair, darker at the roots, swept into a pony tail. Glasses, and a ridge across her forehead where they'd have rested while she was reading. She caught me staring at her, and smiled, and I returned the smile just apologetically enough. No point in antagonising the woman. She'd been friendly so far.

I'd assumed I'd be shown into some kind of room designated for this sort of thing, a sealed unit, a sterile box, but after a couple of minutes' friendly, idle chat, she said "Right then, here it is," flipped her laptop around so I could see it, and pressed play on the pre-trial interview of Pieter Van der Lee.

"Hold it," I said, surprised, and she spun the machine back round and pressed pause. "I thought you were going to show me the transcript."

She shrugged. "They haven't finished typing it up. Delays. Cuts. It was supposed to be on my desk this morning. Thought you wouldn't mind seeing the interview itself."

I smiled. "Thanks. Better than reading it."

And it might have been, if there was anything useful in it at all. But there wasn't. Van der Lee sat there and nodded, said "Yes" and "No", named Fothergill, talked of unspecified abuse on an unspecified number of occasions, and I found myself wondering why the CPS hadn't thrown the case in the bin. There wasn't enough here to convict.

Van der Lee didn't sound like a liar and he didn't sound confused or forgetful. He just sounded vague. He might well be telling the truth, but the truth wasn't the only thing that mattered. Van der Lee would have to take a jury with him, and from what I'd seen, he didn't have the pulling power.

It lasted twenty minutes and as it drew to a close I glanced down at my notepad. No more than half a dozen lines, and not a word that would do much for Fothergill's defence. But I was starting to think he might not need one, and if that turned out to be the case, it would be even better news than a clue or a tell or whatever it was I'd been hoping Van der Lee's interview would reveal.

As I turned my attention back to the screen I gained the distinct impression that the interviewer shared my opinion. The interview had been done elsewhere – in shinier, newer premises than the building I was watching it in, and by a younger, keener prosecutor than Karen Hobart. The questions had come thick and fast at first, but had started to tail off, and by the eighteenth minute the poor woman was reduced to asking whether Van der Lee had anything to add, or whether it would help if his supporter came into the interview room. I raised an eyebrow and Karen leaned over the screen and hit pause.

"His lawyer. The one I put you in touch with. The one I tried to put you in touch with."

"Darren Sutcliffe?"

She nodded. "Van der Lee brought him with – he's entitled to, you know. But he left him out in the corridor the whole time." She laughed. "Would have cost a bit, what with travel time, but if he can afford it, well, it's up to him."

"I'd pay good money to ensure Darren Sutcliffe wasn't in the same room as me," I replied, without thinking, and she laughed in response.

"I don't know the man myself," she said, finally. "But what I've heard from colleagues – well, he's not the most popular lawyer in the region, let's just put it that way. Come on, there's only a minute left."

I returned my gaze to the screen. Van der Lee was shaking his head, explaining that he didn't have anything else to say, that Sutcliffe was fine where he was, that he'd only brought him with in case he was asked questions that made him uncomfortable, but that hadn't happened. And then, as the prosecutor was starting to wind things up and end the interview, a change came over Van der Lee's face.

He was a normal-looking chap. Looked a little older than the fifty-one years he claimed to carry, but Roarkes looked decades older than his real age and no one was accusing him of lying. Bald, but more the baldness of age than the baldness of rampant masculinity. Smooth face, slightly crooked nose. He'd been carrying an expression of vague interest, focus drifting into boredom, throughout the interview, but suddenly his eyes narrowed and his lips pursed and he interrupted the prosecutor with something that looked, for the first time in the interview, like genuine emotion.

"He abused me," he said. "You do believe that, don't you?"

"Yes," replied the prosecutor, with understandable hesitation. The interview had been conducted at an early stage in the process, when the dance between reassuring a victim and trusting every last allegation was a dangerously delicate process.

"He destroyed me. Everything. He took everything from me, that man. Fothergill. He should pay for what he did."

And just as suddenly as it had come, the emotion was gone, and in its place that nonchalant, casual gaze. It had been real enough, though, that change, a spark, a brief

118

flame, and then nothing but embers. I could see now why Karen Hobart hadn't binned the case. Fothergill might not be guilty and I hoped he wasn't, but something had happened, somewhere. Something had been done to Van der Lee. He wasn't making the whole thing up.

Karen turned the laptop back to face her, and smiled. "Funny ending, right?"

I nodded. "Didn't see that coming."

"Nor did we. But look, that's all I can show you right now. I'll send you stuff as and when. If it goes that far."

"Do you think it will?"

She shrugged. "I've got no more idea than you do. But I'll let you know what we decide. Another coffee before you go?"

I looked down at the cup on her desk in front of me. I hadn't had more than a couple of sips; even by office standards, it was a bad coffee. She laughed as I shook my head.

"It's an acquired taste," she said. "Sometimes I wish I'd never acquired it. I'll show you out, then?"

I thanked her, and she accompanied me through the empty corridor and staircase back to the ground floor. As I turned to leave, a thought occurred to me.

"He's got a lot of lawyers, Van der Lee. For a normal bloke. There's you lot –"

"We're not his lawyers," she interrupted, and I nodded in agreement.

"Yes, I get that, but you're on his side on this. If it goes ahead. And there's Sutcliffe. And there's Hartley, the wills guy. What does he need all that for?"

There was silence for a moment, as she digested my question and thought about her response. Eventually she shrugged.

"I don't know. He's a normal bloke, like you say. Normal blokes have wills, don't they?"

"I suppose so," I replied, but I didn't think she'd really answered the question. I thanked her and headed outside.

I sat in the car for a few minutes, thinking, wondering if Karen was watching me from her outsize window, wondering if she was as bemused by Van der Lee's sudden change of character in the interview as I'd been. Wondering about all the lawyers. *Normal blokes had wills,* she'd said. I didn't have a will. Maybe it was time to fix that. Once I'd got some property to bequeath, anyway. Van der Lee had a bar. Maybe *Dervish* was worth something, worth all the lawyers, at least.

Outside the building there was a signal, and one voicemail on my phone, from a number I'd seen written on a notepad in my kitchen the night before. I deleted it without listening, looked up the number for Hartley's offices, and dialled.

"Miller Hartley," said the voice at the other end, bright and cheerful and entirely at odds with the damp, grey sky viewed through the smeared windscreen of an ancient Fiat Uno in a half-deserted out-of-town car park.

"Hello. I was wondering if you could help me. I'm calling on behalf of a friend."

"Yes?" she replied. She sounded intrigued, which was a good start.

"Yes. I wonder, have you heard a mobile phone ringing in your offices? In fact, can you hear one now?"

I waited while she listened out for the sound of a non-existent phone.

"I'm sorry," she said. "I can't hear anything. Have you lost your phone?"

"Not me. A friend. Pieter Van der Lee. I believe he's one of your clients."

"Ah yes, Mr Van der Lee." She stopped, suddenly. Maybe she'd remembered she wasn't supposed to say anything about clients, to anyone, ever.

"Yes. He's in a bit of a state. It's got all his contacts on it. He doesn't remember when he last saw it but he thinks it might have been the same day he last saw Mr Hartley."

There was a pause. I'd been convincing, I thought; I'd always been a decent enough liar, if not a great one, but if I'd learned anything over the last few years it was the art of the bluff. This wasn't the moment to push. This was the moment to let her make up her own mind.

I heard a rustling noise, and stifled a sigh of relief. A moment later she was back.

"Let's see. That would have been last Tuesday. And then again, the previous Thursday. And twice the week before that. Mr Van der Lee has been in half a dozen times since the turn of the year. Is he sure he lost his phone on the day of his most recent visit?"

"I'll check with him," I said, and thanked her for her time. Half a dozen visits in a month. It seemed a lot, to make a will. I filed the thought away, alongside the existence of Darren Sutcliffe and Van der Lee's strange performance in his interview, and moved on to my next stop.

My next stop was Thameside School, Fothergill's place of employment until just a few years earlier. I'd told them I was coming, and Fothergill had been a member of staff there for long enough to warrant a little consideration, so I was expecting something by way of cooperation. I didn't get it.

"What precisely do you want?" said the Deputy Headmaster, Mr Gardiner, a tall, lean man with a stoop, an air of permanent exasperation and the furrow of a thousand frowns etched into his face.

"I'd just like to talk to you about Mr Fothergill, his time here, get as much background as I can."

Gardiner grimaced. We were walking together down a corridor – all white, and newly painted by the smell of it. He paused to shout something incomprehensible at a

121

gaggle of children in front of us; I could see the defiance drain from their faces as they turned and registered the identity of the man berating them. Meekly, they trotted past us and into the asphalt play area outside.

"Here we are," he said, opening the door into his office. He gestured at a chair, and then turned to me, a quizzical and ever-so-slightly menacing half-smile on his lips.

"Are you sure you're not a journalist, Mr Williams?"

I shook my head. "No, no. I'm Mr Fothergill's lawyer. Just looking for anything that might help shed light on these surprising allegations."

Gardiner had sat down behind his desk, and now he stared at me, his eyes hard and focussed, and I was reminded of days in court, trying to relax clients wilting under the remorseless glare of some of the toughest barristers in the country. Slowly and deliberately he lifted a single finger to his chin, and sat there for a moment, gently rubbing at it.

"Yes," he said, finally. "They're certainly surprising. We've had the press sniffing round, and we're not happy about it. But look, Mr Williams." He sat forward, the eyes still fixed on mine. "Fothergill was here forever. As for the era you're looking into, well." He paused, looked away, and then back at me. "There's no one here. Not from that time. I'm sure you can track down old staff, retired staff, they might remember. Fothergill should be able to give you the names himself."

I nodded. I'd suspected as much. It was possible he was lying with that *there's no one here*, but only possible, and if there was anyone, Gardiner wasn't going to help me find them. I tried another route.

"I understand that, Mr Gardiner. I was just hoping there might be something in the records, Fothergill's assessments or appraisals or what have you, anything that might show us what sort of man he was when he was teaching here, how he was thought of, that kind of thing."

Gardiner shrugged. "I suppose that's possible. I'm not really sure. The thing is, Mr Williams, I'm not sure how much help we can be here, but one thing I am sure of is that we don't really want anything to do with any of this. It's highly unsavoury and it's decades in the past and frankly, I don't think it's fair that the school should be associated with something that's not much more than ancient history."

I nodded again. I'd been struggling to place Gardiner, I'd been torn between the bumbling academic and the tyrant, but now I saw he was neither. For all his height, for all his relative power, he was just another petty little man determined to protect his empire, however modest it might be. But my opinion didn't matter. If he had information, if he could get someone to dig through files and find me some information, then he needed the flattery.

"I understand, Mr Gardiner," I said, a broad smile on my face and a nod of empathy alongside. I hoped I wasn't overdoing it. "You have enough to do just dealing with the day-to-day management of a place like this. It's impressive."

I wasn't lying, entirely. It was as far removed from Chalmere as you could imagine, but it wasn't the warren overrun with feral children that I'd feared. It seemed well-maintained, the children quiet enough, for the most part, no obvious blood stains or signs of recent violence.

He nodded himself. "Yes. Well, we have a lot to do, as you say."

"And that's why I was just hoping you might be able to point me in the direction of the files. If there are any. I'm happy to dig through myself."

He smiled, and shook his head. "I don't think so, Mr Williams. We couldn't have an outsider running through all our confidential documents, could we? And besides, the

123

school is due to be inspected in the next month or so. We've just finished getting all of our paperwork in order. I'm sorry, but even if I were prepared to have you look at it, I couldn't let you near it until the inspection's over."

I stood and thanked him, and listened to him apologise, insincerely, and wish Fothergill the best, equally insincerely, and mutter half-heartedly about *the reputation of the school* and *we have spoken to the police already, you know.* Each insincerity, every little obfuscation, all were accompanied by a half-turn, a dip of the head, a glance over my shoulder. Eye contact broken. I'd have torn the bastard apart in court. Roarkes or Colman would have had him for breakfast in an interview room. But we weren't in a court or a police station, and I couldn't do a thing about his lies. Gardiner was a dead end. I wouldn't be getting near those files.

12: To See The Point

FOTHERGILL, WHEN I dropped in to see him half an hour later, was unsurprised. Gardiner had been a lowly geography teacher when Fothergill had finally left Thameside, but he'd been one of a breed, shirts freshly ironed and minds freshly laundered and concerned only with the numbers and the league tables and the *efficient use of resources*. Spending money on music wasn't efficient. Fothergill readily conceded that he'd gone before he was pushed.

He seemed brighter today, in spite of the lack of headway we'd made. His walls had remained insult-free since I'd scrubbed off the last friendly message. Julia had been round to visit, he said, a smile on his face that seemed to hide nothing, to indicate nothing more than simple pleasure at her company.

He had some photographs he wanted to show me. I hesitated, on the verge of making up an excuse; I had better things to do than sift through an old man's memories for the sake of it. And then I remembered that Maloney had people watching Claire and the only reason I was in Oxford at all was to help this man. He needed to be heard: I owed him that, at least. He pulled two dining chairs over to a coffee table and we sat.

It seemed, at first, as if I was to be proven right about the value of the exercise. Hundreds of shots, large groups, classes, the whole school; the occasional individual photo of a favoured student; other staff, both friend and foe. Decades in black and white and colour, and nothing sinister about it, as far as I could tell. After fifteen minutes – there seemed little order to the collection, and we'd jumped back and forth through the years without any discernible pattern – Fothergill sighed and turned to me.

"This is it," he said, and even though I knew precisely what he meant, I feigned confusion, a liar's frown on my brow. "Seventy-seven to eighty," he explained. "Not long after I'd started. A good crop, they were."

Slowly, self-consciously, I dropped my gaze from his face to the picture he was holding. A class, by the look of it, a colour photograph of around thirty children, thirteen or fourteen years old. The same grins and grimaces, the same unbuttoned shirts and high hemlines as would have graced any other school photo from the era. The same minor rebellions. A good crop, maybe, but there was nothing notable about them on the face of it.

Fothergill picked out a face in the front row, his index finger jabbing at it.

"Hawkins," he said. "Jason Hawkins. He's a headteacher, now. Miles away. Cornwall, I think. Decent flautist. And that's Eleanor Simmons. Journalist. I hear her on the BBC, sometimes. Radio four. Does home affairs. Beautiful alto."

He skipped over a handful – he'd been the music teacher, after all, and wouldn't have known all of these children at the time, much less four decades later.

"That lot. Ah, yes." He was tracing a finger around a group of boys on the back row. "Jeremy Bowman and his friends. Trouble, they were."

I reached for the photograph, and he released it. Looking closely, there was little to distinguish Bowman and his gang from the rest of the group. I wondered if these people could possibly have any bearing on Van der Lee's accusations.

"What did they do?"

He shrugged. "The usual juvenile nonsense. Disrupted lessons, shouted, fought a little. Shoplifting. I heard they'd moved onto stealing cars and setting them alight, and there certainly used to be an awful amount of that about. It wouldn't surprise me if it were true. It wouldn't surprise me if they were still doing it now."

I put the photograph down on the table, and he took it up again immediately. "Jessica Hartson. Rachel Jones. No idea what happened to them. Nice girls. Good pianists, both of them. They used to duet together. That's Marine Lambert. Violin. I do wish I'd been able to keep in touch with her."

He was pointing to a smiling girl in the back row. It was difficult to tell, but I imagined she'd have been tall, if she'd been fully visible. A pretty, open face. Fothergill continued.

"Such a bright child. World at her feet. But then, you know, two years later – she must have just turned sixteen. You can guess what happened, can't you?"

Just turned sixteen. World at her feet. *But then*. It didn't take a genius?

"Pregnant?"

Fothergill nodded. "She didn't have the baby, though. I remember telling her she didn't have to, she did have a choice. Then, well, she moved away. From everyone. Off to Lancashire, all by herself. I'd like to think things went well for her after that, but I've seen enough young people trying to make lives on their own to know it doesn't usually work like that. Ah," he said, dropping the briefly wistful tones and sounding suddenly brisk and businesslike. "That's him. Van der Lee."

He stood in the middle row, scowling at the camera, just in front of Marine Lambert.

"And you really don't remember him?"

Fothergill shook his head. "Not at all. I don't even know what he played, if he played anything at all. I wouldn't have recognised him if the police hadn't shown me an old picture when they picked me up."

There were other photos from the same period, individuals and smaller groups, Van der Lee in a few of

127

them but absent from more. There was nothing that shed any light on the child, on the man, on the allegations or the strange alteration that had come upon him during his pre-trial interview. Fothergill had turned quiet, his earlier brightness gone and replaced with something reflective. Nostalgia, I thought. He insisted he was fine, that ever since I'd agreed to take his case on he'd been a different man. That he could *see the point, now*, as he put it. I hoped he was telling the truth. I asked if I could take the photographs with me – I didn't know what I was planning to do with them, not really, although I did have some bizarre notion that confronting Van der Lee with these images of his youth might shake a kernel of truth from him. I left Fothergill sitting in that same dining chair, poring through the rest of his collection, the blank look of forgetfulness broken once in a while by a sudden smile of recognition.

I phoned Mrs Piper on the way to Chalmere, and told her to expect me shortly. I could have started the day there, got it over and done with and then moved onto Karen Hobart and Thameside and Fothergill himself, if there was still any need to do so, but I'd delayed my visit. As I approached the school, as I passed through the open gates, I felt a tension in my stomach, a tight knot that sat there and throbbed, from time to time, as if to remind me that it was still there and wasn't going anywhere until I dealt with it. It had been there all day, but now I could no longer ignore it. I needed to know what Mrs Piper had found out, but I was dreading it, too. I was beginning to like Fothergill, beginning to fall into the usual trap of trusting a client, a journey that rarely ended well. If Mrs Piper's information backed up Van der Lee's story – well, the sooner I found out about it, the better, in theory. I'd drop Fothergill and he'd stop being a different man. Stop *seeing the point*. It wasn't much of a stretch to guess where that would lead. Not after his earlier attempt.

It was brighter than it had been on my previous visit, and the fields were overrun with children, running, shouting, throwing and chasing. A view captured in a painting, a scene from a poem, one of those renaissance Arcadias that Lizzy Maurier had made her domain. A scene, no doubt, from David Brooks-Powell's childhood. And look where that had got him. I parked the car, gave my head a quick brush, had a brief word with myself. It didn't work. The tension was still there.

Mrs Piper greeted me with a cup of tea. She'd remembered the milk and single dose of sugar from my previous visit. I was impressed. Once she'd sat me down in that same armchair I'd endured on my last visit, she strolled casually to the door, took a quick look outside, both directions, and then quietly closed it.

"We don't want to be disturbed, do we, Mr Williams?"

I nodded and tried to look grave. If Mrs Piper was enjoying the subterfuge, no reason to spoil it for her. And then I noticed one edge of her mouth begin to twitch, and I allowed myself to relax into a smile.

"Well, Mrs Piper," I said, "I'm sure there's no one spying on us. But it pays to be careful. There are serious criminal charges involved, after all."

That, I thought, should cover both sides. She nodded and took a seat beside me, in a matching armchair.

"These really aren't very comfortable, are they?" she asked, and then went on before I had a chance to reply. "So, your Mr Fothergill. He really wasn't here very long, was he? And I've found out why."

She paused, and I told myself to relax. Fothergill was a client, not a lucrative one, not one who'd burnish my reputation, not one I'd particularly liked, at first. If it all fell apart right now, it wouldn't be the end of the world.

I might as well have told myself Fothergill was Satan himself for all the good it did. I was, I realised, holding my breath. "Go on," I said, just to get some words out there. Just to see if I could.

"There was a terrible scandal," she began, and my heart sank. "I spoke to Harry DeVries, lovely chap, geography teacher. He helped settle me in, dear Harry. He'd been here a few years when I arrived, he was already a House Master, quite an honour for such a young teacher. He retired, well, it must be ten years ago, but we've kept in touch, he and I."

She smiled, and I found myself wondering what the obvious dalliance between Mrs Piper and Harry DeVries could possibly have to do with my client, whether it had been anything more than a dalliance, whether what Mrs Piper clearly felt for Harry DeVries had been reciprocated. I nodded for her to go on.

"I went to see him, the other day. Lovely place he's in. I do hope, when it's my time –" she paused, the smile still in place, and I thought for a moment I'd lost her, but then she shook her head and went on. "I suppose all that's beside the point. The thing is, he remembered your Mr Fothergill. Said he'd rather liked the man, as it happened. He'd arrived a year or two after Harry, and Harry had tried to take him under his wing, to explain the way things worked. And that was the trouble."

I sat forward. Whatever was coming, it was coming now. She took a sip of tea and continued.

"Mr Fothergill wouldn't play the game. That was what Harry told me. He wouldn't follow the rules."

I frowned. "What game? What rules?"

"Well, I'm not sure if you know how it works at a place like this – how it used to work, at least. It's not quite so bad now. But there's a hierarchy. Everywhere. The children here, their success, their failure, the amount of time the better teachers spend improving their results, the positions in the rugby teams, the captaincy of the cricket teams, the promotion to first violin, even who gets the lead role in the school play. It all comes down to one thing. How much money their parents have given to the school."

I shuddered. I shouldn't have been surprised; if you needed money to get in, it made sense that money would determine how successful you were once you were there. But there was something cold in the way she described it, a matter of simple hereditary economics trumping talent or hard work or anything else that the school might have chosen to value.

Mrs Piper must have seen the shudder, because she shrugged and attempted to explain. "As I said, it's not so bad now, and I'm certainly not going to sit here and try to justify it, because it's an outrageous system. Even Harry saw that, in the end. But your Mr Fothergill, he wouldn't have any of it. He had his own favourites, you see."

I shuddered again, for a very different reason. *Favourites.* That would be how it would start, I imagined. The grooming. With *favourites* and *pets* and *dedicated students* who might need a little more help from a well-disposed teacher. Private lessons. One-on-one. Away from prying eyes.

"What sort of favourites?" I asked, and she shook her head and smiled.

"Nothing like that. Nothing like that at all. He favoured the better musicians. He favoured the ones who actually did their practice. He favoured the children who listened to what he said and at least tried to do it, instead of running off and messing around with their friends and knowing that it didn't matter because daddy would get them a place in the family business whatever happened to them at Chalmere."

There was a bitterness, suddenly, in her tone, and the coldness she'd spoken with earlier suddenly made sense. It wasn't just acceptance. It was anger.

"You must understand, Mr Williams, that I didn't realise any of this was going on. These *rules.* This *game.* Not for years, not until Harry explained it to me. And Mr Fothergill

131

wouldn't have it at all. Wouldn't tolerate it. Harry told me that he'd tried to steer him the right way, because what he was doing, well, it might have been noble and fair, but it was rubbing people up the wrong way. Powerful people. Mr Fothergill wouldn't listen."

"So he was given his marching orders?"

She nodded. "There was quite a scene, apparently. The father of one of the boys turned up and demanded to see him, and had it out with him right there in the corridor, for everyone to see, the staff, the children, everyone. Demanded to know why his son hadn't been selected for a chamber orchestra that Mr Fothergill had put together. They were going on a brief tour over the summer, just England, but still. It would have been quite an honour. Mr Fothergill, apparently, explained quietly and calmly that the boy's playing wasn't quite to the standard necessary, but that he was sure he could achieve it, with practice and dedication. And then the man – this was the thing – the man shouted at him. The words he said, well, they were words that shouldn't be heard in a school, of all places. And Harry remembered how it ended. The father stormed off, and stopped, and turned, and shouted *Who do you think pays for your music department, Fothergill?* And that was it, really."

"That was it?"

"Fothergill was summoned to see the Head Master. There were raised voices. Fothergill was dismissed. He refused to play the game."

I found myself grinning. Fothergill might have told me all this himself – he must have realised I'd find out what had happened at Chalmere. Perhaps he thought it wasn't relevant. Perhaps he thought he wasn't the same man he'd been back then.

For me, it was relevant. A client I liked was a rare thing. A client I liked and admired was like gold dust.

I finished my tea, thanked Mrs Piper for her help and advised her to demand a set of new armchairs. I'd done all I'd planned to in Oxford, I'd met with a measure of success, or, at least, avoided abject failure. I could head home right now, satisfied with my day's work. But while I was in the area, there was something else I could do.

From Chalmere I headed back through Summertown towards the city centre, and then took a right turn into Jericho. Oxford might have changed since my time, but this area had always been one step ahead of the rest of town – the coolest bars, the weirdest clothes shops and cafés, the place the students went to remind themselves that Oxford wasn't just punts and garden parties and Brideshead Revisited. *Dervish* was situated on a side road a stone's throw from Jericho's main street, and yes, it was the bar I'd frequented in my own time, I could see it now, dark and noisy and pregnant with unusual smells.

The place was still closed – I was guessing it wouldn't open until evening – and in the early afternoon, even a winter afternoon, there was enough light to lend it an air of awkwardness, of incongruity, pyjamas in the office, hangover in the interview. *Dervish* wouldn't be at ease till midnight.

In the meantime, though, it was worth taking a look at those pyjamas. I parked thirty yards up the road, checking both ways for a traffic warden before I left the vehicle. I kept my walk casual as I approached – there were a couple of other pedestrians, and a few cars went by, but on the whole it was quiet enough at this time of day and this time of year for a stranger's strange behaviour to be noticeable. I walked past the place, spotting an alleyway that led alongside it, and carried on going until I found myself on the main street. It was busier here, busy enough for me to turn around and walk back the way I'd come without drawing attention to myself, and on the way back I managed to duck into the alleyway without, I thought, being observed.

It was narrow, the wall of the old church on one side and a solid white wooden fence on the other, but a few yards up it took a brief turn to the left, following the contours of the church, and I hit gold. There was a back door here. And it was open. Just an inch or two. But open.

Without stopping to think about what I was doing and whether it was dangerous or merely stupid, I pushed the door back, and it opened silently onto what looked like a store room. Slabs of beer, boxes of spirits, stacked along the walls like an alcoholic's preparation for Armageddon. And another door in the far wall.

My shoes squeaked as I crossed the floor, and caution set in. The door opposite me was closed, so I could cross unobserved, but I tried walking on my toes, and then on my heels, in an effort towards quiet. The heels worked better than the toes, but not perfectly, so I was relieved, when I reached the door and gave it a tentative shove, to find that it was not only unlocked, but also heavy enough to have deadened any noise that I'd made.

There was a corridor outside. Left towards the main bar, part of which I could see through a glass panel in another door at the end of the corridor. I stood where I was, and squinted towards it. If the small square of the bar area I could see was anything to go by, this wasn't your average student bar any more, or if it was, student bars had gone up market. Glass. Steel. Leather. Expensive-looking place.

Right, presumably, led to the kitchen and the office. If I was going to find any clues, they'd be in the office. Not that I was planning on stealing anything. Just observation. That was all I was doing. Simply observation.

I'd just stepped past the open door to a deserted kitchen when I heard footsteps approaching me from in front, and the half second it took me to make up my mind to turn around and duck in through that door were my undoing. He was around the corner and had spotted me before I'd finished turning.

"Hello?" he shouted, and I turned back around to face him. "Can I help you?"

He'd carried on walking as he spoke, so by the time he'd finished his brief question he was just a couple of feet away from me. The nose looked less crooked than it had done on the interview video – those cameras could be cruel. But it was him, the same man, the same bald head and smooth face and a sense of nothing more than vague interest in his eyes.

"Hi." I held out a hand, and he shook it. "Sam Williams. I was wondering if I could see Celia Townsend."

He shook his head.

"Sorry. No one here with that name. What's this about?"

"Hoping to buy a car off her. Must have got the wrong address. She didn't say it was a bar." I turned to leave. "Sorry to bother you."

I started to walk back the way I'd come, and hoped he hadn't spotted my stupid mistake. Not much point making up the name of the person I'd come to visit if I didn't bother hiding my own. Worse than stupid. Two steps, three, four, and I was starting to think I'd got away with it when I heard the footsteps coming fast towards me as he called out.

"Sam Williams, did you say?"

I stopped. No use in trying to bluff this one any further. I turned to face him. The vague interest was gone, replaced by a clear, bright anger.

"Yes," I replied. Nothing more. He nodded.

"I'd get out fast, Mr Williams, if I were you. I'd get out fast and I'd get away and I'd get as far from here as I could."

I opened my mouth to speak, but he held out a finger, one finger, and that together with the anger in his eyes was enough to silence me.

"I know who you are. My lawyer's told me all about you. You've been harassing him, haven't you?"

Open mouth, again. Finger, again, which wasn't entirely fair. My call to Sutcliffe was no more harassment than it was chicken fried rice and a can of beer. But Van der Lee had the floor.

"And now you've decided to go straight for me, have you? Very foolish, Mr Williams. Sutcliffe told you I wouldn't meet you, didn't he?"

"Yes."

"I'd suggest you learn to take no for an answer. You'll regret this little adventure. Now get out. Oh, and Williams?"

He spoke softly, and the rising lilt at the end lured me in, an inch closer, two inches, six, so that when the punch came, a hard low straight into my solar plexus, I couldn't even see the fist.

"You can take that with you and fuck off," he said, standing over me as I lay cowering and foetal on the cold floor. I closed my eyes and tried to brace myself for what I knew was coming next, which bitter experience had taught me would be a boot in the ribs or, if I was particularly unfortunate, in the face, but instead I heard footsteps moving away and the sound of a door closing.

I waited thirty seconds and pulled myself up, clinging to the wall for support. There was no sign of Van der Lee, all that remained of him a throb in my gut that receded even as I slowly walked back the way I'd come. I'd been an idiot, and I hoped it wasn't going to cost me. Or cost Fothergill.

Worse than stupid. Dangerous. Stupid and dangerous.

13: Fallen

I WOKE WITH my heart racing and the certainty that there was someone there in the room with me, with us, someone who meant me harm and had the means to deliver it. I waited in silence as my eyes grew used to a darkness mediated only slightly by the giant green digits on the clock beside me. I could hear Claire breathing, slow and steady, could feel her arm against my side.

I couldn't hear anything else.

A dream, I guessed. I couldn't remember what had happened in it, but it had been enough to wake me sweating, panicking, terrified. I lay there and let my breathing slow and rewound the previous day, the previous evening, looking for something that would set my mind at rest. Something that would let me sleep.

It was 5am. And look as I might, I wasn't going to find anything.

I'd spent most of the drive back to London alternately worrying about what Van der Lee would do, and dismissing the idea that he'd do anything. Sure, he'd told me I'd regret my *little adventure*, but I'd been told I'd regret doing something, or not doing it, or doing it wrong, I'd been told all that so many times it was difficult to take it seriously. I had regrets. But they tended to be my own doing, not someone else's revenge.

The throb had fallen to a dull ache, and I'd almost convinced myself I'd be okay when I got Maloney's text, telling me Claire hadn't left the house all day, and that finished the job, so by the time she opened the door to me shortly after six I was in as good a mood as I'd been in a while. I'd suggested a takeaway but Claire had insisted on cooking, the first time she'd cooked a proper meal in weeks,

137

a chicken stew that made up for in bulk what it lacked in flavour, and was a hundred times better than anything I could have created anyway. I'd washed up and we'd sat down in front of the television with a bottle of wine, and right up to the point I decided I was overdressed, the whole evening had been progressing as well as I might have hoped. I was overdressed, too: I was still wearing the suit I'd spent the day in. So I undressed in the bedroom and hung my clothes up in the wardrobe, checked for a bruise where I'd been punched and was relieved to see nothing there. I was all set to turn around and see where the night led when I caught it.

A smell.

A whiff of woodsmoke.

Just a hint, but as I poked my head further into the wardrobe it grew stronger, until I traced the source to a pile of sweaters on a chest-high shelf. Claire's sweaters. I lifted them out, one by one, sniffed, folded them and returned them, and didn't get a hit until I found myself holding her sweater. The new one. The woollen one.

The one she'd been wearing when I'd gone to visit Melanie Golding.

I heard a step behind me and rushed to put it back, hoping Claire hadn't noticed, hoping my suspicion wasn't going to bring on another panic attack. I turned, and she was smiling, no sign that she'd seen a thing. I breathed a sigh of relief. A shallow one, though, because that was it for me.

Sure, Claire hadn't been out while I'd been in Oxford. But she'd been out the night before, hadn't she? Somewhere unknown, somewhere with woodsmoke and who knew what else. I couldn't trust her, and at the same time she'd hinted that my trust was the only thing keeping her alive. Sure, Van der Lee had made the same threat a thousand others had made idly before. But Van der Lee's solicitor had already threatened to report me to the Law Society, and that was before I'd done anything worth reporting. Van der Lee had punched me in the gut, not that I could blame him. I wondered what he'd cook up for me now.

So I'd let Claire draw me back to the living room and the television, and I'd let her pour me wine, and I'd let her take my hand and press it to her breasts, and I'd let her pull off the few clothes I was wearing and watched while she removed her own, and then we'd made love, and I'd let her think I was there with her, in the moment, although I wondered whether she was there either, or whether this was just one more way to distract me, panic attacks and chicken stews and sex. And then we'd fallen asleep, early, not long after ten, and now I was awake at 5am, and she wasn't, so there was no one left for me to try to fool.

I gave up trying to get back to sleep half an hour later, and fired up the laptop. I'd been thinking back, Van der Lee in that interview, and later at the bar. Sure, I'd intruded, I'd trespassed, I'd made up some bullshit story that any idiot could have seen through, and he was within his rights to be angry. But something jarred. The distracted, bored man in the interview. The man who'd turned, suddenly, convinced beyond doubt of his rightness. And then at the bar, the fury I'd seen in his eyes, but the restraint in his words, in what he'd said and done – because one punch wasn't much, really, not in the grand scheme of things. He could have done more. I'd been expecting him to. And he'd have had the law on his side, too.

I had an account with Companies House – I'd lost count of the number of times a client or a client's enemy or just someone I needed dirt on had tried to hide the truth in a set of corporate accounts that anyone with a computer and a little patience could untangle, if they knew where to look. Untangling Pieter Van der Lee wouldn't take me long.

Dervish was owned by Van der Lee Entertainment UK Ltd. The company was registered at an Oxford address I didn't recognise, but from the postcode it seemed central, which meant it was more likely to be a business address than a residential one. Probably the law firm or accountants who'd set the company up in the first place. Accounts and annual returns had all been filed on time, no penalties for late registration or applications for extensions. Van der Lee was the sole shareholder, and one of two directors; the other seemed, from the reports available, to be one of his employees.

The accounts seemed relatively straightforward: the bar was profitable, if not wildly so; the revenues were great, although the costs seemed a little on the high side, even for a town centre bar. That was it. Everything in order, with just a bit more of it than I'd have expected. What that *bit more* usually meant was money laundering, but I didn't see what money laundering would have to do with Fothergill. I scanned the documents and sent them to Maloney, with a plea for help. Maloney knew bars like I knew kebab vendors, and ever since he'd decided to go straight, he'd made it his mission to learn how a straight business was supposed to work. If there was anything amiss, he'd find it.

I popped my head through the bedroom door. Claire was still sleeping, the duvet clinging to the bed by one desperate edge. It had just gone seven, and there was nothing she needed to be woken for, so I made myself a coffee and sat down to think.

Thinking didn't take long. I needed stimulus, something outside my own mind, something new to throw into the mix. I picked up the envelope Fothergill had given me and let the photographs slide out.

Van der Lee featured in six of them, of twenty from the period in question. I flicked through those six, fast, then slow, staring closely at the face, looking for clues in the eyes or the tilt of the head or the hint of a smile. I found nothing. I caught myself rubbing my stomach, still sore, without thinking about it. The pain was definitely improving. I glanced briefly at the other fourteen, and I couldn't see anything there either, so I returned to Van der Lee and his six, and it was only then, on the fourth time of looking at them, that I spotted something.

It was the girl.

I picked up the large group photograph, the one Fothergill had dissected in such detail the previous day. There she was, in the back row. Marine Lambert. Van der Lee stood in front of her. Her left hand was invisible behind the boy standing beside Van der Lee, but her right snaked down alongside her body and came to a rest on his shoulder.

On Van der Lee's shoulder.

I was surprised I hadn't spotted it when Fothergill had shown me the photograph, but I'd been looking at faces then, just faces. I'd spent so long staring at those faces I could hardly see them any more, and the moment I started looking elsewhere, there it was. A hand on a shoulder.

I picked up the other five. She was in all of them – three photographs in a group of ten or twelve, two in a group of six, one with just three of them. In each case she was beside or immediately in front of Van der Lee, and in each case there was contact, physical contact, and not the sort that could be accounted for by the children squeezing together at the photographer's behest. In one of the larger groups, every other child stood with hands clasped in front, but Marine Lambert and Pieter Van der Lee stood beside one another in the second of two rows, staring stony-faced at the camera, her right arm and his left disappearing into the space behind another child's head which provided just enough cover for those hands to be entwined. They'd grown, by the time this one was taken – they looked fifteen, maybe sixteen, a good couple of years after the class photograph had been taken. But whatever there was between them, whatever there had been at the age of fourteen, it was still there two years later.

Marine Lambert had left. That was what Fothergill had told me. Disappeared into Lancashire. I shivered. I'd done my own bit of disappearing there, not so far back, and I'd lived to regret it. Others hadn't lived at all.

And pregnant, too. Her, not me. Marine Lambert. I picked up those photographs again and the germ of an idea started to form in my head. I spent a few minutes trying to ignore it, to let it grow on its own, to see if it could stand on its own two feet. It could. I picked up the phone and called Fothergill – it was early still, but I didn't think he'd be sleeping. There was no answer. I glanced down at the photographs and remembered Van der Lee's face, in the interview, in his own bar, and without really thinking about it I picked up the phone again and did something stupid.

I knew there would be no one in, not at this time in the morning, but the call went straight through to Darren Sutcliffe's voicemail, as it had done the first time I'd called, and I kept my message short and to the point.

"This is Sam Williams," I said. I was smiling as I spoke. "Please tell Mr Van der Lee that I know about Marine Lambert."

I put the phone down, still smiling, still convinced that what I'd just done was both right and sensible, and the smile stayed in place for the five seconds it took for me to turn to the computer and realise that what I'd just said, its brevity and its opacity, might sound very much like a threat.

I pushed the thought to one side and got to work on Marine Lambert. Fothergill had expressed regret that they hadn't been able to stay in touch, but I wondered how hard he'd tried, and I wondered how difficult it would have been, back then, to find someone who didn't want to be found.

That was then. This was now. And *Marine Lambert?* Not the easiest name to hide behind.

I started with the name and a guess at the year of birth. If the later photographs had been taken in seventy-nine or eighty, and she'd been fifteen or sixteen years old, that gave me sixty-four to sixty-five. But that *Marine*, which had, in its rareness, seemed such a blessing, shaped up more like a curse: all I got were aquatic parks and aquatic scientists and oceanographers and oceanic wildlife reserves, all fields in which the surname *Lambert* seemed frustratingly common. I threw in Lancashire, and that narrowed things a little, but didn't give me what I wanted: a good chunk of Lancashire was coastal, after all. I removed the date of birth and replaced it with the year she'd left Oxford, nineteen eighty, which didn't improve things much. I changed eighty to eighty-one, to eighty-two, figuring that with fewer than ten hits each year I could run right through the millennium in half an hour or so, but I didn't need to, because nineteen eighty-two gave me precisely what I was after.

The hit was from a newspaper article written in twenty-fifteen. The *Blackpool Herald* reported on the final victory of a group of residents who had been campaigning for decades, it seemed, for traffic calming measures on a notoriously dangerous local street. The council had agreed to install traffic lights and road bumps, and the residents were at once celebratory and grudgingly suspicious: for every *vindicates* and *delighted* there was a *believe it when I see it* and an *about time.*

The article listed recent incidents on the road in question, including two deaths and four serious injuries in the past ten years. But the residents had been fighting their battle far longer than that. The reporter had unearthed a letter written to the *Herald*'s predecessor in nineteen eighty-two, in which the furious correspondent had bemoaned the lack of interest in road safety demonstrated by local politicians who were, in his words, "more interested in lining their pockets with the fruits of a morally dubious tourist culture than in the lives of their own electorate."

The letter had been written in response to the death of a young woman on that very street, earlier that month.

The young woman's name was Marine Lambert.

I leaned back into the sofa and sighed, and tried to piece it all together. She'd loved Pieter Van der Lee; sure, they were teenagers, but the story the photographs told was one of teenagers who'd stuck together through the turbulent high school years, and that meant more than just childish lust. She'd loved him; he'd loved her back. She'd fallen pregnant.

I stopped myself. *Fallen.* Why had I picked that word? What did it mean? An accident? Possibly. A trap? Unlikely, if she'd chosen to get rid of it. *Fallen.* A stumble, a slip, something that had happened to her, unwanted and unplanned. I stood and walked quietly to the bedroom door, stuck my head inside, watched the duvet rise and fall with Claire's breath, shallow, calm. Had Marine Lambert fallen pregnant? Had it been something she'd planned, regretted, remedied?

Planned or not, she'd remedied it. She'd aborted the baby and fled north, away from Van der Lee, away from everyone she knew. And two years later she'd died there.

I wondered whether she'd died alone. Whether she'd made friends, in such a short space of time, friends she'd thought about as she lay bleeding in the road, friends who'd stood teary-eyed at her funeral and wished they'd had the time to know her better. I doubted it. What had that angry correspondent written? A "morally dubious tourist culture". Come, spend, leave. A town of transients. She'd been eighteen, Marine Lambert, eighteen years old and, if the photographs were anything to go by, pretty enough.

144

How had she made her way in a town like that? There were enough ways to make a living, but there was one that stood out.

My phone rang on the table in the room behind me. Claire stirred and turned onto her side, and I closed the bedroom door, walked over and snatched up the phone.

"Hello?"

"Are you for real?"

I recognised the voice. I'd heard it an hour or so earlier on his recorded message, after all.

"I'm sorry, Mr Sutcliffe," I began, but he carried on talking over me.

"I don't usually get in this early, Williams," he said, with the air of a man who had a lot to say and was determined to say it. "I've come in earlier than usual, left my wife at home, asleep, slipped out of the house before the kids woke up, which isn't something I like to do, because I like my kids, Williams, I like to see them from time to time if work allows. I've come in early because I've got a shitload of work to shovel my way through, clients with important things they need doing, people who rely on me to get those things done. I get in here early and there's a light flashing on my machine so I pick it up, thinking maybe it's good news, maybe one of those things I need to get done is actually getting done and some rare saint of the legal profession has called up to tell me about it, to brighten up my cold, wet day. And what do I hear? I hear your voice. *Your voice*, Williams. Telling me shit about Marine Lambert."

He paused, for a moment, but I didn't think fast enough to take advantage of the opening. The ground had shifted. *I know about Marine Lambert*, I'd said, and then I'd worried it sounded like a threat. Now I knew she was dead, it didn't sound like a threat. It sounded like a taunt.

"I'm starting to think you've got some kind of problem, Williams. Some kind of obsession. With my client. And I don't think that's appropriate, for a man in your position. Do you? Do you think that's appropriate?"

"No," I said, finally. "Look, I got it wrong. What I said. Marine Lambert. That wasn't fair."

"You're damn right it wasn't fair. You'll be hearing from the Law Society. And if you want to keep practicing, stay the hell away from my client."

And then, nothing, just the dead hum of a dead connection.

14: The Head of the Snake

I HAD BETTER luck with Fothergill, at least. I'd been tempted to call him the moment I'd seen Marine Lambert's name in the *Blackpool Herald*, but I'd stopped myself as I reached for the phone: I didn't know what effect hearing about Marine's death would have on him, and if he had to know, I figured it would be something best told face to face.

But Sutcliffe's call had thrown me, and worse than that, it had put me the wrong side of the line. As I stood there looking at my phone, that dead tone working its dismal way through my hand and up my arm, I found myself looking at my actions from Van der Lee's perspective. I'd turned up in his bar, lied about why I was there, and the very next day I'd called up Van der Lee's lawyer and left a cryptic little sting with him, *Marine Lambert*, his long-dead love, a box-load of memories he probably didn't want opened.

But then, it was Van der Lee who'd opened that box himself. It was Van der Lee who'd brought the nineteen seventies into twenty-seventeen. It was Van der Lee who'd turned, in that interview, from a man with nothing to say to a man with everything to say, just nothing I could understand. I was still standing there when Claire walked in and yawned, stretched, her pyjama top riding up past her belly button, and saw me frowning at the phone in my hand.

"Bad news?" she asked.

I shrugged. "Not sure. I can't figure him out, this Van der Lee guy. His lawyer I've got pinned down: the man's a prick. That's simple. But Van der Lee's a mystery."

"Do you think he's lying?"

I took in a deep breath and tried to think about the answer to that question, to think about it deeply and seriously and ignore the fact that Sutcliffe was indeed a prick and Fothergill seemed, despite my initial reservations,

147

to be both likeable and trustworthy and not the kind of man who'd do the kind of thing Van der Lee had accused him of.

The trouble was, Van der Lee didn't strike me as a liar either.

Sure, I didn't know the man well. Sure, he was hiding something, part of the story, the big part, if I was any judge. But whatever had really happened back then, Van der Lee was convinced by his own line. That was it, that was what I'd seen in the interview. A man who saw himself as the victim. A man who saw my client as the villain. There was more to it than that, no doubt, there were more things unsaid than there were said. But Van der Lee wasn't making it up. Not all of it, at least.

Claire was still looking at me, waiting for an answer, so I shrugged and told her that yes, I thought Van der Lee was lying, because there was too much I couldn't explain in the truth of it. She stared at me a moment, not entirely convinced, and then turned her attention to coffee.

I called Fothergill. I couldn't tell him everything on the phone, but I didn't want to turn up unannounced. He answered straight away, and when I asked him where he'd been when I'd called first thing he told me he'd been asleep, like any normal person at that time of the day. I laughed.

"Listen, I've been looking at those photographs you gave me," I said.

"Loaned you, Sam. I'll be wanting them back."

"Loaned me. Sure. Thing is, I noticed something." I paused, waiting for him to prompt me, but nothing came back. Fothergill wasn't given to wasting his words. I went on. "That girl. Marine Lambert."

"What about her?"

The question came at me fast, like an accusation.

"There's a connection, I think. Between her and Van der Lee. They're together in every photo."

"They're where the photographer put them. The kids didn't get any say."

I thought about that, remembered my own school photos, the pointing and arranging, and then, when the grown-ups' backs were turned, the whispers and the rearranging. Fothergill would have been one of the ones facing the wrong way.

"Maybe," I said. "But it's a pretty strong coincidence. And their body language. It isn't like two people who just happen to be standing next to each other."

I was expecting another argument – I was conditioned to argument, and not because I was a lawyer but because I had a habit of saying things people didn't want to hear. But instead, Fothergill sighed and offered something closer to agreement.

"Hmmm," he said. "Maybe. Maybe. Would that explain things?"

He was asking the question of himself. I waited for him to answer.

"Maybe," he said, again. "I was close to Marine. After she left, too, for a while."

"After she left?"

"Yes. I wrote to her, a few times. She wrote back."

"Where? Where did she live?"

There was a long pause, an old man thrown back on memories gone stale.

"I'm not sure," he said, finally. "She only gave me a post office address. Somewhere in Blackpool."

That tied in with the article in the *Herald*. The sliver of hope I'd been harbouring, the possibility that it was a different Marine Lambert who'd died beneath the wheels of a speeding Ford Fiesta, vanished into nothing. Fothergill continued. "She had a box there. Didn't want anyone knowing where she lived. Didn't want to be found."

"Why not?"

"Her parents. They weren't – well, let's just say they were trouble. And, well, once she'd had the abortion – they were a Catholic family. They wouldn't have taken that well. She needed a clean break."

I wanted to say something, to offer some kind of commiseration, but I had to keep reminding myself that he didn't know she was dead. Instead I just coughed and said "Yes," and let him go on.

"It'll have been tough, for her, all alone. But if anyone could have made it, Marine Lambert was the one. Remarkable girl. She'll have made an extraordinary woman, I suspect."

He'd changed his line since the previous day. He'd been more focussed on the difficulties than whatever attributes Marine Lambert might have possessed. That change would make the truth all the more painful.

"Listen, I'm planning on coming to Oxford tomorrow," I said, before he could reminisce any further, before he could build his vision of Marine Lambert's future into something beautiful for me to tear down when I saw him. "Round eleven?"

"Of course. I'll be here."

Claire had gone back to the bedroom. I returned to the laptop and read that article again. It was neutrally written, professional, the work of a decent journalist who'd gone the extra mile to track down an old letter and give a sense of context to the story. Her name was Eliza Burnett, and I decided to give her a call. If I was going to be breaking the news to Fothergill, the more news I had, the better. I'd deliver Marine Lambert's death like a fist wrapped in cotton wool.

The number for the *Blackpool Herald* given on the website went through to a recorded message saying that operations had moved and providing a different number with a different code. I dialled again, and found myself talking to a switchboard operator at Mercury Regional Press, who, to my surprise, had no difficulty in tracking down Eliza Burnett and was happy to put me straight through.

Eliza Burnett herself said she had a few minutes to talk; she probably thought she might get a story out of me. I hadn't worked out my line before I'd called, and I decided, from the tone of her voice, from the accent that burnished her words with a friendliness that might have been entirely in my mind, to play it straight. No point in lying when I didn't know if I had to.

"Oh yes," she said. "Yes, I remember. You've never seen anything like it. I mean, it's, what, a speed bump and some lights and a camera, and some of them were celebrating like they'd just won the lottery. You could tell it meant a lot. There was this woman crying, I remember that. Said her daughters would be able to play out now. Said they could have their childhood back."

"Yes," I said. "You mentioned her in the article. But I was wondering – you also talked about the accidents."

"Oh yeah. That place was a deathtrap. Thing is, for all the speed bumps and crap, it still is. Young lad got knocked off his bike there last year. He was lucky, just a few broken bones. His mother asked me to write about it but I don't do that patch any more." And she explained how things had changed, since the takeover, by Mercury Regional Press, I assumed. She'd been *relocated* – she said the word like it was poison – to Preston, they all had, the ones who hadn't been sent packing. That was her beat. "Not that I don't prefer it here. It just would have been nice if they'd given us the choice."

I jumped in before she got too caught up in her own local tragedy, and asked whether she had any more background regarding the earliest accident she'd mentioned. "Marine Lambert. Chap wrote a letter about it in eighty-two. You found the letter. I was wondering whether there might have been an article about the accident itself?"

"Maybe," she said, and my heart sank. *Maybe* meant hours with the microfiche and probably no luck at the end of it. There was a pause, while I tried to work out if there was anything I could do to persuade Eliza to do the grunt work for me, whether I had anything local enough to interest her, and then she was talking again. "No," she said. "There was something. I remember digging it up, and if I dug it up and used it then I'd have scanned it, and if I scanned it then it'll be on my personal folders. Hang on."

I waited, again, in silence broken only by her shallow breath and the tapping of her fingers on the keyboard, and tried to remind myself that none of this would help, that it wouldn't add so much as a forkful of meat to Fothergill's defence, that it was just the padding for the big bad news. It didn't matter.

"Got it," she said. "What's your email?"

As I gave it to her I realised I was close to laughing with relief, entirely at odds with what I'd been telling myself a moment earlier. She said she'd send it to me later, and I thanked her, and it wasn't till she'd said goodbye and I'd ended the call that I realised I hadn't explained why I was interested in Marine Lambert's death. She'd never asked.

The morning passed uneventfully, a vacuum punctuated by coffee and desultory conversation, and checking to see if Eliza Burnett's email had arrived. I found I was avoiding Claire's gaze, and forced myself to look at her, head on, to smile when she spoke, to answer her as if I didn't know she was lying to me and had been lying to me for weeks. I wondered suddenly whether she knew I knew, whether this was one of those dances of suspicion, each of us pretending that everything was fine and the miasma of mistrust that had built up between us was just weariness or stress or something that could be easily wiped away. I wondered whether this was what happened with affairs, men and women suspecting and then knowing and not doing anything about it, not saying anything about it, so desperate to preserve whatever they thought they still had that they connived at their own cuckoldry. I shook my head and tried to clear the thoughts away. I was setting traps for my own brain and getting stuck in them without any help from Claire.

I had an appointment with Martins at the station, the one she'd flattered me to get, and even though I didn't trust her and wasn't looking forward to it, I knew I'd go anyway, a blind man walking willingly into a ditch. The fridge was bare – whatever Claire had been doing on her unofficial outings, it wasn't stocking up – but there was tinned soup and bread that hadn't yet turned green, so at least I had something to eat. And so I waited, drank coffee, dipped bread into soup and waited, nodded and agreed and waited, checked my emails and waited, as the day worked its way slowly to the point of my departure like a dribble of paint sliding down a wall.

It said something for Martins that I was looking forward to seeing her even less than I was looking forward to telling Fothergill that Marine Lambert was dead.

It was raining, again, the streets lifeless close to home and even the West End a shadow of its usual teeming self. As I stopped outside the police station I glanced behind and saw, amongst a smattering of lost tourists, a man with grey hair, looking right at me from twenty metres away and across a busy intersection. He glanced down at his phone before our eyes could truly meet, but he looked so familiar, so like all those other grey-haired men I'd been noticing lately, that I almost set off after him. I looked around, briefly, towards the police station, and when I turned back to him he was gone. All in my head, I thought. There were grey-haired men everywhere. I was starting to get paranoid.

My meeting with Martins took place in the same room she and Winterman had interviewed me in, which wasn't a good sign, but this time she was on her own, which meant, at least, that there was nothing formal about the occasion. She'd kept me waiting at the front desk, but only for a minute; she'd offered me a coffee and made it herself, and I couldn't blame her for the fact that it was nearly as bad as the sludge Karen Hobart had given me in Oxford. And now she was sitting opposite me across an interview desk, but she was sitting back in her chair, smile on her face, no tape running.

"So what can I do for you?" I asked, and the smile fell right away.

"What's that, Williams? No *how are you*? No *how's the investigation going*? I thought you of all people wouldn't be able to resist a little dig."

I shrugged. "All out of digs, I'm afraid. All out of chat, too. Work to do."

Her eyes widened in what looked like genuine surprise, but she resisted the temptation to make a dig of her own. Instead, she nodded and outlined the state of the Trawden murder investigation for me.

"Obviously, all of this is between you and me. Not to go beyond these four walls, no pillow talk, I don't want my inadequacies splashed all over the front page. Didn't work out so well for your mate Roarkes. Not having it happen to me."

I nodded. "I'll keep it to myself."

She nodded again. "Right. Well, at the moment we're focussing on John Evans. He's got motive, of course, even if it isn't the purest of motives. His dad only killed one girl, not two, and by the time he got fingered for the one he hadn't done he was dead already."

I seized on that. "The one he *hadn't* done. So you do think it was Trawden all along, behind the Grimshaw murder?"

She shrugged. "Doesn't matter what I think, does it? Trawden's dead, Evans is dead. The important thing is that John Evans believes it. Anyway, he says he's got an alibi, but he's having difficulty proving it."

"You know, people aren't always where it's most convenient for them to be," I said, and she nodded, tongue gliding slowly along her lower lip, again. I felt suddenly queasy, grimaced and glanced down, feigning a cramp in my right leg. By the time I'd given it a rub and looked up again, she'd put the tongue away,

"True, true. Lack of an alibi isn't enough to hang him. He says he was down on the south coast but can't tell us precisely where. Says he was alone, says he'd hitched down, and walked and hitched along the coast, slept rough, spent about a week there. Doesn't know where he was on the day Trawden was killed. He had opportunity, or he can't prove he didn't have it, at least. Puts him in the frame."

"Didn't strike me as the sort to use insulin. More of a fist and boot type, I thought."

I was, I realised, rehearsing the same conversation I'd had with Colman, before she'd walked out on me. This time, at least, my interlocutor stayed put.

"You're right on that. Especially after the incident between the two of you." She sighed. "If we put Evans in the dock and start down the insulin line a jury's going to laugh us out of court. If we even get that far. If we can even charge him. That's why I need your help. I want more out of Evans."

Now I was confused. "But it was insulin, wasn't it?"

She nodded. I continued.

"If it was insulin that killed him and you don't believe

155

Evans could have used insulin, then it couldn't have been him. If that's really what you believe, we're not going to get anything more out of him."

Martins sighed again and looked me in the eye, and I felt we were getting to it now, the meat, the truth of why I was here and what she wanted from me.

"The thing is, Sam, if I can't get anything more from Evans, that puts me in a tricky position."

She'd switched to *Sam*, I noticed. I chose not to reciprocate. "I'm sorry, Detective Inspector." I shook my head. "I understand this is difficult. This case. I know how important it is for you. But much as I'd like Evans out of my hair, I don't really see what you want with him, and I don't see how I can help."

She smiled, now, and that, together with the *Sam*, touched something off in me, some relic of an ancient hunter's instinct that told me I was in the presence of danger. I sat back and waited.

"Okay, Sam," she began. "Okay. Enough of Evans. But on a similar subject – well, I don't think you're going to like this, but I suspect we're going to have to get Claire back in."

I felt my arm twitch and concentrated on trying to look relaxed as she continued.

"I'm aware she's in a –" she paused, searching for the right word, and nodded when she found it, "a vulnerable position at the moment. I'm aware it's difficult. For you, for her. I know she had some kind of breakdown, and part of me thinks it's connected with Trawden, but when we asked her she just smiled at us and shook her head. So what am I supposed to think, Sam?"

She stopped and waited for me to say something. How much, I wondered, did she know? She was right, of course, there was a connection between Claire and Trawden, or *Viktor*, as he'd called himself when he was posing as the father of one of the dead women Claire had been

156

investigating. Did she know about the gun? About Jonas Wolf? Colman knew, but even with the frosty state of things between us, I couldn't believe she'd have told Martins.

"It's not," I said, finally. "It's nothing to do with Trawden." A stone-cold lie. A good thing the tape wasn't running.

She nodded. "The thing is, what with the difficulties you've pointed out, over Evans, we're at a bit of a loose end here, Sam. I mean, the CCTV's useless. And Claire – well, I'll be honest with you, I'm worried. She's got no alibi. Nothing we can verify, anyway. And you know we spoke to her doctor?"

I looked up, sharp, and then back down again. I hadn't known that. Claire had given permission, so it was bound to happen eventually. But I didn't like things being sprung on me.

"And?" I asked.

"Well, according to Doctor Aziz, Claire's been struggling, true, but not so badly that she couldn't have been up and about by the time Trawden was killed."

She'd glanced down, at some papers on the table, presumably for the doctor's name, but now she was staring at me, eye fixed on mine, and for the first time I had the sense that she might actually be good at this, at the bit of the job that involved breaking people, in small, quiet rooms, that involved getting people to say things they didn't want to say. I shook my head and she shrugged and went on.

"And you know, Sam, whatever it was, this breakdown – which seems to have happened right about the time your friend Brooks-Powell got killed, and Trawden got shot, it really doesn't help that she refuses to talk to us about it."

"That's her business."

"Maybe. Maybe it is. But you must understand, on a case like this we have to be seen to be exploring every angle, pushing every door. It's not just me. There are other people

157

involved. There are people who wouldn't mind putting Claire by the flames and seeing if she catches fire. It's about results, Sam."

I'd flinched at the notion of Claire by the flames – it wasn't a particularly comforting image – but my attention had been caught by something else.

"Other people?" I asked, but she declined the invitation to elaborate.

"I even had a phone call with the Grimshaws, you know, for the sake of completeness," she said, with a short, low laugh to end it. I threw out a smile. The Grimshaws had been unlikely killers a decade back. I doubted they'd be any more convincing in the role now. And I didn't need Martins to tell me who those *other people* were – one of them, at least, was obvious.

Genaud. I hadn't seen Genaud when I'd entered and waited and been taken to the interview room, but that didn't mean he wasn't there. Didn't mean he wasn't sitting behind the one-way mirror or listening to our conversation or just waiting to grab Martins when she'd finished with me and find out what I'd said. I hadn't liked the way Genaud had looked at me during the first interview, but I'd been ready to dismiss him. Roarkes' little background talk had made me wary. I didn't like Martins. But I didn't want Genaud taking over.

She was still talking.

"But that's how it is, Sam. Every angle. Which means we're probably going to have to get Claire back in. And I'm concerned how that will affect her."

"She's wrong," I said. "The doctor. Claire's only just got to the point where she can leave the flat."

I knew I was lying again, but that was the line Claire had played on me. It was what I was supposed to think. And I had a feeling for where Martins was heading, a sense of the head of the snake circling back to the tail. I wasn't going to make it easy for her.

"Maybe," she replied.

"And this breakdown. It was – it had nothing to do with Trawden. It's about the past. Claire's past. The distant past."

"I'd like to believe you, Sam. I really would. To be honest, I probably do. But you know how this works. I can't take something like this on trust, just your word, just Claire's word. I need something else. Wouldn't it be easier if we didn't have to get her in at all?"

I tilted my head for a nod, and stopped myself. The head of the snake. I knew where this was going.

"Because," she continued, "that's still possible, I think. If we had somewhere else to look, someone else to look at. And I think you can help there, Sam. I've heard what you did in Manchester, I've spoken to people who say you weren't a complete prick getting in everyone's way, so I'm slightly ashamed that I ever thought you were, but you can hardly blame me, right?"

She was smiling at me now, and as she continued I fought the urge to smile back, to play along, to walk willingly into the serpent's mouth.

"What you did up there, getting people talking, Carson, that sergeant, what was his name, the one who died?"

"Tarney," I said.

"You get people talking. You find an angle. That's what you do, isn't it?"

I dropped my eyes to the table and wondered who she'd spoken to. Not Roarkes. He wouldn't have given her the time of day, and he'd have told me if she'd been asking questions. But others had been involved. Difficult to keep that many people quiet.

Martins was waiting. I decided to let her wait. I could hear noises outside the room, footsteps, the occasional raised voice, the ringing of a phone. After fifteen, twenty seconds of this she sighed and went on with her pitch.

"You know what I'm driving at, don't you?"

I looked back up at her and nodded. I knew what she was driving at, but I was having trouble making up my mind. Getting the focus shifted onto Evans would draw it away from Claire. Getting the focus shifted onto Evans might keep Genaud out of the picture. Getting the focus shifted onto Evans would stop the bastard following me around and turning up outside my flat.

But from where I stood, Evans looked innocent. Evans wouldn't have used insulin.

She smiled at me again. I'd never seen the woman smile so much.

"You can help me break him, Sam. Help me break Evans. He hates you, you know that, right? You're the guy who helped pin Maxine Grimshaw on his dad. You reckon it was Trawden all along. So does young John Evans. Get you and me in a room with the guy, he'll be boasting he killed Trawden within an hour."

My thoughts flew, unprompted, to the man with the grey hair. Maybe I wasn't being paranoid. Maybe John Evans had given up following me around himself and got someone else to do it for him. I was doing the same with Claire. Maybe half of London was having the other half followed. And if Evans was smart enough to get someone to do his surveillance for him, maybe he was smart enough to get them to kill for him, too. The police might buy that, even if I didn't. There were too many good reasons to do what Martins wanted me to do, and not enough not to. But I wanted it on the table. I wanted her to say it.

"You want me to extract a confession from a man you think is probably innocent?" I asked.

"I want you to give me something to work with, Sam. That's all. Something that means I don't have to focus on Claire. Everybody wins."

160

I stood and walked to the door. Before I let it fall shut behind me, I turned back to face her.

"Not everybody," I said. "Not John Evans."

No grey-haired man outside the station, just Evans himself, leaning against the glass wall of a taxi business across the road and starting towards me as I emerged. I shook my head and hurried away in the direction of Leicester Square, and by the time I'd merged with the tourist crowd, he was nowhere to be seen.

Claire was asleep when I got back, one of those mid-afternoon naps that meant either she wasn't back to herself, or she was taking the role seriously. I dropped Maloney a text, and he replied to say she hadn't been out. *Talk to her*, he said, and I told him I'd think about it. Which was yet another lie.

I stood in the bedroom, looking at her, lying on her side, her face turned away from me, blonde hair falling over one eye, and I wondered whether I'd done the right thing, why I'd let John Evans, who probably wanted me dead, take any kind of place over my own girlfriend. I reminded myself it didn't matter: Claire hadn't done it, she hadn't been anywhere near the hospital the day Trawden died, and anyone who thought she had would have a hell of a time proving it.

But I didn't want her to have to face it, Martins, Genaud, the questions, lawyers who weren't me and didn't know the truth. And as for Evans, his innocence, his guilt, it didn't matter what I thought. It mattered what the police thought. Evans had been inside, briefly, for that robbery. He'd have had plenty of opportunity to meet the wrong kind of person there. The kind of person who might stick a tube full of insulin in a hospital patient and walk away. I stepped back and out of the bedroom and looked at my phone, scrolled back to Martins' number, blinked at it for a minute.

161

I called Roarkes instead, and he just told me that no he hadn't made any progress on the building and he wasn't likely to if I kept on calling him every five minutes. *Just ask her*, he said, again, and I gave him my theory, the idea that she knew of my suspicions, might even know of my investigations, that we were all stepping delicately around the unsayable but knowing it was there all the same. He laughed and told me I was overthinking it. He was, I thought, probably right.

I sat down on the sofa and let it wash through my head, Evans, Martins, what she'd said she'd heard about me, what she wanted me to do, Claire, Trawden, David Brooks-Powell. My stomach, I realised, was no longer hurting – it had been hours since I'd noticed any pain there at all. I picked up my phone again, put it down, made up my mind, picked it back up, dialled a number.

"I'm sorry," I said, when she answered. "I was wrong. I need to meet you."

15: A Little Truth

SHE WAS WAITING at a table in the back room of the Sheep Inn. The Sheep was doing good business tonight, by the look of it: I had to shoulder my way past a mob of noisy teenagers and a hefty after-work-drinks crowd in the main bar, and in the back room, half a dozen surly forty-somethings standing, cradling their drinks and staring in quiet hostility at the table in the middle occupied by one woman. She looked up as I approached, and nodded at one of the other seats. There was a fresh pint of lager on the table in front of it.

"Thanks," I began, and Vicky Colman held up a hand before I could say anything else.

"You owe me an explanation, Sam."

I sat, took a sip of lager, and smiled at her.

"I do. And I'm sorry. I should have told you everything. It's just – well, it's personal."

"You can trust me. You trusted me about Claire, and the gun. I haven't said a word about them. I thought we were a team."

"I know. We are. Look, you'll understand when I've explained. Okay?"

She nodded, and I launched into the story. I left nothing out – the pills and the powder, my suspicions, the decision to follow Claire, where she'd gone, the news of Trawden's death and the panic that had followed, the lies and alibis that might have stood their ground for a day or two but were starting to crumble.

"Why don't you just ask her?" she said, when I'd finished, and I found myself going over the same ground I'd been crossing for days with Roarkes and Maloney. I broke new ground, too: I related Claire's comment about Mandy, my fear that she'd go the same way as her cousin,

163

that she was even thinking about it. It felt good to say it out loud, finally. Colman didn't seem entirely convinced by my explanation, but she said *Okay* anyway, and asked me what I wanted from her.

"I want you to find out where she was, what she was doing."

"You know she wasn't at the hospital, though. You know she didn't kill Trawden."

"Yes. I do. But I don't – it's difficult for me to say this, but I've got to. I don't trust her, Vicky. She's lying to me. She's been lying to me for a while. And last time she didn't tell me things, she nearly killed a man."

"Why haven't you asked Roarkes?"

I put my drink back down on the table. "I have. He's not getting anywhere."

"What? With his access? He should be able to find out something like that at the click of a finger."

"I know," I said, trying to keep the frown off my face. "I think he's finding things difficult. Since Helen died."

Colman formed her mouth into a silent "O" and bent down to her own drink, a tall one in a thin glass, with ice and a vibrant blue colouring that reminded me of chemistry lessons at school. When she came back up she was nodding. She'd help. "But I'm not sure I'm the right person. I mean, if Roarkes can't help, what can I do? I can't get hold of information as easily as I could when I was in CID, Sam."

"What about Winterman?" I asked, and regretted it immediately, the crude directness of the suggestion, but she merely laughed and agreed with me.

"Yes. Well, I've been seeing a little of him. He's been seeing quite a lot of me, if you know what I mean. Says they're still keen on John Evans. But they're not ruling out anyone else."

"They're not ruling out Claire. That's what he means," I said. I thought about telling her what I'd been through earlier with Martins, but didn't. I couldn't face an argument about doing the right thing when I still hadn't decided what the right thing was. She gave me a small, sympathetic nod in reply.

I stayed for another drink – Colman had chosen the pub, she was meeting friends there later – and jumped on a bus home.

I got off the bus two streets away from the flat. It had turned cold again, and there was a fine drizzle in the air that dampened my footsteps and gave the impression the whole city was deserted. I'd gone out without an umbrella, wearing a coat that had once been waterproof but had lost that quality long ago, so I dropped my head and increased my pace as I rounded a corner. I heard steps behind me, fast, someone running for the bus I'd just jumped off, no doubt, and then I realised that the bus had long gone, that there was no one about but me, that there was no reason for anyone to be running apart from the rain, and the rain wasn't that bad. I turned, but too late – the fist that had been heading for the back of my head caught my temple, and I fell to the ground, landing on my left side and grunting with the pain. I tried to lever myself back up, but my hands couldn't find purchase on the slippery pavement and I couldn't think straight, my head still pounding from the blow. A shoe flashed past my face and a moment later I felt it, a kick in the ribs, hard but not bone-breakingly hard – the shoe, I realised, was a soft one and probably not designed to break bones. Another kick, same foot, same place, a moment later. I felt a hand snake into my jeans pocket, front right, and come away. Then nothing, for a second, followed by the sound of footsteps again, back round the corner, the way I'd come, the way my assailant had come.

I took four deep breaths and felt the pain in my head begin to recede. The pain in my ribs wasn't going anywhere, though: I'd have some decent bruises there by morning. I pushed myself up and got slowly to my feet. There was no sign of the person who'd attacked me. The whole thing couldn't have lasted more than ten seconds.

I turned and looked the other way. I could almost see my own flat. I felt in my pocket: empty. But it had been empty all along. I had my keys and my phone and a twenty-pound note in the left pocket, the one that had been on the ground and all-but-unreachable to my attacker. I panicked for a second and felt in my back pocket, but it was still there, Eileen Grimshaw's letter. I took a couple of steps and stopped, breathing heavily, willing the pain away. A short break, another couple of steps, easier this time, then a couple more. By the time the number on my building came into view I was managing fifteen steps without a break, my breaths were coming smooth and even, and the pain kept to the shadows until I reached step twelve or thirteen.

I buzzed on the door, and heard Claire's anxious voice a few seconds later.

"Hello? Who's there?"

It wasn't late – not yet eight o' clock – but it was dark and Claire was on her own and, as people kept telling me, *in a vulnerable state.*

"It's me. Can you let me in?"

"Are you okay? Have you lost your keys?" she said, and hit the buzzer before I had a chance to answer. I stepped inside, tackled the stairs and tried to wipe the grimace off my face before she saw me, but it didn't matter: she was standing in the open doorway of our flat, watching me labouring towards her with all the dignity of a drunk in a three-legged race.

"What the hell happened?" she asked, once she'd helped me onto the sofa. She sounded concerned, but there was something else, too. I shrugged.

"What's that supposed to mean?" she said. "Have you

had an accident?"

That was it. Annoyance. She was annoyed with me, as if I were some naughty schoolboy who'd been caught fighting. I was tempted by a throwaway line, *you should see the other guy* or something like that, but when I looked up at her face I could see that annoyance tipping slowly towards anger. It wasn't worth it.

"I got attacked."

"By who?"

"I don't know. I didn't see his face."

"Where?"

"Fitzroy Avenue. Just round the corner."

"Did they take anything?"

I shifted my position slightly, felt in my pockets again, to be sure, shook my head.

"No. They went for one pocket but it was the empty one. I was lucky. Don't think they had time to go for the other one."

She frowned at me, as if there were something unconvincing about it, and I found myself thinking it through and agreeing. They'd taken the ten seconds they needed to bring me down. They'd searched one pocket. There was no one else on the street, no voices, no cars, they'd picked a spot between streetlights, outside an empty office building and blocked from the view of the residential block opposite by parked cars. If they'd wanted the other pocket, they could have had it. Maybe they'd *thought* they'd heard something. Maybe there had been a phantom voice or car or even something as simple as a cat that had saved me my phone and my keys and my twenty quid and probably another kick or two.

"Let me get you a drink."

I nodded and then groaned when she offered me tea instead of the whisky I'd been hoping for, but she was right: there was a faint nausea spreading across my gut, and the whisky would only have made it worse. What with Van der Lee's punch in Oxford – lower down, that one, and less surprising – my upper body hadn't had a great time of it lately. I lifted my shirt and took a look. The area was clearly marked, but the skin didn't seem to be broken. Claire came over while the tea was brewing and pressed gently on each rib, onto each patch of red, and I found myself sucking in my breath and gritting my teeth before each touch and then sighing in relief as she pushed and the most I felt was a little ache, a hint of tenderness.

"Nothing broken," she said, and I nodded. She walked into the kitchen and then back with my tea and a piece of paper.

"This came, while you were out. Earlier."

I turned it over in my hands. Two dozen hand-written lines. The latest episode in the life of Lizzy Maurier, poet, heiress, erstwhile madwoman. It opened, as they all did, with verses from the poem she'd written for Brooks-Powell's funeral.

> *The tears have been shed and the dead are still dead.*
> *All that remains is "Why this?"*
> *And "Will you pass the mustard?"*
> *And "Better late than never."*

> The river's not sacred, the caverns are dark,
> Both damsel and dulcimer dumb.
> The knock on the door's torn the vision apart,
> All the voices are silent, but one.

Following this, as if there were nothing at all unusual about what she'd written, as if prefacing a *wish-you-were-here* with eight lines of soul-baring verse were an entirely normal thing to do, was the latest news from Brittany.

"I think the greengrocer propositioned me the other

night," she began. "Quiet chap, fifties, widower. Seems lonely. He kept putting his arm around me at the bar and trying to steer me away from everyone else. I'd drunk quite a lot, *hélas*, so when he started whispering in my ear I couldn't understand a word he was saying, and I fear I was a little short with him. He seems to have been avoiding me since. Keeps sending the boy out to serve me when I come into the shop. *Quelle dommage,* eh? It would have been just the right thing to round off my little adventure."

She'd signed off there, and I found myself staring at the poem again. She was still sending it piecemeal, but I knew it all by heart: I'd known it since I'd seen it at the funeral. I'd not understood it then. I'd not known who to ask. But then Claire had picked up one of the letters, a fortnight or so back, I thought, seen the verses, and asked me what it meant. I'd told her I didn't know and recited the whole thing, and she'd nodded, gravely, and told me it was Lizzy Maurier's surrender to reality, her admission, finally, that everything she'd put her faith in for decades was a lie. Her mother's infallibility, the words of others, the box she'd put herself in to keep everyone else happy, even her rebellion, her dalliance with Trawden, who'd turned out to be everything he'd said he wasn't, and more. I glanced to the end of this latest letter, to that little hint, *round off my little adventure*, that things were drawing to a close. I could see it, too. Lizzy Maurier back home, colour finally in that sad, wan face, a return of the spirit she'd had before her mother had crushed her dreams and before Trawden had come into our lives.

"Anything interesting?" asked Claire, and without thinking I passed her the letter. There was nothing there that could hurt her, I thought. Nothing to disturb her *fragility*. She read it quickly and passed it back. "Looks like she'll be back soon, then." And that was it. Not a word about the greengrocer. Not a word about the poem.

169

There was nothing to eat in the flat, so we resigned ourselves to yet another takeaway and picked without relish at boxes of meat and rice when they arrived half an hour later. My ribs were feeling better, but the more I thought about my attempted mugging, about the grasp in one pocket and nothing else, the more things didn't add up. There was the grey-haired man. There was Evans, on my phone, outside the police station, outside my flat. And I kept hearing Martins' words, *He hates you, you know that, right*, kept seeing the man, the greasy hair, the scars, the spider's web tattooed across his face.

Evans. John Evans. I could sense him. I could almost smell him, the smell of a man who hadn't changed his clothes in weeks and hadn't washed them in a lifetime, who slept where he was when he felt tired, who went where he wanted and didn't let anyone stand in his way. John Evans, I thought, had punched me in the head and kicked me in the ribs, and I wondered what kind of alibi he'd come up with for this one, and whether it would be Martins or Genaud that would try to break him.

Claire had retreated to the bedroom as soon as she'd finished her food. I reached for my phone and dialled Martins' number.

"Williams," she barked, in lieu of a greeting. "Everything OK?"

"Everything's fine," I said. "I've changed my mind."

"About what?"

"About your proposal. I'll help. I'll help you nail the bastard."

There was a pause, and then a quiet chuckle.

"I knew you'd see sense eventually," she said, finally. "I'll call you tomorrow and let you know where we are."

I started to regret it the moment I'd hung up, and sat there staring at my phone, willing it to do something, to tell me something, to make me feel better about what I'd just

170

done, and as if thrust into existence by my thoughts, an email notification popped up on the screen.

It was from Eliza Burnett, the journalist from the *Blackpool Herald*. I opened it and found no text, no small talk, just a blank email with a pdf attached. I tapped it and there it was. The article. The death of Marine Lambert.

It was stark, factual stuff, not meant for the front page. Blackpool had its share of deaths, accidental, deliberate, the slow, patient work of sickness and age and addiction and obesity. One more woman killed on the road wouldn't have rocked anyone's life, except the people who'd seen it, the people who'd been there, the people who knew her.

She'd been part of a group of friends on the way home from a night out. A night *dancing*, as the journalist put it – there was no name on the byline, nobody had pinned their reputation or career on as unimportant a story as this, just a reference to *our correspondent in Blackpool*. Witnesses had described the group as *noisy and possibly intoxicated*. Marine Lambert and one other member of the group had been crossing the road when a car had come towards them, spotted them, failed to brake in time, hit them head on. The victims hadn't been able to get out of the way in time – there was a suggestion the driver might have been speeding. Whether she was speeding or not, she'd stayed while the ambulance came and waited for the police and given her details and been released and told that the matter would be investigated. Her name, rightly, was not given. Just two names were. Elissa Pengilly, who had been injured and admitted to hospital in a critical condition which had, by the time the article was published, been downgraded to stable but with life-changing injuries.

And Marine Lambert, an employee, like Miss Pengilly, of the Haverstock Hotel in Blackpool, who had been pronounced dead at the scene.

16: A Clean Break

I WAS HALFWAY to Oxford when my phone rang, and I answered on the hands-free without bothering to check who was calling.

"Sam?" said a voice I recognised but struggled to place, and then "Its Karen. Karen Hobart."

I explained that I was in the car.

"Sorry to disturb you. Going anywhere interesting?"

"Your neck of the woods, as it happens. Off to confer with my client."

"Oh," she said, and there was a pause which I fought and failed to interpret. "Right. I don't suppose you could drop in while you're in the area?"

Was she flirting with me? Was that it, the pause, the wheels turning as she saw an opportunity? Or was there more to it than that, something about the case, second thoughts about the friendly face she'd shown the enemy?

It couldn't be that, I decided. That wasn't just a face.

"Sure," I said. "Round lunchtime? I'll call you when I'm on my way."

My ribs weren't hurting any more – the handful of extra-strength painkillers I'd swallowed down had seen to that. But I sensed there was pain of a different sort to come. I spent the rest of the journey alternating between wondering what Karen Hobart wanted to tell me and trying not to imagine Fothergill's reaction when I told him what had happened to Marine Lambert.

In the end, I didn't tell him. I let *our correspondent in Blackpool* do it for me. I followed him to the kitchen – still no new graffiti outside – and let him make me a cup of tea, and when we were sitting down smiling at one another in silence I said "I'm afraid I've got some news for you that you're not going to like," and passed him a printout of the article.

He sighed when he finished. He glanced up at me, blinked, looked back down at the article, and I searched his eyes for tears, but couldn't see any. Richard Fothergill came from a place when men didn't cry.

"That explains it," he said, finally. "Why she stopped writing. I always thought –"

He stopped, stood, muttered "I'm sorry, I'll just be a moment," and walked quickly out of the door and into what I assumed was the living room. I waited, listening out for the sound of sobbing, an angry cry, anything that might give me the excuse to go to him, comfort him, sit him down and make him drink his tea and let him get round to what it was he'd been about to say. But there was nothing. Silence. And then, barely a minute after he'd walked away, he was back, stiff-backed, his face set.

"I'm sorry," he said, again, as he took his seat. "It's come as rather a shock. Which is ridiculous, really." He smiled, ruefully. "It's thirty, what, nearly forty-year-old news. But still. It's a shock."

I nodded at him, waited for him to drink his tea, restrained myself from reaching forward and patting his arm. There was a dignity about him that would, I felt, have been offended by such an action.

"You were about to say something," I said, finally. "You said that explained it. Explained why she stopped writing."

He nodded. "Yes. We wrote to one another. And then, suddenly, she stopped. No reply. I wondered if my last letter had gone astray, so I wrote again, one more time, but there was no response to that, either, so I just assumed that she didn't want to hear from me any more. She had left, after all. She had made a break. I was, I think, her last connection, the one remaining link to her past. I always thought she'd just decided to make a clean break. And what kind of teacher, what kind of man would I have been if I hadn't allowed her that?"

I nodded, and he smiled again and continued. "As I recall, I was happy for her. She'd finally achieved what she'd set out to do. I simply wished her the best, in my own mind, and dismissed the thought of her from my life. In all honesty, until all of *this*, until I started looking at those photographs, the thought of Marine Lambert had barely crossed my mind in decades. Do you have the photographs with you?"

I did. I produced the envelope and showed him what I'd found, what I'd already explained to him, the closeness between Marine Lambert and Pieter Van der Lee, the sense I'd had that there was far more to that closeness than an accident of positioning.

"I do see what you mean, Sam. There is something, isn't there? I wonder that I never noticed it at the time. Perhaps I did. Perhaps it was just another one of those things one observes and then dismisses. They were teenagers, after all. It's not like it's a rare event."

"She was pregnant, you said?"

He nodded, and, as he realised the implications, adopted a grave expression. "Yes. She was pregnant, and yes, if these photographs are anything to go by, Pieter Van der Lee could well have been the father. And she aborted the baby and disappeared. I wonder if Van der Lee ever knew where she went, what had happened. I wonder if he even knew she was pregnant."

"But what would all that have to do with you?"

He shrugged, and turned again to the article. He pointed to a paragraph towards the end.

"Elissa Pengilly," he said. "I wonder if she knows anything."

"I'm not sure there's anything else to know."

He nodded, and we sat and finished our tea in silence.

175

Sitting in the car ten minutes later, I pulled out my phone to let Karen Hobart know I was on my way, and noticed a text from Roarkes.

This has gone on too long, it said. *Tell her. Ask her.*

More of the same. I'd experienced a twinge of conscience, on the way to Oxford, about going behind his back to Colman, about giving up on him and handing the work – work he was only doing as a favour to me – onto someone else. Now the guilt was gone, replaced by a quiet, grim satisfaction. I'd been right. Roarkes was a good man and once upon a time he'd been a good detective, but I needed someone to help me now, not in the past.

Karen Hobart was waiting for me in the carpark outside her depressing office building. Despite the cold and the intermittent rain, she was wearing a knee-length skirt, no tights, a blouse and a flimsy jacket, and she opened the passenger door and slid in before I'd even set the handbrake. Her hair fell loose around her shoulders. The notion that she was after something burrowed into my brain and took root.

"You're taking me to lunch," she said.

"I am?"

She nodded. "You'll thank me."

She directed me to a pub in a village ten minutes' drive away, and as I slaked my hunger and thirst on a pint of lager and a surprisingly good lamb curry I realised she wasn't flirting with me, and she wasn't trying to mine me for information or destroy my client's defence, either.

"A friendly warning," she said, reaching across the table and tearing off a strip of my naan bread.

"What? The food? Seems decent enough to me."

She smiled and swallowed down the bread.

"No. Look, you've got to be careful. There have been complaints."

It hit me hard and fast. Of course. Sutcliffe might go to

the Law Society and tell them all about big bad Sam Williams, but it would be quicker and easier just to tell the CPS.

"Sutcliffe?" I asked.

"Him and Van der Lee. Both of them. Pincer attack. Van der Lee told me he'd seen you at his bar. Is that right?"

I looked down at my plate and nodded. I thought about defending myself, telling her he'd punched me, but there was little point. I'd been in the man's bar, sneaking around, and a punch in the gut was the least I deserved. She continued, addressing the top of my head.

"And Sutcliffe says he's going to unleash the dogs of hell on you if you don't stop harassing his client."

I looked up. "He said what?"

She was smiling, but nodding at the same time. "The dogs of hell. Those were his precise words. Struck me as a little florid for a provincial solicitor. But you get the picture. He actually asked me if I could open a file on you, said he didn't want to bother the police, he had enough evidence himself for a formal complaint or even a prosecution."

I'd put down my knife and fork and was staring at her, speechless, as she worked her way through her pie and mash.

"So what have you done?" I asked, finally.

"Nothing. I told him to leave it. Said I'd have a word with you. Said I obviously wouldn't be opening a file and if he wanted something like that done, he'd have to go through the proper channels. But Sam."

I looked up. She'd set down her own cutlery and was wearing a serious, concerned expression that made me want to walk round the table and give her a hug.

"Sam," she continued. "You seem like a nice man. Be careful. Don't get yourself into trouble."

She smiled and returned to her food, and after a minute I followed suit. She hadn't been impressed by Sutcliffe, by

177

his manner or his sense of entitlement. Van der Lee was a different matter. He was a potential victim of an alleged crime, and I wasn't denying he'd caught me sneaking around his bar. If it hadn't been for the fact that I seemed like a reasonable lawyer just trying to help out his client, Karen Hobart might have chosen to play things differently. I dropped her back at her office, and thanked her, and drove off with a sense that for once, I'd got lucky.

I hadn't checked my phone the whole time we'd been out. I sat in the carpark, watching her walk through the drizzle to the security door and open it with what looked like a well-practiced kick, and fished out my phone. There was a text from Maloney. Two texts. Three.

Call me now, they said. All of them. Devoid of all punctuation or smiling faces, or angry ones, for that matter.

"About bloody time," he said, when he answered a few seconds later.

"What's wrong? What's happened?"

"Claire. She went out. Couldn't follow her."

"Why not?"

"She lost us. Lost my guy. In Euston station. Looks like she got a train out of London."

I beat the steering wheel in frustration, accidentally setting off the horn. I peered through the mist forming on the windscreen, but it was pure wasteland out there. Nobody to hear.

"Shit!" I said. "She could be anywhere."

"Nope."

"What do you mean, *nope?*"

"I mean she'll be back home in a few minutes. I had the guy wait for her at Euston. She got a bus there. Figured she'd get the same bus back, so I just had him stand there where she'd have to go to get it and pretend to read the papers until he saw her."

"And?"

"He just called. She's on the bus. She'll be back at yours in fifteen minutes, probably tell you she's been in bed all day."

"So how long was she gone?"

"Three hours. Three hours from losing her to picking her up again."

"She could have gone anywhere."

I took his silence as agreement. She'd moved things up a gear. Three hours, plus the time to get to and from Euston in the first place. I hadn't planned on lunch with Karen Hobart. I might have been back before Claire. What would she have said then?

"I took a look at those accounts, Sam," said Maloney, a welcome break in my train of thought.

"And?"

"Something doesn't quite add up. Takings are great. Profit's not bad, nothing to shout about. Should be better, last year or so, at least. Which means expenses are high. Higher than they should be."

"That's what I thought. So what do you reckon? Money laundering?"

"Maybe. I need to go through the expenses side again. See what's costing more than it should, make some enquiries. Could be he's just spending big, making the place a bit nicer, pushing up the prices on the other side. Give me a day or so."

A day or so, I thought, as I pulled out of the carpark and into the early afternoon traffic. *A day or so*, as I swallowed down a double dose of painkillers whilst waiting to join the motorway. *A day or so*, as I hit the gas and headed for London. Nothing had happened for so long that I'd forgotten that things could happen at all. But now I'd taken a beating, the threats from Van der Lee and his lawyer had stepped up, and Claire had broadened her range. I sensed things were moving ahead of me, moving out of reach as I

179

stumbled for something to hold on to. I had Maloney and Roarkes and Colman digging around for answers, but I needed them fast.

Anything could happen in a day or so.

17: Rage

SHE WAS IN bed when I got back. There'd been an accident on the M40, near Wycombe, too far from home for me to plot another route, and what should have been an eighty minute journey had taken nearly three hours. It was five o' clock, and Claire was in bed.

I stuck my head in through the bedroom door. She was awake, at least. She turned to me and gave me one of those wan smiles, and I prepared myself for the lies to follow, the *haven't left the bedroom*, the *it's been a tough day*, the bullshit I'd have to nod at and force myself to smile through. I wondered whether there would ever come a point when one of us would tire of it, this stupid, pointless dance. *Tell her*, Roarkes had said. *Ask her.* I was tired of it already. But I wasn't ready to risk ending it. Especially given where that end might lead.

It turned out I was wrong. Claire hadn't just been out, she was happy to admit it.

"I made it to the shops today," she said, brightening up a little, and I stretched that smile across my face.

"Fantastic. What did you get? Where did you go?"

"Just the High Street. Got some food in. Don't want to get completely dependent on takeaways, do we?"

I sensed a rebuke, but a mild one. I could have done some shopping. I could have cooked a little. I hadn't. I'd been too busy trying to work out what my girlfriend was hiding from me. I shrugged and asked her how she was feeling after her trip out. Her trip *to the High Street*. I emphasised the words, my own little rebuke, a joke she wouldn't get anyway.

"Not so bad. How was Oxford? Anything useful."

I returned her shrug, and remembered how things had been a few months earlier, when she'd ask me how my day had gone, and I'd tell her, in detail, and she'd prod me for more of those details and I'd think of something that had escaped me. She'd wanted to know everything. I'd wanted to tell her. I opened my mouth to say something, to tell her about Marine Lambert, the pregnancy, the tragic death, the connection with Pieter Van der Lee. And then my phone rang and I looked down and it was Martins' number, and I answered it anyway, because if I couldn't get angry with Claire then maybe I could get angry with Martins.

"Hello Sam," she said, utterly friendly and normal, and not a hint that she'd recently convinced me to help convict a potentially innocent man.

"Hello," I replied. I felt my ribs. Maybe not innocent. Maybe not innocent at all.

"Any chance you could come in tomorrow?"

"Have you got him? Have you pulled him in?"

"Not yet," she said, and I felt something bubbling up inside, something I couldn't yet name but had to do with everything, with a sore gut and a lying girlfriend, a dead murderer I'd hated and more than one dead lawyer I'd liked, with John Evans and Roarkes and Colman and Maloney and Melanie Golding and Genaud and most of all, with Martins herself. I forced it down.

"I thought we had a deal," I began, but she cut me off before I could say any more.

"It doesn't work like that, Sam. You know it doesn't work like that. It's not just down to me. Why don't you come in and I'll explain everything?"

Genaud, I thought, and, then stopped myself. Genaud might just be a convenient excuse for Martins. It was bubbling up again, and now I could put my finger on it.

Rage.

I glanced behind me. Claire had her face in her phone, apparently oblivious to my conversation. I stared at my own phone, shaking my head as a volatile brew of anger and disbelief coursed through my veins. I counted to ten, silently, waiting for it to disperse, ignoring the distant, tinny sound of Martins asking if I was there, if I was okay, if I could come in and chat. I couldn't think of the words, but eventually I just said "I'll come in when you've got Evans," and killed the call. I turned – I'd conducted the entire conversation standing in the bedroom doorway, facing the living room, as if not being able to see my face would somehow mean Claire wouldn't be able to hear what I'd said. It didn't matter. She was frowning at me.

"Everything okay, Sam?" she asked. She looked tired, again, real tired, not pretend tired, and I remembered Martins' threats. She hadn't pulled Evans in, and without him, she'd have to turn her attention elsewhere. Elsewhere meant Claire. In her *vulnerable state*.

"Yeah. Yeah," I said. "Fine."

I turned and walked into the kitchen, grabbed a beer from the fridge, sank into the sofa. I switched on the television. I needed to empty my head.

My head wouldn't empty. Claire hadn't left the bedroom, must have picked up a book or her phone or just fallen asleep, because I couldn't hear a thing from her. I had Roarkes and Maloney rattling around my brain telling me to ask and tell and wait for an answer, I had Pieter Van der Lee and Sutcliffe chasing Roarkes and Maloney round and whining and threatening, I had Martins turning circles, ever tighter, making deals I didn't like and breaking them when it suited her, I had Claire scuttling around behind the lot of them, never quite in view. And then, unexpectedly, I had Fothergill on my phone.

"Are you okay?" I asked.

"Yes, yes. Fine. It's just been on my mind."

"What has?"

"Marine Lambert. What happened to her. Do you think

it was an accident? Do you think maybe there was anything more to it?"

That notion hadn't even crossed my mind. There wasn't room for it in there.

"No. No, I don't," I said. "You read the article. And it was a notoriously dangerous spot. Dozens of accidents there, over the years."

He sighed. I could hear it across the line, a long, slow, the-worst-has-already-happened kind of sigh. "I'd just love to know. What really happened. Not just how she died. Everything else."

"Leave it with me," I said, and even as I said it I was kicking myself, because finding out what had happened to Marine Lambert might make Fothergill feel a little better but it wouldn't help with his defence or Claire's mental state or getting Martins off my back. "I'll see what I can get."

And the moment he was gone, I was back on the laptop, looking up the friend, Elissa Pengilly, who still lived in Blackpool, apparently, and ran a guesthouse there.

I dialled the number under her entry on Google. A woman answered, coughing and trying to speak at the same time.

"Elissa Pengilly?" I asked.

"Who wants to know?"

The voice was harsh, sixty-a-day and then some.

"My name's Sam Williams. I'm a lawyer. I'm working on a case for a client and your name has come up in connection with certain matters."

Keep it vague, I thought. Hold out the promise of something good.

"Someone died?" she asked. "Left me a fortune?"

So much for vague.

"No, it's not that. My client has been accused of a crime, and he thinks there may be a connection with someone you knew, nearly forty years ago."

184

"You coming up here?" she said, suddenly, interrupting my flow.

"No, I don't think so."

"So you're not a paying guest and you haven't got a rich man's will for me. Got any money for me?"

"It's not about – " I began, but it was too late. The line was dead. Elissa Pengilly had hung up on me.

Silence, still, from the bedroom. I crept to the door and took a look: Claire was asleep. I lay down beside her, fully clothed, and shut my eyes and tried to chase that cast of rogues and liars out of my head. And for a moment, I succeeded, but only because they were replaced with the biggest bastard of them all.

Edward Trawden. Dead Edward Trawden.

I lay there, my eyes open, now, but I couldn't get his face out of my head. Smiling, every time. I hadn't seen him get shot, hadn't seen the effect of the bits of lead that had made it past Brooks-Powell's body. It might have helped if I had.

I gave it five more minutes and then rose, quietly, and walked back to the sofa. Before I sat down I reached into my back pocket.

The letter was still there. I picked it out and read, again, about Eileen Grimshaw's cold years and her thaw and her advice for Melanie Golding. And there was more.

We had some peace, you know. When Edward Trawden was convicted. I've told you that you must not feel guilty, and I stand by that. But when he was released, that day in court – I have to tell you, what you did, what you and poor Elizabeth Maurier did, that day in court, it robbed us of our peace. It tormented us. And yes, I know. You were doing your job. You were acting in the service of the law. You were trying to prevent a miscarriage of justice. But justice isn't that simple. I know you saw it, too – that her scales have weights on both sides. That for every victory there is a defeat, that every victory is in itself a defeat. I don't know why you left Mauriers, so suddenly, so soon. But I like to think that it had something to do with us, with Trawden, with justice.

I put the letter down. This wasn't the first time I'd read it, or even the fifth. But it still surprised me, her perspicacity, her apparent ability to see inside my head and understand what was happening there better than Elizabeth had done, even though I'd been working with Elizabeth every day, even though I'd as good as told her. I remembered their faces, Eileen and Bill Grimshaw. Turning, as the judge made his announcement. Turning, as beside me Elizabeth Maurier bowed her head in solemn false humility before the idol of the law. Turning, as in the dock a smile spread across the face of Edward Trawden, a free man at last. Turning towards me with a look I could hardly describe, a look that made me feel like I'd brought it all back, that Maxine's death was fresh and new and violently here. That I'd as good as killed her myself.

Trawden had turned, too, he'd turned to me in the pub, later on, a glass in each hand, smiling. "Here's to Robbie Evans," he'd said. That image had sat in my head for years, behind the horrified faces of the Grimshaws.

I put the letter down on the coffee table and heard a stirring from the bedroom. It was time. I picked the letter back up, walked to the kitchen, found a box of matches in a drawer.

When Claire walked in thirty seconds later, all that remained of Eileen Grimshaw's letter was smoke and a heap of black that could have been anything, sitting smouldering on a plate beside the sink.

"Why?" she asked. She didn't ask what it was I'd burned. She didn't need to.

"You know the way you sleep half the day, barely leave the flat?" I asked. I tried to make it sound like this wasn't

186

an accusation, like underneath I wasn't saying *you know the way you sneak around and lie about where you've been?*

She nodded.

"That's how you deal with your pain," I continued. "This is how I deal with mine."

She narrowed her eyes at me for a moment, and I wondered if this was it, finally, the end of the dance. But then she shrugged and said "Fair enough. But I still think you should write back. I think you owe them that."

She turned away from me, reached into a cupboard, pulled out a box, moved onto the fridge. The kitchen was her territory. I swept the burnt letter into the bin and went to lie down on the bed. I closed my eyes again, saw the flames dancing before them, picked up my phone and called Roarkes.

"I had nothing this morning. I've got nothing now. Ask her," he said, and hung up, and I closed my eyes again and this time, miraculously, I fell straight to sleep.

I was woken by my phone a few minutes later. I hadn't been dreaming, or if I had I couldn't remember what I'd been dreaming about. I saw Colman's number flashing at me from the bedside table and snatched up the phone before she could give up.

"Sam," she said, before I had a chance to say my name or *hello* or anything at all, and went on before I could confirm. "I need to see you. Tonight."

"Why?"

"News, Sam. I've got news."

18: A Small Bag

CLAIRE WAS STILL in the kitchen when I emerged five minutes later wearing the same clothes I'd fallen briefly asleep in. She was stirring something on the hob with one hand, glancing over to it every now and then, her main focus the book open on the counter beside her. As I approached she turned, noticed me, nodded and looked back at the pan on the hob.

"What's cooking?" I said, and she gestured at the book. I stood beside her and looked at it, at a recipe for an oriental steak dish I'd never heard of that sounded better than anything I'd eaten in weeks. I took a sniff. Smelled good, too.

"Don't suppose that'll keep?" I said.

"Why's that?" she asked,

"Because I've got to go out. Sorry. Colman."

She didn't reply. I was only an inch or two away from her, and it occurred to me that given the way things were between us, this ought to make me uncomfortable.

It didn't.

I reached out a hand, circled her waist, pulled her gently towards me, kissed the back of her head.

"I'm sorry. It smells fantastic."

She turned away from the pan, finally, and looked at me, right into my eyes, as if searching them for an answer to a question she didn't dare ask out loud. "Don't worry," she said. "It'll keep."

Colman was waiting for me in the Sheep, again. Same room, same table. This time she had a bottle of beer and a bowl of chips in front of her. I got myself a beer and ordered chilli con carne and sat down opposite her.

"Cheers," she said, and knocked her bottle against mine.

I'd been sitting at the table for no more than five seconds, but already I could tell she was in a good mood. I thought about Claire, at home, about that steak dish she was making, about the smell of her hair when I'd kissed the back of her head, and felt a wave of resentment sweep through me.

"Well?" I asked. "What did you need to see me about?"

She cocked her head to one side and grinned at me. *She's drunk*, I thought, but there were no empty bottles, no empty glasses, just the one beer she'd only just got started on.

"I've got news for you, Sam. Proper news."

"You said. What kind of news? What are you talking about?"

The grin fell from her face about the same time that wave of resentment ran out and I realised how unreasonable I was being. She was only here to do me a favour.

"I'm sorry," I said. "Bad day. Not your fault. Please. Tell me what you've got."

She nodded. "The building. I know who's in it."

"And?"

"And it's the National Crime Agency."

If I hadn't been sitting down, I'd have fallen to the floor.

She explained a little more, as I took some deep breaths and started to regain my composure. She was smiling. I reckoned she'd been looking forward to that little bombshell.

"Sorry it's taken me so long," she said. It had taken her less than twenty-four hours. "I've got to be careful how I milk Simon. He reckons he's onto a free ride."

"Isn't he?"

She laughed. "Well, yes. I guess so. But you know how it goes. A girl can't give everything away all at once. Not if she wants to keep hold of her CID access."

"So," I said, anxious to move onto more important

189

matters. "The NCA?"

She nodded. "Yup. The NCA. The big boys."

"Any idea which division?"

"Nope. Working on it."

So Claire had gone to visit Britain's equivalent of the FBI. I could see why Colman was smiling. It might not tell us much, but it was good news. It had to be good news. No one would believe Claire had been involved in Trawden's death if she'd been visiting the NCA at the time. I hadn't believed it in the first place. This had to put her in the clear.

But at the same time, it threw up more questions than it answered. The NCA had a remit as wide as crime itself. What the hell was Claire doing there? And why had she come out looking so angry?

It occurred to me, as I bought us two more drinks and turned all that over in my head, that I had news for Colman, too.

"Anything odd happen to you last night, after you left the pub?" I asked.

"No. Why?"

"Because I got beaten up on the way home."

She looked me up and down, a frown on her face.

"Nope," she said. "You're just the usual kind of ugly. Didn't do a very good job of it, whoever they were."

I laughed. "It was over fast. I'd have thought it was a mugging, but they didn't get anything and they didn't really try."

"So what, then?" She stared at me, eyes boring into mine, for a moment, then nodded. "You're thinking Evans, aren't you?"

"Makes sense, doesn't it? The guy hates me, he's been hanging around outside my flat trying to talk to me, he tried to get me outside the station yesterday, he won't –"

"What was that?" she said, interrupting my self-justificatory stream of consciousness. "The station?"

I waved her away. "Went to see Martins. She summoned me. Had to go."

"And you really think Evans did it? Hit you?"

"Yes. Well, he's the most likely candidate, anyway."

There was a brief silence, broken only by the sound of Colman chewing away at her chips.

"I don't buy it," she said, finally.

"Why not?"

"If he's committed murder – *if* – then punching someone in the head, well, it's a bit of a step down, isn't it?"

I shook my head. "If he's smart enough to kill with insulin then he wouldn't be stupid enough to go full psycho on me."

She shrugged, and for a moment I forgot that she was helping me, I forgot that I wasn't sure of anything, not when it came to Evans, and I felt it again, that anger and disbelief. I didn't care what Coleman thought.

"Well, you might not buy it," I said, "but Martins does. She's pulling him in."

"What?"

Her mouth had fallen open, a handful of chips grasped between her fingers, paused mid-air.

"I told her I'd help her break him. Evans. I'll sit in on the interview and get the truth out of him, and he'll stop bothering me and Martins'll stop bothering Claire and she'll have her suspect wrapped up in time for tea."

She put the chips back in the bowl.

"Are you fucking kidding me?"

I shrugged, her own shrug right back at her. "Well, I know I didn't kill Trawden, and I know Claire didn't either, so if it's got to be between the three of us, then Evans gets my vote every time."

She finished her chips in silence, and after a couple of minutes I found myself going back over what I'd just said and wondering why I'd said it. It wasn't like I believed it.

191

"I'm sorry," I said, finally. "The truth is, I need Martins off my back and I need Evans to stop giving me grief, and this way I'll get what I need. You and I know there's no way a jury's going to send him down for injecting insulin into Edward Trawden. They'll take one look at him and acquit. I just need some breathing space."

She smiled at me and said "Okay. Just as long as you know what you're doing," and we left together twenty minutes and another drink later, talking of other things, things that didn't really interest us or concern us or have us waking, cold, hearts pounding in the dark. I thanked her and said good bye, and she said she'd try to find out some more about that building, if she could, and neither of us said anything more about John Evans.

There was a text on my phone from Maloney, saying *call me*, so the moment Colman had turned the corner and disappeared from sight I did.

"I've found something," he said, and my mind jumped straight to Claire.

"What Claire's been up to?"

"Nope. Not that. Your bar."

It took me a moment to remember. "*Dervish?*"

"That's the one. Pieter Van der Lee. There's something a little odd there."

"Go on."

"There are some new payments. Outgoings. Five thousand a month."

"Right, what, some new supplier?"

"It's possible. But it's high. And there's no sign of anything coming in to balance it. No big new earner. Could be some big investment, but I can't find anything on the assets side to match it."

"Who's the payment to?"

He paused, and I heard the sound of papers being turned over.

"The Restoration Company, Leeds, Limited. That's it."

"Leeds?"

"Yup."

I thought, for a moment, about what I'd seen behind that glass panel. Steel and leather and more glass. An expensive job. I remembered the grand reopening.

"It's nothing," I said. "He had the place done up. Relaunched eighteen months ago. It'll be that."

"No it won't."

"Why not?"

"Because that's all accounted for already. The builders and designers and decorators and the people who got the new tables and chairs, they were all paid in advance or when the work finished. But these payments only started a few months ago. And he's not a billionaire. No one's going to give a bar owner eighteen months plus credit. Bars aren't reliable enough for that."

I took a moment to turn it all over. It was a stretch. Chances were it had nothing to do with Fothergill. Chances were nothing I was looking into had anything to do with Fothergill, chances were Marine Lambert and Blackpool would be a dead end and this would too.

"Thanks," I said. "I mean that."

"I know," he replied, and ended the call.

I saw neither Evans nor the grey-haired man on the way back to the flat, which was a bonus, and no one attacked me, which was even more of a bonus, because I'd drunk more than I'd realised while I was digesting Colman's revelations about the NCA and trying to defend my deal with Martins, and I was less steady on my feet than usual. I stumbled up the stairs and spent a minute trying to get the key in the lock, and then found myself falling forwards as the door opened away from me. I stopped myself before I landed on Claire.

193

"Sorry," I said. "Hope I didn't disturb you."

"I was asleep. How much have you drunk?"

Her hands were on her hips, her chin pointing towards me in challenge, and I was drunk, no doubt about it. I'd done little more than pick at my chilli, I'd had a pint with my lunch and a couple more with Colman, plus something short she'd got me which I hadn't much liked but had drunk anyway. I could hear Roarkes in my ear, hear Maloney, hear Colman, all of them saying *just ask her*. I could hear myself making deals I didn't like with a DI I couldn't stand to protect a woman who was lying to me. I could hear Claire herself, telling me about her cousin, could hear myself reply, listening out for hints and threats, hearing things that hadn't been there at all, conjuring fears from nothing. Suddenly, I'd had enough.

"Where have you been?" I said. She stared at me and pointed to the bedroom.

"I just told you. I was asleep."

"I don't mean now. I mean the last week, the last fortnight, longer. What have you been doing?"

She'd taken a step back, but the chin was still up and I could see her hands curling into fists.

"I've been recovering from a nervous fucking breakdown. I've been shopping. I've been in to see Detective Inspector Martins. You know all that."

I shook my head. "No. Not that. What else?"

"What else? What the hell are you talking about?"

The alcohol was hitting my body, forcing me to lean against the wall, but my mind had started to clear in the last few seconds, and what I could see didn't tally with what I'd expected. She could have caved. She could have floundered, uncertain. She could have had another panic attack, a real one or a clever fake. She could have started on about Mandy, again, about suicide and trust. Any of them I'd have been prepared for. I wasn't prepared for this. I reached through the last remnants of the fog in my mind and asked myself if I really wanted to do this, and the answer came clear and fast. I'd already done it. There was no going back.

"You've been out. When I went to Melanie's. You got on the tube. When I was in Oxford – today, for Christ's sake, you can't have forgotten that already – you were up and about getting trains from Euston. Before that, even, you were up when you said you weren't."

She was shaking her head. It didn't matter. I pressed on.

"And when Trawden died. That day. You remember that day? You weren't home then, were you?"

She'd stopped shaking her head and now she was just staring at me.

"What are you talking about?" she said, again.

"You got the tube to Southgate," I replied, and suddenly she'd crossed the distance between us and was standing in front of me, jaw set and mad as hell.

"Have you been following me?"

I kept my mouth shut and tried to stare at her, but I couldn't stop my eyes sliding around the room, searching for refuge.

"I asked you a fucking question. Have you been following me?"

I shrugged and started trying to prepare an explanation, she'd left me no choice, I'd been worried, I'd not known what else I could do, but I didn't get the chance to deliver it.

"After everything I've just been through, and the one person I should be able to trust is *following* me?"

She'd turned – she wasn't talking to me, she was addressing the television and the wall behind it.

"Just – just another controlling *man*," she spat, and turned back to face me. So trust had come and gone, and what followed it wasn't suicidal despair, as I'd feared, but anger. "Trying to manipulate me. Trying to make me your

195

instrument. After everything that happened. I thought I knew you."

"I was just – "

"And you think I'm going to sit there and let that happen? *Again*?"

"You don't understand," I said, feebly, but she just stood there, staring at me, shaking her head. I opened my mouth to continue, but I couldn't. There was a question in her eyes and I wasn't sure I could answer it.

Who the hell are you?

"Get out," she said. She turned and walked from the living room, into the bedroom, and I stood there leaning against the wall beside the door, and less than a minute later she was back with a small bag.

"Here's your clothes. Some of them. And your toothbrush. We'll arrange for you to pick up the rest."

My senses had finally unglued enough for me to say something.

"Please. Can't we just talk about this? Honestly?"

"No. Not now. Just get out."

"Please?"

She shook her head. "No. I've asked you nicely. I don't want to have to remind you who pays for this place when you're off in Manchester or Oxford or wherever you're working and not getting any bloody money. I don't want to have to remind you who you've been living off for the last six months. But it looks like I just did."

She thrust the bag into my arms and I took a step back. The door was still open – it had been open the whole time, and as she approached me I stepped back again until I was through it and into the hall.

"Claire," I started to say, but the door had slammed shut before I'd even got the word out.

PART 3: TALK OF THE DEAD

19: The Lucky One

THERE WAS HARDLY a soul on the train with me. I counted half a dozen spaced evenly through the carriage, a woman in a suit with her laptop out on the table in front of her and buds in her ears, a man in torn jeans lounging across two seats and asleep before we'd left Euston, an anxious-looking couple with a toddler right at the far end. And me.

I'd woken at four, to the Grimshaw dream. For ten years I'd been haunted by it, a nightly visitation which woke me wracked with guilt, Bill and Eileen Grimshaw turning to me, the same look they'd worn in court plastered across their faces, only they weren't in court now, they were in my bedroom or my office or wherever it was I'd fallen asleep. And they weren't silent, the way they'd been silent in court. They spoke to me, a single voice from two mouths, a single word, and they pointed at me as they spoke. *Guilty*, they said. *Guilty*. Over and over. *Guilty*.

I hadn't had that dream in a year, and now it was back.

So I woke, gasping and wretched, and turned to look at the big green numbers on the big old clock radio and check whether I'd woken Claire, and the clock wasn't there, and neither was Claire. It took me a moment to remember where I was.

I was at Parker Long House. I was in Maloney's spare bedroom.

I'd stood staring at that door, at the door to my own flat, eyes boring into it as if with enough effort they'd be able to see Claire standing behind it, and she'd be able to see me, and we'd carry out some weird silent reconciliation with a heavy wood-veneer door between us. She'd kicked me out. She couldn't have kicked me out. She couldn't have kicked me out, so I'd stand there for a minute and eventually she'd open the door and she wouldn't have kicked me out after all.

I stared at the door for ten minutes before I turned, lifted the bag she'd thrown at me onto one shoulder, and walked slowly downstairs. As I took the second step I heard a sound, a mechanical twist and slot, and turned again, but the door was still shut. She'd locked it, that was all. Then the tinkle of metal on metal. She'd locked it and thrown on the chain.

Maloney had been sympathetic, at least. I'd called him the moment I hit the street and he'd told me to come round and stay at his until I sorted myself out. I'd thought about taking the car, but the keys were in the flat and I didn't think Claire would be keen to see me so soon. So I walked, got on a bus, walked a little further and got on another bus and by the time I'd reached Parker Long House I was as sure as I could be that neither Evans nor the grey-haired man nor anyone else had followed me there.

Maloney had greeted me with a tumbler half full of cheap scotch and told me everything would be okay, and I'd agreed with him that yes, everything would be fine, just as soon as I managed to speak to her and properly apologise.

He'd looked at me like I was an idiot.

"No," I'd said. "She's right. Isn't she?"

He'd put a hand on my shoulder and taken the glass from my hand – I was on my second by then – and as I attempted to stand he'd pushed down, firmly.

"I need to go and explain," I'd said.

"Not now."

"I need to tell her. I need to prove I'm not who she thinks I am. I'm not that man."

Even as I said the words I looked up into the face of Maloney, Kevin Maloney, a man who'd hired people to follow my girlfriend on my instructions, and I thought maybe I was that man after all.

199

"Not now," he'd replied, again, and I'd given up trying to stand and slumped back down in the chair.

"Okay," I said, taking the drink back from Maloney and gulping it down fast. "Okay. But it's time to stop following her."

He'd nodded.

So I'd woken up in Maloney's spare bedroom, one of Maloney's spare bedrooms, possibly the one Claire had managed to find a gun in, although I hadn't asked, and I'd checked the time on my phone and shut my eyes tight and spent twenty minutes trying to get to sleep before I'd given up. Then I'd looked up the time for the first train to Blackpool, checked my pocket for the spare set of keys Maloney had given me the previous night, found a scrap of paper and a pen in his kitchen and written him a short note explaining where I was going.

I called Claire three times before we hit Milton Keynes, and the phone just rang the usual nine times before it diverted to voicemail. I didn't leave a message. I tried again just after Crewe, half past seven, two hours after we'd set off, with the couple and the toddler now gone and replaced by an ancient woman with a huge, heavy suitcase nearly as ancient as she was, a suitcase I'd taken from her and heaved to safety without a word of thanks. This time it rang once and then informed me that the person I was attempting to call was not available. There was no option to leave a message.

Claire had blocked me.

Nothing happened for the next half hour, and then my phone rang and I snapped it up and answered, praying it would be Claire.

"Don't hang up," said Martins, and I couldn't hold back a sigh of exasperation.

"What do you want?"

"I thought you'd want to know. We've got him."

"Evans?"

"No, the Loch Ness Monster. Of course Evans."

If she was trying to draw me into a friendly chat, she'd caught me in the wrong mood. All I said, in response, was "About time."

"So when can you get here?"

"Not for a while," I replied, but she was still talking.

"Because we'll keep him in as long as we can, but unless we get some of that Sam Williams magic, we're not going to get enough out of him to charge him, are we?"

"I'm on the –"

"And if we can't charge him, we won't be able to hold him, will we?"

"No, of course not, but –"

"The good news is he's already admitted harassing you, but that's not much, is it? Not enough to keep him."

She stopped, finally, and I thought about that punch, my head, my ribs, and whether that really constituted *not much*, whether *harassing* was really the word for it, and wondered whether I should argue. Instead I said "I'm sorry. I'm on the train to Blackpool."

"What the hell are you doing there?"

"Work. Actual paying work."

"Hmmm." She didn't sound convinced, which annoyed me more than it should have done, because for once I was telling her the pure unvarnished truth. "You're supposed to be here helping me question Evans."

"Am I some kind of mind-reader now? How was I supposed to know you were pulling him in today?"

"If you'd listened to me yesterday instead of hanging up you might have got an idea."

I paused and realised she was right. I'd killed the call. Maybe Martins had been about to explain that it was just a matter of delay, just a few hours, half a day, nothing more.

Maybe I'd let my anger get in the way.

"Yeah," I said. "Sorry about that. Listen, see if you can get an extension. Speak to the super. You're questioning the guy about a murder, not a little punch-up in the street. You should be able to get another thirty-six hours. Get that, and I'll come in tomorrow."

"I'll see what I can do," she said. "I'm up against it here. I'll let you know."

I rose as we drew into Preston, and the old woman caught my eye and nodded towards her suitcase, so I sighed and heaved it out again, along the carriage, out onto the platform, where I prayed there would be someone there to meet her. There wasn't, so I found myself obeying her unspoken instructions – she communicated by pointing and the occasional nod – and dragging the case up a set of stairs, across the platforms and down again, where I finally consigned her to the care of a taxi driver who was unlikely to be as patient as I'd been. Still not a word, just a nod, as they pulled away. I wasn't sure she'd even told the driver where to take her.

I'd been unable to sleep on the train, my mind forcing itself, exhausted, through the events of the previous evening, from Colman's revelation about the NCA building to me standing staring at a door, and then back to the start, over and over. I hadn't eaten a thing or had any coffee, I was tired and hungover, and I'd hoped to use the fifteen minutes I had at Preston station to get a hot drink and maybe a sandwich, but now those fifteen minutes were two and there was a queue at the one place that seemed to be selling anything. I found the right platform just as the train to Blackpool pulled in, and I was there less than an hour later.

Elissa Pengilly's guesthouse – *Avalon*, it was called, without apparent irony – was only twenty minutes' walk

202

from Blackpool North. I managed to find a stand selling coffee and took a chance on the single stale croissant that was all that remained of their food offering, and I fought my way against a stiff wind and a steady drizzle to make it to *Avalon* in fifteen. Two streets back from the sea it was cold, and somehow still close to dark at half past nine. The door was painted blue and cracked in several places, and even the sign hanging outside was falling to pieces. I rang the bell and stood shivering for a minute. There was no sign of life in the guesthouse; there was no sign of life in any of the buildings opposite or beside it. January mornings were always going to be quiet in Blackpool. I rang the bell again, and a moment later the door opened towards me with a hard shove and a woman stood there, squinting at me.

"What do you want?" she asked.

Elissa Pengilly was a mountain of a woman, her face broad and unlined, her hair pulled back in a bun so tight you could see the roots straining to free themselves. I put her around sixty, but she could have been anywhere from thirty to eighty, really.

"My name's Sam Williams. I called the other day."

She nodded at me. "Aye. I remember. Lawyer."

"That's right."

"You said you weren't coming up. But here you are."

"Here I am."

"You staying?"

"I have to be in London this evening." I offered an apologetic smile. "I was wondering if we could talk."

"Not if you're not staying." She stepped and reached to close the door.

"Wait," I said. "How much do you charge?"

She paused, her hand still on the edge of the door, and looked at me, still in the crumpled suit I'd been wearing the previous day, no luggage, nothing except a paper bag carrying the remains of the croissant which had been too dry to eat after all.

"You don't look much of a lawyer to me. Reckon you can't afford much. A tenner, it'd be, to the likes of you."

I reached into my pocket and drew out a ten-pound note.

"I just want to talk to you. Half an hour. No more. Let's get a coffee and talk."

"Breakfast," she said. "I'm sick of the kitchen 'ere. Get me some breakfast and that tenner and you can have a half hour."

Billy's Café was no more than a hundred yards away, but it took close to fifteen minutes to get there, Elissa Pengilly limping, labouring over every step, stopping every fourth to catch her breath, stopping twice on the way to roll a cigarette which she smoked as she walked.

"Sorry," she said. "I struggle in winter."

I didn't imagine she'd have found it much easier in summer, but I didn't say anything.

Billy's looked filthy from the outside but was cleaner in, and did a decent coffee and an extremely welcome bacon roll. Elissa Pengilly went for a full English, but I couldn't complain, especially at two pounds fifty. The place was close to full – apart from Elissa herself, the only people I'd seen since I'd left the station were in *Billy's*, and they all seemed to know her and greeted her with a wave or a friendly word.

"So," I said, when we'd sat ourselves down at a narrow, rickety table, so close to the one beside it that I found my already-sore ribs poked by the stray right elbow of a teenager with a shaven head every time he shovelled more beans into his mouth. "I was wondering if you could help me."

She smiled, and I thought there was a chance the whole trip hadn't been for nothing, and then she looked down at the plate in front of her, so full the bacon hung over its edges, and said "Food first, business later. Don't they teach you manners in London?"

I thought about telling her that I wasn't actually from London, that home, originally, was Reading, but she was already halfway through a sausage, wouldn't have noticed if I'd spoken, wouldn't have cared if she'd noticed.

After five minutes of serious, almost violent chewing, she set down her knife and fork and looked up from her plate.

"So what did you want, then? There isn't a rich man's will in it for me, you said. What can someone like me do for a fancy London lawyer?"

"I was wondering," I said, my heart racing out of all proportion to the importance of the conversation, "whether you remembered Marine Lambert."

She nodded. "Of course I do. Nearly died lying in the road next to her, didn't I? Not likely to forget something like that."

"Can you tell me what happened?"

"It was thirty-five years ago," she said, and I slipped a hand into my pocket, thinking another ten-pound note might do the trick, but she saw the movement and shook her head. "No need for that. I'm not like one of them grasses. I tell people what I know. You pay for my time. That's all."

"So?"

"So, she was drunk. She got drunk and she had new heels on so she fell over crossing the road. She was holding my arm when she fell, so she pulled me over with her. Next thing I remember there's blue lights and people crying and the bloody pain. I remember the bloody pain all right."

"So it was her fault? The accident? It was Marine's fault?"

"Too right it was." She paused, looked at me, down at her empty plate, back up again. "No," she continued.

205

"That's not fair. She was drunk, but we were all drunk and we were all wearing stupid bloody heels – last time I wore a pair of heels, that was – and maybe she fell over, maybe I fell over, maybe it was one of the other girls. I don't know. It might have been her. It might not. Doesn't really matter, does it?"

"No," I said. She was right. It didn't matter at all.

"Thing is, she was the lucky one."

I'd just lifted my coffee to my lips as she spoke, but I put it straight back down again, so fast it spilled out over the rim and onto my shirt. Without a word, Elissa Pengilly picked up a paper napkin from the table, leaned forward and dabbed at the drops before they could make their way any further down.

"Can't have you ruining that fancy suit of yours, can we?"

"No we bloody can't," I replied. "Only one I've got. And you know what we're like, us fancy London lawyers. One of us walks into a room with coffee on his suit, the rest won't speak to him for a year."

She laughed at that, sat back and roared briefly but loud enough for heads to turn.

"You're not that fancy, are you? Not really. That suit hasn't seen an iron in a while, I can see that from here."

I nodded, anxious to return to the moment before I'd spilled my coffee. "No, I'm not. Wish I was, sometimes, but you've seen right through me, Ms Pengilly."

"Elissa. Ellie. You can call me Ellie."

"Thanks, Ellie. But you were saying she was the lucky one. She died in that accident. Doesn't sound that lucky to me."

She'd been leaning towards me, but she sat back now, with a sigh. "Oh, that's the easy way out, isn't it? Dying. Believe you me, she got the good end of the deal. She's out of it. I'm not. Thirty-five years on and I'm still in pain."

I remembered her limping to the café, and without thinking glanced down at her legs.

"Aye," she said. "Broke the pair of 'em. Half a dozen places. And the hips. Can't remember which bits of me are metal and which are bone these days."

I nodded in sympathy. "Sorry to hear it. Must be terrible."

"It's terrible all right. But you didn't come all the way up here to listen to an old woman moaning about her hips, did you?"

"You're hardly old, Ellie. But no, the truth is, I came up to find out about Marine. Did she live round here?"

"Oh no. Not her. St Anne's for Marine Lambert. Too good for Blackpool, she was." She spoke without bitterness, in spite of the words. "Had a little flat there with one of the other girls from the hotel, I've forgotten the name."

"That was the Haverstock Hotel?"

She nodded. "Right. Out on the front. Not there any more, of course, but it was a nice place. Bunch of us worked there and it didn't matter if you lived in St Anne's or Morecambe or Preston, one of the lasses lived all the way out there, but the Haverstock was in Blackpool and if we were having a girls' night out, we had it in Blackpool. It was a girls' night out when the accident happened."

"Anything unusual about that night?"

She shook her head. "No. Nothing, really, not until the accident. They said the woman might have been going too fast, but I don't know, do I? All I know was this," she gestured to her legs. "And Marine. Oh, we had some good fun, those nights out, those bars and clubs. We showed 'em." She laughed, and then stopped, suddenly, silent. I thought about jumping in again, asking another question, keeping the momentum going, but I had a sense this silence was more than just a pause for the sake of it. There was

207

something underneath it. I waited, sipped at my coffee, waited some more.

"Still," she said, after a minute or so. "It was a shame about the child."

20: Things Left Behind

SILENCE, AGAIN. THERE was noise, outside the little bubble we'd created, Elissa Pengilly and I. There was conversation, there was the tinkle of fork against plate, the grind of tooth, the sizzle of another round of bacon, the shouting in the kitchen. I knew it was there, but I couldn't hear it. All I could hear was that sentence.

It was a shame about the child.

I ventured a look upwards. She was watching me, thoughtful.

"You didn't know," she said. It wasn't a question. I shook my head.

"No. I didn't. What happened to the child?"

She leaned forward again, a hard look on her face, and I realised that what I'd just said might have come across like an accusation. I opened my mouth to explain, but she was already talking.

"Well I could hardly take him, could I? Three months in hospital and when I got out, well, my job had gone, my flat had gone, and the boy had gone, too."

"Gone where?"

"Council. They put him in care. I'd have helped, if I could, but I couldn't, and really, it wasn't my fault, was it? None of it was my fault. And it wasn't like we were best friends, me and Marine Lambert."

She was still watching me, suspicious. I needed her back on my side, and I opted for the easy route.

"Do you want something more to eat?" I asked. "Bacon buttie?"

She nodded, and by the time I'd returned from ordering it she was sitting back, looking more relaxed. I ventured another question.

"What about the father? Couldn't he have taken the boy

209

in?"

She shook her head. "No. Marine told me the boy wasn't wanted. Father wasn't interested. There were some right little shits around back then. Still are, way I hear it."

The sandwich arrived, and she set to it with the hunger of a woman who hadn't eaten for a lot longer than ten minutes. I waited for her to finish, laying out questions in my mind, a plan, a flowchart that might lead to an answer. I'd thought Blackpool was likely to be a dead end, but that was before I'd heard about the child. She dabbed at her mouth and started talking before I had a chance to ask my first question.

"She was a funny one, that Marine. I mean, we'd come from all over, us girls. Not just her that wasn't local. Can you guess where I'm from, originally?"

She sounded pure Lancashire to me, no trace of an accent from anywhere else, but the name was a clue.

"Cornwall?" I said, and she nodded.

"Aye. There was a Scottish lass, there were a couple Londoners, like you, there was even one from bloody Poland, and back then Polish people might as well have been Martians for all we knew about them. But Marine Lambert was the only one who didn't talk about it."

"Didn't talk about what?"

"Her past. I said to her once, I said don't you want your parents to see their grandson, and she looked at me like I was talking Chinese or something. She said no. Said she didn't want anything to do with them. Didn't want anything to do with any of that bit of her life. I got hints, you know, from time to time. Got the idea they were drunks, her parents. Once when she'd had a few, we were in the Rose and Crown, that's closed now too, and no great loss, she said it reminded of her at the local back where she'd grown up and she hadn't liked that one little bit. Said her dad's friends used to feel her up there. Said he didn't do 'owt to stop 'em. She didn't want anything to do with them and didn't want anything to do with the father of her own lad. So no. We never got in touch with him. With any of 'em."

"Do you have anything of hers?" I asked, conscious that this was a delicate question, that it might prompt more suspicion and set me back another bacon sandwich or two. She stared at me, but her jaw wasn't set the way it had been when she'd thought I was accusing her of abandoning her friend's child.

"What's all this about, then?" she asked, and it hit me that all the obfuscations I'd planned for precisely this question wouldn't get round Elissa Pengilly for a second.

"I have this client," I replied. "His name's Richard Fothergill." And I told her everything.

She sat back when I'd finished – she'd leaned towards me as I told Fothergill's story, hanging on every word – and glanced at her watch. She'd offered me half an hour for my tenner, I remembered. We'd been longer than that already. I went to put my hand in my pocket but she shook her head.

"So you're helping some old paedo, are you?" she said.

"No. I'm not. He's not. He's innocent." I found myself believing it as I said it, which was a good sign. Elissa Pengilly nodded and bit her lip, lines suddenly appearing from nowhere as her face creased into a frown. "But the man who's accused him – the man I think was probably the father of Marine's son – he's not a madman. Something hurt him back then. And whatever it was, he blames my client for it."

She stared at me for a moment, and then she nodded. "Truth is," she said, "I did feel guilty. I mean, like I said, it wasn't like there was anything I could do, at the time, I mean. I didn't like to think of him all alone, his mum dead and him not knowing where he was or where he was going. But what could I do?"

I shrugged in agreement, and she continued.

"Thing is, last year I was cleaning up the store room, and I come across all her stuff."

"You had her stuff?"

She nodded. "Aye. Girls she lived with sent it me, after she passed, after I got out of hospital. Said I'd known her better than they did, and that might've been right but it didn't mean I'd known her well. So they sent it me, and I must have forgotten about it and put it in a load of boxes and then it came with me when I moved, and came when I moved again. So last year I found it and I got to thinking, maybe the boy should have it, he'd be a man by now, maybe he should have all this stuff, so I tried to find him, but I didn't have a chance. I mean, how do you find some lad who could be anywhere? So I was all set to give up, and then I thought, how about the father?"

"Marine's father?"

"No, why would I think of 'im? No. The lad's father. I remembered his name all right, funny name it was. Van der Lee. And I remembered the city. Oxford. Same bloke who's after your Fothergill, right? So it was easy enough to find 'im. And I sent it. The lot. Everything she'd left behind."

"Which was?"

"Nothing valuable, if that's what you mean. Loads of letters. Some documents, the little lad's birth certificate, that sort of thing. But letters, mostly."

"And did he get in touch with you, Van der Lee?"

She laughed. "He'd have had a job. Didn't send 'im my name or address, did I? Didn't want to get mixed up. Done my bit."

I nodded, turning it over in my mind. It felt important, these documents and letters, felt like another piece in a puzzle that was slowly coming together. I rose to my feet, lost in thought and hardly aware of what I was doing, and found myself thanking her for her time and offering another tenner, which she declined. I walked with her, back to *Avalon*, and I didn't mind the minutes it took, the pace of it and the pauses for her to roll another cigarette, because I spend most of those minutes working on that puzzle, trying a piece here and a piece there and taking them back out again, slowly and patiently, when they didn't fit.

Elissa Pengilly turned to me, before she closed her front door.

"I don't really know what you're looking for or how you think it'll help you, Sam Williams. But I hope you find it."

I thanked her, and turned to walk away, but she hadn't finished.

"And if you ever do find that lad, well, I hope he's turned out okay. I really do."

I thanked her, again. A light drizzle had sprung up, blown into my eyes by the sea breeze, coating my hair in fine cold droplets. I headed back to the station, through it all, the waking town and the rain and the wind, oblivious, lost in the puzzle.

I stayed like that most of the way back to London.

21: A Plausible Killer

MOST OF THE way. Not all of it. After a couple of hours I remembered there were other things going on in my life, more important things, for me, personally, than Marine Lambert's son. There was Claire. There was Evans, who was hopefully kicking his heels somewhere dark and cold and wouldn't be emerging into the sunlight until I'd figured out how to deal with him. Evans wouldn't be a problem for another day or two, I figured; Martins would have got the nod to keep him in by now. But the Claire business couldn't wait.

I called Roarkes and arranged to see him, and shortly before three I was sitting opposite him in his office in his new station.

My first impression of the place was that it wasn't very Roarkes. It was new, shiny and modern, nestled in underneath the roar of the North Circular a stone's throw from Wembley. A convenient location, if you wanted to be somewhere else in a hurry. Roarkes' office was clean and almost austere – a desk, a couple of chairs, a filing cabinet, white walls, cream carpet. He'd been there a few weeks, more than enough time to put his tired, grubby stamp on the place, but he didn't seem to have bothered. He greeted me with a smile that didn't fit him any more than the office did, and I found myself wondering where the man I knew had gone.

"So what can I do for you, Sam?" he asked.

"I need to talk. Got some things to tell you about. Got some questions to ask."

"Go ahead."

So I told him everything. Fothergill and Van der Lee and Marine Lambert, not that it was any interest of his, but I wanted him to see the whole picture, everything I had going on, which bits fitted where. I told him about Evans. And finally, I told him about Claire.

"So, I did what you've been on at me to do. I did it, Roarkes."

"You did what?"

"I confronted her. I told her I knew she'd been sneaking about, and I asked her where she'd been."

His eyes widened. "Sneaking about? Is that what you said?"

"No. I didn't use those words. But she got the message."

"And did she tell you?"

"Yeah. She told me to get the fuck out of the flat. She told me I was manipulating her, like I was Trawden come back from the dead. She chucked some clothes in a bag and slammed the door on me. Got to say, that was some advice you gave me."

"Hmm," he replied. "Yeah. Sorry." And then he fell silent. I waited a minute, hoping he'd come up with something useful, but nothing came.

"I'm still worried about her, Roarkes," I said, finally, and he shook his head.

"Where's the Fothergill case taking you next?" he asked.

"I don't know. I need to dig a bit more into this kid. Just because the old lady didn't find him doesn't mean I can't. And I want to look into Van der Lee again. That bar. The restoration work. The company in Leeds. Doesn't add up."

"You're not going to get in his face again, are you?"

I'd told him about our little conversation in *Dervish*. "No. Not this time. I'll tread carefully. But it's Claire that's on my mind, Roarkes, and I'm losing her. I don't know what she's doing or where she's going, and I'm worried she's going to do something she'll regret."

"I wouldn't worry, Sam. She's not stupid."

"It's easy for you to say that. You didn't find her with a gun outside the Old Bailey."

"And then she realised she'd been manipulated into being there in the first place. That was a mistake. Everyone makes mistakes. Only stupid people make them twice, and like I said, Claire's not stupid."

I stared at him and shook my head, as he continued.

"I mean it. She's tougher than you think she is and she's smarter than you'll ever be. Leave it. She can look after herself. Get yourself up to – where did you say it was? The company that did the bar up?"

"Leeds."

"Get yourself up to Leeds and find out what your man Van der Lee's been paying them for. It'll probably end up being expensive leather chairs, but you never know. The only thing you should be worrying about as far as Claire's concerned is how to get your apology right."

"Have you been listening to a word I've said?" I asked, and he smiled at me and nodded. "Last time I left her to it she nearly killed someone. That was a mistake, and what was it you just said? I'm not stupid either. I'm not making the same mistake twice."

"Listen, Sam, you've done everything you could. You've used all the resources at your disposal and you still haven't been able to figure out what she's been up to. You've asked her face to face and she's kicked you out. I get that you're worried, but there's no point being worried when you can't do anything about it."

"All the resources?" I said. He'd got my back up. He frowned and I went on. "Yeah, I suppose that's true. I've got this DI who's supposed to be a friend and all I ask of him is to find out what's behind a building on a road in the middle of London, because I'm worried my girlfriend's going to kill someone, and what does he give me?"

The smile was back on Roarkes' face, and all that did was fire me up even more. I could feel my face growing warm as I continued.

"So it's a good thing I've got other, more competent friends in the police force, isn't it?"

"What do you mean?"

"I mean Colman. Vicky Colman. She's been helping me, too. Been helping me for half as long as you have, and she's not even in CID any more, but she still managed to find out about that bloody building."

"Did she indeed? And what did Vicky Colman tell you about it?"

"It's the NCA. National Fucking Crime Agency. She got that in about a day. What the hell have you been doing, sitting here on your arse watching the cars go by?"

I'd been hoping to shift that grin from his face, but instead he just laughed.

"NCA? The NCA?"

I didn't reply.

"Well I never," he said. "And she got that in less time than I've had?"

I nodded. I'd thrown everything at him. The least I'd expected was a bit of righteous indignation, a little wounded pride at the fact I'd asked Colman for help when he was already working on exactly the same task.

"I'm impressed, Sam. Martins shouldn't have kicked that girl off her team. I wouldn't have done."

"She wouldn't have been working for you in the first place, Roarkes. She's better than that," I said, before I could bite the words back. It was unnecessary, and it was untrue. If Roarkes had come calling, Colman would have bitten his hand off.

"Let's call her, shall we?" he said, as if I hadn't uttered a word, and without waiting for a reply picked up his phone and pressed a button.

"I need to reach Vicky Colman, please. Uniform. What station is she at now, Sam?"

"Holborn," I muttered.

"She's working out of Holborn. Put me through to her mobile, please."

He put the phone down and hit the button for the speakers, and a moment later Colman's voice boomed out.

"Vicky Colman here. Who is this?"

"Vicky," said Roarkes, the same bloody smile in his voice as the one on his face. I tried to remember whether they'd ever met, face to face. I didn't think so. "It's Detective Inspector Roarkes. I'm sitting in our office with a mutual friend. He tells me you've been doing some rather successful freelancing."

I shot Roarkes a look of disgust and leaned over the phone.

"Hi Vicky. It's me. Don't worry. You're not in trouble."

"I'd better not be," she replied. "Anyway, I'm not sure I know what Detective Inspector Roarkes is talking about."

Roarkes leaned his head to one side and frowned at me, and I sighed and leaned back over the phone.

"It's okay, Vicky. You might as well tell him the lot. He knows about the NCA, I've already told him."

"You might have warned me first," she replied.

"Yeah. Sorry about that."

"So what else have you got for us, Vicky?" said Roarkes, and I registered that *us* with a curious blend of satisfaction and resentment.

"That's it, Detective Inspector. NCA. Still trying to figure out who she went to see there. Sam says she came out looking pissed off, so I'm guessing she didn't get what she came for, but it would be good to know, right, Sam?"

"Right," I said, and then stopped and thought. "No. Don't."

"What do you mean, don't?"

Roarkes jumped in.

"I think our good friend is telling you to drop it. Is that it, Sam?"

I waited for a moment – the last thing I wanted was to give Roarkes the satisfaction of being right yet again – but he *was* right and there was no getting around it.

"Yeah. Drop it, Vicky," I said. "Claire's kicked me out. I asked her straight out and she told me I was – well, let's just say she didn't take kindly to being followed about and questioned like some kind of terror suspect."

"Are you sure?"

I waited, again. Roarkes stared at me, unreadable. I'd called off Maloney already. What difference did it really make if I found out what was in that building?

"Yeah," I said, again. "Time to let it die."

Colman called as I was trudging away from Roarkes' station through a rare break in the rain.

"I've got two questions for you," she said, the moment I answered. "First one, are you one hundred per cent certain Claire had nothing to do with Trawden's death?"

"Yes," I said. "Of course I am. Don't be ridiculous. She was at the NCA. We've been through all that already."

"I know that. And I know she's your girlfriend –"

"I'm not so sure of that. Not now."

"Stop being so bloody negative. You'll get her back. As long as she's not locked up for murder. Yes, I know she's your girlfriend. And I know she wasn't actually there, on the scene."

"So what's the problem?"

"Who's to say she wasn't there sorting something out?"

"At the NCA?"

There was a pause, while she digested the implications of what she'd been saying. If you were going to plan a murder, an NCA headquarters wasn't the first place you'd go.

"Yeah, fair enough. But she might have arranged something in advance."

I'd considered much the same thing myself, at one stage. But I didn't tell Colman that. Instead, I asked her what had brought on this sudden burst of suspicion.

"Well," she said, "the NCA. It's a bit bloody convenient, isn't it?"

I couldn't argue with that. A ready-made alibi if ever there was one. But that wasn't news. We'd known about the NCA for a while, now.

"What else?" I asked.

"Evans."

"What about him?"

"They brought him in."

"I know." I refrained from setting out my own role in Evans' arrest. Colman could add two and two herself.

"Which was a stupid, pointless thing to do, but anyway. They're going to let him go."

"WHAT?"

I couldn't hold it back. Bringing Evans in might have been stupid and pointless, Colman was right about that, but letting him go was just doubling down.

"He's got an alibi after all."

"What, one of his junkie mates has shown up with the goods, have they? Come on, Vicky. He's not got an alibi."

"He has, you know. He was seen. By witnesses. Independent ones."

I waited. I didn't like the sound of this.

"Stood on the top of a cliff somewhere near Bournemouth, like he was about to jump off it. Passer-by managed to talk him down. There was even a small crowd there to see it happen."

"And these people, they've identified the man as Evans?"

"Well, no. Not as such. But it's the right place, and Simon says he admitted it, this morning, said he went down there to top himself, would have done it if this woman

220

hadn't turned up and talked him out of it. It's even in the local paper, apparently. Right day, right time. *Suicide Averted*, it says. They don't say anything about the bloke, Evans, I suppose they wanted to protect his privacy, but Martins' lot are going to follow it up and they're pretty much certain it'll check out."

"Shit," I said, quietly. "But what about everything else? What about beating me up?"

"Are you sure that was Evans?"

"Yes," I said. That was a given. I'd been attacked on the street and it had been Evans that had attacked me, so I'd given in to Martins and agreed to help her if she picked the bastard up, only now she was letting the bastard go before I had the chance to crack him.

"So maybe it was him, Sam. He can't be the only person who's wanted to give you a good kicking in your life, can he? Doesn't mean he's a killer."

I'd thought much the same myself. There wasn't a thing she was saying I could disagree with. Evans wasn't a plausible killer. Not this killing, anyway.

"Do you think they'll hold him until I get there?" I asked. I was clutching at straws now. So what if they did? Evans had an alibi. I wasn't going to crack him.

"Not a chance. Martins couldn't get approval to hold him any longer. If he's not out now he will be shortly. What with the alibi, and Genaud –"

"What's Genaud got to do with it?"

"Genaud was the one arguing for Evans' release. Stood there in front of the superintendent, Simon said. Martins saying *can we keep him in* and Genaud saying *don't let her*. Said Martins was too close, apparently. Said she was trying to cover up her own failures, that Evans was just a convenient scapegoat. Simon thinks he wants to take over the case. One thing's for sure. He definitely wants Evans on the street, and it looks like he's got his way."

"Shit," I said, louder this time. "But really, what's this got to do with Claire?"

"Don't you get it?"

"No."

"She's the only one left. Fuck knows why, but they've bought your Maloney alibi. Lizzy Maurier was in France. Evans was standing on the edge of a cliff. As far as CID are concerned, Claire's the only one without a solid alibi."

"But the NCA –"

"We've been through that, Sam. She could have planned the whole thing in advance. And there's something else, too."

"What?"

"They've found someone on CCTV. Figure in nurse's uniform, only it isn't one of the nurses. Hanging around the corridor outside Trawden's room."

"Who is it?"

"They can't make out the face."

"Well it can't be Claire."

"So you keep saying. You're sure, are you? You're sure you've got the right time, the right day? You're sure she was in that building right when Trawden was killed?"

"Yes," I said. It was about the only thing I was sure of. We fell silent, the pair of us, and I was about to thank her and ring off and try to get hold of Martins, whatever it took, when I remembered how she'd opened the call.

"Two questions, you said. We've done Claire. What was the other one?"

"Roarkes."

"What about him?"

"That thing you said, about dropping it, not trying to find out any more, the building, what Claire was up to. Was that just for his benefit?"

Drop it.

Leave it.

222

Kill it.

I opened my mouth to say the words, and then I stopped, and thought, for half a second, and something completely different came out.

"Yes," I said. "Keep on digging."

22: Crossed Out

I GOT BACK to Maloney's around five. Everything was a blur, between calling Claire and getting that same damned voice telling me she was unavailable, and calling Martins and getting nothing at all – eight rings on her mobile followed by dead air, fifteen on her direct line before I gave up, four different sergeants and constables answering the public line and assuring me with varying degrees of sincerity that yes they would pass on my message and yes they understood this was an important matter that couldn't wait any longer and yes they'd have the detective inspector call me back as soon as she was available. I even tried Winterman, twice, but he was no more accessible than his boss. And back to Claire, still *unavailable*, which seemed to me a decent description of where she'd been for weeks. Where she'd been from the beginning, as far as I was concerned, because for all that she'd made parts of herself available, the surface, the likes and dislikes, the laughter and the easy tears, her body, of course, for all that, the inner truth had always been hidden.

Evans had tried to kill himself, that was the line, now, that was his alibi. Fothergill and Evans. Not Claire, not yet, not ever, I imagined, but I couldn't dismiss the possibility. More in common than I'd thought possible. And yet they were alive, all of them. Marine Lambert wasn't. Nor was David Brooks-Powell. No one ever seemed to get what they wanted.

Maloney was out, again. He hadn't left a note – no reason for him to leave a note, really; he'd told me I could come and go as I pleased, and he'd be doing the same, and if our paths crossed from time to time, so much the better.

There was a kebab shop on the corner, a good one, and I ventured out at eight for an extra large donner and chips.

224

When I'd finished the food I spent another fifteen minutes trying Martins and Claire and then I lay down on my bed and forced my mind back, to Fothergill and Van der Lee and Marine Lambert and her son. There were a number of pieces, but not too many; on any normal day I felt I'd have been able to slot them into place in minutes. But now there were other factors, distractions, threats and fears, and every time I thought I'd found a good connection, up popped Claire, slamming the door in my face, or John Evans, doing the same with his fist, or Martins, with her useless deals, or Genaud, sinister and silent.

I called Fothergill and related my encounter with Elissa Pengilly, and I could almost hear his jaw drop when I told him about the child.

"So what do you reckon?" I asked, when I'd finished. I was pleased with myself. I'd managed to push everything else into the background, and now, briefly, I could bask in the knowledge that my long-shot trek to Blackpool might actually have paid off.

"We have to find that child," he replied. I'd been expecting that.

"He won't be a child now. And it won't be easy."

"I know. But I know you can do it, too. I can't believe it, Sam. She never mentioned the child. I thought – well, I assumed she'd had the abortion. She'd never said otherwise. Naturally, I – well."

"I understand. I'd have thought the same."

"We have to find that child, Sam."

I switched on the television in Maloney's living room and found myself drawn into a nineties cop show that hadn't weathered well. I gave it twenty minutes, which was nineteen more than it deserved, and then I tried Claire again.

Instead of ringing once and going straight through to

225

that *unavailable* message, it rang on. Four, five rings. And then it was answered.

"Sam," she said.

"Claire. Thank god. I've been worried about you."

I hadn't been worried about her, not that sort of worried, not the *I-can't-get-hold-of-you-where-are-you-have-you-had-an-accident* sort of worried that might have made sense if I wasn't already used to not knowing where she was or what kind of trouble she was getting into. But the words just came out that way.

"You need to stop trying to call me, Sam."

"I know, but –"

"No, stop talking, Sam. You need to stop talking and listen to me for once. I need some time. You need to give me some time. I'm not ready to talk to you yet. When I am – *if* I am – I'll let you know. Until then, well, you've got to be patient."

"Okay," I said, even though it was anything but.

"I know that's not easy for you. Being patient. I'm sorry. But you're going to have to wait. Goodbye, Sam."

"Goodb –" I began, but she'd already gone.

Claire was a dead end, but Martins was still out there, and I spent another hour trying to reach her before I gave up and crawled into bed. I closed my eyes and fell asleep almost immediately – I'd been up since four, travelled most of the way up the country and back down again, and had a few surprises along the way. It wasn't long after ten, but nothing was going to keep me awake.

The phone woke me half an hour later. I reached for it, instantly aware of my surroundings and my situation, and almost dropped it in the darkness when I saw Martins' number on the screen.

"At last," I said, when I managed to get it back in my hand and hit the big green button.

"Yeah. Sorry. Been a busy day."

"So I gather. Well? You got Evans tucked up over there waiting to talk to me tomorrow?"

I knew she hadn't; Colman hadn't rated her chances with the super, not after the alibi and Genaud and her recent history of failure.

"I'm sorry, Sam. We had to let him go."

"What?" I tried to throw a little surprise into my voice, a little shock and fear, but I was too tired to play games and it came out long, low and slow, disappointment more than anything else.

"We couldn't hold him any longer. Super wasn't having it. He had an alibi, Sam. It looked like a good one, too."

I half-listened while she described the alibi, the clifftop, the passer-by, the crowd of witnesses, the same scene Colman had given me earlier that day. She didn't mention Genaud. If anything had beaten her, it would be the facts, not a rival. I tried to picture her, sitting in her station, surrounded by tired subordinates, no collar, no real suspect, a day or more lost, but even though I'd been there more than once and seen her more times than I cared to recall, I didn't see her or her station at all. I saw the nineties police from that nineties television show, all big teeth and stupid fake accents, and I found I was having to work hard not to laugh out loud.

"Okay," I said, when she'd finished. No use fighting it. Even without Genaud, she hadn't had a chance.

"But there's – well, there's been a complication, Sam."

I didn't like that *Sam*. I didn't like that *complication*. I waited.

"Well, while we had him in custody we had uniform take a look at the last place he'd been staying. Some bloke's floor, one of his connections, friend of a friend. We didn't have a warrant, but the bloke didn't want any trouble and I guess he didn't have any drugs on him either, because they

227

didn't find any."

She tailed off.

"And?"

"And they got back just after we'd let him go."

"What did they find? You said there'd been a complication. What are you talking about?"

"He had the newspaper there."

"What newspaper?"

"The Clarion. The local Bournemouth rag."

"Okay, well, he'd been down there, hadn't he? Backs him up, I suppose."

"Not exactly." I waited, again, and after a nervous cough, she continued. "It was the edition that described the suicide attempt. Right time, right place, just like he'd said."

"So what's the problem?"

"It didn't describe him."

"That's fair enough," I said. I was trying to convince myself just as much as I was trying to convince Martins, and I had to keep reminding myself that it didn't matter, that whether he'd been on the top of a cliff or in the middle of London, Evans wasn't a plausible insulin killer. "Why should they describe him? They'd want to protect his privacy, right?"

"Yes," she replied. "That was what we thought. We'd already seen the article online, anyway, when we checked out the alibi. We knew there was no description."

"So what's the problem?" I repeated.

"Well, he had the paper. With the article in it. He tells us he's down on the south coast, and first, second, third time we talk to him he's got no alibi, doesn't remember where he was that day. Then we pull him in again – and by this time he's managed to get himself a copy of the local rag – and suddenly he remembers exactly where he was and what he was doing, and not only that, there's a crowd there to witness it."

"What are you driving at?" I asked, even though I knew it, even though I could feel it filling my veins and turning my blood to ice.

"Well, if I were a decent cop with a suspicious mind – and I'm both of them and more, as you know – I'd assume he hadn't been on the south coast at all. I'd assume he'd got hold of the paper and looked for some local event he could tie himself into at the same time Trawden was killed, and he'd found one, even better, found one that mentioned a stranger and didn't describe him. I'd assume he'd turned someone else's near-tragedy into his own alibi, and he'd had us for fools."

"Right," I said. I felt cold, colder than the weather or the city outside. "So – when you had him in custody, did you mention me?"

"Of course we did. We could hardly avoid it, could we? I told you yesterday he'd coughed to harassing you. You're part of the case, whether you like it or not."

A car alarm went off outside and I jumped up, staring wildly into the darkness and listening to the shouts and the cars and the normal, everyday noises. Evans wasn't the killer. That was the important thing. Not what Martins thought. Not the alibi. Evans couldn't be the killer. Martins was still talking.

"And you said he'd attacked you, so –"

"I thought he'd admitted that."

"No, he admitted the harassment. Following you about. Making calls. Grabbing your arm. Nothing about fists and boots."

Evans couldn't be the killer. But even before all this, he'd hated me. Now I'd got him arrested and locked up for the day, he wasn't going to like me any more.

"So you're pulling him back in, right?"

A silence. The alarm outside had stopped, and I could hear her breathing down the line.

"Martins? Did you hear me? You're telling me his alibi was bullshit. Have you got him back yet?"

"I'm sorry, Sam. We'd love to. But he's disappeared."

I dropped the phone. Somewhere in the black I could hear her voice, high and thin, "Sam? Are you there, Sam?" I stumbled over to the door and switched on the light and snatched up the phone before she could hang up and disappear herself, become *unavailable* again at the one time in my life I actually needed her.

"I'm here."

"We'll find him. We've got everyone looking. I mean *everyone*."

"Okay. Just make sure you do."

"There's something else, Sam."

I hated it, the way she kept using my name, the way we were suddenly friends, the obviousness of the ruse.

"What?"

"They found a list. The uniform, the ones who did the search. Evans' mates place."

"What list?"

"A list of names. Yours was on it."

"Who else? What were the other names?"

A pause.

"Martins?"

"Trawden was at the top."

"Right. Who else."

"Akadi. Blennard. Elizabeth Maurier."

My mind was racing, but the connection was obvious enough.

"All connected with the Grimshaw case," I said.

"Yes."

"And all dead."

"Yes."

"All except me."

Another silence, and then, quietly, the final nail.

"They were crossed out, Sam. The other names. The dead. Every name was crossed out. Every name except yours."

After Martins had apologised, for the hundredth time, and assured me for the fiftieth that she was doing everything she could to bring Evans back in, she finally got round to offering me protection.

"I'll think about it," I said. Evans was a real threat, I was sure of it, and protection sounded good, but I'd remembered something even better. I was at Maloney's. No one knew I was at Maloney's — I hadn't told Martins, I hadn't told anyone, and Claire might guess, Roarkes and Colman, too, but Evans wouldn't have a clue.

I was safe here. For now.

I called Claire, to warn her, but I was back on the blocked list. Even texts wouldn't get through, so I dropped her a short email, *John Evans thinks I set up his Dad, he's after revenge, be careful.* I signed off with a couple of *X*s, not something I'd done before, but it couldn't hurt.

I'd dropped off quickly, earlier, but now, after hearing from Martins, I couldn't sleep. I lay there, trying to think of something that wasn't connected to John Evans, but he'd hemmed me in, with that list. Every time I narrowed in on someone else, a name from the list elbowed its way in. Marine Lambert with her infant son became the Mauriers, mother and daughter. Fothergill pleading his innocence turned into Trawden. Maloney and his history of dealing drugs gave me Akadi. It didn't matter which way I turned. There was no escape.

I picked up my phone and scrolled through the news, but there was nothing interesting enough to keep my attention. I lay back down and stared into nothing, resigned to a night of fear and useless thought.

I woke at midnight to a fierce pounding and shouts from

231

outside. I pulled myself up and out of bed, fumbling in the dark for my jeans and my t-shirt. Even dazed by sleep I worked quietly and without light. Whoever was out there, I wasn't going to make it easy for them.

The shouting was confused, more than one voice, indistinct and indecipherable, but by the time I was half-dressed I could hear *"Open up!"* and a few seconds later *"Sam Williams!"* and as I slipped on my second, elusive shoe, *"Police!"*

I hoped Maloney wasn't back yet. He wouldn't thank me for bringing the police to his door.

When I opened it a minute later Genaud was leaning in, towards me, already halfway through it. I took a step back, involuntarily, and by the time I'd recovered he was inside.

"Mind if I come in, Sam?" he said, and smirked at me.

I did mind, I minded on Maloney's behalf, but he was in already and I had the feeling he wouldn't be here if he didn't think he could get a warrant, or at least make life so difficult we'd let him anyway. I shrugged.

"Thanks," he said. There were two officers behind him, a man and a woman, both young, both in uniform. Neither of them had made any move into the flat.

"What do you want?" I asked. Genaud smirked at me again. With both of us standing, I saw he was short, shorter than I'd realised and several inches shorter than me. That thick layer of hair didn't reach all the way up; there was a bald spot in the middle, which gave me a strange sort of comfort.

"Just a chat, Sam. Just a chat. Evans is out, did you hear that? Got an alibi. And you're hanging out with the man who provided you with your alibi. That's convenient. Maloney around, is he?"

I ignored the question, focussing instead on Evans.

"From what I hear, Evans' alibi isn't all it should be. From what I hear, he's on the loose and he might have

232

made it up. From what I hear, he made a list, and every person on that list is dead, and every name is crossed out. Every name except mine."

"Oh, I don't think you need to worry about Evans, Sam."

Another bastard using my first name. It was bad enough when it was someone I liked, but lately it had been people I didn't. Martins had done it to ingratiate, to soften me up. With Genaud there was a naked malice to it. He'd taken half a step forward, but this time I stood my ground, so there were just inches between us.

"Right. I don't need to worry. The man's a suspect in a murder case and he hates me and he's attacked me once already. And you let him out. You can tell me I don't need to worry when you've got him under lock and key. Until then, I'll decide what I need to worry about."

He laughed, a short low chuckle, a laugh from smoke-filled pubs and dark corners and bloodstained pavements.

"You don't sound too pleased about it, Sam. Shame. Where's Claire? Not with you? Had a bust-up, have you?"

I shrugged, again. He continued.

"I was wondering if you had anything to say about her alibi. Not that she's got one. Not anything to shout about, anyway. Home by herself. Got any thoughts on that, Sam?"

"How did you know I was here?"

He laughed, again.

"No? Not going to help me nail your girlfriend, Sam? Shame."

He turned around, and took a step away, back through the door.

"I asked you a question," I said.

"There's a murder investigation going on, Sam. Unlike Martins, I'll use all the resources I've got. Common sense. CCTV. Idle talk. Good night, Sam. I'm sure we'll be seeing each other again soon."

233

I let the door fall shut as he walked away. This time I knew I wouldn't sleep. *No one knew I was at Maloney's.* That was the one thing I had.

And now it was gone.

23: Restoration

I SURPRISED MYSELF with a solid four hours' dreamless sleep, but I only managed that because I'd made a decision. London wasn't safe. I'd been fine in Blackpool – I'd been fine because Evans had been in custody and the idiots hadn't got round to letting him out, but even if he'd been out, even with me at the top of the list, I was out of his reach and untraceable. Blackpool had distance. London wasn't safe.

Leeds, I thought, might be safe.

Maloney was making coffee as I emerged from my bedroom at seven next morning.

"Hear you had some company last night," he said, passing me a cup, and I filled him in on Genaud's visit.

"Micky Genaud," he said, thoughtful. "I remember that fucker all right. Don't cross him, Sam."

"That's just what Roarkes said. Reckon I'll keep out of his way. Leeds today."

Maloney nodded.

"Good move. Keep yourself busy."

The tube was busy, another day of cancelled trains and closed stations forcing half of London into one enormous bottleneck of human flesh, squeezed into every corner of every carriage and platform they could. That should have made me feel safer – even feet away, Evans couldn't have got to me – but I couldn't shake a sense of dread or stop myself seeing violent intent in every eye that fell on me. Kings Cross was just as crowded, with the added danger of advertising boards and kiosks and pillars for a would-be assailant to hide behind. I felt every nerve in my body, a piece of string woven tight round each organ and muscle and joint, and I didn't let it ease off until I'd taken my seat on the train north, removed my coat, stood, paced up and down the carriage three times checking every occupant of every seat, and satisfied myself that Evans wasn't among them. I closed my eyes as we trundled through the suburbs under a slate-grey sky, and found myself drifting off to sleep again.

I was woken by my phone. Colman had news.

"It's a whole bunch of departments," she said. "They don't like people knowing they're there. That's why it was so difficult to work it out. Although it still doesn't explain why I managed to crack it and Roarkes couldn't."

Evidently she wasn't letting that one go.

"Cybercrime," she continued. "Witness protection. Money laundering. Child sexual exploitation. Human trafficking. They're all in the same building. Could be any of them."

There were some good candidates there, some teams whose jobs matched Claire's interests well. The last two in particular. Child sexual exploitation. Human trafficking. Of course, she'd come out of that building without the thing she'd gone in for, that much was clear. But what had she been looking for?

I changed the subject and told her about Martins' call, the list, Genaud's friendly visit.

"I don't like that bloke," I said. "I get the sense he isn't on the level."

She laughed.

"I get the sense he's one dirty fucker and he'll do whatever it takes to get the result he wants. And that won't always be the right result, either."

"He's after Claire."

"That matches what Simon told me. Listen, yesterday you told me to carry on looking into the building. I've done what you asked. I can dig some more, if you think it'll help. With Genaud on the warpath it's all getting a bit more serious."

"I think it was pretty serious when Trawden got killed and we were all pulled in to tell Martins where we'd been."

"Yes, true. But Genaud makes things different. So do you want me to carry on looking into it?"

I remembered my call with Claire – not so much *with* as *listening to*, really – the previous night. She needed time. She didn't need me checking where she'd been and what she'd been doing. If I was going to prove I wasn't the man she thought I was, I'd have to stop being that man.

"No," I said. "You've done enough, and I'm grateful. I really am. But I think it's time to drop it."

The rest of the journey passed without incident, and there was still half an hour of morning left by the time the taxi dropped me off outside the offices of the Restoration Company, Leeds, Limited. Leeds wasn't what I'd been led to expect, what years of television documentaries and sad news stories had impressed upon me, or at least this bit of it wasn't; none of that gritty urban decay, no streets overflowing with litter and boarded-up windows. Instead I was faced with wide roads, trees, parks, and right in front of me a large, imposing Georgian building set in its own grounds. In former times, an estate or country retreat, I guessed. If this was the Restoration Company, furniture looked like a good game to get into.

There was a low red brick wall separating the grounds from the pavement outside, and within, a taller wire fence with a wrought iron gate set in it, and a short driveway that led up to what looked like the main door. I stayed close to the wall as I stepped onto the driveway, and instead of advancing to the building itself, followed the wall round. The fence died away abruptly after the first corner, but I figured they didn't need it. I counted six windows per floor on the side of the building I was facing, and four floors, but none of the windows were open. I continued round the next corner to the back of the building, following a stone pathway set into the grass. I could hear the trickle of a stream nearby, out of view, and see a single willow off to my left. As for the building, just the same sets of windows and a small white door, also shut. The doors at front and back, it seemed, were the only ways in or out.

Of more immediate concern were the cameras. I'd spotted one set high on the fence as I entered, but it wasn't until I turned and looked back the way I'd come that I saw its twin, lower down and mounted on a ball that would allow it to swivel and change the field of vision. Attuned to what I was looking for, I found five more on the building itself and another three on the fence. Whoever Van der Lee was paying, they took their security seriously and had the resources to pay for quality.

Russian mafia, I thought, for no reason other than the fact that they were all over the place these days, television dramas and breaking news and fingers pointed at politicians everywhere. If social media were to believed, the Russians owned most of Britain already. Another piece for the puzzle, possibly, but I couldn't see where it would fit in with Fothergill and Marine Lambert.

I completed my circuit, took a breath and strode up to the door. I had no doubt they'd already seen me, and I hadn't really expected to get all the way there without interruption, but whoever was in there watching seemed content to let me snoop around. Maybe they had nothing to hide. Maybe they were confident I wouldn't find it.

The door was closed, with a large white button beside it, which I pressed. There was no sound, but a moment later the door opened from within, and I was greeted by a man who redefined my sense of big.

Close to seven foot, I reckoned, as I looked up at him, white shirt, dark suit, dark hair, five o'clock shadow creeping in before noon. Behind him was his twin in blonde. And behind them both, sitting in a leather armchair beside a wooden table that had *priceless antique* written all over it, another blonde, a woman, around my own age, I figured, with cheekbones that could cut glass and a smile I didn't trust for a second.

She stood, and the two men took a step back and allowed her to approach me.

"Welcome to the Restoration Company, sir," she said, in an accentless voice, a professional, blue-chip voice. "Do you mind me asking what your business is here?"

I glanced at the two men, at the room I was in, a vast, high-ceilinged entrance hall with a chandelier in the middle, portraits on the walls, and wood panelling to match the table the woman had been sat beside. I tried to work out what I should say, what story would work best, who I'd come to visit and what the nature of my appointment would be, and then my eyes came to rest on the woman and her smile and her eyes, which seemed to be telling me she knew everything already, and that decided it. Whoever these people were, they were too smart to fall for my usual bullshit. They had me on CCTV, so they could figure out who I was if they didn't already know. And if those two men got to work on me, they'd know everything they wanted to in minutes anyway.

"It's complicated," I said. "It'll take a while."

"Please, take a seat," replied the woman, and gestured to the chair she'd been sat in. She pulled out another, a modern artefact of twisted metal I hadn't noticed, and sat beside me. "Now, Mr –"

"Williams. Sam Williams."

"Mr Williams. As you may have noticed, we're rather cautious here at Restoration. I'd be immensely grateful if you could explain your presence."

The two men had drifted away behind me, but I could

sense their presence, between me and the door. And something about the way the woman spoke, the way she smiled, the way her eyes bored into mine as she asked me to *explain my presence*, made her seem more dangerous than that pair of giants anyway.

"I'm a lawyer. I have a client who's been accused of historic sexual abuse – and yes, I know that's terrible, but of course everyone is entitled to a defence, and I happen to believe he's innocent."

I'd thrown in the line about entitlement and innocence because people tended to need it, people tended, in my experience, to hear the crime and jump straight to trial and conviction and prison, to assume the worst. But she hadn't even blinked.

"Do you mind telling me your name?" I asked. A name might soften her, I thought.

"Certainly. I'm Mrs Hargreaves."

"Well, Mrs Hargreaves," I continued, aware that the name hadn't softened her at all. "The man who's accused my client has not been particularly forthcoming with the details of the alleged crimes, and I've come to the tentative conclusion that these crimes are entirely non-existent and that something else happened, close to forty years ago, which my client is entirely unaware of, but for which he is being blamed by his accuser. The accusations of sexual assault are merely a device for his revenge, as it were."

I'd slipped, without noticing it, into the refuge of formal, legal English. It seemed appropriate. I realised, as I concluded my brief monologue, that other people knew where I was, that at least one ex-gangster and at least one police officer were aware of my location. I saved that for later use.

Mrs Hargreaves nodded. "And how does that concern us here at Restoration, Mr Williams?" she asked.

"Well, the trial is going to be long and complicated,

probably quite a high profile affair." It had occurred to me that *high profile* might help, too. If I gave the impression that I was a name to be reckoned with, they might assume my disappearance would leave some uncomfortable ripples behind. And people who hid behind walls and locked doors and giants tended not to like publicity. "And it would be best for all concerned if matters could be concluded before it reaches that point. So I and my colleagues have been investigating the financial affairs of the gentleman who's made the accusations – a Mr Van der Lee – and we've found that he's been making substantial payments to this business for the last few months."

I kept a close watch on her as I said the name, *Van der Lee*, but she showed nothing at all, not a smile or a widening of the eyes or even a blink. She might have been manning the reception desk, or whatever the Restoration Company equivalent of a reception desk was, but she was a lot more than the receptionist.

"Now, my colleagues are aware of my visit to your –" I looked around the room again, searching for the word, and found it – "establishment, although I understand the police haven't reached the same point in their own enquiries. It would be immensely helpful," I continued, "if you could let me know precisely what Mr Van der Lee has been paying you for. I assure you I have no interest in anything else that goes on here. No interest whatsoever."

I stopped and set my mouth and fixed her with what I hoped was a confident, appraising look. I'd done all I could. I'd made it clear, I hoped, that I knew there were things hidden inside the building that might not be entirely above board. I'd made it clear that I didn't care. All I was interested in was Van der Lee.

Mrs Hargreaves nodded, briefly, and rose from her chair.

"Come with me, please," she said, and a shadow fell

241

over me as one of the giants approached. I'd be going with Mrs Hargreaves, then.

I followed her to a door at the far end of the hall, down a short corridor to another room, an expensively-furnished but otherwise entirely normal-looking office. The giant stayed two steps behind me the whole way. Mrs Hargreaves invited me to sit – a small sofa this time, against a wall, with a coffee table beside it, and asked me if I wanted some tea or coffee.

My mouth, I realised, had gone dry. "Some water, if you don't mind," I said.

Mrs Hargreaves turned and walked back the way she'd come. The giant followed her. They hadn't shut the door, the pair of them, I could, if I'd wanted to, have got up and walked away, made it as far as the front door, out of the front door, with luck, and as far from the Restoration Company, Leeds, Limited, as my wits and strength and resources could take me. Except the other giant was probably still there, still standing by the front door waiting for me to do precisely that. I was probably closer to the small white door at the back of the building than the one at the front, but I didn't know the layout of the building or whether that door was locked, and if I couldn't get out fast I probably wouldn't get out at all. The giant who had followed us had no doubt taken up position by the back door, anyway.

I was trapped. I was sitting in an office surrounded by people who might be Russian mafia, might be anything, really, but whoever they were, they needed high security and anonymity and were prepared to maintain that anonymity at all costs. I'd just walked in and fired a bunch of stupid questions at them. And now I was trapped.

At least I wasn't in London, I thought. At least I wasn't watching my back, checking John Evans wasn't following me, knowing without a shadow of a doubt that he *was* following me and that when my guard was down he'd be at me again, boots and fists and the rest, and I tried to laugh, but I couldn't, because John Evans wasn't a killer, I was sure of it, and these people, this Restoration Company, they might well be killers. They had the calm certainty of people who'd do whatever it took to get what they wanted, and if it took killing, killing it would be. I'd have taken John Evans and his fists and boots over a quiet chat with Mrs Hargreaves every day.

She returned a minute later, a jug of iced water in one hand and a glass in the other, and poured the water in the glass and put the glass in my hand and sat down opposite me and frowned, the first sign of anything other than cold calculation she'd shown.

"Tell me, Mr Williams," she said. "What precisely do you know about the Restoration Company?"

I leaned forward and took a breath.

"Nothing," I said. "I don't have the faintest idea about your company other than the name and the location and the fact that Pieter Van der Lee has recently started paying you five thousand pounds a month. I don't even know what you do, what the name's about, what you actually restore."

She smiled again, a surprising smile, one with a warmth I hadn't thought she possessed.

"People, Mr Williams," she said, and nodded, the smile still on her face. "We restore people."

24: Déjà Vu

I MUST HAVE given myself away, my surprise, the relief that had flooded through me with her smile, even if I didn't understand her words, because she laughed, suddenly, and I noticed the glass in my hand and realised I hadn't drunk a drop of it yet. I took a sip as she continued.

"Would you like me to explain, Mr Williams? We don't usually like to let people know what we do here, but I have a feeling you're not the type to give up easily."

I nodded. *We restore people.* It didn't make sense, but it didn't sound like the mafia or like anyone who would kill me sooner than let me walk out alive, and suddenly, neither did Mrs Hargreaves herself.

"You're a lawyer, you said. You must have come across plenty of people who seem like a blot on society, when the truth is they're its victims. People with potential but no opportunity. People who made the wrong choice, once, and haven't had the chance to correct it."

"Very much so," I replied. I knew the people she was talking about. Half of my clients, since the Mauriers days, had fallen into that category. The other half had made their own decisions and stuck to them willingly, but I didn't think Mrs Hargreaves wanted to hear about them.

My phone rang, a sudden shrill burst from my pocket, an unwelcome intrusion from the outside world. I picked it out, registered Colman's number, and rejected the call. Colman could wait.

"We help those people, Mr Williams," she continued.

"Sam, please."

She nodded. "Sam, then. We restore them. There are shelters for the homeless and rehabilitation centres for alcoholics and drug addicts all over the country, as I'm sure you know. And many of them do an excellent job. But many

244

of them don't. And we – well, I like to think we do a little extra."

"Such as?"

My phone rang again, just as she was about to answer me. Colman, again. I rejected it, again, put my phone back in my pocket, and then I fished it back out and switched it off. For the first time in weeks it felt like I'd managed to get away from my problems. Evans couldn't find me. Even Genaud would struggle. Martins probably didn't care, Claire didn't want anything to do with me, and Trawden could only die once. It was temporary, sure, a brief respite from the fear and confusion that would hit me the moment I set foot outside Restoration, but while I was in here, I'd use it. "I'm sorry," I said. "Please go on."

"As I'm sure you can imagine, a lot of these people have other problems, problems that might be associated with their addictions or not, problems with the police and other authorities, with families, educational issues, that sort of thing. We don't just deal with the drugs and the alcohol. We deal with everything."

It sounded too good to be true. "How on earth do you do that?"

"I'll take it from the beginning, shall I? I'll give you an example. Hypothetical, of course."

"Of course."

"We'll receive a recommendation – usually from a social worker or a police officer –"

"The police know about this place?"

She smiled again. "Of course. The police love us here. We take their problems away. So, someone comes in – we need their consent, they have to come in voluntarily, but we're good at persuading people to give us a chance. They get a full workover. Medical, psychological, the lot. And then we start on the external factors. We speak to their relatives, the victims of their crimes, the local councils and

245

police forces and everyone else with a stake or a concern or just a grievance, and we spend our time and sometimes our money smoothing things over."

"What do you mean, smoothing things over?"

"Well, at the most basic level, we'll persuade a retailer to drop a shoplifting prosecution. We'll get the council to stop hounding someone for unpaid tax. It's easiest with individuals, people who've been robbed, that sort of thing, they're not some faceless business, so they can make up their own minds, and we can usually convince them that it's in no one's interest to keep going after our clients. We get in touch with employers, where it's appropriate, and we try to work with them so they can give our clients a second chance and a leave of absence while they're rebuilding themselves. And then there are the emotional issues. We speak to spouses, parents, children. We find out what interaction there's been, what these people have been doing, what they haven't been doing. We facilitate reconciliations where that's both possible and desirable, and where we think it isn't, we make sure there's a clean break and support for our client."

"Where are they? These clients?"

"They're here, for the most part. We don't take on more than fifteen at any one time. They have their own rooms, their own privacy, there are common areas, too, there's entertainment for them, and we bring in teachers and vocational trainers for those who could benefit from them."

"And they don't leave the place?"

"Oh, they can leave. When they first arrive, they sign up to our contract. That usually entails not leaving the premises for a certain period – it might just be forty-eight hours, while we're evaluating them, it might be weeks or even months if we think they need more time to prepare for healthy interaction with the outside world."

And I'd mistaken these people for the Russian mafia. I

smiled, at the thought, and she caught my smile and frowned.

"Does this amuse you?"

"Not at all. I'm impressed. I'd like to hear more. It's just – well, when I saw all the security, and your guards –"

"Welfare assistants."

"Your welfare assistants – well, I must admit, I had the sense you were some kind of organised crime outfit. Russian mafia. Something like that."

She laughed. "I hope I've set your mind at rest on that score."

"Very much so."

"We're entirely above board. Nothing dubious going on here."

"And how can you afford it?" I gestured around myself, at the tasteful, expensive fittings, at the door and what lay beyond it. I wanted to believe her. But the place stank of money. And money made me twitchy.

"Restoration began life as a private clinic." She shrugged, almost in apology. "A refuge for the wayward sons and daughters of the rich and famous. But times have changed, Mr Williams. Sam. The rich and famous aren't as selfish as they used to be. One of our alumni decided it wasn't right for the benefits of a place like this to be withheld from those without the resources to get in. She persuaded others of the merits of her cause. Between them, they set up a foundation, which funds a number of things, including the *pro bono* work we do on this site. In addition to the income we receive from the foundation, we have access to certain charitable donations, and we means-test the clients – where they can pay, or their families are willing to pay, we charge them. But apart from that, it's free. And as I was saying, we don't keep them in all the time. Reintegration is an important part of what we do. Our clients need to be able to get out. They need to go to work,

247

if they have jobs, to go for interviews if they don't, they need to see family, if it's right for them to do so. That's the deal we make with them. We'll get you back on your feet. In return, no drugs or alcohol. We're strict on that. And our results – well, I don't like to boast, but our results are incredible. We've been operating this model for eighteen years, and we have figures for rehabilitation and recidivism that even we find difficult to believe."

"And that's why the police like you," I said, drawing the connection between their success and their popularity.

"Precisely. Put bluntly, we keep the crime rate down."

"And what's Van der Lee's role in all this?"

She shook her head. I'd thrown the question out fast, as if it followed naturally from everything else we'd been talking about, and hoped she'd answer it without thinking, but Mrs Hargreaves – she hadn't, I realised, reciprocated on my first-names offer – was too smart for that.

"One other thing we offer our clients is complete confidentiality," she said.

"So there's a client involved?"

"I think we've taken up enough of your time, Mr Williams – Sam. Don't you?"

I shrugged, defeated. I hadn't got everything I'd hoped for. But things, I felt, were starting to come together.

I turned on the phone as I walked away from the building – Mrs Hargreaves had accompanied me to the door, and one of the giants, the blonde one, had opened it for me with a flourish that didn't suit his frame.

Five missed calls, all from Colman. And one text, from Fothergill, *Please do everything you can to find the child, Sam, this is important, possibly even more important than my case*. He was right, I felt; the child and the case were bound together – if we got to the heart of one, I was sure we'd crack the other. I found Colman's number again and hit dial, and then looked up and cancelled.

There was a man walking towards me on the pavement. He was twenty, thirty metres away, moving slowly, looking around himself and down at the ground. He hadn't noticed me yet, but in a few seconds or less, he would.

It was Van der Lee.

I stopped and tried to think of a line, but I didn't have time for anything convincing, and after my performance in his bar he wouldn't believe anything I told him anyway. I'd been ready for anything, right up to the Russian mafia, but I hadn't expected Van der Lee himself, which was careless.

He looked up. I could see him trying to place me, could pinpoint the precise moment, the exact fraction of the specific second in which recognition dawned and his expression, confused with an undertone of sullenness, turned to rage. He took four paces towards me and without thinking I adopted a defensive stance, left foot forward, elbows in, fists up by my jaw. Then he stopped and turned and stormed back the way he'd come, so fast I had to adopt a half-walk, half-jog, just to keep up. He kept going for a hundred yards or so, then turned a corner, and I slowed down. There was little point following the man halfway through Leeds, and if he kept the same pace up he'd lose me before long.

As it transpired, I didn't have to follow him halfway through Leeds after all. I'd all but given up on Van der Lee and returned my attention to my phone when I noticed movement in a parked car in front of me and to my left. It was him. I stopped, instinctively, and took a step back towards the driveway of the nearest house. I crouched down, not that the open air offered much by way of cover, and crept forward, and found that the lack of cover didn't really matter.

Van der Lee had his face in his hands. His shoulders were moving up and down, jerking fast and uncontrollably.

I couldn't hear anything through the thick glass windows of his year-old BMW, but it was clear even from here that he was sobbing.

I turned and walked away, back round the corner, stopped and tried to consider my options. I could go home, pretend I'd seen nothing, pretend none of this had happened. Or I could take a chance and approach the man directly.

I stood there for a minute and turned over those options and the possible outcomes of each. I'd made up my mind and taken the first steps back towards the corner and what might end up being another one of Van der Lee's fists when my phone rang again. I cursed, looked down, expecting Colman, saw Maloney, and answered, because I'd learned over the years that Maloney never called without something to say.

"I'm sending you something. You'll want to see it."

I was walking backwards, back out of sight of Van der Lee's car. "See what?" I asked, keeping my voice low.

"We followed her."

"What do you mean?"

"Claire. She went out again. We followed her."

"I thought I told you to drop it. I'm sure I told you to drop it."

"Yeah, you told me to drop it, I didn't drop it, so it's on me, right? You didn't know."

"Why?"

"Why didn't I drop it? Because you were right. She was hiding something. She needs watching."

I sighed. "Okay then. So you're still following her. Where's she been."

"Milton Keynes."

"Milton Keynes? What the hell's in Milton Keynes?"

"If you stop talking for a second I'll tell you."

He was right. I pushed back the next question I'd been

about to ask and waited.

"Right. She drove to Milton Keynes. Took your car. New housing development just on the outskirts. Parked outside a house, looked like all the others. Rang the doorbell. Bloke answered. She went in, spent half an hour, came out alone."

Thoughts were rushing through my head, flashes of light like a train in a tunnel. Her family? An affair? Maloney had told me to shut up, but he'd gone oddly silent.

"Any idea who the bloke was?" I asked.

"We got a photo of him as he opened the door. I'm sending it to you now."

He killed the call, and a second later I heard the ping as a text hit my inbox. A picture message. My finger hovered over the icon, ready to touch it, but a sense of déjà vu swept over me, without warning, and I paused. I knew it already, I knew what I'd see there, I knew what she'd done.

Not child sexual exploitation. Not human trafficking.

The people she'd gone to see at the NCA ran witness protection. And she might not have got what she wanted out of them, but she'd got it from someone else, because she'd found him.

I touched the icon, and there he was, half-hidden behind a door, but recognisable. A young, dark-haired man – a couple of years older and heavier than he'd been in the last photo I'd seen of him, but there was no doubt. Same face. Same grin. Same carefully trimmed stubble.

Claire had found Jonas Wolf. Claire had been to see Jonas Wolf. She'd been in there half an hour and come out alone.

Last time I'd stopped her. This time I was too late.

Claire had killed Jonas Wolf.

25: Too Late

I STOOD THERE staring at my phone for a full minute before I got moving. I spent most of that minute contemplating my own stupidity. It should have been obvious. She'd tried before. She'd been focussed on Wolf to the point of obsession, she'd tried to kill him, she'd failed. She'd had a breakdown. She'd recovered. She'd started lying to me. And I hadn't drawn the clear conclusion. It was the same obsession driving her again.

The last ten seconds or so I spent admiring her ingenuity. I knew she was smart, I knew she was a good journalist and once she got the bit between her teeth she was close to unstoppable, but witness protection should have been one of the few things that could bring her to a halt.

And then I was running, without any sense of where I was heading, but running back round that corner, past Van der Lee's car. I caught a glimpse of him as I passed, watching me, his head turning to follow my progress, a look of bewilderment on his face.

Thirty seconds later I turned another corner. Traffic was light and my nerves stretched to breaking point, so the sound of a car approaching from behind set off all kinds of alarms. Without slowing, I glanced back over my shoulder, praying that Van der Lee hadn't picked this particular moment for a face-to-face, but it wasn't Van der Lee's grey BMW crawling slowly up the road, it was a battered Citroen with a taxi light on.

Still running, I exhaled hard in relief, and just as the car drew level with me I stepped out into the road, forcing the driver to jerk sharply to the side, and shouted "TAXI!" as loud as my struggling lungs would let me. The car carried on five, ten yards, and then, as if in answer to my prayers, indicated left and pulled over.

"You bloody idiot, I could have killed you," said the driver as I slid into the back seat.

"Sorry about that," I panted. "Could you get me to the station?"

"No problem. Just watch where you're running in future."

I nodded, and he turned back to the road and switched on the radio. More bad memories – the last time I'd been chasing after Claire I'd turned on my own radio and heard the news break about the shooting, Brooks-Powell's death, Trawden's brief stay of execution. I found myself listening intently, certain the next item would be live from Milton Keynes, I could hear the anchor in my head, *and now we go live to our South of England correspondent*, and the reporter on the scene, *this quiet, everyday street just like a thousand others across the country*, the shocked neighbours who'd *never imagined something like that could happen here*, the tight-lipped senior detective telling the world that *at this point all we can say is* nothing at all, or nothing useful, not that it mattered, because I knew what had happened.

Claire had killed Jonas Wolf.

I pulled up Colman's number and dialled, and before I could say anything, before I could tell her the truly important stuff, she was telling me things that didn't matter any more, things that had seemed like everything minutes earlier but were now nothing at all.

"I've been trying to get hold of you for hours," she said.

I tried to interrupt, but all I managed was "Yes, sorry," before she continued.

"I've been talking to Simon," she said. "He's told me everything."

She paused here, and that was my chance, but I was still catching my breath and hadn't known the opportunity was coming, so all I did was gulp back some air and open my mouth before she was going again.

"They're going to arrest Claire. It's Genaud. He's forced it through. Not sure how happy Martins is about it, doubt she gives a fuck, to be honest, although she wouldn't like other people making decisions on her case. But that's not the point," she said, as if I'd insisted it was, "the important thing is they're going to take her in. I know, you're thinking *what about Evans?*" – which I wasn't at all; for the first time in days Evans had been entirely absent from my mind – "and they can't find him, but they're not looking too hard now because they've finally managed to track down someone who was at the scene, the attempted suicide, you know, and she had Evans down to a *T*, even the tattoo, not that you'd forget that, right, and Simon got hold of the chap who wrote the article in the local rag, the *Clarion,* and he said all the witnesses said the same thing, dirty-looking bloke with a spider tattooed across his face, and they couldn't really print the description because it was so distinctive they might as well be naming him if they did," and now I was getting sucked into her narrative to the extent I found myself thinking this was unusually sensitive behaviour for the press, "so now they don't have anyone except Claire," and I closed my eyes for a moment and saw ashes against the lids, specks of white in the darkness, and felt the car slowing and opened them again to see we'd hit traffic and still no sign of Leeds station, "so they're going to pull her in. They're going round to the flat this afternoon," she said, finally, and stopped, and waited for me to answer.

"They won't find her there," I replied. "I – she –"

I was lost for words, suddenly, so full of the one thing I had to say that I couldn't say it.

"Why not?"

"She's gone to Milton Keynes," I managed. "She's gone to kill Jonas Wolf."

"You're taking the piss, right?"

I took a couple of breaths.

"No. No, Vicky. I wish I was."

And then I told her everything Maloney had told me.

"Shit," she said, when I'd done.

"She's miles away, Vicky. I can't get to her the way I got to her in London. And she's been in and come out already. I'm too late."

"You can't be sure."

The car drew to a halt, a swarm of red lights in front, and I exploded into a wild, unfocussed rage.

"Don't be a fucking idiot!" I shouted. "Of course I can be sure! Of course she's killed him! It's the only fucking thing she cares about. And now she's done it."

Silence from the phone. The lights receded and we moved on, slow but steady. I felt the rage ebbing away. I glanced up, and caught the driver staring at me in the rear view mirror. He held the look for a moment, before returning his focus to the road.

"I'm sorry," I said.

"It's okay. I know you're stressed. I'd be stressed. But you've got to try to stay calm while we think our way out of this."

The rage had gone, but in its place was a horrible cold emptiness. *Despair*, I thought. This must be what despair felt like. I wondered why she hadn't said it yet, the obvious thing, the need to alert the authorities, to let someone know, someone other than Vicky Colman, someone who wasn't personally involved, and then it hit me. She wasn't trying to figure out how to get Claire out of trouble. She was trying to figure out how to tell me we had to let the police know Claire was a murderer, where she'd committed her murder, who she'd murdered, why and when and how. She was trying to figure out how to say all that and anticipating my rage, again, anticipating argument and rebuttal and refusal.

255

Colman didn't realise I'd gone past the point of argument miles back. It was too late. I knew it was too late. She couldn't say it, but I could say it for her.

"We've got to tell someone, Vicky. The right people. We have to let them know."

"I know." I'd been right. She almost sighed the words. Relief.

"Who should I call?"

"It's okay, Sam. I'll make the calls. I'll let the right people know and I'll tell you as soon as I find out anything new. Do you have the address?"

I cursed silently – I'd forgotten to ask Maloney for the address, and he'd forgotten to give it to me – and then I held the phone out and flicked to the photo he'd sent me and there it was, Harlington Crescent, MK19, he hadn't forgotten at all. I read it out to Colman, and she said goodbye and promised, again, to let me know as soon as she heard anything. And then she was gone.

At the station I had what felt like my first piece of luck all day, the train pulling in as I dashed onto the platform, the carriage half-empty, a table to myself. Not that it mattered, a small slice of good fortune, being early, being on time, beating the clock. The clock had already beaten me.

I tried calling Claire anyway. My number was no longer blocked, by the sound of it, but it rang and rang and no one answered and when it came to leaving a message, I couldn't think of anything adequate to say. I tried Martins but she was *unavailable*, as she always was when I actually needed to speak to her. I wondered what Colman had said, how she'd put it, who she'd called. Probably not Martins. Probably best I hadn't got through. I tried Roarkes, for all the good speaking to him would do, but his phone rang and rang, too, and he hadn't even bothered to set up his voicemail, so

I gave up on the third attempt. I got hold of Maloney and the two of us had a loud and heated argument about where I should be going and where – I'd checked the stopping points shortly after I'd boarded, and there was no easy way to get to Milton Keynes from Leeds, but I'd decided to leave the train at Stevenage and get a taxi, no matter the cost, there were more important things.

Maloney told me I wasn't thinking straight, she'd already left Milton Keynes, she'd be on her way back to London by now or possibly there already.

"Possibly?" I said, and waited. There was a quality to Maloney's silence, I could hear it even under the noise of the train. Another piece of bad news coming.

"We lost her," he said, finally, and suddenly nothing else mattered, nothing at all, just that I had to find Claire and the one person who should have known where she was didn't.

"These people you've been hiring," I said. "Are they fucking IDIOTS?"

I shouted the word *idiots*, shouted it from behind teeth clenched so tight I could feel them fighting to press through one another and take out my brain. And then, as quickly as it had come, the rage was gone.

"Sorry," I muttered. I glanced around the carriage while I waited for him to answer. Most of the people on it were wearing headphones or lost in their own screens, but three or four were staring at me, looking away as I met their eyes, all but one, a thin, frail-looking lady with a few wisps of white hair escaping from the shawl that covered her head, who returned my look without fear or shame, gazing down her long nose at me and frowning. Maloney was talking again.

"Listen, you need to go to London. If Colman's right that they were looking for her anyway, they might have picked her up already. I'll go to your place. If we can get to her before the police do we can keep her underground until we can figure out what to do."

I couldn't help laughing at that one. "Figure out what to do?"

"Yeah. See if we can get her out of the way for a bit. Till the dust settles."

"She's wanted for murder! Two murders, now. It's a bit late for all that."

I'd forgotten, for a moment, that I was on a train, I'd forgotten the other people, I'd shouted again when I should have been whispering. I glanced around, again, and this time the three or four had become a dozen, and even the old lady averted her eyes when I turned her way. I shrugged, a pointless gesture if ever there was one, and returned to the call.

"Just find her," I said. He started to reply, but my phone gave a beep, and I held it away and checked the screen. "I've got a call coming through," I said. "It's Colman. Maybe she knows something we don't. I'll let you know."

I cut him off, hoping he'd do what I'd asked, and opened the line to Colman.

"It's okay," she said, right away, and even though I didn't know precisely what was okay, whether Claire had committed no murders or just the one, or whether it was something else entirely, I felt my entire body relax and realised I'd been stretched like a guitar string ever since Maloney had first called.

"What do you mean?"

"I spoke to local CID. Didn't want to get Martins involved, certainly didn't want Genaud to hear about it. Gave them the address and even while I was talking to them I could hear people shouting at each other, it was like I'd just hacked NASA or something. They had a team round there in minutes and I insisted on staying on the line the whole time."

258

"And?"

"And Wolf's fine. He answered the door, invited them in, offered them a cup of tea. Must have freaked out the neighbours, armed police in body armour swarming all over their quiet suburban street, but it's okay. They asked him what had happened, who'd been in, and he admitted he'd had a visitor and his cover was shot, but he wouldn't say who it was and he insisted he was fine and not to worry about it. Claire must have been long gone by then, I suppose."

So Wolf was alive.

"What about Genaud? He still wants her for Trawden, right?"

"Yes. We still have that problem."

I liked that *we*. Claire and Colman had met just once and hardly exchanged a word, but Colman knew more about her than even her closest friends. And Colman was on Claire's side. On *our* side.

"What should I do?"

"If she's on her way home, they'll pick her up before she's through the front door. I take it you've been trying to reach her."

"Yes."

"No luck?"

"Right again."

"Go straight to the station then. You can't help her if you're not there. Go straight there and I'll keep trying to find out what's going on. See you later."

"Thanks," I said. I meant it.

There were another ninety minutes until we hit London, and I spent them trying to reach Claire and Roarkes, apologising to Maloney and explaining what had happened, keeping my voice a little lower as my heart rate returned to something approaching normal.

Wolf was alive.

I didn't know what it meant, any of it, I didn't understand even a fraction of what was going on in Claire's mind, but she hadn't killed Wolf, and she'd been with the NCA the day Trawden had died, the very hour he'd died, and despite what Colman and everyone else seemed to think, I knew she hadn't *arranged* that one either.

Of course, knowing that and proving it were two very different things.

As we hit the London suburbs I thought about trying Martins again and decided against it. Genaud might be enemy number one, but Martins wasn't too far down that list herself. It didn't matter, anyway: my phone was out of juice and I didn't have a charger with me. So I spent the last half hour staring out of the window as familiar landmarks raced by, places I'd driven past, streets and corners I'd walked on, stations I'd staggered to, drunk and uncertain where I was, at unpalatable times of day.

I was up and off the train the moment it came to a halt, grateful I didn't have a suitcase with me, hit the tube, and emerged two hundred yards from Martins' station barely fifteen minutes after I'd arrived at Kings Cross.

"Can I help you?" asked a young woman I hadn't seen before, standing at the small desk I'd waited behind the first time I'd been to visit Martins, in the wake of Elizabeth Maurier's murder.

"It's okay, I can see myself in," I said, sidestepped her in the very spot Evans had shoved me with his shoulder, and hit a corridor that I hoped was the same one I'd been through before, the one that would lead me to Martins' interview room and, I suspected, Claire. I kept on walking, kept my head down, expecting a challenge from the side or in front at any moment, but when it came it was from behind me.

"Ah. I see you're here."

I turned. Martins was standing in the doorway of the room I'd just passed.

"We need to talk about Claire."

"I'm sure we do," she replied. "I don't believe we had an appointment, Sam."

"I think we're a little past that, Olivia," I said, and she grinned. I looked for the wolf in that grin, but I couldn't be sure it was there. Maybe she was just getting better at hiding it.

"Not to worry. Come on through."

"Is she here?" I asked, and was answered by another voice, from behind me – from the direction I'd been heading in initially.

"No," it said.

I took a step towards Martins, away from that voice, and turned. Genaud wasn't smiling. Genaud didn't need to smile to get my nerves going. Even blank-faced, he had the look of a man who'd rip your leg off just to get your shoe. "No, she's not here yet. I'm not sure you should be here yourself, though – unless you're representing the suspect?"

He smiled now, and all the wolf I'd been looking for in Martins was there in that smile. I shook my head.

"I just need to speak to her – to you, to all of you." I was floundering. I didn't have a plan, I hadn't been able to make a plan because I didn't have a clue what was really going on, and I needed time alone with Claire to find out.

"I should probably tell you just to fuck off out of my station," he said, and I heard a noise behind me, the sound of air being sucked in between teeth, a bitter sound I associated with Roarkes more than anyone else, and I turned, but it was just Martins. "Your girlfriend'll be along in a minute," continued Genaud. "We sent uniform round to get her, but she wasn't at the flat – I suppose you knew that, right? But it didn't matter. She called half an hour ago and told us she was coming in." More noise, from behind, doors opening and closing, familiar voices. "Ah, speak of the devil," he said, and I turned, and there she was, standing in the middle of the corridor, looking at me, her face unreadable.

Behind her, eminently readable, jaw set halfway to resolute but pulled back by a frown that looked somehow apologetic, stood Roarkes.

26: When You Can Get It, You Get It

I STOOD WITH my mouth open for a moment. Roarkes caught my eye and shrugged. Claire remained unreadable – no, that wasn't it. It wasn't that she was unreadable at all. It was that there was no vulnerability, no brittleness, just Claire herself. The real Claire, with a solidity to her I hadn't seen for months. She was still pale – she'd been varying degrees of pale as long as I'd known her – but the fragility had gone.

I turned to Martins, but she seemed as confused as I was, her mouth twisted into a question she wasn't ready to ask. Only Genaud had found his feet.

"What the fuck are you doing here, Roarkes? I thought they had you handing out parking tickets outside the Olympic Stadium."

Roarkes laughed, politely. "It's Wembley, Micky. Otherwise you're almost spot on."

"I don't give a fuck where they've put you out to stud, Roarkes. You can fuck off with everyone else. I've got a warrant for *her*." He jabbed a finger in Claire's direction. "The rest of you can piss off out of my investigation."

Martins finally jerked into life. "*Your* investigation, Detective Inspector? I don't think so. I think you'll find that for all your influence, this is still officially my case. Not that I haven't been grateful for your help."

Genaud turned his face slowly in her direction, adorned with something that looked very much like a snarl. I'd found myself in the surprising position of cheering on Olivia Martins, but I didn't know how long the cheering would last. She wasn't beaten, but from everything I'd seen and heard, Genaud still had the winning hand. And he didn't seem the type to fold lightly

"Yes," said Roarkes, as if nothing had happened, as if

263

the little internecine spat we'd just witnessed were an everyday CID custom, which for all I knew it was. "I quite understand your reluctance to have me here, to have any of us here. And I do get that your interest is in Claire and you don't want anyone else muddying the waters." His politeness was disconcerting, almost mesmerising, and I found myself falling into his rhythm, accompanying his cadence with nods and tiny tilts of the head. "I'm not going to interfere," he continued. "I'm not going to do or say anything, except where I can assist you." That *you*, I noticed, was directed at both of them, at Martins and Genaud. He had a job to do and he couldn't yet be sure who he had to do it on. "And Sam," he turned to me, and I flinched as though he'd delivered a fist instead of my name, "I'm sorry."

More noise from further up the corridor, a door opening and closing, and now Winterman was here, taking up his post beside Martins, arms crossed, ever loyal.

I turned back to Roarkes. *What are you sorry for?* I thought, but I didn't say it. Claire's expression had shifted, she was smiling now, a big blank smile, and I remembered all the powder, all the drugs she hadn't taken, and wondered whether it had all become too much and she'd decided to take them all in one go. A shout from the entrance lobby, and the door swung open yet again, revealing Vicky Colman and the young officer who'd been stationed at the front desk, standing behind Colman and wearing a nervous, apologetic smile. Genaud swore under his breath. Martins laughed.

"You too?" she said. "Christ. We might as well put up a bloody board outside. Open to the fucking public." The words were angry. The voice wasn't. "Come on," she continued. "There's an interview room down here that'll probably squeeze us all in."

"This is ridiculous," muttered Genaud, but he turned as

Martins walked past him and fell into step ahead of me, ahead of Roarkes and Claire, ahead of Colman and Winterman, who were eyeing one another suspiciously. I turned to catch Claire's eye and she looked away immediately, the way the people on the train had looked away, and I wondered whether I'd turned myself into a pariah. I turned to Roarkes instead.

"What did you mean? What are you sorry about?"

He shrugged, and then, like Claire, like everyone else, he looked away.

We followed Martins into an interview room, a larger version of the one she'd questioned me in twice, but otherwise close to identical. There was one table and four chairs, but no one made a move towards any of them. Instead we stood, all of us, alone or in little groups, Martins and Winterman to one side of the desk, Roarkes and Claire to the other, Genaud standing by the door scowling, me in the corner. Colman shot a look at me that told me she didn't understand what was going on any more than I did, and made her way over to my corner, which felt surprisingly reassuring.

"Right," said Genaud, but Roarkes had come for a reason and wasn't going to let anyone, even Genaud, get in his way.

"If you don't mind delaying the actual questioning for a few minutes, I have something I need to show you." Again, he was switching his attention between Genaud and Martins, hedging his bets, unsure, still, who was going to come out on top. "Sam, you'll want to see this too. It might explain a few things."

"Like fuck we're delaying things," said Genaud. Now he was angry, properly angry as opposed to merely aggressive, and I detected a hint of an accent, something northern, but as far from the soft Yorkshire roll of Claire and her family as you could get. Further north. Border country. Further than that, perhaps. "I've waited long enough to get her in." He pointed, again, at Claire, and I expected her to recoil, at least to flinch, but instead she just smiled and I thought again about the drugs.

"You've hardly waited at all, Genaud." Martins seemed to be enjoying this new role, the reasonable one, and I wondered whether it might suit her better than the bad cop she'd been playing. I remembered the first time I'd heard her voice, through a mobile phone in a service station telling me Elizabeth Maurier was dead and asking me what I'd been talking to her about. I'd heard it then, the false depth, a magician's prop in reverse, the sense of a hidden chamber when the reality was nothing more than what was in front of you. She'd always played a role. "I'm the one who's been running this case."

"Great fucking job you've done of it," grunted Genaud, and Martins smiled at him, and his scowl deepened.

"The fact is," she continued, "that we have our suspect here now, and she's not going anywhere until we let her go, so it won't do any harm to hear what her – Roarkes, what precisely is your role in this?"

Roarkes shrugged again. I was starting to get sick of his shrugs. "Just a friend."

"Right," said Martins. "A *friend*. Well, let's listen to what Ms Tully's *friend* has to say for himself, see if it sheds any light on proceedings, and if it doesn't, you can go and get your thumbscrews. Okay?"

Genaud threw his hands up in disgust, but he didn't say anything.

"Thank you," said Roarkes. "Have any of you seen the news in the last fifteen minutes?"

I shook my head. Everyone else followed suit, except Genaud, who said "Of course fucking not." Colman tapped me on the shoulder and I bent down so she could whisper

266

in my ear.

"I saw them waiting outside, looking at Claire's phone. They must have been waiting for this, whatever it is."

I nodded and looked up. Roarkes was looking at me, at me and Colman, waiting. I nodded again, at him, and he put his phone down on the desk, face up.

"If you wouldn't mind watching this," he said. We edged forward, closer to the desk so that we could see the phone. I heard another grunt of disgust from Genaud, but he moved with the rest of us, craning over Winterman's shoulder for a better view.

The screen was paused on a familiar red and white logo, the BBC breaking news symbol that had brought me reminders of David Brooks-Powell's death, Serena Hawkes' death, sad tale after sad tale. I looked up at Claire again, that disturbing calm and sincerity seeping through every pore, and prayed I wasn't going to be seeing more of the same now.

Roarkes hit play. The view cut to the studio, a woman I didn't recognise reading straight to camera, with the screen behind her showing an image of the scales of justice. I prayed a little harder. The woman on the screen started talking.

We are just getting news of simultaneous raids in four locations in connection with a long-running human trafficking investigation.

I glanced up. Claire had turned to look at me, and her smile seemed to broaden still further, to include me in it, somehow. I turned back to the screen,

We understand that three arrests have been made and police are still looking for one further individual. The case is said to involve the smuggling of women and girls, some as young as fifteen, from a number of countries into the United Kingdom, where they were sold to the highest bidders. It is thought that in at least three cases, the women were subsequently murdered.

I switched my attention to Claire. The serenity was

there, but I'd been wrong about the blankness. She was intent and focussed. Just not on anything in the room.

What makes this case particularly unusual is the nature of the information which led to these raids being carried out. Reliable sources have informed us that a witness, living under police protection and with no further obligations to the authorities or charges pending, approached the police voluntarily with the identities and addresses of his former colleagues, and agreed to testify against them.

Roarkes hit pause.

There was a moment's silence, and then Genaud telling us he didn't give a fuck about any of this and Martins shouting him down and Roarkes apologising, again, and Colman laughing, actually laughing, as if this were all just the punchline to a long and painful joke.

I looked at Claire. Claire looked at me. There was a question in her smile now. The shouting and apologising and laughing died away, and in the quiet that followed I spoke.

"I thought," I said, but I didn't know how to end it. I wasn't sure what I'd thought. That she'd killed Wolf, at first. That she was going to kill Wolf, if she hadn't already.

"I know what you thought," she replied, the first words she'd spoken since her arrival at the station.

"I thought you were going to…" I continued, and stopped again.

"Yes, I know." The smile had gone, and I couldn't tell what she was feeling, if she was condemning me for what I'd imagined, if this a continuation of the last argument we'd had, or something new. "But I'm past that."

"You never said. You didn't say a thing."

"I wasn't ready to talk. I told you that."

"Are you ready now?"

She paused and looked around the room, as if realising only at that moment that we weren't alone, that we'd been having this conversation across five other people, all of them police officers.

"I think so."

Something had occurred to me, while she pondered my question, and now I had one of my own.

"This wasn't the first time, was it? The first time you've been to see Wolf? They've made the arrests. They couldn't have done all that if you'd only just got him on board."

She shook her head. "No. Today was a formality, really. I wanted to tell him it was about to go ahead and make sure he hadn't changed his mind."

"I can't believe it."

She pointed to Roarkes' phone, the image paused, the woman on it turning to face the screen behind her. "You've just seen it. It's real."

"I'm proud of you," I said. I meant it. She smiled, again, not the vague smile or the intense smile of earlier, but her old smile, Claire's smile, the smile I'd fallen in love with.

"It's justice, isn't it?" she replied. "Not always. Not for everyone. But when you can get it, you get it, right? Like Maxine. Like Fothergill."

So she'd been listening to me. All those weeks and months when I'd thought she was just nodding away, hearing a quarter of what I said and caring about a quarter of that, she'd been listening all along.

And then the spell was broken.

"Can someone please tell me," asked Genaud, "why I should give a fuck about any of this?"

I looked to my side. He was bent over the table, jabbing his finger at the phone, his bald patch on display. I raised my eyes to Martins, opposite him, her face curled into a frown that cleared, as I looked at it, into a semblance of a smile. She was starting to get the point. Roarkes cleared his throat.

"You should give a fuck, Genaud, because this goes to

269

the heart of Miss Tully's alibi."

"She doesn't have an alibi!"

"No, she didn't *tell* you her alibi because there were sensitive, important matters to be dealt with and she couldn't be sure you were going to keep your mouth shut. Any of you." Roarkes stood back and turned to include Martins in his address, and her eyes widened as if affronted. "Here," he continued, and pulled a sheet of paper out of his pocket, dark where it had creased. "Don't worry. This is just a copy. It's a written statement from various senior figures at the National Crime Agency confirming Miss Tully's whereabouts at the time of Trawden's murder."

He stretched to pass the paper to Martins, but Genaud reached in and grabbed it, unfolded it, scanned it, grunted and handed it to Martins himself. She read it out loud.

"At least four officers were witness to Miss Tully's presence on NCA premises on the seventeenth of January between the hours of noon and one pm. Her appearance was memorable in that she obtained access to the building without an appointment or appropriate clearance, demanded sensitive information, refused to leave voluntarily when denied said information, and departed only when threatened with arrest. We understand that Miss Tully subsequently obtained the information she sought, and will be reviewing our internal procedures to ensure that no future breaches occur."

I caught Roarkes' eye as Martins read the final sentence, and he looked away. All that time he'd insisted he couldn't find out what was inside that building, and he'd been the one who'd found it for her. No doubt he'd been the one who'd "subsequently obtained the information", too.

"You knew about this, didn't you?" said Genaud, and I turned to face him, to argue my innocence, but he wasn't looking at me.

He was looking at Martins.

"You've been wasting my fucking time, wasting everyone's fucking time, first Evans, now this." He'd raised his voice, he was shouting, now, and no one had thought to close the door to the interview room. I could hear footsteps outside, more than one set, slowing, taking up station within earshot of our little conversation.

"I knew nothing about this," said Martins. "Why do you think I wanted to focus on Evans? I told you it wasn't Claire, but you wouldn't listen, would you?"

"This isn't over," he replied, turned, and stormed out of the room. I stifled a laugh. Genaud couldn't have been more wrong. Wolf was alive. Claire had the mother of all alibis for Trawden's death. It was over.

Martins herself I couldn't get a read on. Angry, I'd have expected, because Genaud was right. Between them Claire and Roarkes had wasted Genaud's time, but they'd wasted a lot more of Martins'. She was frowning, but there was none of the fury I'd seen in her before and knew she was capable of, none of the rage she'd thrown at Colman before she'd kicked her off the team. And she'd not done that thing with her tongue, either, the slow glide along her lip that made me so uncomfortable.

"Thanks," she said. She was looking at Colman.

"Thanks for what?" replied Colman.

"For getting my message through to Sam."

"What are you talking about?"

"Winterman told you Genaud was pulling Claire in, right?"

Colman looked at Winterman, who gave a brief nod.

"Yes," said Colman.

"And who do you think told Winterman?"

"Well, you did, obviously."

"In the knowledge the message would reach you and you'd pass it on to Sam. Look, I knew something was going on. Not this, obviously." She gestured at the NCA

271

statement, on the desk beside the phone. "All this is playing hell with my brain. But there was more to Claire's shit alibi than sitting around doing nothing. I didn't want it to be you," she was talking to Claire now, "and I'm glad it wasn't, but Genaud said he was going to send you down and I wanted your boyfriend there to make sure nothing happened that shouldn't happen. Turned out we didn't need you, Sam."

"You were just using me to get to Sam? And you knew about this?" Colman had turned to Winterman, hands on hips, a look on her face that said it would be good for Winterman if he didn't and better still if he was a hundred miles away. Winterman shrugged, nervously, and edged an inch or two away from her.

"Leave it, Colman," said Martins. "You were using Winterman to get information out of me, out of everyone else as far as I can tell, I knew it, he knew it, so don't stand there and play the innocent. I could have called Sam directly, but I'd warned him about Genaud before, he knew about Genaud, he knew about the interest in Claire, and besides, I reckoned I'd used up all my goodwill with him. You wouldn't have believed me, would you?"

I shook my head. If Martins had called me up and told me they were pulling Claire in I'd have worried, sure, but I'd have put it down to another one of her games, a threat or a promise, the prelude to another deal I wouldn't want to make and couldn't be sure she'd keep her side of. She'd been right to come at me through Colman.

Winterman glanced at his watch, tapped Martins on the shoulder and whispered in her ear. She nodded. He left without another word, glancing back at Colman and turning quickly away again when he saw the look on her face.

"No, the more interesting thing is Claire's alibi and who knew about it and why they didn't tell me in the first place," continued Martins. She'd turned to face me, the familiar annoyance etched across her face.

"I didn't know. You think if I'd known I'd have let it get this far?"

"But *you* did." She was looking at Roarkes. Then back to me. "And even if you didn't know about this nonsense with Jonas Wolf, you knew something. You lied to me. As for you," to Claire, now, "you've been lying from the start, and you might think you've had good reasons, but I could have the lot of you charged with wasting police time, for starters. Might even get that jazzed up to perverting the course of justice, obstructing an officer, the kind of thing even you wouldn't want on your record, Sam."

"You won't, though," said Roarkes, and suddenly she smiled at him and shook her head.

"No. I won't."

Roarkes hadn't finished.

"There's something else, Sam."

He was wearing a sheepish look that didn't suit him. "Another apology?" I asked.

He nodded. "I've only just found out myself, so you can't really blame me."

"You'd be surprised what I can blame you for."

He smiled and raised his hands in a gesture of acknowledgement. He was, I reflected, very fortunate that everything seemed to have turned out fine.

"The NCA had a report. A man watching their building."

I met his eyes and flicked mine towards Martins. She didn't know I'd followed Claire that day. She didn't know my alibi was as rotten as anyone else's. She might not be so willing to forget those charges if she found out. Roarkes cleared his throat.

"Anyway, they're nervous about that sort of thing. So they sent someone to watch you."

"Who?" I asked, before I realised. The grey-haired man.

Not Evans. Nothing to do with Evans.

"Some guy. I don't know. Eventually they joined up the dots, connected you with Claire, decided you were harmless and called him off."

And there was me thinking it was my move to Maloney's that had buried my tail. We stood there, the five of us, watching one another, watching nothing at all, letting everything we'd heard and said sink in.

"You're not the only ones with work," said Colman, suddenly, breaking what was starting to become an uncomfortable silence. "Got to run."

I thanked her. Claire did, too. "Well done," said Roarkes, as she walked past him, and she nodded but didn't reply.

"Good work, officer," said Martins, but she didn't even get the nod.

I pulled out the chair nearest me and sat down. Four people, four chairs. The others followed suit a moment later. The door was still open, and we could hear shouts from outside, the sound of something hitting a wall, the sound of a door slamming shut. Martins smiled.

"Genaud's used to getting his own way," she said. "Useful lesson for him, this."

"Watch your back, Detective Inspector," said Roarkes.

She nodded. "I will. Colman did well, then, did she?"

"Yes," I replied, and Roarkes said the same thing at the same time, and Martins nodded again and rested her cheek in one hand. It had been a long few days.

"You know, don't you?" she asked. She was looking at me again.

"Know what?"

"Who killed Trawden."

I shook my head. "No. I don't know and I don't think we ever will. I don't really care, either. It wasn't me and it wasn't Claire, it wasn't Evans, that'll do for me."

She frowned at me, and shrugged. "I suppose you're right. We're out of suspects. Through the A list, anyway, and the B list is so long we'll never have the resources to get through them. We'll keep the case open for a while, but only for form's sake. It's not like anyone really cares."

We left a minute later. I held back as Martins and Roarkes exited the room, and found Claire beside me. She didn't say anything, but as we walked down the corridor together she threaded her right arm through my left.

We weren't quite finished. The corridor was narrow, and as we approached its end the door in front of us opened and John Evans walked in, a detective behind him. He stopped in front of me and held out his right hand.

"I'm sorry," he said. There was a gentleness to his voice I hadn't expected, not after everything he'd said and done, not after everything else I'd imagined.

I took the hand and shook it, briefly. "Me too," I replied, and he dropped my hand and walked on. I turned to see him enter an interview room, and called out to Martins in front.

"I thought you were done with Evans. Out of suspects, you said."

"We are. Just formalities now. He heard we were after him and handed himself in at the local station, they sent him here, we'll send him home again. Wherever home is. You were right about him, Sam. He's no killer. Wouldn't hurt a flea."

I thought back to the kicking I'd got, to the list with my name on it and all the dead crossed out, and considered arguing, but decided against it. There was no point now. And Martins was still talking.

"It's a shame, really. Addiction, suicide attempts, murderer for a dad, he's got the deck stacked against him, that one. Never really had a chance."

"Come on, you two," called Roarkes, already opening

the door in front of us. "I think we all deserve a drink."

27: Between The Lines

I APPROACHED FOTHERGILL'S street nervously, but I needn't have worried. No fresh graffiti on the wall. No half-dead client on the floor inside.

It had been two days since we'd left Martins' station, and a day and a half since Claire and I had staggered out of the pub, having put a barely-conscious Roarkes in a cab home an hour earlier, and with unspoken agreement gone back to the flat together and to the bed together and barely left it since. I'd made some comment, the following morning, about going back to Maloney's to pick up the rest of my things and she'd shaken her head.

"No, not yet."

"Can't live without me?"

"It's not that, Sam. It's lovely having you back."

"It's lovely being back."

She laughed. "But I'm not ready to have you *back* back, if you see what I mean."

"So what am I doing here now? What was I doing last night?"

"You're staying over. And you can stay over tonight, if you want. It's just –"

I'd leaned over and kissed her, stopping her in her tracks, and not broken the kiss for nearly a minute.

"I understand," I said, when we finally came up for air. "You're not ready to call this a permanent thing. I hope I'm not waiting too long, mind."

"Me too," she replied, and pulled me in for another kiss.

We'd left the bed for food, for drinks, and for personal hygiene. I'd left it to take a few calls and make a few more.

The first surprise was Evans. I recognised the number and hesitated for a moment, but I figured if I didn't answer now he'd just keep ringing until I did.

"Can we meet, please?" he said.

"What for? Going to beat me up again?"

He laughed, but he didn't apologise. "No. I just need to talk to you."

I looked over at Claire – I hadn't left the room for this one, hadn't seen it coming. "Maybe," I replied. "I'm not ready. Not yet. I'll call you."

Claire asked who'd been on the phone, and I explained, and she understood my reluctance, and everything felt like it had felt months earlier, when things were normal, before Wolf had appeared, before Trawden had resurfaced.

Except my stuff was still at Maloney's.

The next call was even more of a surprise, so much so that I stood up the moment I realised who I was talking to, and found myself reaching down and grabbing the side of the bed for support.

"Mr Williams?"

I took a few breaths, enough to regain my sense of balance and reality, and stepped outside the room.

"Mr Van der Lee. I really wasn't expecting to hear from you."

A nervous laugh echoed down the line, and I tried to picture it in the mouth of the man who'd delivered that punch into my stomach. I couldn't. And then I saw him again, on Karen Hobart's screen, in his interview, and it seemed more fitting.

"I'd like to see you."

I took a sharp breath, removed the phone from my ear and stared at it. I didn't recognise the number, but that was Van der Lee's voice alright.

"You didn't seem so keen last time. In your bar."

Only after I'd said the words did I remember that the last time I'd seen him hadn't been in his bar, but outside

Restoration, sobbing and staring in confusion as I ran past like a man possessed.

"Things have changed, Mr Williams. You know about Restoration."

"I know a little. I don't know much."

Not my usual tactic – I'd always had success pretending I knew more than I really did. But something in his voice told me this wasn't a battle that needed winning.

"If you're willing, I'd like to talk face to face. And I'd like you to bring Mr Fothergill with you, if he's amenable."

"Will your lawyer be present?"

"No. I don't think that's necessary."

I felt something in my neck and back, a sense that things were either unravelling or coming together, but I couldn't work out which it was. This was either very good or very bad. I stalled.

"Are you sure that's a good idea?"

"I've thought it through."

"It's not exactly protocol, in these matters," I said. I wanted to blurt it out, to tell him the very fact of this meeting would destroy his case, but I opted for something softer instead. "I'm not sure the CPS would approve."

"I looked you up, Mr Williams. You're not really one for protocol yourself, are you?"

"I'll speak to Fothergill. See if I can persuade him. Where would you like to meet?"

Oxford, I assumed. Somewhere mutually convenient, for the two of them at least.

"Leeds. The Restoration Company. Tomorrow, if you can."

I confirmed his number and told him I'd call him back. I tried, when I called Fothergill a minute later, to dampen things, but there was no dampening the man. He'd been at me to get things done and find things out since the moment he'd heard about the child, an obsession that seemed to

279

have become more important to him than the case, than his own future. He was more than happy to meet his accuser. I called Van der Lee back and fixed on a time. And by ten o'clock next morning I was parking the car outside Fothergill's house.

He emerged before I'd got the handbrake on, carrying a small paper bag and a bottle of water. I looked at them as he opened the passenger door and climbed in.

"Sandwich," he said. "I don't like those service stations."

I hadn't brought my own packed lunch, so after a couple of hours steady driving and idle conversation Fothergill had to endure Woodall Services after all, looking on with an air of disgust as I wolfed down a KFC meal and picked up a bar of chocolate and some crisps.

"Want some?" I asked, pulling open the salt and vinegar as I hit the motorway again.

"No, I don't think so."

"Why did you appoint me?"

We were doing a steady fifty through the roadworks, but the road was quiet, and I risked a glance to my side as I asked. He was frowning, turning things over in his mind, trying, no doubt, to work out how he could phrase things sensitively. I decided to make it easy for him.

"I'm under no illusions here, Mr Fothergill. I'm no one's idea of a first class lawyer, particularly when it comes to historic sex crimes. And you're not a fool. You'll have done your homework."

He laughed.

"I did. I did my homework and then some."

"What was wrong with your appointed solicitors?"

"They didn't care. Just wanted me to plead guilty so they could move onto the next thing. They told me it was the environment."

"What environment? What do you mean?"

"The public mood. I'd been named. People knew. And in the *environment*, as they put it, that made me guilty. Whether I was actually guilty or entirely innocent didn't matter. Everyone's going to assume you are. Even, they said, the jury."

I clicked tongue against teeth in disgust and disappointment, and he went on.

"So, as you've surmised, I did my homework. You were cheap, to be frank. But more importantly, you have a reputation for not taking things at face value. And you seem to have a habit of finding out what lies at the heart of things, Mr Williams. I liked that."

I liked that, too. If I couldn't be the best lawyer out there, at least there was something I could hang my hat on.

"And," he continued, "I was right, wasn't I? You found out about the child. You found out about this company, this Restoration place, and whatever it is we're going to learn today, we wouldn't have been learning it if you weren't prepared to look in unusual places."

I found a parking space as close as I could to the Restoration building, but it was still fifty yards, which might, I thought, be a challenge for Fothergill, but the cane was no more than an accessory as he strode along beside me. It was a bright day, the first bright day in months, it felt, and he gazed upon the wide streets of suburban Leeds with an almost childlike wonder. I hoped his optimism wasn't about to be crushed under the weight of Van der Lee's history.

We were greeted by Mrs Hargreaves, both of us by name, and not even a hint that she and I had met before. The blonde giant leaned against the wall beside the main door, and when I caught his eye, he winked at me, which I hadn't been expecting at all.

Mrs Hargreaves showed us into a decent-sized room

281

with a pair of a big sash windows, a couple of doors down from the office she'd spoken to me in. She ushered us inside, but she didn't follow us in.

Van der Lee was waiting for us.

"Sit down," he said to me. He was sitting himself, in an armchair beside an occasional table. There was one other armchair, and a small metal contraption that, of the three of us, was probably best suited to me. I sat. Van der Lee nodded at Fothergill, who approached with his right hand outstretched, but didn't stand or extend a hand himself, and Fothergill retreated to the other armchair, a confused frown on his face, the limp back, suddenly, and the cane more than just a prop. I wondered whether this was real, whether the fast pace of our walk to Restoration had taken more out of him than he'd let on, or whether it was all for effect.

"It's time to let everything out," said Van der Lee, when Fothergill had settled himself down and rested the cane against the side of the chair. "Time for a bit of truth."

"Does this mean you're asking the CPS to drop the charges?"

"That rather depends on the next half hour or so, Mr Williams."

I nodded. I couldn't ask more than that. And as I'd already hinted, the very fact of this meeting, at Van der Lee's instigation, would put a big dent in his case if he did choose to proceed. I glanced out of the window, and Fothergill followed my gaze, towards the willow tree and the unseen stream. The grass shone in the sunlight – if I hadn't known, I might have thought it was August out there, not February.

"Last September I received a package from someone in Lancashire. I don't know who and I don't know why. But it contained some interesting items."

"Elissa Pen –" said Fothergill, but I waved an arm at

him. Van der Lee had the floor. We'd say our bit when it was time.

"There was a letter with it from someone who said they'd known Marine. Marine Lambert. You remember her, don't you?"

Fothergill nodded. Van der Lee continued.

"There was a child. A child I'd never known about. A child whose very existence had been hidden from me until that moment. My son. There were documents, photos, certificates, letters, the usual paraphernalia of a life half-lived. Some of those letters were from you, Mr Fothergill. In fact, it seems you were her most loyal correspondent."

"I did write, yes," said Fothergill, and looked over at me. I shook my head. *Yes* and *No* would suffice, for now.

"Marine was on her own at the time, as far as I can tell. She may have been living with other people, but more out of convenience than friendship or anything meaningful. She was working at a hotel, her pay slips were in the package. Cleaning rooms, that sort of thing. And she was a single mum. But Marine was clever. You remember that?"

"Yes."

Two birds flew towards the willow tree, paused there, briefly, and flew on. Pigeons. A moment later, a man appeared on the path, heading our way. He, too, noticed the birds, and stopped for a moment to follow their progress before continuing along the path. Van der Lee was silent, watching me watching the man watching the birds. The man disappeared from sight. Van der Lee continued.

"She'd have pulled herself back up. She'd have made a success of herself. Might even have come back down, might have let me know where she was, might have let me meet my son, one day. If she hadn't died."

"I'm sorry," said Fothergill, and Van der Lee shot him a look that would have turned sugar sour.

"My son wasn't even two when his mum died."

283

"We know all this, Mr Van der Lee," I said, leaning forward, anxious to move on to the things we didn't know.

"Of course you do," he replied, which threw me, and I sat back again. "I tracked him down. It took a bit of work and a lot of money, but I did it. He'd been through six care homes and eight foster homes. That's fourteen homes with fourteen sets of people. *Fourteen!* Can you imagine that?"

I shook my head. It was a sad story, but it was the same sad story that repeated itself every day, a thousand times, all over the country.

"He didn't turn out well, my son. You wouldn't, would you? Not with that start. When I found him he was on the streets, in Leeds, of all places. He had a criminal record and a drug habit and a justified feeling that the world was against him."

"I'm sorry," said Fothergill, again, but this time Van der Lee didn't look daggers at him. He just ignored him.

"And I hadn't known. Hadn't known about his existence. If I'd known, I'd have found him, I'd have found him when Marine had died, and I'd have taken him in, and none of this would ever have happened."

He stopped, looked out of the window himself, and stayed there, staring at the grass and the willow for what felt like minutes. He turned, finally, to Fothergill, and spoke softly.

"But you knew."

Fothergill's face twisted, lines of bewilderment and disbelief all over it.

"You knew," continued Van der Lee, and suddenly he was crying, heaving, almost choking as he carried on talking through the tears. "I begged her to keep that baby and she said no, she was going to get rid of it, and the next thing I find out she's disappeared, she's left Oxford, even her parents don't know where she is. I didn't know she'd had the baby. I didn't know I had a son. He never had a father.

And for most of his life, he didn't have a mother, either. Look at what this has done to him. It destroyed him."

Cold years, I thought, Eileen Grimshaw's letter hitting me from out of the blue. Cold years for both of them. Fothergill was crying too, now, and I tried to look beyond the frailty and the cane and see if there was anything calculated behind it, but there wasn't. The tears were silent, but real enough, the same tears he'd no doubt shed when he'd read about Marine Lambert's death and withdrawn to his living room, silent, again, so I'd assumed he was just taking a moment to compose himself.

"I didn't know," he said, finally. "I never knew about the boy. Until Mr Williams told me, the other day, I didn't know a thing. I swear it."

"And I thought to myself, this is abuse." Van der Lee was either ignoring Fothergill's protestation of innocence, or he just hadn't heard it. "You abused me. You denied me my child. You abused him. You denied him his father."

"No," said Fothergill. The tears had stopped as suddenly as they'd come, and he spoke quietly and calmly, the years sitting on his words and lending them an air of careful consideration. "I didn't know anything about the child. Please, Mr Van der Lee, listen to me. I knew nothing of him. I knew that Marine was pregnant, that's true. And true, too, that I knew she intended to leave. I tried to persuade her not to, but she wouldn't listen to me. You must remember what she was like. She didn't listen to anyone if they didn't tell her what she wanted to hear."

Van der Lee had been shaking his head, face down to the floor, but he stopped now and glanced up. There had been, I thought, in the moment before he looked back down again, a trace of a smile on his face. A sad smile, but a smile nonetheless.

"She wouldn't listen, Mr Van der Lee. And she wouldn't tell me, either. She wouldn't tell me who the father was, and

285

it wasn't really my place to ask, not more than once, anyway. I thought – it's a terrible thing to hear, and I'm sorry – but I thought I'd convinced her not to have the baby. I thought there was no baby, and even if I'd known there was, I didn't know who the father was so I couldn't have told you anyway."

"What about the letters?"

"What about them?"

"She must have told you."

"You've seen them, haven't you? You've got them. Elissa Pengilly sent them to you."

"Your letters to her. Not hers to you. For all I know there were pages there about the boy, about what he –"

"What was his name?"

I couldn't help the interruption. *The boy, the child, my son*, it was all too impersonal.

"Gregory," replied Van der Lee, and then went on. "She must have mentioned him in her letters. She must have mentioned me."

Fothergill shook his head. "You've seen my letters to her, you say?"

"Yes."

"Have you read them?"

"Yes."

"Is Gregory mentioned there? Even once?"

Van der Lee shook his head, but didn't say anything.

"What does that tell you?" Van der Lee frowned, and Fothergill pressed on. "Don't you think I'd have asked? If she were writing to me about her son, about you, Gregory's father, don't you think I'd have asked after Gregory? Don't you think I'd have made it my business to find out what you were doing and pass the news on?"

Silence, again, from Van der Lee, still staring at the floor, looking up, occasionally, at me, at Fothergill, at the willow tree, and back down again.

286

"Of course I'd have asked, and told, I'd have done all that. But I couldn't, because I didn't know. I didn't know any of this. I didn't even know where she lived – you've seen how I addressed the letters, to a post office box. She wouldn't give me her real address for fear I'd tell her parents where she was. And then the letters stopped, and I assumed she'd just got bored of me, because who's interested in writing to their old music teacher when they're grown up and have a life of their own, Mr Van der Lee? I had no idea about Gregory. I had no idea Marine had died."

Van der Lee stood, and before I'd fully registered the movement, he'd advanced to where Fothergill sat, head in his hands, unaware of the figure standing over him until he saw the shadow at his own feet. I started to stand up myself, sure that this was it, that the same punch that had bruised me and left me aching for a day or two would drop Fothergill to a place he wouldn't be getting up from. Van der Lee's right hand began its descent, and I was halfway across the floor when I saw it wasn't shaped into a fist.

An open hand. An open right hand.

It had fallen so slowly, before I'd known what it was, but now, suddenly, it was on Fothergill's shoulder, clasping, hard but not, from Fothergill's reaction, painfully so.

Tears fell from two faces. Fothergill's own right arm was out, now, and Van der Lee had sunk to his knees, and both of them muttering the one word over and over again, at first in response to each other and then together and then drifting apart again, so that the overall effect was something akin to a Gregorian chant, something deeper and bigger than the word itself.

Sorry.

They stayed like that for a few minutes, the word coming quieter and less frequently as time went on, until finally Van der Lee turned to me and said it again.

287

"I'm sorry, Mr Williams."

"What for?"

"For punching you."

I laughed. "I was in your bar. I'd sneaked in and I didn't even have the brains to come up with a false name. I deserved the punch."

"Not then." He shook his head. "London."

I gaped.

"I think I might have kicked you, too," he continued. "I really am sorry."

"That was you?" I asked, struggling to connect what should have been obvious. Van der Lee had already hit me once. Evans had shoved me with his shoulder and grabbed my arm. If I hadn't been obsessed with Evans, with anything that would justify Martins' looking away from Claire, I'd have known from the start it was Van der Lee.

He nodded. "It was a difficult time. You'd left that message about Marine. I didn't know what you knew and what you were going to do with the knowledge."

I rubbed my ribs, remembering the kicks, remembering how I'd felt afterwards. I smiled.

"Well, these things happen," I said. "Let's call it quits."

I hadn't noticed the pot of tea on the table beside Van der Lee's chair, but Fothergill had, and he was already busy pouring three cups and asking Van der Lee what he'd like with his. He'd remembered my milk and one sugar.

"What happened to him?" asked Fothergill, when we were sat back down and everyone breathing normally, thinking normal thoughts, drinking tea. "You don't have to tell me, not if you don't want to, but after you found him, all his problems, it feels like something I have to know."

Van der Lee smiled. "I think you just saw him," he said.

I looked across at Fothergill, frowning, both of us, he shaking his head, me starting to do the same, and then it hit me.

"The man on the path? Outside?"

Van der Lee nodded.

"But he was – well, he was wearing a suit," I continued, aware of how absurd that sounded, but unable to think of anything else. "He looked like anyone, like a man coming home from work. From a decent job, too."

Van der Lee nodded again.

"But how?" asked Fothergill.

"They're good here. Really good."

I thought back to clients past, violent men, fools and addicts. "No one's that good."

Van der Lee shrugged. "Well, these guys are. He was clean within six weeks, they'd got him a job within one more. Data stuff. He's always been good with computers, apparently. It's just thirty hours a week, low-level stuff, but it's a start."

I shook my head. It was barely believable. But I believed it.

28: From Ashes

ROARKES SEEMED MORE his usual self tonight. Full of apology – I'd had it up to here with the apologies, from him and Claire for lying to me, from Martins for doubting me, from Fothergill for getting me punched and kicked and from Van der Lee for doing the punching and the kicking.

I told Roarkes to can the apologies, and he did, but he couldn't resist telling me all about it anyway, the lies and the obfuscations, the blind alleys and the why and the how. It had been bullshit, the lot of it, the idea that he'd been put out to pasture, the slow fumblings towards the truth about the NCA building, a man playing a role.

"You played it well," I said, and raised my glass. "I thought this was the new Roarkes. Old man."

He laughed. "Credit where it's due. It was Claire's idea. I just did what I was told. I'm sorry –"

"I told you to stop saying sorry."

"Yeah. Well, it just comes out, okay? Truth be told, I enjoyed it. Not lying to you. But finding Wolf. It was a challenge."

"So you've still got it, Roarkes. Well done."

I hadn't meant that to come out the way it had, clouded with bitterness. Roarkes raised an eyebrow and switched the subject back to Claire.

"It wasn't that she didn't trust you. It was that she didn't think you'd trust her, you wouldn't think she was stable enough to get involved in something like this, in finding Wolf, in talking to Wolf, in persuading Wolf."

"I didn't. She was right. She made me promise to trust her. She kicked me out of the flat because I couldn't. I was right not to. And wrong at the same time."

Bitter, again. I didn't mean it, the bitterness. We'd talked it all through since, apologies exchanged, lessons learned.

Our relationship all the stronger for it, she'd said, and even though it sounded like the kind of thing her old life coach might have said, it had the advantage of sounding true, too. Roarkes was sitting back, one arm raised, ready to leap to her defence, so I smiled and shook my head. "It's okay," I said. "It's history."

How she'd talked Wolf round was still something of a mystery. Photographs of the girls, she said. Guilt. I didn't think guilt would work on a man like Wolf. I had a different theory. If Claire had found him, then his previous associates probably would, too, some day. They knew he'd already saved his own skin once, testifying for the Crown and sending down people who had once been friends and colleagues. The way I figured it, it made sense to get them behind bars before they got him shot or stabbed, and Claire was just there at the right time to make it happen.

But none of that really mattered. There was talk that one of the men was already considering changing his plea to guilty, just nine days after the arrests. Claire was free of it, finally – happy for the first time in months. She was back at work – back today, for the first time since before Brooks-Powell had died. She'd told me she was looking forward to it, to stories that came and went, that blew over in a day or a week, maybe longer, but not years. Not long enough to take over her life. She'd told me that, and looked me in the eye as she was saying it, and – again for the first time since Brooks-Powell had died – I'd believed her.

I'd been over at Maloney's before I'd hit the pub with Roarkes. I'd picked up a bag, some clothes, a toothbrush.

I was moving back home tonight.

Roarkes looked smart. Suit and tie. It was a good look for him, the look he'd worn a year or so back, when he'd been travelling the country cracking the toughest cases and turning up on television to tell us all about them. Back before Manchester, before Serena Hawkes. Back before Helen had died.

"Nice suit," I said, and he laughed.

"I don't have to pretend any more, right? And at a certain point you've got to come out of mourning."

I nodded and went to the bar to top us both up.

I'd made it back to Melanie's house, the night before last. Claire had insisted, after I'd told her about the last time, the files, the guilt that had hit me at being alive when David was dead. She'd even come with me, had sat on the sofa with Melanie drinking expensive wine while I pored over document after document at the table in front of them, four hours' worth, sober while they drank and drank until they were halfway to unconscious and I was halfway through the files, a job well begun if not yet done.

Finishing it wouldn't be the end of the world.

"Colman called," I said, setting two pints of lager on the table. "Said you'd offered her a job."

Roarkes drank, long and deep, before he looked up and answered me. "Seems wasted in uniform, that girl. If Martins won't have her I sure as hell will."

"She asked me what I thought of you."

"And I have no doubt you gold-plated me."

"I told her you were senile, you couldn't be trusted, and your best days were behind you."

He laughed. "No need to sugar-coat it, Sam."

"I told her she could do worse."

"Thanks."

"Truth for a truth, Roarkes. How come you thought of Vicky Colman? There's plenty of decent cops who'd do well in your team."

"Truth? I rate her. She gets things done. Not by the book, but you know me, Sam. I'm not so fussed about the book. There are times when you have to toe the line, there are times when you have to cross it. She doesn't know which times are which yet, but that'll come with experience. If she comes with me she'll learn to be a good detective, and she'll learn which dodgy lawyers to run a mile from when they come begging favours."

I ignored the jibe. "And that's all?"

"No. Martins called me."

"Martins? Olivia Martins?"

"She's not so bad, you know."

I remembered what Martins had said about Roarkes, yesterday's man, the same things I'd just said about him, only not in jest. I remembered her apologising and taking those things back, doing all she could to get Genaud's attention away from Claire, doing all she could to warn me when it was too late. Maybe Roarkes was right.

"She'll be a decent cop herself, one day," he continued. "She's learned an important lesson. It's not all about the big wins. She's as good as shut down Trawden's murder, and she knows the truth about Elizabeth Maurier and the other three, although she'll never admit it in public. She called me and recommended Colman, said if I had space on my team I could do worse than take her on. I said I'd think about it. Did you know Colman's seeing that Winterman guy? Martins' DC?"

I nodded. The fact that Colman and Winterman were still together was possibly the most surprising thing about the whole affair, Colman, who went through men like I'd gone through kebabs before Claire had put the brakes on that habit, Colman who'd been so outraged, at first, when she learned that she'd been used as a messenger. Winterman had got through to her, apparently. They shared a pragmatism and an honesty about what they'd do to get the job done. They were, I thought, remarkably well suited.

"Thing is," said Roarkes, on a roll, "Martins really rates

her. Colman. Said she regretted getting rid of her. Said she'd take her back herself, but she doubted Colman would agree to work for her again."

"No. She has a very particular idea of what kind of DI she wants to work for, and Olivia Martins it isn't."

"Maybe." Roarkes took another drink. "Maybe Olivia Martins isn't the woman she was a few months ago. And I'm not going to be doing this forever."

He drained his beer, and when I stood and offered him another – I was buying, apparently *I* owed *him* a favour, according to Claire at least, although I was fairly sure it was the other way round – he shook his head.

I'd spent most of the previous day in Oxford. I started at Chalmere, where I surprised Mrs Piper with a box of truffles and an enormous orchid. I'd called earlier and checked with the head – Mrs Piper was a fan of orchids.

"Zygopetalum," she breathed, stroking the thick purple lips with an almost sensual fervour. "It's beautiful. Thank you."

"No," I replied. "Thank you. My client's in the clear. And if you hadn't found out what you did, I'd never have known what kind of a man he was. I probably wouldn't have trusted him."

"I'm glad to have helped."

She returned to her orchid, bent down and seemed to whisper to it, then remembered she wasn't alone and straightened up, the prim school secretary again.

"Would you care for some tea, Mr Williams?" she said, but I declined. The best thing I could do for her would be to leave her and her zygopetalum alone together.

Next I dropped in on Fothergill, who seemed chipper enough. He was going through those old photographs when I arrived, putting names to faces and musical instruments to names, compiling a list.

"I'm thinking of getting in touch with one or two of them," he said. I couldn't think of a good reason not to.

From there I'd driven to Jericho and stopped at *Dervish*, through the front door this time, although it was closed. I rang the bell and the door opened for me, and Van der Lee made me coffee and apologised, again, for the punches and the kicks, while I explained what was about to happen.

"You're sure you don't want to bring your guy along? Darren Sutcliffe? You never know. CPS won't be too happy with you. Can't predict what they'll want to do about it."

He shook his head.

"Can't stand the man."

"Why'd you hire him, then?"

He shrugged. "Well, you know the whole story now. I wanted someone to keep the CPS at arms' length if they started asking difficult questions. Sutcliffe never bothered asking me any questions at all. He was just a wall, really."

"Well, it's possible you might actually need him now."

"I'll take my chances. And I'll have you with me, won't I?"

"I'm not your lawyer, Mr Van der Lee."

"It's Pieter. Call me Pete."

"Okay, Pete. But I'm not your lawyer. And I can't be unless I get Fothergill to sign off on it. And I won't let him do that until the CPS have dropped the charges against him."

"Chicken and egg, then."

I nodded. "Chicken and egg."

Roarkes was looking at his watch.

"Got somewhere to be?" I asked. It was only eight o'clock. I'd assumed we were going to make a night of it. I'd told Claire not to expect me back until well after midnight.

He flashed a smile at me, a grin I couldn't read, a grin

295

that didn't make sense on the face of the Roarkes I knew. "Oh, I'm expecting a call, that's all. May have to dash. I think I'll have that pint after all. If you're buying."

If you're buying. I was pretty certain it would have been a half if I wasn't.

From *Dervish* we'd driven straight to our meeting with Karen Hobart, who'd not even tried to hide her astonishment as the whole story came out, interrupting every thirty seconds with exclamations and expressions of disbelief.

"So," I said, "I believe Mr Van der Lee would like you to drop the charges against my client, if you can."

She'd turned to him, eyes still wide. "Is this true? This story Mr Williams has just told me?"

He nodded. "Every last word. I'm sorry I wasted your time, Ms Hobart."

"It's Karen," she said, and I knew then that things were going to be just fine. "You know I could ask for charges to be brought against you, Mr Van der Lee?"

He nodded again. "I do. I can accept that. It's been – well, it's been difficult."

"I can see that." She paused, turned to stare at me, searching, I thought, for a signal, a hint that things might not be as we'd presented them. I smiled at her, and a moment later she shook her head and returned the smile.

"I'm sure we can smooth it all over," she said. "I'll get the paperwork started. You'd better let your Mr Sutcliffe know he's out of the picture."

I asked Van der Lee to go on ahead; I wanted a minute alone with Karen Hobart. I waited until I could hear his footsteps on the stairs.

"Something I've been meaning to ask you, Karen," I said.

"Go on." We were both standing, me by the door, she

leaning against her chair, head tilted up towards me, anxious to hear what I had to say.

"I don't mean to be rude about your colleagues, but, well, in my experience the job of a CPS lawyer is to make life as difficult as possible for her opposite number. As far as I can see, you've gone out of your way to help me. Why?"

"You've got it all wrong, Sam," she replied. "The job of a CPS lawyer is to get a conviction if we can and get a case dropped as soon as possible if we can't. I don't like wasting time and money and ruining people's lives if they're never going to see the inside of a courtroom anyway."

"Don't they measure your success on conviction rate?"

She shrugged. "Maybe, but they're not going to fire me, so I'll carry on doing things the way I've always done them. But there is something else you should know."

"What?"

"It's personal, too."

"What is?"

"The reason I decided to help you. The reason I let you see the video, the reason I warned you about Sutcliffe, the reason I'm going to make sure no one goes after Van der Lee for wasting our time."

"Go on." I was intrigued, now.

"I knew Serena Hawkes."

I took a step back, coming up against the hard jamb of the door into my spine. "How?" I breathed.

"We were at law school together. We were quite friendly, really. I'm still in touch with Pauline."

I remembered Pauline. Serena's sister. I'd spoken with her at Serena's funeral.

"I was there, Sam. At the funeral. I actually remember seeing you there, talking to Pauline. Talking to Thomas Carson and his wife."

"Why didn't you say anything?"

"Why should I? That's the past. It didn't end well, and I

297

didn't think you'd thank me for dragging it back up again."

"So, why?"

"Why did this make me predisposed to help you?" She smiled as she spoke.

"Yes."

"It ended badly. Serena died. But you did your best, Sam. Everyone who knows what really happened in Manchester knows you did your best. You tried to help my friend. She died, and you suffered for it. I thought you deserved a break."

I vowed it as I left, as I shook her hand and took those dark steps to the cold, miserable corridor downstairs and Van der Lee waiting for me in my car outside. I vowed to remember her words and believe them, to let them comfort me when I doubted myself, to let them be there, double spaced in bold caps, when I doubted other people. For every Trawden, I thought, there were a hundred Karen Hobarts.

Halfway through his next beer Roarkes stopped, suddenly, shoved a hand into the pocket of his jeans and pulled out a ringing phone.

"Got to take this," he said, and then, mouth to the phone, "Hello Priya. Yes, of course I haven't forgotten. I was hoping you hadn't. When does your train get in?"

He paused. I tried to meet his eyes, but he was looking determinedly away, down at the table and then, when my waving hand entered his field of vision, twisting so that he was facing away from me entirely.

"I'll see you then," he said, returned the phone to his pocket, and turned slowly back to me.

"So," I said. "Detective Sergeant Priya Malhotra's in town, is she?"

"Ah, yes. You remember her, then?"

"Oh yes, Roarkes. I remember DS Malhotra."

I could hardly forget her. The woman who'd been dragged into Roarkes' mess of a case when no one else was willing to help. Malhotra had cracked the mystery around Carson's finances, which was credit to her brain, but what stuck in my mind more than any of that was her driving, towns and villages passing in a blur, the music – her *beats* – pounding away, out of Manchester into the Bowland hills and the mystery that awaited us there.

"We're just tidying up some details on the Carson case," said Roarkes, his face half hidden by his beer glass. "Priya was due in London for a few days, which saved me the trip to Manchester."

Priya. He'd called her that from the beginning, not the usual barked surname or vicious epithet he reserved for most of his junior officers and plenty of his superiors. The suit and tie made sense, now. So did the reluctance to stay in the pub with me all night sinking beers. The Carson case was dead and buried, had been for weeks. I thought about pushing him a little further, but there was no need. I knew what I knew, and Roarkes knew I knew it. Instead, I nodded and finished off my drink.

When I'd got back from Oxford there had been another letter from Lizzy Maurier. The conclusion, it seemed, of her poem.

> There was a secret.
> *Better Late Than Never.*
> There was a life.
> *Better Late Than Never.*
> There was a voice.
> *Better Late Than Never.*
>
> It sang. It sings still.
> And no one will hear.

I remembered it from David Brooks-Powell's funeral. I remembered driving away and stopping, distraught, climbing into the woods and staring at the hills and the mist and reciting it to the wind, hoping for solace, getting nothing at all. I hoped it had brought something more to its creator.

I read on. It had done.

I'm coming home, she wrote. *I was wrong. Wrong about everything. Wrong about you and David, wrong about Edward Trawden, wrong about my mother. Most of all, I was wrong about me. I still, I believe, have things to write. Things to say.*

And so I am coming home to say them.

And someone, somewhere, will hear.

I smiled as I handed it to Claire. "You know what it means, right?" she asked, and I shrugged.

"No one ever knows what Lizzy means. You've probably get a better idea than anyone else. But if you ask me, it means she's better."

I stood, ready to leave, wondering why Roarkes wasn't doing the same, racing off to his rendezvous with Priya Malhotra. Instead he sat, a quarter of a pint of lager fizzing gently in front of him, and looked at me.

"In a hurry, Sam?"

"I thought you were."

He shook his head. "It's okay. I've got half an hour."

I sat back down. "Another drink?"

"No. But tell me about Leeds. You got the guy to drop the case, right?"

"Yes."

"How?"

I made him wait while I bought myself another pint –

just because he wasn't drinking didn't mean I couldn't, and all this talking was thirsty work – and worked out whether I *could* tell him everything, the truth about Pieter Van der Lee and Marine Lambert and their son. Eventually I decided I could. Roarkes had nothing to do with Van der Lee, there was no reason for them ever to cross paths, and he was a police officer, after all.

So I told him everything. Restoration. Gregory Lambert – that was the name he went by, a name under which his father was proud to know him. Elissa Pengilly and the letters that had started it all. As I spoke I thought about that, about how one woman's attempt to put a piece of the past behind her had dragged that past kicking and screaming into the present, how it had come close to costing Fothergill his life, how, ultimately, it had brought everything neatly together. Back to the start. I thought of births and of deaths, old and new. Of thaws and rebirths. For Claire. For Roarkes. For me, too, perhaps. I told him of the building and its cameras and the pair of giants guarding it like dragons in a fairy tale. I told him of Mrs Hargreaves, whose first name I'd never learned. I told him of my race back to London, past Van der Lee, sitting in his car and sobbing, and of our return, three of us in a room listening to old truths and learning that everything we thought we knew was wrong. I told him almost everything that had happened in the nine days since we'd left Martins' police station in a haze of wonder and the glow of victory.

But there were things I didn't say.

I didn't tell him about the little conversation I'd had with Mrs Hargreaves alone, while Fothergill and Van der Lee continued their tears and their reminiscences. My enquiry about cost and practicalities, and whether they might have space for another resident. I didn't tell him about the call I'd made that night to Melanie Golding, who had more money than she knew what to do with and was anxious to put that right. I didn't tell him about the conversations I'd had with John Evans, who hadn't beaten me up after all, who was, it seemed, the man Martins had said he was, the man with the deck stacked against him, the man who'd never had a chance. Evans had explained the list to me, finally. People he wanted to talk to. People who might be able to tell him something about his father. The names were crossed out, but it wasn't John Evans that had killed them. Instead, Trawden and time had robbed him of every last name but mine. He'd spent most of his life worrying he'd turn out like his father, but he knew next to nothing about the man.

So I'd agreed to meet John Evans. I wasn't sure how much use I'd be – I'd never met Robbie Evans, all I really knew of him was the discredited testimony of a liar. But I owed his son that meeting. I'd tell him the little I knew, and I'd make him an offer. A suggestion. He was struggling – he'd admitted that on the phone. Addiction and petty crime and a lack of education. He needed some stability in his life. He needed a place to start anew.

I didn't tell Roarkes any of this. I'd told Claire, of course. There were no secrets any more. Claire knew everything.

Well, almost everything.

There was something else. Something I'd remembered, right back at the start, the day after Trawden had been killed. Something I'd remembered, but everyone else seemed to have forgotten.

Before she was just a name in the newspapers, a photograph on the courtroom steps, a face red with days and weeks of tears, Eileen Grimshaw had been a nurse.

I hadn't told Claire that.

And I hadn't told her what Eileen Grimshaw's letter had said. The way it had ended.

The cold years seem endless; the thaw brings their end. But you don't forget. You never forget. And courts and police officers and newspapers and lawyers may think they know the truth, but we know. We truly know, you and I. We will always know and we will never forget. And our cold years may have passed, but they were painful. Too painful to be allowed to return.

So you understand what I must do. You understand that in the end, justice must be served.

I considered acting in silence, but you, of all people, had to be told. Had to understand. And ultimately, it will be in your hands. All of it. Your choice. You may give this letter to the police, if you wish. You may bury it or burn it. You may lock it away and save your choice for another day.

Whatever you choose, justice will have been served.
Yours sincerely,

Eileen Grimshaw, SEN.

The letter was ashes. For all her talk of choice, she remembered the look we'd exchanged all those years ago, and she knew I remembered it too. There had never really been any choice.

We chatted idly for another twenty minutes, Roarkes glancing at his watch from time to time, fiddling with his tie, even, on one occasion, disappearing to the toilets and returning with his hair noticeable tidier than it had been. His cold years were upon him already, but he seemed to be handling them well, if Priya Malhotra was anything to go by. I'd keep Roarkes on his toes. Colman certainly would.

I watched Roarkes, half-listening as he told me about a stabbing that had taken place not thirty yards from his Wembley station, a case he'd be passing on to Colman if she took up his offer quickly enough, but I was thinking about John Evans, now. Cold decades, that man had been

303

through. His thaw was coming. I thought of Pieter van der Lee and Gregory Lambert, whose cold years were, I hoped, behind them. I thought of Melanie Golding, who had cold years to come, who'd been living through them for long enough already. Only now could she show it.

We all had cold years to come, I thought, those of us who weren't living through them now, those of us who hadn't lived them and come out the other side. My mind turned to Claire, who would be back by now, who would be curled up in front of the television or lying in bed reading. I smiled to myself, as Roarkes stood and said goodbye and left for the start of his own thaw. We all had cold years to come.

The best we could hope for was that we wouldn't have to face them alone.

A Message From the Author

I very much hope you've liked what you've just read. You've made it this far, which is a good sign, but you never can tell. You might just be a sucker for punishment.
Either way, if you're interested in joining my reader group – where you'll find exclusive offers, competitions, snippets from work in progress and next month's lottery numbers*, please head over to my website and fill in the details.

If you did enjoy this book, please consider leaving a review on Amazon. I can tell people how great it is as much as I like, no one's going to believe me. You, on the other hand, have impeccable taste, and are as honest as the day is long.

*Actual lottery numbers may differ from those published.

Also by Joel Hames

DEAD NORTH

Two dead cops and a suspect who won't talk.

"intelligent, intricately woven" - S.E. Lynes
"It's going to leave me with a thriller hangover for some time." -
John Marrs
"a white-knuckle, breathlessly-paced read that also has heart." -
Louise Beech
*"A pacy thriller, rich in voice and with gratifying degree of
complexity."* - John Bowen

Once the brightest star in the legal firmament, Sam
Williams has hit rock bottom, with barely a client to his
name and a short-term cash problem that's looking longer
by the minute. So when he's summoned to Manchester to
help a friend crack a case involving the murder of two
unarmed police officers and a suspect who won't say a
word, he jumps at the chance to resurrect his career.

In Manchester he'll struggle against resentful locals, an
enigmatic defence lawyer who thinks he's stepping on her
toes, beatings, corrupt cops and people who'll do anything
to protect their secrets. On its streets, he'll see people die.
But it's in the hills and valleys further north that Sam will
face the biggest challenge of all: learning who he really is
and facing down the ghosts of his past.

*He's working someone else's case and he's in way over his head. But
sometimes you need the wrong man in the right place.*

NO ONE WILL HEAR

**Four murders
Four messages
One chance to catch a killer.**

Renowned human rights lawyer Elizabeth Maurier lies dead, her body mutilated, her killer unknown. For DI Olivia Martins and her team, it's a mystery. For the victim's daughter Lizzy, a poet and academic with a shaky grasp on reality, it's a tragedy. But for Sam Williams, the man Elizabeth fired a decade ago and hasn't spoken to since, it's a whole new world of pain.

Elizabeth's death has stirred a sleeping past back to life. Former clients are darkening Sam's door, old enemies returning, ancient cases reopening. It doesn't help that DI Martins is on his case, the press are dogging his every step, and his girlfriend's behaviour is increasingly erratic.

But Elizabeth's murder is just the start. As Sam reluctantly digs his way back into the past, more truths will crumble into lies.

More certainties will shade to doubt.

And more innocent people will die.

THE ART OF STAYING DEAD

A prisoner who doesn't exist.
A lawyer who doesn't care.
A secret buried for thirty years.

Meet Sam Williams. Lawyer, loser, man on the way down.
Sam's about to walk into a prison riot. Meet a woman who
isn't what she seems. And wind up on the wrong side of
some people who'll stop at nothing to keep him quiet.

**Sam thought things were going badly yesterday. Now
he'll be lucky to see tomorrow.**

*Read what Amazon customers are saying about The Art of Staying
Dead...*

"A brilliant read for thriller action readers"

"The suspense is perfectly timed and believable, the
atmosphere and characterisation spot on"

"The well-thought-out plot moves along at a relentless
pace"

"A pacy thriller with a rich seam of laconic humour"

"Engaging, fast-paced and genuinely thrilling"

VICTIMS – A SAM WILLIAMS NOVELLA

The trick is to save one without becoming one

Young lawyer Sam Williams is riding high. He's got a job
he loves, a girl he wants, and the brain to win out every
time.
But Sam's about to find out that he's got enemies, too.
And figuring out which one wants to hurt him most isn't
as easy as it seems.

*Victims introduces Sam Williams, hero of international bestseller
The Art of Staying Dead and Dead North, ten years younger than
we last saw him, and a lot less wise.*

CAGED – A SAM WILLIAMS SHORT

Promises come with consequences.

Binny Carnegie doesn't want her *notorious* night club shut down. Lawyer Sam Williams wouldn't normally care, but it's his job to fix Binny Carnegie's problems.
Fixing this particular problem might be more trouble than it's worth.

Caged is another snapshot of Sam Williams, hero of international bestseller The Art of Staying Dead and Dead North, back in his formative legal years at Mauriers.

Please note that Caged is a short story, not a full length novel.

BREXECUTION

There are thirty-three million stories on referendum night. This one has the highest body count.

Dave Fenton sleeps by day and drives a taxi by night. As the counting commences in the most important vote in Britain's history, one passenger leaves something in his cab.
Something secret.
Something explosive.
Something so dangerous there are people who will stop at nothing to get it back.

From Downing Street to the East End via the City and a whole bit of the country that isn't London at all, BREXECUTION is a fictionalised account of the closing days of June 2016. Politicians, bankers, cabbies and crooks - some will win, some will lose - and some won't make it past the first day of Brexit.

From Joel Hames, author of international bestseller The Art of Staying Dead, comes a thriller you'll want to put your cross on.

BANKERS TOWN

The number 1 bestselling financial thriller, "A real page turner - a hugely enjoyable, often funny, always intense thriller of a book"

"This time everyone else had their ducks lined up and every last duck had "Alex Konninger" written in bold marker-pen on its forehead. If I didn't crack this fast, those ducks would be shot, shredded and rolled into pancakes before you could say hoi sin sauce."

Everything's going rather well for Alex Konninger. He's drifted his way into a big-money job in a top-tier bank, and if he doesn't always play by the rules, he's hardly the only one. Alex doesn't know it yet, but he's got a problem, a whole army of problems, in fact, and they've all picked this week to jump on him. He's losing control, his past is about to catch up with him, and he doesn't know who he can trust, because someone wants him out, and it looks like someone else wants him dead.

In a world of bonds, bodies and blackmail, not everyone will make it to drinks on Friday.

Welcome to Bankers Town, the explosive thriller from Joel Hames

Acknowledgements

I PLAN TO keep this brief: there are so many people who have helped with this book, as with all of my books, that to list them all by name would take a whole new book. So instead I shall begin by offering my praise to a number of friends and fellow authors: the marvellous John Bowen, the wonderful Susie Lynes, the brilliant Joanna Franklin Bell, the outstanding Rose Edmunds and the awesome Ray Green, each and every one of them thoughtful commentators and sounding-boards, and souls with whom I have shared the delights of victory and the torment of defeat.

There are readers, and there are readers, and then there are **Readers.** Tracy Fenton and Helen Boyce certainly fall into the latter category. Tracy's THE Book Club on Facebook has provided exposure for many an author and wonderful reading opportunities for thousands of members. As if that weren't enough, Tracy doubles – or should that be trebles? – as both a blogger and a blog tour organiser, and throws informal advisor and all-round potty-mouthed friend into the mix for the hell of it. Helen Boyce is an indefatigable admin and contributor to TBC, but more than that, she's a tireless and remarkably effective evangelist for authors and books of all types, and most importantly, a friend, both personally and (if an author is really entitled to use the word) professionally. These people are the best allies for authors and readers that any of us could hope for. The whole team at TBC are due my thanks and the thanks of many an author.

I've mentioned bloggers – if there's one thing a writer needs, it's a reader, and if there's one thing likely to get us that reader, it's a decent blogger. I've been blessed with some of the best, both for this book and those that came before. I can't mention everyone, but please know that the very fact that you read my books is miraculous enough. Writing about them, and writing nice things, on the whole, sharing those things, well, that's just cup-overfloweth stuff.

As for you, gentle readers (and the rougher ones, too): please give yourselves a pat on the back, on my behalf. You never cease to amaze me by buying my books and reading them and reviewing them and telling your friends about them. All I can ask of you is that you never stop.

And finally: my wife and best friend, Sarah. My children, Eve and Rose, delights even when they're far from delightful. My parents, Valerie and Tony, ever supportive. My family and friends, in the writing community and outside it. Thank you all.

Printed in Great Britain
by Amazon

29141968R00189